The Suspects

Richard Wright

Published by Richard Wright
Seaford, Sussex, UK
Suspects@harbroe.org

First edition, 2018
Second impression

ISBN: 9781980763260

For my long-suffering wife Judy who with my help has made our home resemble a comfortable library.
With thanks also to those Scouts, Venture Scouts, Leaders, Students, Teachers and everyone else who, over many years, have taught me that people of 13 and above *can* be trusted to do the right thing. You just have to leave them to it.

The people and events in this book are not based on anyone, living or dead. They are a product of my imagination. If they remind you of anyone you know, that is coincidence. So there.
The places are not based on any real places either, but if you think of Heathfield Park in Sussex for its being walled and private, and Friston Forest for its size, its hills and the village, it'd be a good start.

Contents

1   The Decision

"To camp? Who with?"

"Oh, just the Suspects."

"Well, possibly…"

I'd been at the school, the main school rather than the Junior, for ages. Well, nearly three years. That made me fourteen. Oh come on, it made me thirteen years and eleven and a half months. In those three years naturally I'd got to know everyone else in my school Year quite well, and those in my class particularly well. We were all used to the school and its peculiarities and knew well how to work the system. To our advantage, naturally.

There was a group of us, just six of us, who were really good friends, all of a 'type', guys in whose veins life and mischief flowed in equal quantities. We never committed anything that would really get us into trouble – well, we tried not to – but there were the usual little things that went wrong; pranks that people believed we might have been involved with in some way. Usually they were right. For example, it was said that when together we could not be trusted in the unguarded presence of glue. Or board markers. And if one of us was seen with a piece of chalk teachers knew that it should be taken off him immediately and he should be required to retrace his steps. And remove the graffiti.

Some of the staff viewed us with exasperation and those particular teachers were always cautious when we volunteered an answer in class, because they never knew if the comment was going to be serious or a joke. These were the teachers who were really surprised when we did well at tests and exams. Oh yes, none of us was stupid, because if he had been he wouldn't have been one of us.

Other teachers were inclined to 'jolly us along' – even when we thought they were meant to be getting serious with us. And those teachers we liked for being normal, human. As happens in half-decent schools (there's an admission!) each side of the desk got on adequately well with the other.

Then one day one of the staff, driving out of the car park, came to a decidedly wobbly halt so that she half blocked the busy main road. When asked what the matter was she said that it felt as if her car had square wheels. An investigation showed that all the car's wheel nuts had been loosened. Each wheel was loose, hence the wobbling.

The next day we were all told at Assembly how lethal this could have been, how it could have resulted in accident and death. And then the inevitable question: who had done it? I knew I hadn't, and just hoped none of the other five had either. All right, the woman who owned the car wasn't the most popular of teachers. But none of us would go to those lengths. We weren't stupid, as I've said. Nor were we vindictive.

Well, no one was going to say anything, were they? In the face of the silence the Headmistress spoke again.

"I want to see the usual suspects in my office immediately…" and she named us. The six of us. Each of us got an independent grilling from her and each said the same, that we hadn't done it, that none of the others would have done it because we weren't that sort of person, it would have been stupid, and we hadn't a clue who might have done it.

We met afterwards.

"*Did* any of us do it?"

Arif, the usually quiet one, was tactful in his phrasing. And each of us gave, scornfully, his own version of 'no'.

"It'd be stupid," said Alex, whose usual reaction to any accusation would be to go off on one. "And if we had they'd soon find out and accuse us… Oh."

We had to laugh. But there still followed two weeks of suspicion, even on the part of some of the more decent teachers, and finally ended up with interviews with the Police. Mud was being slung at us from a number of directions and some was starting to stick. Even some of the other kids in the school thought we were to blame. We talked about it all the time, comparing notes on how bad things were getting and trying to think who at the school might have been responsible.

Finally Tom, our informal leader, said we should get our parents involved and set up a meeting between them, the Head and the Police.

All through this, whenever people were talking about us, they were calling us "The Usual Suspects", following what the Head had said. Unfortunately everyone then knew the six boys they meant.

Amazingly, the meeting happened, thanks to Tom. Parents

were indignant. Parents mentioned that in Britain people were innocent until proven guilty. The Head said that we had a history of mischief so it was hardly surprising that we should be under suspicion. The Police advised caution and said that this wasn't mischief, it was a criminal act, and there was no reason to assume we'd done it. And anyway as the wheel nuts had been professionally tightened after a tyre change two weeks previously and checked by the garage a week later, it wasn't likely that any of us had the strength to undo them. And where would we have hidden the spanner to do it anyway?

None of us had been expecting help from the Police, so looked gratefully at the Sergeant who'd been press-ganged into coming to talk.

"But..." started the Head.

"But nothing," retorted Tom's mum, a lady as short and tubby as Tom was tall and thin. It must have been something about the family – not the girth but the ability to take command of a situation. Tom was a natural leader to us. He didn't set out to act that way, it was just that we relied on him to be right. "They have done nothing. I know Tom wouldn't, and he wouldn't make or remain a friend of anyone who was silly enough to go to those lengths. I trust them all and if the school *really* knew them, they'd trust them too. They may be mischievous but they're not evil. Look elsewhere, Headmistress! Your usual suspects are not to blame in this case. Look for some unusual ones. I'm sure the Police are looking outside the school too."

The Headmistress subsided. She had little option in the face both of the Police and of Mrs Bishop's impressive appearance and manner. News spread round the school that we were off the hook.

Two weeks later a man was arrested. It seems that the teacher who owned the car had refused his offer of marriage and he wanted to get his own back or prove himself, or something.

We all learnt from it. Parents learnt their sons weren't naturally bad; the Head learnt that we weren't evil, and we learnt that teachers had private lives.

But we made a joke about being The Usual Suspects, despite our parents' disparaging looks. Gradually the joke spread to teachers and students alike. If something went wrong,

3

anything from a chair disintegrating in class to a fire in the town, someone would say "Oh, it's the Usual Suspects," and we'd all laugh. Nobody really suspected us, not now, and of course it wasn't us.

Well, the chair might have been.

Being a group like that meant that we had protection from the more unpleasant elements in the school. It wasn't planned like that: it just happened. People were inclined not to argue with the red-headed and impetuous Alex who, at fourteen and a bit, was solidly built and inclined to... well, react. He also had a father who was a solicitor but whose aim was to help people. That made him a lot of friends but little money, but it also meant Alex was instinctively fair – and when it came to arguments he could talk the hind leg off a donkey. Tom, an old man of nearly fifteen, thin and whippet like, with near blonde hair, had such a likeable demeanour that just his being there stopped most unpleasantness before it started. Others of us helped in any way we could. Me? Haven't a clue. Perhaps I was the natural victim the others protected although I was known to speak back quite strongly on occasion and amaze the 'attacker'.

Looking back, we were one of those groups of close friends who must have been hell to teach, except that we egged each other on in trying to keep ahead of whatever the teacher was trying to get over to us. It was a sort of competition, in a way. There were times when the others in our year groaned when one of us put his hand up.

Doesn't that sound like a load of crawlers? It wasn't like that, not at all. It was just that we inevitably talked about things, helped each other out with homework all the time, but naturally competed in the classroom. Teachers soon got wise to us and usually chose others to answer the questions, and we realised what they were doing and grinned to ourselves. It didn't stop us adding "I knew that!" when the answer had been given. And indeed, sometimes we did. Maybe usually we did.

It was coming up to the summer holidays and we'd got together at break to find out what we were going to do over the next six weeks. None of our parents were that well off, mainly thanks to the recession, and they seemed all to be economising on holidays. But the prospect of six weeks' boredom after the first week or so of being able to get up late was a distinct turn-off.

"There's the beach," said Arif. He was the eldest of us, black haired, coffee skinned, tall and thin. Of Indian descent.

"Stones," I said. He looked at me.

"It's all pebbles. They hurt."

"Wimp."

"They still hurt."

"Fishing?" asked Joe.

"Boring," said Alex. "Can't be arsed."

"What then?" asked Tom. "Sky diving? Caving? Scuba?"

We all looked at him. Had he come into some money without telling us?

"Who's paying?" I asked uncertainly.

"Not me," he said, "I'm not made of money."

I punched him, but lightly; he was bigger than me. We scuffled, until someone said "Farter's looking this way."

Mr Windebank walked up to us, raised his eyebrows, and walked past.

"He's not bad really," said Alex.

"There are worse," Tom confirmed, "and we're taught by some of them."

"I might be caving later in the holidays," Steve offered.

"Scouts?" Tom asked.

"Yep."

For once no one teased him. We were envious.

"What about camping?" growled Joe. He wasn't really growling as such, it's just that his voice had gone from high thin treble to a deep bass almost overnight, and it still made us laugh a bit. In other respects he was normal: just over fourteen but quite tall, and like me had boring mid-brown hair.

"Where?" I asked.

"Only one place," said Steve. "The forest."

"It's private," said Tom.

"It's big," said Steve. "No one'd find us in there if we were careful. And the Scouts got permission to go in there some time ago."

"What, camping?"

"No, just for a hike."

"What's it like?"

"Oh, wooden."

"Stupid."

"Yup."

"But I mean, what's it like?"

"Well… how do you describe forest that nobody goes in unless they're allowed to? It's wild. Lots of trees. Firewood on the ground…"

"Firewood? Are we going to start fires, then?"

"Don't you want to?" asked Steve.

"Well yes," said Arif, "but I mean – fires."

"Fires," Steve aped him. "What's wrong with fires?"

"Nothing – nothing at all. I just never thought…"

"We could take stoves," said Tom.

"What's Emily Long doing?" asked Joe, though it had nothing to do with us camping. Emily was one of those who looked down her nose and sneered at anyone younger than her. She seemed to be universally disliked except by a few girls her own age and attitude, and a few older boys who, we thought, had pretty poor taste. This time she was at the railings, talking to some man. We were too distant to see more.

"Who cares?" Alex dismissed the occurrence. "Probably her new boyfriend."

And so the discussion continued until we were yelled at to come back to the classroom again. I didn't know why they bothered to try and teach us anything on those last few days before the longest holiday of the year. The poor idiots who'd had to take exams had either left or were meant to be starting their next year's course, and the rest of us were just hanging in there by the skin of our teeth. And that applied to the tired looking teachers too.

We'd come to no real conclusions so we arranged to gravitate to Tom's house the first afternoon of the holidays, the afternoon being chosen "to give me a chance to wake up before you get there," as Tom put it.

"What are we looking for?" asked Alex when we were convened.

"Somewhere to camp of course, Ginge," growled Joe. Alex hated being called Ginge, despite his declarations of being happy with having deep copper coloured hair.

"Ha ha, Growler," Alex responded, hurriedly making up a nickname for Joe. "I mean, do we have a clue what a camp site looks like?"

"Caravans, tents, girls in bikinis, old men letching at them…"

"You letching at them, you mean."

"Somewhere secluded, water, somewhere to swim, wood, near enough not to have to travel far, level area, somewhere for ball games…"

We all looked at Steve, the quiet one, now nearing 15, who had let it slip once that he was in the Scouts and got a lot of stick about it for a time before we all got used to the idea. He seemed to have suddenly opened up. Even Tom opened his mouth to say something, then shut it again while he thought.

"He's not wrong. Is there somewhere like that?"

"Dunno," said Steve. "When we were in there we were too busy trying to find our way around to look for campsites."

"Should we go and look?" I asked.

"How about a map?" asked Steve.

"Map?" It had never occurred to me.

"Yeah. You know, the sort of thing you look at just before you get lost."

"You might. I'm quite good at them," said Arif.

"I was talking about Mum, in the car, navigating," I told him.

That struck a chord with all of us.

"Got a map, Tom?"

"Nope."

"I have," Steve volunteered, "I thought we might be needing one."

"Where?"

"I shoved it down my trousers to get it out of the house. My parents don't know I've got it."

He produced it, and we all studiously avoided it in view of its storage history. He spread it on the floor. Soon, despite misgivings, we were all poring over it.

I don't know what made me look at the tops of the heads as their owners knelt there. It was one of those moments of realisation, but of something so trivial that it couldn't matter less. But I'd never looked before at the colours of my friends' hair except Alex's in-your-face copper colouring. Sounds silly, doesn't it? But that's what I did for a few seconds. So I can tell you that they ranged from Arif's jet black, straight hair all the way through the spectrum to Tom's near blonde of the short, slightly wavy variety, passing through a straw (Steve), a mid-brown (Joe) and Alex's copper. I wondered briefly why I hadn't had interesting coloured hair, but then nobody notices boring old mid-brown, like Joe and me.

I looked back at the map. They were scanning their way around the forest. It was really the estate which had belonged to what was now a more or less ruined stately home. We'd heard a little about it. Interestingly it happened to have a small village right at the edge of it – we knew about that too. The hamlet was more or less normal and anyone could go there. The rest of the land was private, separated from the hamlet by a hedge, and from local and main roads by a wall which ran for miles. We knew that entry through the hamlet was not going to be possible, as we'd get hounded off by anyone watching. So a less official approach would be needed. But from where?

"Look!" Tom exclaimed, "There's a pond or something." He pointed to a small blue splodge on the map.

"Looks tiny," I said, "What is it, a cattle trough?"

"It's definitely a pond. Cattle troughs aren't marked, I don't think. And they don't have streams running in and out of them. It should be big enough to swim in. And – look." Steve pointed. "There's a cliff or something behind it. That means it'd be sheltered, at least from that direction."

"You sure?"asked Joe. Steve was adamant.

"We need to go and have a look," Tom decided. "How do we get there?"

Steve was allowed to look closely at the map. After all, it was his shorts that had hidden it.

"Can we get over the wall there?" he asked, pointing to the road where it was closest to the pond.

"One way of finding out," said Joe, sitting up. "Get on a bus and go there."

The road concerned was one of the busiest in the area, linking us with the next town along. Buses were frequent. We checked round and found that some of us had money for what we thought the fare should be, not that we used buses very often since transport was generally provided by bikes or parents. High finance amongst the six of us provided loans and sub-loans, and we made our way to the bus stop.

That was fine until we realised no one knew what stop to ask for. The driver sorted that one out by charging us to the next stop beyond the area we described, telling us that there weren't any official stops along there but to let him know when we wanted to get off.

"Coming back, are you?" he asked.

Tom, first in the queue, admitted that we were.

"Just put your hand out as soon as you see the bus and he'll stop. They do it like that 'cos no one hardly ever gets on or off along there."

We hit the top deck and Tom told Steve to get the map out.

"Why do you have to stick it down there? You're not smuggling it out of the house now," he asked. Steve just shrugged and opened it.

The rest of us chatted until we got to the outskirts of the town but then were interrupted by Steve who abruptly told us to shut up so he could concentrate.

"Shout out any obvious features," he ordered us.

"Thirty limit sign." "Pylon." "Lamp post," (the speaker got a glare). "Hill in the distance." "River." "Brick wall starting." "Pylon." How he got any information from this verbal machine gun effect I hadn't a clue.

"Pylon, a bit closer."

"Ah…. Yes, we're there. No, I don't mean we're there, I mean that's where we are, here." He pointed to a spot on the map.

"You mean we're neither here nor there… sorry."

"Shut up, Arif, I'm concentrating."

"We're going up a hill."

"I know, I know; then it'll flatten out a bit, then the road bends to the left, then we get off. Come on, downstairs. Let me go first and I'll tell the driver where to stop."

Reading a map and going downstairs on a swaying bus takes a skill that Steve didn't have, and he nearly fell down them. The driver slowed. Steve went to talk to him and he sped up again.

Just below the top of the hill he spoke to the man again, and the bus stopped. We chorused our thanks and coughed in the cloud of fumes as the bus sped away. Opposite us a tangle of hedge stood, and we had seen from the bus that fields stretched away behind it. We were more interested in the old high stone wall at our side.

"We actually need to be a bit further on," said Steve, "but just down there are some trees. I thought we could climb over

9

behind them so we couldn't be seen from the road."

"Good thinking, young man," said Tom.

Steve, just a month his junior, nevertheless grinned.

We went to the trees, chose our moment and then used Arif, the tallest, as a halfway point to clambering over the wall. Fortunately there was nothing to damage us on its top or on the other side, so we all dropped down safely, leaving Tom, next eldest after Arif, to haul Arif up. They dropped down and joined us. We were in.

2   Arrival

It was like entering another world. Traffic noise from the road behind us had become muted. At our back was the wall. In front of us the trees blocked our path rather more effectively than the brickwork.

"Now what?" asked Arif, dusting off his clothes from the wall's debris.

"Ask The Scout," suggested Alex.

"My job was to get you here," Steve retorted. "I've done that."

"Your job was to get us to the pond," Tom corrected him. "And none of us has a clue. I suppose you've brought a compass, along with the map, have you?" It was said sarcastically, and it was comical to watch his face as Steve brought one out from his pocket.

"Okay, okay… I'm sorry." Tom looked resigned. "Do you have the rest of the Ordnance Survey in another pocket, or is that it?"

"That'll do, if I can remember how to use it." Steve looked at the instrument anxiously, then at the map which he'd opened out again having landed second from the top of the wall. We crowded round the map.

"We're here," said Steve, pointing. "These are the trees just behind us and that's the top of the hill."

"Where?" I asked, because I couldn't see any mark.

"See the contours? They open out there and there aren't any more until over the page when they start to go down again."

Well, I knew what contours were, but I'd never really looked at them with the intention of using them in mind. I had the same view of them that I did of ironing boards, if you see what I mean.

"Anyway," Steve continued, "if we go right, between the wall and the trees, perhaps we'll find somewhere that looks promising."

'Something promising' proved to be where the line of pylons crossed the wall and headed off downhill. From our position by the wall the lie of the land had been hidden by the trees, but they'd been cleared underneath the wires and it looked as if we could struggle down beside the scrub that was flourishing there. Eventually it proved easier to walk just under the trees where the scrub was less thick.

According to Steve, whom we soon termed 'falling man' because he watched the compass so constantly that he kept tripping over things, the wires were going in roughly the right direction for us; that direction being downhill. At times quite steeply downhill. We had lost quite a bit of height when Steve came to a halt and the pylons turned sharply left.

"Ahh," he said as if we all knew what the problem was. He looked up when there was silence. "We need to go straight on down, then a bit right.

"Ahh," Tom echoed. "That'll be through those hedges, then?"

"Looks like it," Steve responded. "Lead on, will you? I'll keep watching the compass."

"And falling over," reminded Alex. He got The Look.

I should explain that The Look was used by us first at school so as to avoid being accused of calling someone very rude names. It was so effective, now we all knew what it meant, that it had entered common circulation, so to speak. And it saved people getting hit.

It was a fight, the next bit. But after not too long we were back under the main tree cover and able to make better progress; down, always down, until Tom held up a hand and tried to lift his right foot, a combination that nearly led to his following Steve's example. With some considerable arm waving to balance himself he retrieved his foot from suddenly-soft ground.

"Sod that"! he said elegantly. "Can't get down there."

"That's our direction," Steve pointed out, unaware of the problem.

"You go first, then."

Steve looked up, saw Tom's wet trainer and said: "Ahh…"

By a process of careful testing we discovered that there at the foot of a small ledge in the hillside, about a metre high, the rock we could see marked the start of the wetness. Above the rock the ground was dry; it was only at its foot that it became wet.

"Spring," I observed.

Someone just had to say 'boinggg'. It was Joe.

"Just a minute…" Steve was back at the map again, this

time stationary. "It says 'spr.' Here. It's a spring, and if it's the same one I know exactly where we are. There are two more this side of this long hump. Let's go down the other side."

And on we went, trying to keep the lighter green of the soggy ground in sight. There came a point when we thought we'd lost it completely, and had to double back at the cost of some effort. But when we found the lighter green foliage it was to discover that it had become a small stream.

"Ahh…" said Steve.

"You've found us again?"

"Yup," he said happily, "or at least I know where it goes."

"Oh? Where?" asked Alex.

"Over that little cliff and down into the pool."

There was a silence.

"So you mean," Tom started, "that we have to follow it, fall off the cliff and drown in the pool?"

Steve looked up again and grinned. "If you want. But I'm going to turn right again and join the track that's marked, which goes down the hill and ends up by the pool.

Tom just raised his eyebrows.

"If I'm in time I might try and haul anyone who's gone the other way out of the water, but it does depend…

The other four and I looked at each other and engaged in a short skirmish with him, which nearly resulted in the map and compass getting lost.

"Come on guys," he spluttered, spitting out some leaves which seemed to have found their way into his mouth, "it was only a joke. You can come down my way if you really want."

We did, and found that the so-called path was actually little more than a hint of one. What there was of it led steadily downwards and we could see the trees thinning in front of us as the gradient levelled out. It continued past some thick thorn bushes and rather boggy area to where we could see space between the few remaining trees and bushes.

Tom stepped out of the trees and immediately stopped, causing the rest of us to cannon into him. But we spread out and looked round and I felt my mouth drop open.

Ahead of us was the pond. That's what we assumed it would be from the map. We were not expecting an expanse of water about 200 metres round. We were only partially expecting the 10 metre cliff to our left, or the small waterfall that fell down it on to rocks before taking the final tumble into the main lake. And we were not expecting to find a flat area between the encircling woods and the water which was screaming at each one of us: "camp on me!" The ancient tree that had sheltered the ground there, causing the lack of undergrowth, lay at the back of it, with its root system exposed and providing a sheltered area.

"Wow," said Arif, rather unnecessarily.

"I think we've found it," Joe agreed.

"We've got water, we've got a place to camp, we've got wood for a fire. The only thing we don't have is somewhere to play footy," said Alex.

I was just gobsmacked at how special the place was, and how it would be to wake up in the morning and look out at all that. It must have impressed the other five too, because no one said anything for some time.

"When do we come?" asked Tom, untypically quietly.

"Tomorrow?" asked Steve. "It'd be good to get the Explorers along 'cos this is so good, but I think I'd rather just keep it to us."

"What do we need?" asked Tom.

"Tent. Pots and pans. Food. Matches," said Steve.

"Sleeping bag." I offered.

"Anything else?" asked Arif.

Steve frowned. "There's bound to be a lot more. Let's get back and make a list from what it says in some of my Dad's old Scouting books."

"You and your Scouts!" said Joe, though not as scornfully as he had at other times.

"They got you here, didn't they? And stopped you falling down the cliff."

There was no answer to that. We hauled ourselves back up the hill and struggled through the undergrowth. This time the pylon line was our wayfinder and Steve fell over less often. Tiredly we hauled ourselves back over the wall and flagged down the next bus. Arrangements were made to meet the following morning at Steve's to get a list of needs ready, we separated at the bus stop in town and each returned home to face parental criticism for having missed tea.

Three days and a lot of shopping later found us back at the

bus stop with parents' hard-won and grudgingly given permission to camp 'if you can promise me faithfully it's as private and safe as you say' or versions of the same. And no, we hadn't told them where it was, only that we were on some private land owned by friends of one of our parents. And no, that wasn't really true either. Okay, it was a lie. But how else were we to get out of parental reach and have fun? It wasn't as if anything was going to happen to us. And I think they were still a bit sorry for us after the incident with the teacher's car. Maybe even admired the way we'd dealt with it together.

As well as the illicitly gained permission we each had a rucksack. Some of these had been borrowed and many were far too large for the person carrying it (apart from Tom and Arif who were tall enough). Shared amongst them we had two tents, food, cooking equipment and utensils, food, water purifying tablets (despite our protests), sleeping bags, food, sleeping mats, matches, food, gas stove ('in case it rains, dear'; parents sometimes choose to ignore weather forecasts), lightweight tarpaulin for a shelter, and food. With added bacon.

All of this had been shared so that we were all equally burdened. We could hardly move.

I was dreading the long trek down to the pool but knew it would be worth it once we were there. We all realised that Steve would be in his element and we'd have to do what he said, because he'd camped plenty of times before. I'd only been with my parents when I was much younger and the others were similarly inexperienced. At least this time we each had money for the fares and had even returned the loans to each other from three days previously. The bus driver looked taken aback when he saw the size and weight of the packs we carried, and more so when we asked to get off at somewhere that appeared to be in the middle of nowhere.

"You aren't camping in the old Manor Estate, are you? Private that is, and you'll get chucked out."

Tom, the ambassador, just smiled at him; he shrugged and issued a ticket. Single this time.

Getting over the wall with the gear was a nightmare. For some reason I had been deputed to sit astride its top and pass the rucksacks over. Taking the weight of the first one as it was passed up nearly pulled me off and I was glad when Alex climbed on Arif's back and sat facing me to share the loads. We thankfully dropped each of them to the waiting catcher who was at least fairly successful in preventing them from hitting the ground and breaking the contents.

Having finally reassembled all the people with their packs on the correct, unofficial, side of the wall, we broke out some lunch; logical as it was by then four o'clock in the afternoon. It had taken us all morning to share things out, remember things we'd forgotten, unpack the things that parents thought we'd need but didn't, and then repack them when Tom's parents told us that we really should. (In other words, if we didn't take them, our parents would get to hear about it).

Conversation stopped as we ate, and stayed stopped afterwards as we realised that the first break in the silence would probably mean we'd have to start moving downhill. So long was the silence that it was only broken by the call of a loud bird of some sort, astonished to find six people behind its wall. It shouted out the news to all and sundry and woke us up.

Groaning, we dragged the heavy rucksacks on to our backs and started staggering down the hill. It's a journey I'd rather forget, so I won't dwell on it. We arrived, that's the main thing, and the campsite looked just as wonderful as it had when we'd first seen it. Thankfully we struggled free of the rucksacks and collapsed on to the ground. Bottles came out of rucksacks. We sat gathering our strength for the next effort.

After some discussion we decided that the two tents should be upwind of the fire. Inevitably it was Steve's suggestion based on where he insisted his tent would be. We pitched them – with his help.

"Now you need to get wood," he commanded. "I'll build a fireplace." We looked at him. Surely a fire just needed a heap of sticks and a match? We put it to him… okay, Alex started an argument.

It appears that a fireplace does need to be built if you're going to stop the fire spreading to the surrounding woodland, your tents, and you. We left him to it and looked for wood.

Coming back was oddly like returning home to find your bedroom's been repainted. Two tents were supplemented by a line of string between them. A third, small pop-up tent which, we were told smugly, was for our stores had appeared. In front of all was a fireplace built of rounded stones which Steve had gathered from the pond – we knew that because they were still wet. In it he had piled a cone of wood. It looked like something out of a boys' adventure book. Seeing the wood starting to come in he told us where to put it – "Not near the fire, idiot, or it'll get hot and burn."

"Isn't that the idea?" I asked flippantly, and got The Look again.

He was enjoying being bossy and taking Tom's place as unofficial leader, though he was more direct. Tom did it by suggesting the best way: Steve just told us what to do.

He bullied us into getting our gear into the tents – after an argument about who was sharing with whom, of course. I ended up with Alex and Arif, leaving Joe, Tom and Steve to decide who wasn't going on the outside, by the walls, in their tent. He'd also told us that we needed to dig a large hole behind a bush, downwind of the tents, to use as a loo.

We protested, but all he said was "Where are you going to 'go' then?"

We dug. We left a roll of toilet paper there. We returned to the fire which by then Steve had lit, though he wouldn't tell us how he'd done it. We had a cup of tea and shared out some biscuits that someone had squirreled away.

And we wondered why it wasn't as light as it had been. I looked at my watch. "It's nearly eight o'clock," I exclaimed. "How about cooking?"

After the inevitable arguments about what, and by whom, Tom and Alex set to and cooked, watched by Steve,. It may have been only spuds and tinned mince but it was ours, we'd cooked it, and it was on a fire. And there was a lot of it.

"I'm not carrying any food back up that hill," said Tom.

Then Steve made us wash up. "It's like being at home," complained Arif. "I'm bullied into things there too."

By that time it was almost dark. Steve had given up on the instructions for the night, or at least for the moment. We sat around the dwindling fire and chatted, the pauses growing longer and longer, until we became aware how quiet it was. The little crackles of the fire, miscellaneous rustlings, the water falling down the cliff, the occasional insect and night bird – they were all we could hear. The large, bustling town, and home, seemed a million miles away.

From bravado, because we were on holiday and away from parents nagging at us to get to bed, we stayed up, just sitting, until I felt I just couldn't last out any longer. I laid back on the ground. And yes, the air temperature was still warm enough to make it pleasant.

I suppose it was seeing me do that that made Joe yawn and rumble something about going to bed. He stood, and so did the others. Tom stretched down an arm, I grabbed it and he pulled me up – I was half worried that he'd get me half way and then let go as he'd probably have done at school. But the place, the time, the darkness had all contrived to make the moment special.

Sounds soppy, I know. But there are moments you instinctively know are points in your life which you'd be hard pressed to recreate. This was one of them.

We each found a bush – downwind – and then crawled into the tents. I was asleep before the others had finished muttering about hard ground.

3   First impressions

They were still muttering the next morning. Or maybe they'd just restarted. There seemed to be an argument in the other tent about getting firewood. Since I was once again in need of a downwind bush I called out to tell them I'd go once I'd got dressed. I crawled out, bleary eyed, to find myself alone. No one else was up. The fireplace, the washing up, the pool, all were as we'd left them. Quiet, unspoilt. Then I noticed the birdsong, the sound which was so much louder than when we were at home, and stood amazed.

Finding a bush was a painful experience as I was still barefoot. It was also quite cold since I was still just in underwear. I suddenly hoped that the others wouldn't have had time to dress before I got back or I'd doubtless be the butt of comments.

There was a rustle in some bushes just upwind of me and I looked in alarm. A pair of liquid brown eyes looked back, even more alarmed. A crashing, and the deer was away like the wind.

Back at the camp the conversation was starting, so I hurriedly entered the tent and grabbed some clothes. A few minutes later and I was away searching for wood. It was good to be on my own for a change, especially after witnessing what the woods might have in store for someone who moved quietly.

After some few minutes of trying to creep round and gather firewood I realised that it was either wildlife or breakfast, and made a conscious effort to be more effective as a fuel collector. Once more there was a crashing from the undergrowth but this time the eyes were those of Alex, though it was the copper hair that I actually saw first. He grinned.

"You snore," he said as a welcome.

"Do I? I didn't hear it."

That floored him for a moment.

"Got much?

"What?"

"Wood."

I pointed to the pile I'd collected so far and he nodded. We continued, and our return to camp was welcomed by Tom and Steve. Despite that they sent us back out again to collect more.

At last, under instruction from Steve, breakfast was cooked

and eaten, and declared good. Steve also instructed us that we must wash up unless we wanted to eat off dirty, insect-licked plates at the next meal.

We washed up.

There was a discussion about what we were going to do. After a lot of to-ing and fro-ing we decided to walk down the stream and see where it ended up.

As we left the pool and the campsite we had to climb down beside a series of small waterfalls. That sounds a lot more exotic than it is; they were small falls and the rocks they fall over were on an easy gradient. It was easy going for quite a way, but further down the going became difficult again. More and more we were forced to follow close to the stream's banks so that wherever they had crumbled away we were tripping and almost in the water. The banks gradually became higher and at last we had no room to walk without being in the water itself.

"Oh... what?" exclaimed Tom, "we'll have to climb out of this. Unless anyone wants to get their feet wet."

"We could paddle," I offered.

Steve looked at me scornfully. "Have you seen the rocks in there? Sharp as knives. You'd need your shoes on."

"Well?" I tried to bluff him out.

"Well if you've got more than one pair, I haven't. So forget it."

"We can climb up the bank," Tom's even voice commanded.

It wasn't so much a climb, more a scramble over small rocks that dislodged as we tried to use them as footholds, threatening the head of the person below. We soon decided that one at a time would be safer. The small bushes were more reliable as holds, though our legs were scratched by the time we reached the top, gasping in the heat which hit us.

The little gorge had been cool, shaded as it was by foliage for most of its length. At the top we had found a wide expanse that had been cleared. Tree stumps showed through young gorse bushes. A wide rutted track led away from the area, heading off downhill. We could just see over the trees to the right of the stream. In the far distance were a group of houses in a line.

Steve referred to the map. "That's the little village. We don't want to go there or we'll be chucked off."

"Where now, then?" asked Joe.

Steve looked round. "Really, we need to go on to the other side of the gorge to avoid it. Or we could head back through the woods and find the back of the estate."

"Sod struggling down that cliff and up the other side," said Alex. "Too much like hard work and too hard on the knees."

"Looks like the far reaches then," said Tom, looking round at us as if daring anyone to disagree. He led on, then handed over to Steve, the one who actually stood a chance of finding where we were going.

"Looks like there's another blue spot up at the back," he informed us. Unfortunately he was looking at the map instead of the ground at the time and caught his toe in a rabbit hole. We didn't laugh as he measured his length on the ground, honest. "Falling Man," I muttered. He ignored me.

The map was easy to find but the compass seemed to have flown away. We were about to give up on it when Arif saw a reflection of sunshine from just inside another rabbit hole. "Grand Theft Compass, Rabbit Indicted," he intoned in an American accent. Steve picked it up without a word and limped off. We followed.

He stuck to the direction his compass told him, though if there was any hint of a path we used it. Fortunately the trees here were older, further apart, so that finding our way was not as much of a struggle as we had experienced the day before. The journey led gently, persistently, upwards, a fact brought home to us when we started breathing harder than we thought we should be.

"I'm knackered," panted Alex eventually, as we entered a sort of clearing.

"Drinks and a biscuit all round," suggested Tom, and for once we obeyed without an argument.

Just as we had the previous day, we were reluctant to start moving again and lay for some time where we'd stopped at the edge of the clearing. The sun, once again hot, shone through the leaves far above us with a dappled effect, and a gentle breeze came to us across the clearing. Even the most dull spirited of people would have been privately affected by the peace, the warmth, the absence of human noise; and we were not dull of spirit.

"It's a bit special," rumbled Joe, and then there was silence.

We lay still for a while, drinking it in.

There was a movement opposite us, where the trees restarted. Cautiously I looked up. What I saw made me freeze and I hoped no one else would move or exclaim. A deer stood there, wary, snuffling the air. His antlers were, I suppose, fully grown; certainly they were an impressive sight. I wouldn't have liked to be on the wrong side of them.

He seemed not to see us, and dropped his head to nibble at some grass. This was the sign for others to appear; other, smaller deer with no antlers. His wives. They too bent their heads to graze.

I watched enthralled as this scene was acted out barely thirty metres away and hoped that the others were watching too. To have checked whether they were would have meant moving my head and spooking the deer.

My body was horizontal, my head was raised. That works for a few minutes but after any amount of time you realised that breathing is difficult and your neck muscles are aching. Cautiously I lowered my head and as slowly as I could sat upright. And I mean slowly. Unfortunately even such a gentle movement upset the small bottle of water at my side and it fell over. Immediately I was the focus of twelve large, scared brown eyes, and a moment later there was a thumping of hooves and they were gone.

"Phew!" Alex exclaimed as he sat up and bent his neck one way and then the other. "My neck was aching. I don't know how much longer I could last."

"Me neither," I admitted, "My water fell over. That's what scared them."

"I said this place was special," said Arif. "What a sight! I've never seen deer that close before. And that buck – incredible."

By this time we were all easing aching necks and backs.

"We'd better get on," said Tom, "they'll not be back here today."

We continued, wondering what else we would see on the way. There were two similar clearings we stumbled across, but although our approach was as silent as we could manage we saw no wildlife. Finally we came to the wall, the estate boundary. Of the blue spot there was no sign. "Damn," said Steve.

"Which way now?" asked Tom.

"Dunno… I need to think."

There were no comments to this, for a change.

Joe looked over his shoulder at the map. "Are those two clearings shown? Did we go in a straight line between them?"

"No, they're not, and yes… well, I tried to. But it's not easy when you have to keep veering away to avoid things."

"Can you tell which way's up?"

Steve looked at him scornfully. "North's up!"

"What I meant was, which way is uphill on the map?"

Steve pointed uphill, to our left. "That way."

"Yes," said Joe patiently, "but how does the map show it? How do the contours show it?"

"Ahh..." He looked back at the map. "Contours by the wall, going up… Here?"

"Maybe."

"But it goes up everywhere, including the other side of the wall."

"Yes, but if we go up and get to the highest point, that'll show on the map. Then we know where we are."

"I hate smartarses," said Steve after a pause.

We continued climbing, not without some grumbles, until we could see that the ground started falling away again. Around and in front of us light was visible through the trees, but there was no way of seeing any distance because of them. Behind us was the wall, beyond which the hill continued upwards. Steve spread the map out again. This time all six heads bent over it.

"Here's the boundary wall." He pointed at the map. "The contours look like they come up this way - " he pointed again "- but where do they start down again?"

We looked all along the wall. At one point there was a sort of complicated, multiple upside-down U of the brown lines. I pointed it out with dim memories from an age-old geography lesson. "Is that it?"

Steve looked. So did everyone else. "It must be. It's a sort of spur. The wall crosses it, it keeps going up the other side, and this side of the wall it goes down both sides. So that's where we are.. Phew."

I was rather pleased with myself, but nobody said anything.

"The blue splodge is down there, away from the way we came, so let's go!"

"Hang on," said Tom, "there's a stream or something

crossing the wall there. We could go on along here until we find it, then follow it down to your splodge."

Steve looked again, just said "okay," and folded up the map again. This time, we went. Within ten minutes or so of descent there was a rusty set of bars at the bottom of the wall which let a small stream through, a stream which had made a shallow cutting for itself over the years, exposing the rock. We followed it, but cautiously, remembering the sudden drop we'd found in the way when we were first exploring for our camp site. And sure enough there came the noise of a waterfall through the trees as we wound our way down. The ground became rockier, and steeper. We veered off the direct line of the stream and continued, seeing the rapids – for want of a better word – to our left. They ended in a short fall into a pool, similar to that in our campsite but smaller.

"We could have camped here," said Alex.

"Ours is okay," Tom told him, "and this is even further from where we crossed the wall."

"We could eat here though," he said. "And how about a swim?"

The climb to the summit had made us hot, hungry and thirsty. The pool, being in a natural hollow except at the opposite end, was a sun trap. A swim was certainly an attractive thought.

"Are we allowed to?" I asked. The youngest always makes the silly comment or asks the silly question.

"Seeing no one knows we're here and hasn't actually told us we can be, I'm not sure that matters too much."

He had a point.

"No towels. No swimming things," said Joe.

"You could skinny-dip," suggested Arif. We just looked at him.

"I notice you said 'you'…" Tom commented.

"Well yes, naturally I wouldn't."

"Naturally nothing. We're not skinny-dipping and that's that."

"Good."

"What?"

"Good. That means if we go in in our underwear I can swim too."

The pause was to try and work out the logic in that.

"How do we get dry?" asked Alex.

"In this temperature? We just wait, I should think. We'd be dry in five minutes."

We looked at each other. Eventually Tom shrugged and started pulling off his shirt.

The first foot in the water caused a loud shout. And some of the language that followed as more and more skin was submerged should have turned the air blue. Had we been at school every one of us would have faced a suspension, I should think. Warm, it was not.

We managed about ten minutes maximum in the water before coming out and basking in the sunshine, then running round in circles to get some warmth into our bodies again. We had no idea where that water had been but had we heard it was pumped straight from the Arctic we'd not have been surprised. Except that it wasn't salt.

Lying at last on the warm ground, drying, was a relief, even if the occasional breeze was inclined to make us shiver theatrically. When dry enough, we hurriedly and as privately as possible removed the still-damp underwear and climbed back into normal clothes, then settled back down to have lunch.

It was warm in the hollow, and after a hot climb, a cold swim, a pasty and Penguin lunch, it was inevitable that we just lay back and sunbathed. The small waterfall at the head of the pool drowned out any other noises apart from the few investigating insects, so it was hardly surprising that we all dozed off.

A voice in my dream told me it was nearly four o'clock, and did so in such a tone of shock that as I woke to ask who was shouting I wondered why it was so light at that time of the morning. Realisation and memory returned and I shaded my eyes to see what was happening.

The others had also been jolted awake, apart from Joe who was looking accusingly at us as if he had been the only one not to sleep.

"You've been asleep for an hour," he complained. We should be getting on."

"How about you, Joe?" I demanded. "You weren't asleep, then."

"Well… okay then, but we still should be getting back."

He was right. We had to try and navigate our way to our

own pool. Steve dug out the map again.

"Don't we just follow the stream down?" asked Tom.

Steve made no answer, just looked at the paper. "No," he said finally. "This stream isn't ours. It joins ours, but further down, near the hamlet. Too near. We need to cut across to ours."

He dug in his pocket for the compass and played with it, then looked at it and reeled off three numbers. "That's our direction."

"Fine," Tom said witheringly, "care to point to it?"

Steve looked at the compass, held it level in front of him and swung slowly round, stopping as he was facing the bottom lip of the pool. "That way."

"You mean, we need to get over the top of the waterfall," said Tom.

"Suppose so. That way, anyway."

"That way, or anyway?" joked Alex.

"Pity you didn't tell us when we were swimming," Arif complained. "We could have got dry that side."

"Pity you didn't ask me when we were over that side," retorted Steve.

"Did you have the map with you?" asked Arif innocently. He got no reply.

The stream's exit proved to be the start of a shallow slope of boulders. The water ran through and under them rather than over, so we were able to cross without getting wet. Not even 'Falling Man' lost his footing. At the other side we waited for him to point out the direction again, and followed on.

Despite the best efforts of the undergrowth, which here was rather thicker than we'd experienced in the morning, we made quite good time, and only an hour later found what we assumed was our own stream. Of our camp site there was no clue, though.

"We've followed this once, all the way down to that steep valley," said Steve. "Anyone remember this bit?"

None of us did.

He looked at the compass again. "It's flowing in the right direction to be ours, and only the two are marked... If we were near that look out point it'd be a lot deeper. I think we go upstream. I can't believe we'd be so far above our camp site that we wouldn't remember it from the first days."

"'The first days'… he made it sound as if we'd been marooned there for years. We turned left and climbed up beside the water. And there, round the stream's next bend, were 'our' little waterfalls. We climbed, and the sight of the tents was a tonic.

"Ten minutes' rest and we start wood collecting, and I'll start a fire," Steve bullied. We all groaned theatrically.

4   Eviction

It was actually only twenty minutes later that I raised myself and went to find a bush – my bush: it seemed only right. Avoiding the places where others had 'been' I managed to collect some good armfuls of wood and was pleased to pass Alex and Joe doing the same on my way back, even if they were doing it reluctantly having been told to by Steve. He and Tom were feeding the fire and Arif was chopping something into a billy.

"Mum did a curry for us," he explained. "It's all right, it's a proper Indian one, not the English version that takes the roof off your mouth."

"Why are you chopping it into the billy?" I asked.

He looked at me pitifully. "That's onion, wazzock. You fry it first."

"You mean it's not a curry?"

I dodged the piece of chopped onion he flicked at me and went to sit by the pool. A ring of ripples was visible, and I looked for what had caused it. There was nothing. I looked away, distracted by a noisy bird up on the cliff by the waterfall and when I looked back there was another ring of ripples.. Again I scanned the surface, then kept watching.

Nothing.

Alex called from behind me. I turned.

"Oh, it's all right," he said, "I've found it."

I turned back. This time there was an audible 'plop' as something fell into the water. I looked round and found Joe trying to look innocent. The others were looking down and I just knew they were trying to make their laughs invisible. I called them some rude names. Joe laughed. "Your face when you saw the ripples - and when you realised what it was!"

Steve told me it was dangerous to fight near the fire, even in fun, so we stopped. As I looked away, brushing the usual leaves from my clothes, there was another ring of ripples on the water.

"Who is it this time?" I asked, witheringly. They all gave versions of 'not me'. It had obviously not been Joe, who was at my side, or I'd have seen him. I looked back, and this time saw the ripples start.

"There's fish in there," Joe growled.

"Fish for dinner tomorrow," I called to the others.

"Don't count your fish before they're hatched," said Joe. I looked at him.

"Caught?"

"That too."

The fish came up a few more times and we watched it. Then we sat and watched it. Then we just sat. At last there was a call from Arif and we went to eat.

Given Arif's family background we shouldn't have expected the usual curry take-away standard of curry, so often just violent spice and no meat, His mum had done us proud, and even the occasionally fussy Alex said it wasn't bad. We decided we didn't need anything afterwards. Actually, we didn't decide. We just lay back where we were and made satisfied noises and no one thought to mention apple pie (my Mum's offering). I was glad, not because she can't cook, but because I wouldn't have been able to face any more food.

As usual we were bullied into washing up, this time to Arif's mum's standards as well as Steve's. He told us she'd never cook for us again if we didn't.

Once again, we lazed around afterwards, until Steve 'suggested' we collect firewood for the morning. Now used to his 'suggestions' we set to and amassed a great pile, which prompted him to continue the cooking fire and to suggest we all sat round it. And we did, chatting, arguing and just being silent as the mood took us, until once again we found keeping our eyes open was a problem.

I slept like one of the logs we'd collected. It was way past dawn when I woke and was pleased there seemed to be no one else conscious before me. Carefully getting from the tent I thought to start the fire but there were no matches visible. Instead I sat and watched the pool again and was just starting to wish I'd got more clothes on when there was a yawn behind me. Arif.

We cooked, ate and washed up as before, then discussed a route for the day. Steve mentioned the old, mainly dilapidated manor house again; he was almost sure it was uninhabitable. It sounded interesting, so we equipped ourselves with sandwiches and drinks and set off.

The going was difficult, as usual, and we almost immediately got lost. The ground was mainly downhill to our right if we were to follow the dead reckoning Steve wished on us. But the terrain was so thick with brambles and general undergrowth that we could only hope we were on the right "path", even if there wasn't one. We'd been struggling for about forty five minutes when the terrain seemed to be getting, if not easier, then less overgrown. Trees dominated, as ever, but the ground became almost springy with the depth of leaf mould on it. Alex suggested a halt and we were glad to sit, two each to a tree, and remove some of the thorns from clothing and skin.

It was while we were each drinking that we heard footsteps. Fast footsteps, not human. Thinking again of deer we stayed as still as we could, but no sign of anything moving could be seen. Soon peace returned, bottles were put away and we cautiously continued in what we thought to be the right direction – even Falling Man was puzzled.

We crossed still more of the same woodland. It felt cool, ancient, and increasingly sun-dappled. Walking inevitably caused us to disturb the leaf mould, so thick it was, and a constant muffled rustling accompanied our progress. So used did we become to the sound effects that when a deep bark sounded just behind us we all jumped.

Turning, cautiously, we found a Labrador watching us. As Labradors go he was quite slim, and appeared as surprised to see us as we were to see him. He just watched us, with that engaging grin on his face that the breed often shows.

Arif broke the silence by greeting him like a long lost friend. And cautiously the two approached, met and seemed to like each other. We knew it was all right when, after a few moments of stroking, tickling behind the ears and so on, the silly animal rolled over. Arif just grinned and scratched the chest. We crowded round and still the dog just grinned at us.

"Where does he come from?" I asked, more in wonderment than with any hope of a reply.

"No collar," said Arif quietly, as if he was still talking to the dog.

I looked at him, puzzled.

"No collar, no tag," he explained.

I nodded, feeling rather silly.

We were happily making a fuss of the dog who seemed to have no better way of enjoying himself than to be petted by a load of strangers, when there came a shout in the distance. At once the dog stiffened, rolled upright, got to its paws and gave an answering bark. Just one. And there started a surreal conversation; every minute or so there was a shout, and the dog answered back. And each time the shouts were closer.

We looked at each other.

"Do we pretend we're not here?" Alex asked.

"Pointless," said Arif, "The dog will find us anyway."

"True," muttered Tom. "And it'd probably look worse if we were searched for rather than just discovered."

So we just sat there, talking to the dog, who was still very friendly – he just gathered in his muscles periodically to bark an answer to the next shout.

When the shouts were near, he ran from our caresses and vanished from the clearing. We heard some sort of human greeting, tinged with reproach, but it wasn't in English. A man appeared in the clearing, saw us and froze.

He was tall and thin, bearded, with deep set eyes; one of those people who you instantly like. Yet his voice when he spoke was far from friendly.

"What are you doing to my dog?"

We looked. No one was expecting that; but then no one was expecting *him*. Arif answered. After all, he was the dog-whisperer.

"Is he yours? He's super. And he came to us. He's fine, as you can see."

The man looked at him, no doubt taking in his dark face, black hair and like so many others, making assumptions.

"Hmm. He was too far away from me, and seeing you here, where you should not be, he is trying to find you, no doubt. But what are you doing here? You must know the estate is private and we do not let people in."

We all knew the only person who had been there before was Steve, and heads swivelled to look at him; a point that wasn't lost on him.

"Er.. well, I have been here before. With the Scouts, when they came to do orienteering. There wasn't a problem then."

"A special, that was, and agreed by the villagers. You have no right to be here. And you, as a Scout – you are one, I suppose – should know that and respect it."

"But surely, if we're not doing any harm...?"

"And how does anyone know you are doing no harm? *If* you

are a Scout and *if* you know how to behave in the countryside that may be fine, for you. But still you are forbidden to come here. And these others are not Scouts. So they are even less welcome. What are you doing here? And what would you have done to my dog?"

It was Tom's turn. "We're just walking, exploring. Watching nature. Enjoying the forest. We don't get out to country like this often. And your dog? We were saying hallo to him – he's very friendly. We were going to try and find the old house, to have a look at it, see if it was as dilapidated as people say it is. He would have come with us, I'm sure; followed us, you know."

The man looked at him. Nodded. "Well, you'll have to leave. You're not allowed here, and that's that. It's not just me, it's the people in the village. If they knew you were here they would call the Police and tell your parents, and that would not be good."

"But we were... Ow!"

Tom had stamped on my foot. I never did finish the sentence.

"We'll have to collect our stuff from over there," he said sadly.

"Do that. Then follow me. And Scout or not, finding your way around here is difficult, and if you did run Lars would find you, and with him would be the people from the village. And me."

"Who's Lars?" asked Joe.

The man nodded at his dog. To give the dog his due he seemed just as happy to see us as he had to start with.

We let this sink in, then retreated to the trees and our packs.

"Gather round," hissed Tom. "Don't let him think we're talking. We can't escape, but we can get back in later. Don't tell him we're camping here."

"Is that why you stamped on my foot?" I asked indignantly.

"Yes. You were going to mention getting stuff from the tents."

I had no answer to that.

We had no option but to follow him. If we'd run, the whole hamlet could have been called out, so far as we knew, and our parents involved, and that would have been that. He – and Lars – seemed to know their way well; unsurprisingly, I suppose.

From what I could remember of our planned route before we had met Lars, we seemed to be still following it, so I wondered if we were headed for the old house after all. My thoughts were answered by the appearance through the trees of extensive roofs; extensive and damaged roofs, roofs that had no option but to let in the weather. There were comments between us. The man heard.

"Nobody lives there now. It is too damaged. The last of the owners died many years ago. But there is a cottage I have kept in good condition."

"So… can I ask…" started Joe, "… what you have to do to be here?"

The man looked at him. "Only those from the village can be here. I told you."

"But if we were friends of one of the village, what then?"

"But you are not."

"But if we became friends with one. Or… or with you?"

The man looked at him, and for a moment I wondered if there was a smile about to appear on his face. But it seemed to be a non-starter.

"You trespass here and ask me to befriend you so you can stay here? You have cheek, *mijneer*."

"Is that Ge… No, it isn't German. That would be Mein Herr," I said.

"*Nee*… No. I will not speak German. It is *Nederlands*, Dutch you would call it."

I nodded. "It is a softer way of saying it than German."

"I will not speak German, though my Father did. But it did not help him in the war."

We paused. The conversation seemed to have gone out of our comfort zone.

"In the… in the war *here*?" I asked.

"No. He and my Mother were in Holland. I was small then. The Germans came for him. My Mother hid; she did not know he was in the house when they came or she would have made him hide too. He had been in the Dutch government, but mostly he had been helping English soldiers to escape."

There was another pause.

"Wow," said Alex. "He was brave."

We had nearly reached the cottage, where Lars was now waiting, panting, tail wagging, with an expectant look on his face.

"So you weren't born in England?" asked Tom.

"I was born in Nederland. The war ended when I was just a boy."

"So... you came over here?"

"Huh! On my own, yes, at twelve years old! My mother came over with my step-father."

"Oh..." said Tom. But Alex wasn't so easily satisfied.

"Holland must have been horrible then."

"People were starving. The Germans had made sure of that. An English officer came to us and took a fancy to my Mother, and he was one of the sons here." He indicated around him.

We were now gathered around the cottage door. Lars scratched at it, wanting to go in.

"He's thirsty," said Arif.

The man shot a look at him.

"You have a dog?"

"No, we are Muslim, and anyway my parents say one would be too much of a tie. But I wish I did have one."

"He likes you."

Arif grinned. "I make friends with most dogs."

A pause.

"I suppose you want a drink too," said the man, walking to the door and opening it. It hadn't been locked, I noticed casually.

"Please. It's been a long time since we had anything." Tom was exercising his right to talk for all of us.

The man and Lars vanished into the cottage. We hung around uncertainly, wondering whether we should follow him. But he was soon back, carrying a dog bowl and a bucket. We followed him, prompted by a wag of his head, as he walked round the cottage to its garden.

We were all shocked to encounter an oasis of a well tended, colourful, genuine cottage garden. There was a rumble of "wow...", and he stopped to look back. This time there was indeed a smile on his face.

"Few people have seen my garden. It is my hobby."

He crossed to what we thought was the garden's 'water feature', a brick-built, wooden-roofed well, complete with winding drum, rope around it and a handle to turn. But rather than just looking at it, the man hung the bucket on a hook attached to the rope, and started to wind it down.

"But…but do you get your water from here?" asked Steve.

"Water to the House was cut off years ago when nobody would pay the rates. There was nobody left to pay them."

"So you have no water…" Steve said.

"Of course I have water! Better water than ever came from tap. Here…" He beckoned to Steve. "You have muscles. Wind it up for me."

So Steve grabbed hold of the handle and wound. Fast. Turn after turn of rope wound itself over the drum, and he got slower and slower, panting, red faced.

"Someone else's turn," he gasped, and would have let go of the handle had it not been for a shout from the man.

"Don't let go!"

Steve looked at him, then at the handle, and despite his panting, grinned. Joe stepped forward and carefully took hold of the metal, and continued winding until the man stopped him. The bucket was unhooked, the well covered again, and we followed him once again to the door.

"Wait there. I'll bring out mugs."

He went in. We stood and looked at each other. His head popped out again.

"And no running off while I'm in there!"

The idea had occurred to us, but then we knew that the dog could find us and, more importantly, find the tents. At least this way we would stand a chance of climbing back over the wall where we first got in and getting them. Sleeping another night in them, even.

So we were still there when he returned with a variety of mugs which we eagerly filled and drank from. He was right about the water. It was totally unlike the stuff that came from our taps; this tasted cold, pure, like nothing we had encountered. Apart from...

Arif said: "We were on holiday in the Lake District once, and the water from the stream from the fells tasted like this. It was so good, we bottled some."

"You mean, to sell?" asked the man.

"No, to take home."

He nodded. "Soon run this dry if you bottled it to sell."

He collected the mugs. One fell from his hands on the way to the cottage. Arif went, picked it up and took it into the kitchen. The man met him just as he'd entered and rather abruptly ushered him out again, putting the mug down by the door.

"Come on," we were ordered, and had no option but to follow him downhill. At one point the dog darted off into the woodland, barking excitedly, but he was called back. He obeyed, but you could tell he was puzzled as he kept looking back to where he'd been.

"Hunting?" asked Arif.

"Yes, we do." And with that he shut his mouth as if he'd said too much. He led us, wordlessly, down a path that became wider and more worn until at last rooftops could be seen. Without delay he led on; the path became a track, then a dust road leading past the inevitable houses. Fortunately there was no one else around, though these buildings were obviously well cared for and lived in.

We rounded a bend to an anonymous turning on to a metalled road.

"Just down there," we were told, "and you will find the main road. It has been nice talking to you but please remember this is private land. If the Scouts want to come back your people can make arrangements but that is it."

We muttered variations on "Er…well…okay…goodbye…" and he turned his back and walked back, disappearing round the bend.

"Well," said Tom, "that's that… for today."

The last few words were said in a quiet voice for our ears only. He held his finger to his lips, turned and walked towards the road.

5   The problems start

Not until we were on the bus heading homewards would he let any of us speak.

"We'll have to fetch our stuff, of course," he said as an introduction.

There was a chorus of comments at that stage, indignant comments about allowing us to be bullied into just leaving the estate.

"Don't be idiots," he said when he could make himself heard again. "If we'd kicked off he'd have been really bolshie, and probably someone would have mentioned camping gear. This way we've said nothing about *not* going back and have a campsite ready to go back to when we want. No one ever goes that far into the estate nowadays; we'd have seen the tracks if they had. No, this way we can camp again, make sure we stay up the back out of his way, and leave when we want to."

"What about the food?" asked Alex.

"Mostly tinned and packets left. We ate the fresh stuff, apart from your apple pie, Matt. Milk we can take back with us." Joe was pretty positive about that.

"What's up, Arif?" I asked. He had been staring out of the window taking little notice of the chat.

He shook himself. "It was in his kitchen. Over on the table… you didn't see it."

"See what?" asked Joe.

"I don't know…"

That prompted a chorus of comments, mainly derisive.

"I mean, I'm not sure. It was something… I've seen it before, but I can't think what it was."

Tom looked at him. "What are you talking about, Arif?"

"I don't know, I tell you. There was something – some things – in his kitchen that I'm sure I've seen before but I can't remember where. And somehow it's important. But – well look. I'll Google around a bit and see what I can find."

We looked at him hopefully, but his phone was out of charge, just as ours were.

"Should have turned them off when we were there," growled Joe.

"We're going to have to do some explaining," said Steve.

"Just tell them we've run out of food," said Steve.

"Well, that's nearly true," Joe answered with a grin. "*And* I need a shower."

"That's true," we all said. It was inevitable, really. We grinned, and moved carefully out of his way.

"When are we going back?" I asked, aware that quite a lot of my clothes were still in the tent. Their absence would be noticed.

"Tomorrow? Couple of days when he's forgotten us?" Alex was keen.

"See what the weather does," Tom said. "We can look at the forecast tonight and see what's what."

One by one we left the bus. I was right; that evening when the parents came home my clothes were missed and I got a bit of a lecture about irresponsibility. The truth nearly came out, but I thought about the consequences of saying 'private land' and 'not allowed there' to them, and bit my tongue.

The weather forecast made me glad we had returned. Thinking back to how we'd left the tents, I was also glad that Steve had insisted we'd secured them. Secured them as well as it's possible to 'secure' any tent. They should at least stay dry, something I was able to tell the parents confidently when they started grilling me again.

During the gaps in the rain that week we managed to get out of our respective houses a few times to visit each other, but it wasn't the same as being back in the woods and on the estate. I found myself getting bored, despite it being only the second week of the holidays. It was on one of the excursions to visit someone and hang out, this time on a trip into town, that Joe, Arif and I were stopped by three men.

There are a very few people I instantly dislike. These were three such, each unlikeable in his own way. It may have been the sneering attitude of one, or the way we were looked at by the others, but dislike them we all three did.

"Hallo *boys*," said the sly eyed one. "You go to the Community School, don't you?"

"College," I reacted before my better judgement kicked in. The other man sneered down at me.

"*College* of course." He said it with a humourless, condescending laugh that made me want to punch him. "That's where Emily Long goes, isn't it. We have an arrangement with her."

It was the way he used the word 'arrangement' that made me squirm.

"Do you?" said Arif, taking charge, to my relief. "What sort of arrangement?"

"A *business* arrangement," he was told sarcastically. "An arrangement she enjoys and earns her money."

"And some of her friends could help her as well," said another, "and earn some money. You could earn some yourselves if you can introduce us."

"Oh really?" Joe growled. The man looked at him calculatingly.

"Sounds like you might already *know* her. Or more of her friends perhaps."

"Course I do," said Joe, "we go to the same *college*."

"You know what I mean," said the sneering one. He might have done: Joe might have done. I hadn't a clue.

"You tell any of the good lookers who are close friends of Emily's that there's money to be earned. Lookers, of course. These boys will know." He nodded at Arif and Joe whilst somehow managing to sneer at me.

"But mind you only tell them. And tell them to go to the Plough on a Wednesday after 8 and ask for Gerald. And no telling anyone else. It'd be horrible if anything happened to you."

There was a shock to the words. It sounded like a threat. Arif's turn to look him in the eye. "What d'you mean by that?"

"Just that. After all, we know Emily, and we know where she lives. And we know where you three come from too. So no telling parents, no telling Police or anyone else. Just the girls."

The words I wanted to shout back at him failed me. I wasn't used to being threatened by an adult – not one I didn't know and who wasn't a teacher, and one who meant more than 'detention' when he said "if anything happened…". The other two said nothing either, as the three men walked away from us.

We just looked at each other. Well actually we tried our best not to, but kept catching each others' eye anyway. What they'd hinted at was something outside my experience, something that I knew existed but which wasn't something that was mine to contemplate. Not yet.

"Now what?" said Joe. His voice broke the mood. I shook

my head to clear away the doubts. It nearly worked.

"We can't just do nothing," said Arif. "I don't know about you, but although I haven't much time for Emily – or some of her friends – I'd not trust those men with her. It sounded like they… they wanted to…"

"They did," said Joe, as if it was obvious. "I'd heard her talking about getting some weekend work while school was on. And by her smirk and the way she didn't give details it was certainly not a paper round or shop work."

"And they want us to get her friends in on it too?" I wondered.

"The 'game' needs a good supply," said Joe.

"How do you know so much about it?" I asked, half worried that he might be involved himself.

"Dad's in the Police. Well, he's Support, but he gets to know things, so I do too."

"They don't know he's Police," said Arif, "and nor did we."

"You don't." Joe gave a sort of non-smile. "No. And I wasn't really going to tell that man, was I?"

We talked round it for a few minutes and decided the best thing would be to see Tom and get his input. It started raining again on the way, so by the time we knocked on his door we were soaking. His mother wordlessly threw towels to us so we could at least dry our hair while we were talking.

Tom, too, was silent after we'd finished. Then:

"We've got to go to the Police, of course."

"But they threatened us!"

"But they wouldn't actually *do* anything."

"How do you know?"

"It wasn't you they were threatening!"

He had no reply to that but asked: "Well, what do you suggest?"

"We don't know," I told him. "That's the trouble. If we tell anyone they could come after us. Or do something to Emily."

"Someone needs to do something," said Tom eventually. "And we can't just troll round to the Police Station and ask to talk to someone."

"I suppose… I suppose I could ask Dad," said Joe. "He's used to keeping things quiet. It's part of his job."

We looked at him. Although the man had said 'no parents, no Police', he wasn't exactly Police. And I thought that if I told the story, well, he wasn't my parent, either. I started to think more hopefully about it.

So, not without some misgivings, it was agreed. I would go to Joe's in the morning. Arif would come round after a while as if by accident. We'd all go swimming after that.

But I got a call from Joe that night to tell me his Dad wouldn't be there in the morning; he was on a case. "Come round late afternoon, about five or six. He should be back then. Or we could go swimming this afternoon and all end up at mine. I'll tell Mum you're coming for a meal. Arif too."

That sounded more positive, and probably the three of us going to someone's home for a meal would be less suspicious. I was a bit jittery, though.

Some others from the school were in the pool, including Emily, to my surprise. She saw me looking at her and gave the same sort of sneer that the men had – I hadn't a clue why. For Joe she seemed to have more of a favourable glance. In fact a positive stare, at times. I wondered if she realised. She was with some friends of hers; some from our class, including one or two who I thought really...well, nice to look at. I wondered if the men would like them. I shuddered at the thought.

They all left before us. At last we were free to swim without worrying.

Later, as we walked away from the pool, we rounded a corner and almost bumped into two of the men who'd spoken to us.

The creepy one laughed. "We've just seen Emily and her friends, and they say you haven't spoken to them about what we said."

It was an accusation. I just looked at him, and could feel my face reddening. Arif came to the rescue again.

"We'd have had to shout to do that in there," he told the man. "I mean, we could have, but who knows how many Police there are helping their kids to learn to swim?"

He received a look which should have reduced him to a skeleton, but the two said nothing and headed off towards the pool.

"Whew!" I said when they were out of sight. "Well done, Arif."

He grinned at me. "I can be quick off the mark sometimes."

Joe's dad wasn't home when we arrived. His mum, one of

those calm, easy-going people who seem unphased by most things, told us that he could be back at any time. "It depends what's happened," she told us.

Joe confirmed it. "Unless there's been something major, he's usually pretty good but it could be any time up to seven."

We had settled down to a meal that the unflustered Mrs Hammond seemed to conjure up effortlessly when her husband finally arrived. He looked a bit shocked to see two extra people there, but grinned at us and sat down.

"Dad," Joe started immediately, "we need to talk."

His Dad almost choked over his first mouthful. When he had recovered, and finished it, he looked at Joe.

"I thought that was meant to be my line for you, when there was something that you'd done wrong?" There was, though, the suspicion of a laugh in his voice so I knew not to take it seriously.

"It's serious, Dad," said Joe. "I wouldn't ask at a meal if it wasn't, would I?"

His Dad nodded. "Not another false accusation, is it?"

"What?"

"Like the one that got the six of you that nickname."

I cottoned on first. "The Usual Suspects? No, nothing like that."

"Good. May we finish the meal first? Or is it so urgent that I need to stop eating so I can make notes?"

"You'll need to make notes, Dad. But we can eat first."

"You're all in this together, are you?"

"Yes," I said without thinking.

"No," said Arif. "We're not in it at all. Nor is Joe. And we don't want to be."

Joe looked at him gratefully. His Dad's eyebrows rose.

"Hmm. Perhaps I'd better hurry so we can get to the bottom of it, then."

"It's not *that* urgent. Not as in *immediate*." Joe wanted to smooth things over. His father looked at him, nodded, and the conversation turned to our camping trip.

"Just as well you came back when you did," Mr Hammond told us. "The weather is set to carry on being foul over the next couple of days, but it's better after that."

And so we carried on, talking about trivial things, until we were all full and Mrs Hammond was declining offers of help with the washing up.

"It goes in the dishwasher, thanks, and it sounds as if you need to talk before these two have to go back home."

So it was that Arif and I started to tell Mr Hammond the tale. I could see him becoming increasingly concerned as we went on. Joe, as we'd agreed, said nothing, even when asked a direct question by his father. Arif or I would always jump in with a response first.

When we'd finished he was silent for a moment or two. Looking suddenly at his son he asked the simple question we hadn't expected. "Why have you said nothing at all through this story? It's not a question of you not believing it – it's you they spoke to first. But you've said nothing, not even answered any of my questions."

Joe wriggled uncomfortably, but had to answer.

"They said that we mustn't tell anyone, not our parents, not the Police. You aren't Arif's or..."

His Dad interrupted. "I see. So you thought you couldn't talk because that would mean that you'd told your parents. Fair enough, but you might want to look at it differently. You're honouring a demand made by these people. But they're not honouring a demand made by the Law and by decent people anywhere. So how does that work?"

Joe sat in silence for a moment. "Two wrongs don't make a right?"

It was his father's time to be silent.

"Look, Dad, we're in the middle of this. They were serious when they threatened us that if we told anyone they'd get even. Somehow. But we can't just leave it. And they expect us to talk to these girls to get them to... well, you know."

"Tell me exactly what they said, please."

It took some time, but we were able to get the words over to his Dad so he could write it down.

"What are you going to do with that now?" asked Arif.

"We have an investigation going on. There's much you've said that ties in with what I've heard, but there are some nuggets that the Police themselves will want to know. And..."

"But they *can't*," I exclaimed, horrified. "If they get to know what those men have said to us, they'll know where it all came from. Us."

Mr Hammond looked at me. "The Police aren't so stupid,

Matt. One of the first things they'll probably do is visit various pubs, which might or might not include the Plough. And it may be on a weekday, or a weekend. It may be in uniform or not, or both. It'll be a chance encounter. And if they find underage girls in there, well, action will be taken. You have no need to worry."

"What should we do, Dad?"

He thought. "Firstly, nothing. If you see any of the men, tell them you're trying to do what they ask but... but that it's the school holidays and not everyone is about. Then once I've been able to talk to Plod... sorry, that's technician-speak and mustn't be repeated ... the guys in the Force itself, I might be able to tell you more."

There was silence as we digested all that, but he went on:

"Don't forget that just as the girls' safety is the most important thing, equal to that in the minds of the Police will be the safety of any youngster at all involved. So don't worry: no chances will be taken."

That, really, was the end of that for the night. Later, Arif and I walked home – for some reason he wanted to go past my house. I turned at the door to say goodnight. He grinned, and hung there for a moment.

"Plod!" he said, and we both laughed.

6 Plotting and Amy

We had decided to try and make sure none of us went around alone. It seemed safest, even if the Police – Plod – were aware of us and the potential dangers. We discussed it all freely, at least when we knew we couldn't be overheard. On the second day after our visit to the Hammonds Joe asked Arif and me if we'd like to go round for a meal again that night. Parents were contacted and once again we sat down to Mrs Hammond's cooking.

"Police are very interested," Mr Hammond confirmed to us afterwards. "They're fairly happy that contact between you and them should happen with me as middle-man. They do want written statements from you three, though. That should mean that you needn't appear in Court…"

We looked at each other, horrified. That was what we knew we had to avoid, otherwise the men would know who it was who gave them away. We knew enough about gangs and so on to realise that even if these people were caught their friends could come after us.

Mr Hammond saw our faces. "Statements are only to keep the paperwork trail intact," he said. I didn't have a clue what he meant. He tried again.

"The Police have to have all the right paperwork, otherwise the case will collapse. What they need is information written by you that they can keep without it appearing in Court. The results of the raids on the pubs will make sure these men believe it was just bad luck or coincidence that got them, not anything you've done."

We digested this.

He hesitated and started again: "They've also suggested that one of you, Arif perhaps, talks to one of the other girls at the school, preferably somewhere and at a time when the men can see you. There's nothing to stop you, Arif, from sounding out a girl about Emily Long and see how much she knows, and what her attitude is. They don't want to get anyone into trouble, someone who's not guilty, but it might be that one of her friends is unaware of the situation. You could tell her they've asked you to ask her if she was interested in making money, and you're doing as they asked. You should also tell her that you know that she wouldn't want to be involved in anything like that. If that's true."

Arif thought for a moment. "I'm not sure if she's a friend of Emily's, but there's Amy. She's okay, and often hangs around the shopping centre when she's bored. I could talk to her."

"I'll leave that to you, then, Arif. Just don't put yourself in danger. And please keep me posted about what's happening. We can always meet here, or at your place if your parents don't mind."

"My parents don't know. Not yet, anyway. And I want to keep it that way." We knew his parents, and their view on Arif's few entanglements with officialdom.

There was more, of course, but it didn't last long.

We heard nothing for a day or two, and each went his own way, usually with parents – much to their surprise. Normally we tried to avoid parental trips out, especially shopping. Mr Hammond phoned eventually and Arif and I met each other and walked to Joe's house.

Arif was quiet, quieter than usual, which meant he was almost silent. He looked embarrassed when asked what he had to report.

"I spoke to... to Amy," he admitted. And it sounded rather like an admission rather than a report. "She knows Emily but she says she tries to avoid her. Doesn't like her. She wanted to know why I wanted to know, and asked if I had anything to do with Emily. In *that* way. You know."

He paused, even more embarrassed. "I was so horrified at the idea that I almost shouted 'No!', and it was then that I saw someone in a shop doorway nearby. A bloke. Just standing, listening. So I led her away a bit to the middle of the market place and talked quietly and... well, I may have said too much."

"Okay, Arif, calm down," said Mr Hammond. "What did you tell her?"

"That we thought Emily was into prostitution and some men had asked us to see if any of her friends were interested in doing the same. And that I was talking to her about it because we'd been threatened that if we didn't try and get other girls they'd do something to us."

He stopped again. We waited.

"She asked who the others were and I told her, and she said we should go to the Police. And then I told her we had..."

Our mouths dropped open. Or it felt like it. He carried on, wretchedly. "She asked why I was talking to her and I told her that I knew there was no way that she would be involved or want to be involved or even think about being involved. And I told her she mustn't tell anyone 'cos if she did we'd all be in danger."

We watched him, willing him on.

"It was odd," he said slowly. "At first she looked shocked, then she smiled, and then she asked how she came in to it then. So I told her she'd already done what was necessary by meeting me and I was sorry to have bothered her."

He stopped again, and this time didn't want to go on.

"What did the man do?" asked Mr Hammond.

Arif looked at him as if startled. "Oh him… he'd vanished by the time we left."

"How much longer were you there?" he asked.

"Oh… er… I don't know."

"Five minutes? Ten? Half an hour?"

He thought. "I got home at half past four."

"And what time had you met?"

"I'd arranged to meet her at three."

"So if she was on time, you spent an hour and a quarter talking to her."

"S'pose so," he muttered.

What on earth could they have been talking about all that…. And then my mind suddenly clicked. Those soppy films my mother loved so much came flooding into my mind and I had to do a reality check. Arif? With a girlfriend? But he was one of us. He was also the eldest of us… oh well.

"Well, it probably persuaded the watcher that you were doing a good job on persuading her, so that's taken the pressure off all of you," Mr Hammond said. "And it may have done you a different sort of favour too, Arif. Can you carry on keeping your eyes open, guys, and tell us if there are still people watching? And anything else?"

It was only the next day that Arif called my land line. He'd heard from Amy, who'd had a man come up to her and ask her to come to the Plough that Wednesday where she'd learn a lot to her advantage that her "boyfriend had told her about yesterday". She had been non-committal, saying that her parents liked her to be indoors early during the week. Arif was so embarrassed again that he could hardly say the words, so I cut him short and asked what Amy was going to do about it.

"I don't know," he admitted. "I've got to phone Mr Hammond later and ask. I was so worried about her and what she'd think that I don't know what I said. But I've got to speak to him and then phone her back. On her mobile. Her parents don't like boys phoning the landline. Or her mobile, come to that. But she can go out and then make a call. Oh, Matt, what have we got ourselves into?"

"How old is she, then?"I asked, though it had little to do with the problems.

"Oh, our age, I suppose. Why?"

"Just wondering if she was as old as Emily."

Our age... his age, or mine? Hmm.

"Tell me what happens with Joe's Dad," I said. He promised he would.

Hours later, almost when I was looking at the clock and wondering when one or other parent would mention bed time, the phone rang again. Mr Hammond, asking for me. My puzzled mother gave me the phone and I vanished into the kitchen with it to get some privacy.

"Arif's phone has been stolen from him," he told me. "Don't call it or text it, please, and don't use yours. Take the battery out. If they've got the number they might be able to trace it and somehow bug it. I'm having to say the same thing to all of Arif's other contacts to say the same, and it's a long job. Some parents are having kittens and it's difficult persuading them that it'll only be for a few days.

"You see, we think it's all happening on Wednesday. This Wednesday. And now I need to talk to your parents, please, because we need you out of the way then, starting early that morning. I mean really early. It's best if you're all out of circulation before these people get up. So I'm in for a bumpy ride."

I returned the phone, and listened as voices raised in alarm, then returned to puzzlement, and then to anger.

"And where do the Police think they're all going so as to get out of the way?" asked Dad at last. And then I knew what we had to do. I signalled to Dad until at last he stopped shushing me and asked Joe's Dad to hang on.

"We'll go back to the camp!" I exclaimed. "It's so deep in

48

the woods no one will find us there."

He looked at me for a moment. "I can't take the chance," He said, "and we don't even know where it is. It could be that this friend of yours whose parents own it could be something to do with these… these…*people*."

"Dad, it's not a chance; well, it is, it's our only chance. We can't all just make arrangements to go away to some hotel, none of us can afford it." I hoped he wouldn't pick up on where the camp was.

"And how do we check on you? Tim tells me all your mobiles may have been hacked into. And where is this camp, anyway?"

Fortunately the phone squawked again. Dad jammed it back to his ear and listened.

"That's a point," said Dad. "That'd be quite cheap."

They talked for a lot longer, but it's difficult to draw full conclusions from one side of a conversation. At last Dad rang off.

"Well," he said, "you have got yourselves into trouble again. And this time it's even more serious. But you should have told us, and we could have gone to the Police. It's very bad to hear all this from someone else. Too bad."

"Dad, the men said 'No parents, no Police', and threatened us with what might happen if we did tell you."

"What threats did they make?" asked Mum indignantly.

I thought back. What had they actually said? Well…

"Well, they knew where we lived, and Emily knows us, and you, and… well, they didn't exactly say what," I ended lamely.

"Yet you got to the Police through Tim – Mr Hammond – and he seems to have stirred things up. We…"

The phone rang again. Arif, for me. But Dad asked him all sorts of questions about what his parents thought now they knew, and it was some time before I got the phone.

His parents had gone spare. They had wanted to call the Police themselves and complain, and he nearly had to shout at them before they came to their senses. And in his sort of Muslim household children *never* shout at their parents. He was not very popular, to say the least. But he got really agitated when he told me that he couldn't call Amy's mobile, nor she his stolen one. If they were really – er – getting involved with each other I could see that was a problem.

"How did they get it?" I interrupted.

"I was with the parents, in a shop, and someone picked my pocket." I nodded, not that he could see.

"So where are you going?" I asked. "Are your parents taking you away somewhere?"

"They think I should just stay here, indoors," he said rather bitterly. "That's not going to happen. I'll just go back to the camp."

"So am I. Early Wednesday morning. First bus."

"*First* bus? What time's that?"

"No idea," I admitted, "but we need to get back before they realise we've gone."

Dad was signalling to me. "Just a sec," I told Arif.

"You can't go back there unless we know where it is, and who owns it," he said.

"But Dad, it's…"

"No. Who owns it, and where is it?"

"Dad, if you went and spoke to them, and one of those men was following, it wouldn't be safe any more, would it? So if I told you…"

I swallowed. It had just come into my mind.

"…Anyway, Lars lives there, Steve has been there before, and Arif is a friend of Lars's, would that do?"

He thought. "So both Arif and Steve know him, then?"

"Yes. I mean, we all do now. Obviously."

"And it's not Lars – is he Norwegian, or something? – who has told these men about you? How can you be sure?"

"There's no way he knows Emily or the men. The men only know about us because Emily goes to the same school as us."

"So this Lars – what's he like?"

I thought. "Well, he… his family are Dutch, came here at the end of the war. They don't get out much."

"End of the war? So he's quite old, then?"

"About your age, I suppose."

"This isn't funny, Matt."

"Sorry. But I don't know how old he is."

"If he came here in 1945, he's getting on for eighty."

"Well… I suppose so."

"I imagine he'd be quite glad of the company. And he's hardly likely to do anything… Okay, then. If you want to go there it'll get you out of the way. And if one of you has a cheap phone with a loaded card in it, we can make sure you're okay once a day and you can phone us in an emergency."

I looked at him, then turned back to the phone. Arif sounded highly amused.

"Talk about thinking on your feet," he said. "That was good and I only just managed not to roll on the floor laughing. Okay, I'll work on my parents again. Can you phone round to the others?"

We agreed to meet at Joe's the following day to make final arrangements.

The remainder of the evening seemed to be spent by Dad on the phone. I could only imagine the surprise on the other Suspects' faces as they were told that someone, a friend of Arif's called Lars, owned the land we were going to be camping on.

The following day, Tuesday, we each made a mobile call to each other, arranging swimming. Despite what we'd all said, Mr Hammond had changed his mind and told us to do that so that if the phones were being hacked, it looked like normal behaviour. He told us to come back to their house, all of us this time, but not to mention that on the phone. We should see if we were being followed, and if not, go straight there.

So that's what happened. Though they didn't stop us, we spotted some of the men watching us, so spent some time window shopping and walking on a bit; then as if accidentally, walking back the way we'd come. Whether they didn't want to talk to six boys at once, I don't know. But eventually we saw them walking away from us as if they'd given up.

At Joe's, we found the Hammonds' dining table loaded with full shopping bags.

"You'll not be staying long, guys," he told us. "Put some clean clothing in a small bag, then be watching your front door from 6.30 tomorrow morning. Except Joe and Tom, that is. I can take three and Mrs Bishop the others. And don't be late. We're taking you to wherever this camp is. We'll drop you there with this food and you're off. You shouldn't go short for a few days."

"But Dad," exclaimed Joe, "that'll mean you know where it is."

"So will Mrs Bishop," he said grimly. "And that's what's going to happen. If you're camped a long way from where we drop you it'll still be secret, so if they capture us and try to torture the information out of us we still can't tell them."

There was a silence at this.

"It... they wouldn't do that. Would they?" Alex sounded a bit quavery.

"No. It won't come to that. People like that don't deal with adults; they're cowardly. We'll be fine. And we'll phone you on that mobile every evening at 6.30. So only switch it on at 6.25, then off again immediately. If there's an emergency, obviously use it then. That way you won't run out of battery."

We went home shortly after, separating into twos and threes so we were walking alone as little as possible.

7   Return

Six in the morning doesn't exist. Half past seven only exists in term time because of breakfast and school, and even then I'm not really awake. So being woken by a father (for a change) at six in the morning was not at all welcome, especially as I'd not slept very well. I'd been too busy worrying about us, my parents being tortured, and having to be careful in camp. Eventually I surfaced, just enough to have a drink and some cereal, then sat with my pre-packed bag watching for a car.

When it appeared, with Mrs Bishop at the wheel, I said farewells to parents and 'hopped' in as requested, to find Tom and Arif there but equally brain-dead.

As we left the outskirts of the town Mrs Bishop said in a voice that would cut through a heavy metal band: "We have to find Mr Hammond. Steve is the one who can recognise where we're going."

As we had no idea whether he was in front of us or behind, we thought this might be a problem, but at last came to a car at the side of the road. We thought it might be the one, as there was no other traffic around. And so it turned out to be. I looked around and could just see the trees which shielded our route over the wall.

"This is the Estate wall," Mrs Bishop said.

We couldn't disagree. No one said anything.

"Are you sure you've got permission to camp here?"

"Mum," said Tom, "our tents are in there, and that's where we were before. It's fine, honest."

"And whatever the case, we can't take them back now," said Mr Hammond. "We have to trust that they know what they're doing. What concerns me is that there's no entrance."

"It's behind those trees, Dad," Joe answered. "Best if you vanish quickly, just in case someone sees you and remembers six boys being dropped off here."

His father looked at him, and said something quietly. Joe grinned and said something back, equally quietly. Mrs Bishop raised her eyes to heaven and started getting bags from the back of the car. With the food and our clean clothes there was going to be quite a haul down to the tents, and although I was starting to wake up I wasn't looking forward to it. Oh, *being* there would be fine. We had to get there first.

Goodbyes were said and we waved them both out of sight before Tom led us towards the trees. We'd nearly reached them when a bus passed us.

"Damn!" said Alex, echoing the thoughts of us all.

"Did you see how many people there were on it?"Joe asked.

None of us had.

"We'll have to hope no one noticed us, then."

There was nothing we could add to that so we just continued towards the wall, our 'entrance' to the Estate. I was elected top man again, being the lightest, though Alex was once again hoisted up as well. We hoisted the first bag to the top and were about to drop it over when Joe shouted "NO! Eggs!" So just in time I hauled the bag up again.

"Why haven't we got any eggs?" Arif asked.

"What?"

"Joe said we had no eggs."

Tom gave him The Look. We were obviously waking up at last.

We hauled Tom up; he straddled the wall and carefully let himself down, dropping to the ground so as to receive the bags. Despite some near misses we managed not to spill anything. Finally, everyone else was hauled up, with the quite solid Arif last. We were in.

With no real exploration to do, no camp site to find and decide on, and no particular plan in mind apart from being away from the local problem, it was a very leisurely wander downhill, with frequent stops to rest, towards the camp. Shopping bags, I decided, were more unpleasant to carry than a heavy rucksack. At least a rucksack doesn't cut into your fingers whilst at the same time bashing against your legs. There were quite a few mutterings amongst the rest of the Suspects about them and as before it was as well that no parents or teachers were around to hear.

Eventually Steve had a brainwave, retrieved an evil looking folding saw and cut a few thickish branches into 30 cm lengths. With the carrier bag handles looped over them you held the wood and were no longer in danger of slow amputation.

Finally rediscovering the little cliff and the soft ground at the start of our lake was like realising that you've found the end of your own street. Actually approaching the tents gave me the same sense of relief that I'd get when I saw our front door getting nearer when it was raining.

Seeing the tents were still standing, all intact, zipped up and welcoming… well, it was really like coming home. We opened them, let the musty smell disperse, then flopped down on our beds. It had been silly o'clock when we were woken and we needed some beauty sleep. Well, I needed a pee. The beauty sleep came afterwards.

We didn't really sleep, honest, just lay there resting. And someone had to say, after what seemed all too short a while: "What's for lunch?"

I just about summoned up the energy to roll over and look at the watch that I'd put on top of my kit. 11.00. Lunch? I called out the time.

"Up at six, breakfast asleep, nothing since? And you think it's not lunchtime?"

You have to admit I had a point. But still nobody moved. Not even The Scout aka Falling Man aka Steve.

I next looked at my watch at midday. I had been increasingly uncomfortable for some time. Even with the tent open it was hot in there. The sun, absent earlier, had come out and was at its full July strength. I was roasting. I was also fearsomely hungry. I struggled out and looked around. Everything was as we had left it, including the new plastic bags of food that we had brought with us. Surely they should have been kept cool? I started putting things in the tiny stores tent which, if tidy, was even hotter than outside. Finding some milk, I thought I'd better tell Steve about it.

Hauling on his foot brought forth some words which might well have been heavily criticised had they been heard by parents, but at my insistent questioning he became less bleary-eyed and told me to tie string round the handle and suspend it in the pond. When I said "How will we find it again?" he got rather impatient, but at least struggled free from the tent, waking the other two up as he did, and before long it wasn't just the milk that was in the lake.

No, I don't mean that I was too.

Some of the other things we'd brought needed 'refrigerating', so were waterproofed with my help and held in the water with stones and made retrievable by string. Clever, I thought.

Having woken him, it seemed only fair that we should get some lunch ready together. Actually, he bullied me into helping him, which I suppose was inevitable.

We all needed something to eat, a fact that everyone else decided once they saw signs of food being put on plates, just out of their reach from the tent, of course. But neither the deepest pleading nor the most dire threats persuaded either of us to push the food nearer to the recumbent figures. It was a little like feeding time at the zoo without both the bars and movement from the animals.

They emerged. We ate.

When it had all been cleared up to Steve's satisfaction, Alex discovered, to everyone's mirth, that the toilet paper we'd left by The Hole had all but dissolved in the rain. His increasingly impassioned pleas for a replacement caused an argument about who was going to deliver it, and a game of catch developed with it. I dropped it first, so was detailed to go and cautiously deliver it to the victim from a safe distance.

"What now?" asked Arif when Alex had returned and endured some interesting comments.

"Well…" started Steve. We listened.

It seems he had been reading up on some old Scout stuff and had discovered a way of making a table. "You see," he finished, "It would bring things off the ground so it's easier to do things like washing up."

How six people, quite intelligent people, can get into such a mess with just sticks and string was quite remarkable. We started off by constructing a cat's cradle – that's what my old aunt would have called it. It was Joe who started laughing first as he took a look at the mess we'd made, and before long we were all in near hysterics. Even Steve, whose idea it was.

"We've got to do better than that," he gasped, trying to catch his breath. "A primary school could do better."

We tidied up under Tom's direction – well, suggestion – and started again. This time Steve's descriptions were better and we actually ended up with something reasonable, even if it did slope down one way.

"It's a draining board, so it should slope," I said. "Otherwise how's the water going to drain away?"

"Possibly between the sticks it's made of?" suggested Tom. "Or are you going to put a piece of ribbed metal over it so it looks more homely? Then the water could run down toward the washer-up and get their feet wet."

That didn't impress anyone greatly..

Not content with a table for washing up, we searched around for some logs to use as seats, with varied success. Mine turned out to be so rotten that it collapsed as soon as I sat on it, sending woodlice everywhere.

"Evicted by the bum of Matt," murmured Arif, "A fate worse than death." Most of the others found something that would do. There was a lot of checking for insects and rot before they were rather carefully set up and used for the first time.

"Now all we need is a table to eat off," said Steve, ever the optimist.

"You going to make one?" asked Alex, whose pride had suffered badly during construction of the cat's cradle.

"We need some more wood for cooking anyway," Steve announced, "Otherwise there'll be no dinner tonight."

"We've only just eaten!" Alex complained.

"Maybe, but I want another meal before tomorrow even if you don't."

The next hour – how does time go so quickly when you're trying to find your way round and not get lost? – was spent picking up wood for the fire and keeping an eye open for possible pieces for a table, though despite Steve's hazy description from the book he'd looked at we didn't really know what we needed. The bits we took back were considered by The Scout and mainly just added to the burning pile.

Finally, despite our slowness and, to be honest, our laziness, there was enough wood. Enough at least for a bit. As Steve pointed out, we didn't really want the woodpile to take over the campsite. He thought there might be enough to use to start another table, but we were tired by then, and hot. Although it was late afternoon the day seemed to be getting hotter. We – those of us who had found one – flopped on to our seats and stretched.

"How about a swim, then?" Tom said suddenly.

We looked at him, expecting something else.

"Where?" asked Steve, eventually.

"Well…derr…in the lake?"

"Anyone else coming in?"

There was a chorus of "why not" and "okay then". Only Joe

was silent.

"What's up, Joe?" asked Tom.

"Still no swimming things," he muttered.

"Skinny dip, then!" called Alex on his way to the tent. It was the second time at camp that he'd made the comment, a point not lost on Joe whose accusation was returned by a rude sign.

"Underwear again?" asked Tom.

"Hmm... possibly."

"There's no girls here."

"I know. But... oh, all right then."

In fact only two of us had proper swim shorts. Arif and I were properly clad, Steve, Tom and Alex had ordinary shorts and Joe wore some rather risky underwear type trunks which inspired a few choice comments – which he returned with increasing good humour.

The water, after the heat of the afternoon, was freezing, just as it had been before in the other stream. But this time we got used to it and had a good swim and a game with the ball we'd brought, though Arif had to shush us on occasion.

"You'll bring the dog here – Lars – and the old man after him."

We tired after a while, dragged ourselves out and got dried and dressed properly. Wet shorts – and underwear - were strung up on the line that Steve had run between the tents. He started a fire and he cooked, this time with Alex. Tom remembered the phone call, switched the horrible, cheap little thing on and reported in. No problems were reported back. The Police had not contacted anyone, so as far as we knew all was well.

Sitting round the fire later, after eating and the inevitable washing up, the conversation naturally turned to the expected raids. We "supposed" our way around all sort of possible happenings, but were glad that we were in this anonymous place and safe. The chat subsided as the fire did, and once again we were quietly yawning our heads off. In fact none of us lasted very much longer. The day had started desperately early, it had been reasonably active, especially the swimming, and we were tired. Once in the tent and in my sleeping bag, it must have taken me about 60 seconds to unconsciousness.

Because of the early night it was logical – at least to me – that I would wake early. Unfortunately my metabolism didn't agree with my reckoning. The first thing I knew it was light and I was being hauled out of the tent by Alex, whose gentle method was to pull heartily at the end of my sleeping bag. The resulting tussle stopped when someone pointed out that fly-zip-less pyjama shorts are not the most decent things to wear when in public. I subsided, red faced, back to the tent, got dressed and went to find my bush.

"What's happening today?" I asked when we'd cleared up after breakfast. There's nothing worse than having a Scout with you when you're at camp, apart, that is, from a smug Scout. Steve was running what is called a tight ship, apparently, and was enjoying every minute of bossing us around. On the other hand, everything seemed clean, we were eating well, and all at the same time, and we were all – well, I suppose content is the word.

"We could go up the other side of the estate, I suppose," said Tom. "We've done most of this side as far as it's safe. And whatever happens we mustn't get chucked off today. It's Thursday and if anyone's been arrested their friends will choose today to ask us questions."

And so we went exploring again. This wasn't nearly as interesting as our other forays. We were camping a fair way from the main house, but all our explorations – except the last when we had been discovered – had been a similar distance from it. Our journey took us well away from the old centre of the estate into areas of scrubland that probably had seen no human footfall for years.

Or so we kept telling each other, trying to weave a story of mysterious no-go areas where wild beasts roamed. When, in response to that, Joe mentioned unicorns, we all fell about laughing. Unfortunately the gorse was very thick there and stumbling about trying to regain a straight-ish face was an uncomfortable experience.

"It's all right for you," he said when we had regained sanity and many scratches, "You don't have to live with an eight year old sister."

Everything the estate's grounds could throw at us that morning, it did. Brambles and scrubland, cliffs and drops, a pond, and finally the boundary wall.

"What now?" I asked when we were standing beside it. "We can't just climb over it, we'd be seen."

"Why not get someone up there to look over and tell Steve what's around? Joe, can you make a support, then Matt can climb on Arif's shoulders. Don't get more than your head over the top, Matt, or someone in a passing car will notice." We could hear the occasional vehicle, muted, from our side.

Well, I got up there in a wobbly sort of way, with Arif complaining I was heavier than when we'd first got over the wall to explore. I looked around.

"What can you see?" asked Tom impatiently.

"Well, there's some grass, then the road, then some more grass, then a line of trees," I told him. There was a scuffling from below me and I found I was being let down to the ground.

"You're too heavy," said Arif. "And if that's all you can see it's not worth busting a gut to hold you up there."

"Is that really all you could see?"

"Yes, Tom. It's just that, until the road curves, in both directions."

"Which way did it curve?" The Scout was at work with his map again.

I thought. "To the right to the right, and to the left to the left."

I got The Look, even though I knew exactly what I meant.

"Come on," said Tom, "we do need to know, you know."

"It's what I said. Looking right, it curves to the right, gradually. To the left, it curves to the left, rather less gradually."

"So we're on a bend."

"Yes."

"Why didn't you say so?"

"I did. But not in those words."

There was a pause, one of those where you wonder if there was going to be one of our very few real arguments coming on. The morning had thrown so much at us by way of obstacles that we were all a bit fed up by now, and if it had been safe to climb the wall – which was uncomfortably high just here – and walk around it until we found our entrance behind the trees, we would have happily done so.

Steve was looking at the map still. "I *think* we're here." He pointed to an area of road. We all gathered round to see. "If we walk to our right, we should come to what the map shows as the beginning of the hill down towards the houses. We can strike in from there and keep right, there's a track on the map. That'll take us towards the tents.

"Lunch?" Alex asked. We had sandwiches with us.

"Why not?" said Tom.

Lunch was followed by sitting against the wall and resting, though not for long as we were in the shade there and that day was not as hot as some had been. When we started feeling that autumn was on us we started off again. Annoyingly in a way, because I knew he'd just get even more smug, Steve was right and at the top of a gentle incline a path led away from the wall. We wondered why, but Joe noticed the new brickwork let into the old and guessed at a previous gate in it.

Knowing that we had to pass rather closer than before to the old house and therefore to the old man, we kept quiet. It was a relief, after about half an hour, to find an overgrown path to our right. We followed it, only to find it became so overgrown that we were soon once again struggling to get through. There were muffled comments as we were scratched and stung, and were moaning about how stupid shorts were when Tom shushed us, warning that we were getting too loud for safety.

We eventually found the tents again, and not without relief. It was good just to flop down and rest. Here with the shelter of the cliff to one side, the old tree roots and the wood on the other, the temperature was higher than when we stopped for lunch. In fact it was almost uncomfortably high again. Steve's plaintive comments about someone lighting the fire so we could brew a cup of tea fell on deaf ears – probably including his.

We ended up doing nothing for the rest of the day, at least until the temperature had fallen to something like normal. One by one we stirred, looked around and thought we'd better do something. "Something" turned out to be getting wood and cooking a meal, and we did very little after that either. The Scout bullied us into clearing up and stowing the perishables in the lake again, and we just lay around the fire until it seemed a decent time to struggle into the tents. It was still hot, and by now we were seasoned campers so left the tent flaps open for the sake of ventilation. The early morning of two days previously must have affected us all more than we expected, because once more I was asleep within seconds of lying out flat.

8   The Ankle

I came to suddenly, uncomfortably. I was sure there had been a shout yet now all I could hear was a low murmur. I blinked myself into wakefulness and looked round. A dog. Lars. Talking to Arif... well it looked like it. Arif was watching him, having "said" something. We were all awake by then.

"He licked my ear," explained Arif. "I shouted and he jumped back, but he's okay now. Aren't you, Lars?"

I could have sworn the dog grinned for a moment.

But – my brain was catching up – if Lars was about, this meant the man was nearby too! Before anyone else spoke I just said "Shh!"

There was no sound. No one was calling the dog. None of us spoke.

"The old man must be near," I whispered, "We should be as quiet as we can. Maybe Lars will go and find him and they'll go back home."

But Lars, having greeted his old friend, backed away and looked at Arif expectantly, and all he could do was look at Lars. The dog took a few more steps away, heading into the wood, then looked over his shoulder.

This sort of thing only happens in kids' films. A dog wants someone to follow them and behaves just as this one was actually doing. I'd only partly believed it when I'd watched films like that, and even then thought it just the result of good training. But I could see that's what Lars was aiming at. As if to underline it, he whined, looked into the woods again, then round at Arif, then back to the woods.

"He wants us to follow him," said Arif unnecessarily.

"Could be a trap," said Alex, who had crawled from the other tent and had an unpleasantly small amount of clothing on.

"The dog isn't *that* clever," Arif told him. "He could be told to go to us, possibly, but not to get us to come back with him. I think we should go with him."

Lars had grown impatient, it seemed, because he gave a loud bark, then walked off into the undergrowth, stopping only where a bend in the path would have hidden us from view.

"Anyone coming with me?" asked Arif, rather accusingly.

It turned out we all were. Hurriedly, without even too many

mutters of "bloody dog, disturbing a night's sleep", we dressed and headed off after the black dog. To give him his due, he made sure we were able to see where he was going, never too far ahead, and always pausing as we pushed through the low branches and clumps of bush that had been our pleasure for most of the previous day. Steve had the presence of mind to use the compass to see what direction we were travelling, just in case we got lost, I supposed. After about half an hour of fighting with nature, and trying to assure the dog we were not being slow on purpose, Lars barked again. We caught up with him. He stood in a partial clearing; partial because the area was covered with branches that had fallen over many years. We looked at Lars and there, at his feet… paws… was the old man. He was not moving, and even from where we stood he looked pale.

"He's not dead, is he?" I found my voice was quavering.

"We need to check. Have you got the phone with you?"

None of us had.

Tom gingerly picked his way over to the man, followed by the rest of us. It became clear as we went that the going was difficult; we were walking on a very old rabbit warren, the top parts of which were delicate in places and just gave way under our feet. With occasional mutters of annoyance we reached the man. He certainly didn't look good.

"His eyes are closed," said Tom. "Arif, just be by his head, and hold his shoulder and I'll check him over."

Carefully Tom laid his head to the man's cheek and held it there, then sat up again. "He's alive," he said with very obvious relief. "I can feel breathing."

"Would this be the problem?" asked Alex. We all looked. The man's right leg ended, not at a normal ankle, but at an ankle that came to a stop, then continued to the foot sideways from where it should be. I swallowed, hard, when I looked at it.

"That must hurt," said Tom. "What do we do?"

Silence. Lars whimpered.

"We've got to get him to his cottage" said Tom slowly, "but how?"

"Well if we've *got* to move him," said Steve, "and we shouldn't, really because the Paramedics should come to him. But if we *have* to, then we can make a stretcher our of our shirts and a couple of sticks. There are enough around!"

"How?" asked Arif.

"Get a couple of long sticks – about two metres each, and I'll show you. Take your shirts off, all of you. Look," he continued, "we need that phone. Who's quickest? Joe. Can you find your way back?"

"Okay," Joe replied. "If I take the map I might be able to find my way easier."

"Okay. Let's have your shirt first. When you get there dial 999 and tell them we have someone unconscious and with a peculiarly shaped ankle, and get them to send an ambulance to the cottage in the Estate. Then come back. With the phone. Got it?"

Joe nodded. "I'll be as quick as I can. Should I see you at the cottage?"

"Yes. That's where we need to take him."

Joe sped off, back the way we had come, following the directions Steve had given him.

Not without some difficulty we cleared the ground behind him of sticks and other bits and pieces. Only then did we lay the shirts flat out by the side of the old man's body. One of the poles we found, and which had been tested to prove it was strong enough, was threaded through the body of each shirt and up one arm. The loose end was tucked in below the victim as far as we could without moving him. But he stirred not a muscle.

"If we can roll him over he'll be more or less lying flat on them. Then we put the other pole up the other side and lift." Steve knew what he was doing, it seemed. Again.

When that was done Tom gently shook the shoulder he could reach, so that when the man opened his eyes he would see him and Arif. But nothing happened. Tom shook again, and as gently but as loudly as he could said "Can you hear me?"

Still nothing.

"Well, all we can do is to roll him on to the stretcher and hope he stays asleep, or unconscious, so that he doesn't feel the pain. Look, somebody needs to hold that ankle absolutely still… well no, not still, just so it stays in the same position with the leg as it is now. Matt? Can you?"

I didn't think I could. I didn't want to be the one who saw it drop off, or gave the man so much agony that he woke up, screaming. I hesitated, but swallowed again and agreed in a small, scared voice.

That was the first really difficult part of it. Tom put us all where he thought we should be, with one at the man's back to take the weight on his knees as the body rolled over, me at the ankle, Alex, Steve and himself gently rolling the unconscious man over. It wasn't easy. It wasn't quick. It wasn't without incident. It wasn't helped by Lars emitting a mix of a growl and a whine when he could see we were trying to move his master.

Trying to avoid moving his injured ankle was the most frightening thing I've ever done, before or since. I think I managed it, but if I did it was by a concentration level I'd never been guilty of before. Along with luck. But roll him over we did, and then had to shuffle him up and down so as to get enough of the shirts under him to allow the second pole to be worked up through the other side.

Once done, we stopped to take stock.

"Now all we've got to do is get him down to his home, where hopefully the ambulance will pick him up," said Tom.

"Is that all?" asked Alex with a grim smile in his voice.

"Now, Matt, while we lift him, one on each corner, you need to do your bit with that ankle again. Tell you what, if we've got enough handkerchiefs or something, we could tie his legs together and pad them so they're apart, so the good one keeps the bad one still. I've seen that done."

And so we did. And we were so grateful that the man was unconscious because it obviously meant moving the two feet closer together.

Finally we were ready, lifted the four corners nearly at the same time, and I did my best to make sure the injury was stationary.

"Which way?" asked Alex.

"Lars? Home, boy!" Arif knew just the way to get directions and to find the route. We thought we remembered the way from being marched along it before, and by the very man we were now carrying, but to be able to follow Lars was a bonus. Fortunately it was a reasonably well-trodden path from there on, with little undergrowth in the way except in places. We just had to be exceptionally careful where we placed our feet, especially in the clearing where the man had injured himself, and to make sure we didn't go too fast.

After a bit Tom called a halt. "We need to even things out a bit, give everyone a swap round." he said. He'd been thinking, and with as little time wasted as possible he told me to take over from Alex, who swapped sides with Arif, who swapped with Tom, who swapped with Steve, who took over from Alex, who was stationed at the man's feet, which effectively meant having a rest.

It was during this second leg of the journey that there was a groan from the stretcher, which we were carrying at the level of our legs so we could be as smooth as possible. Steve heard it just after Lars did, and called a halt. Lars shouldered his way in to look at our patient. We shuffled forward to a flatter bit of ground and were about to set it down when Steve said, with alarm: "No! Put it on your knees so he doesn't get on to the ground. The man groaned again. Lars whined and licked his face. Arif spoke to him and held him back a little.

A pair of eyes, pain visible in them, looked at the dog, then at Arif.

"What happened?" a slurred voice asked.

"You fell and have injured your ankle," Arif told him gently. "We're taking you to the cottage, where there should be an ambulance coming." He looked up. "Someone should run on ahead and make sure they stay there."

"Alex?" asked Tom. "Or Matt?"

"I'll go," Alex volunteered. I was quite relieved.

"Are you okay to carry then, Matt?"

My arm was aching, but I nodded anyway. "Can we change sides again?" I asked.

"Sides?" asked the weak voice.

"We're taking you on a stretcher," Arif said. "It's not going to be comfortable, but it's the best we could do."

"Stretcher? But who… I told you not to come back."

It wasn't an accusation, more a comment, the way he said it.

"Probably a good thing we did," said the quick thinking Arif, "otherwise you'd have died out there. It was Lars you can thank for coming to find us. He knew where we were."

"Lars…" and he gritted his teeth in pain as we lifted the stretcher again … "he's a good dog."

"He's a lovely dog," Arif confirmed, "and I'm going to look after him while you're in hospital."

"Hospital? But I can't stay there… the dog, hunting…"

His eyes closed in pain again.

"Shhh," said Arif. "We'll work it out."

"You don't understand."

"I think I do. Trust me."

"Are you the Scout?"

"No, that's Steve. He's here."

The head nodded, eyes still closed.

"Thank you…"

It was enough.

In the long, jolting journey he was sometimes conscious, sometimes not. We stopped quite a few times to change sides and ease aching arms, and to make sure Lars was still on the right path – not that we'd have been sure what to look for. We may have come this way when we had been marched out of the Estate before, but really couldn't be certain. Really, the dog was our only guide.

Finally, with great relief, we saw roofs ahead, and the resulting relieved comments jerked our patient from his unconsciousness.

"We are here?"

"The old house is in sight."

"Hmm…"

But when we reached the old, semi-overgrown, sweeping drive that ran past the cottage there was no sign of an ambulance. Nor had Alex heard one. We found a patch of soft grass at its side and very, very carefully put the stretcher down.

"What now?" asked Tom, usually the first to know what to do."

"People in the houses have phones." Came faintly from the stretcher.

"We've already phoned," Tom told him. "One of us went back to our camp and called on our mobile."

The pained eyes blinked. "Camp… phone?"

"It's a long story," said Tom hurriedly. "But yes, we had a mobile there and Joe ran back to use it to call an ambulance to come here. He should have got there and called, and it must be on its way by now."

He was having difficulty at taking that in, I could see. We waited for perhaps another five or so minutes. Lars had been lying as near to the patient as we would allow him, and seemed fairly content with that even if he did look anxiously at his master from time to time and give a gentle whine. Suddenly he looked up, ears cocked forward.

And then we heard it too. The unmistakable sound of a siren.

Tom stood. "I should have thought of it earlier," he said. "We need someone at the houses to direct it up here. Stay there."

And before anyone else could answer he was away, speeding down the drive.

Apparently there was a knot of people around the puzzled ambulance crew by the time he reached them, all denying any knowledge of a call. When he appeared there was a rather angry, puzzled reaction from them, tinged with astonishment as he was dressed just in shorts, his top having been donated to the makeshift stretcher. He took charge, though, as he always somehow managed to. Mentions of Lars' master and a broken ankle shut up any who were still muttering, and before he knew it he was in the cab with the two Paramedics and being rushed up towards us.

It was a very welcome sight. They stopped a short distance away and the Paramedics jumped out.

"Hallo... can you tell us your name?" asked one of them.

"Nils Lundgren." He muttered. The man looked confused.

"Sorry – could you repeat that?"

He did.

"He was born in Holland," Tom offered.

The paramedic nodded. "Got that."

They checked him over, not where the obvious break was, but everywhere else; all down the back, all over the head, down the arms, down the legs... but when one of them lightly touched the ankle there was a shout of pain. Lars growled. Arif comforted him as best he could.

"Entonox?" said one of the Paramedics.

"Definitely," answered the other, and rose to go to the vehicle.

The gas calmed our patient and he gave a smile at last when Arif appeared in his line of sight.

"I turn you off, and you save my life.. Thank you."

Arif smiled back. "Couldn't leave you there, could we?"

"And will you really look after my dog, and...and... but how do you know about... about the hunting?"

"I just saw them from your door when we were here, just

before you closed it. And of course I'll look after Lars. And I'll visit you and tell you how things are going."

"That gas is wonderful… can I have some more?"

The paramedic obliged.

We watched, relieved, as the experts scooped him on to a two-part, proper stretcher, took him to the ambulance and set to work. We felt a bit deflated, and were worried when several out-of-breath people appeared, I supposed from the hamlet.

They ignored us and crossed to the ambulance.

"What's happened?" asked someone.

"Broken ankle," replied one of the men tersely.

"How did he do that?" came the stupid question.

"You'd better ask those lads. They called us and brought him down here. Now, sorry, but we need to tend to him in private. And keep that dog away, please."

The door shut.

The group looked over at us, and one of them came over.

"What are you doing here? It's private."

"We rescued Mr…er…Lundgren from the middle of the estate where he fell. His dog found us and we made this stretcher and brought him here." Tom was on good form, and sounded confident.

"Er… But what brought you here in the first place?"

"Aren't you more interested in what's going to happen to Mr Lundgren?" he replied.

"Don't be cheeky. You're trespassing."

"We're saving his life," I shot in, thoroughly roused. "If Lars hadn't found us – if we'd not been there – he would have died. As it was he was unconscious when we found him."

The woman turned from me as if I'd said nothing and spoke to Tom. "We don't welcome people here. Not unless they've been invited."

"As Matt says," replied Tom, "if we hadn't been around to rescue him Mr Lundgren would have died. I think you'll find he might invite us, don't you? I should ask him."

I could tell he was angry. The woman just looked at him.

An ambulance door opened. "He wants to talk to you." The paramedic nodded in our direction. We and the woman headed to it and climbed gingerly aboard. The man looked at us and smiled faintly.

"If my young friend will look after Lars, and do what is

necessary, I'd be very grateful. Mrs Elliott, they have my permission to be here, and I'm more grateful to them than you can believe. They tell me I'm going to the hospital, so if anyone wants to visit they come there."

"We're off now," interrupted one of the Paramedics. "Everybody out. And if anyone wants to know whether Nils' life was saved by these lads you can take it from me that it was. He's been out overnight as it is. Another day and a night would have killed him almost for sure. So these guys need a medal, not criticism."

He came out, and was about to close the door. A weak voice could be heard.

The man turned back to us. "He wants one of you to come with him."

We looked at each other. "Tom?" asked Arif.

"I'll go if nobody else wants to. Arif needs to stay to look after Lars. Will you be all right without me?"

"Yes, Dad," Alex responded, his spirit returning with a typical put-down. He got The Look, not just from Tom but from the annoying Mrs Elliott. But Tom was grinning as he climbed up into the ambulance. The door shut and off it set, leaving us facing a group of the local residents again.

9   First Hunt

There was a call from the edge of the woodland, and Joe reappeared, dishevelled, hot and out of breath. Mrs Elliott seemed to be put off by yet another of us being there.

"Haven't they come yet?" he panted.

"They've come, dealt with him, and gone again. You were quick."

"Where is he? And where's Tom?"

"Both in the ambulance," I told him.

"What's wrong with Tom?"

"Nothing. Mr Lundgren – Nils – asked him to go with him."

We turned our back on the knot of chatting locals and disappeared back up the driveway, intent on getting out of reach of any further comments.

And so, now we were as complete a team of Suspects as possible without our natural leader... it's odd how none of us had ever said anything that hinted that he *was* our leader. Not in private to Tom himself nor between ourselves. Yet without him there was always something missing. We were not quite a rudderless boat, but it was that much more difficult to decide what our next actions should be.

"Where's Lars?" asked Arif suddenly.

We looked around. No sign. Without saying anything, Arif started back.

"Arif, wait!" called Joe. "What was that shout that the old man used when we first met the dog?"

Arif stopped. "I don't know," he said unhappily. "I was trying to remember. Sounded like two words."

"Sounded a bit like "o-e"" I said.

"Call it," suggested Arif.

"Better coming from you, really." I didn't want to make myself a fool.

So he took a deep breath and gave voice in a low bellow. Then we waited. And there was a scrabbling in the bushes and a panting Lars appeared, but from the direction of the old man's house.

"Phew!" said Arif. "I thought he might be chasing the ambulance. Come on then, Lars. O-e."

The dog looked at him, then barked. We all laughed, and,

and with spirits higher, returned to the old man's... Nils'... little cottage.

"Need to get him a drink," said Arif.

"I need one too," I said. "In fact we probably all do. Do you think we can go inside?"

"Don't think we have an option," said Joe, "and if I don't have something soon I shall need an ambulance of my own."

"No, indeed, and there's something I need to check." Arif was suddenly eager. I remembered his saying that there was something he knew, but wasn't certain about. We followed Lars' black tail once more and soon found ourselves at the cottage. It seemed wrong to barge in with no introduction or permission, but with Lars scratching at the door and looking round expectantly it was the same, somehow, as having knocked at the door and being invited in.

The door was unlocked. Indeed, a closer inspection showed that the ancient lock mechanism had seen no use for many years. It was cool inside, and a relief after the mounting temperature outside. We looked around for the tap, and the sink, only to remember that the water had to be drawn from the well.

"I'll go," I announced. "Alex, can you help?"

He just nodded, following me outside with the bucket that stood on the draining board. We followed the procedure Nils had shown us when we'd first met him and we soon had a supply of that clean, cool nectar that as townies we'd found so unexpected. Lars was first, then Joe, then the rest of us.

Arif had been looking round Nils' kitchen, really examining everything, and now we had drunk and were all together – minus Tom, of course – he spoke.

"I know what Nils and Lars were doing when we found them."

The rest of us just looked at him.

"He collects truffles. Lars is a truffle hound."

If he'd told us that Nils drove steam engines around the estate we couldn't have been more puzzled. To me, truffles could be found in packets in sweet shops; they were chocolate things that were rather nice, but expensive. They were obviously made, not found. I told him so.

He looked at me with that I-know-something-you-don't expression we often used between us (and, more rarely, to our teachers).

"A *real* truffle is a fungus. It's extremely valuable to good chefs and therefore restaurants because of the unique flavour it imparts to specialist dishes, and is greatly sought after by gourmets. It is difficult to find, but there are some dogs who can be trained to detect it using their advanced sense of smell."

Silence.

"And where did you get all that from?" I asked.

"Google."

"So…"

"Just a minute," Alex interrupted, "You think that Nils is roaming the woods looking for mushrooms? And then selling them to posh cafes?"

Arif looked at him pityingly. "I don't *think* it: I know it. Look." He walked over to one of the closed cupboards and reached out a basket, which he put on the table. Lars gave a whine and stood, pointing directly at it.

We crowded round and looked. Inside were some of the most ugly pieces of dark… stuff …we had ever seen.

"You sure they're not actually… er… *from* Lars?" enquired Alex with disgust written all over his face. It took us a moment or two to realise what he was getting at, and four of us immediately backed away from the basket.

"Well," said Arif loftily, "If you don't want to hunt for some more, with Lars, and hopefully sell it, I will, and I'll be able to afford a new iPhone to replace my stolen crappy phone within about two months."

There were mutterings.

"Er…" Steve started. Somehow we all knew what he was going to say. We listened anyway.

"This is Nils' way of making some money. We can't just walk in and take it from him because he won't be here for a bit."

More silence. But there was a grin on Arif's face.

"So we should carry on collecting the stuff, and sell it, and give him the money?" said Joe.

"Yes, and keep a record of what it makes, what we've had to spend out of it, and so on. And deal with the money so it's safe."

"Safe from what?" I asked suspiciously.

"Safe from theft by the people in the hamlet. They must

know he collects and sells it, and it could be they're looking for an opportunity to get at it." Steve was being – well, the voice of our consciences. This wasn't anything to do with his being in the Scouts, it was just him. He was just naturally honest. Unfortunately. I could have done with some money. But he was right, of course, and we all knew it – as did Arif who had been the first to mention a new iPhone.

"So how does he sell it?" Joe asked.

"Don't know that," Arif admitted. "If Tom had his phone we could call him at the hospital and get him to ask Nils."

"First thing is to find some more," said Arif. "There's not much in here."

"Could that be what they were looking for when we found Nils?" Steve asked.

We agreed that was the most likely reason for them both to be in such a remote part of the estate. Agreement had nearly been reached that we should return to have a look at what was there when there was a knock on the door, which nevertheless opened without any of us saying a word. Lars gave a short bark. Two of the women from the houses, whom we had seen at the ambulance, marched in and pulled up short when they saw us.

One of them, who was dressed to go and work in an office, or so it appeared to us, glared at us.

"Hasn't taken you long to make yourselves at home, has it?"

Since we were standing round the kitchen sink, talking, that was hardly an accurate description. We waited, saying nothing.

"Well? Nothing to say for yourselves? This house needs to be locked up so that no one else can come in uninvited."

I could sense Alex of the ginger hair getting wound up. Someone needed to say something before his spring released with a snap. Fortunately Arif looked calmly in her direction.

"And who would be looking after Lars?" he asked.

"You know perfectly well he's in hospital."

"No, that's Nils - Mr Lundgren."

"Who is Lars, and why can't he look after himself?"

"Lars is the dog. Mr Lundgren's dog. As you know Mr Lundgren so well you'll know his dog, surely?"

Without so much as a blink she continued. "He'll have to go into kennels, then. And you need to leave the estate now."

"And you will be paying for the kennels?"

"What?"

74

"Kennels have to be paid for. We can't, and our parents can't be expected to. So you would have to pay as it was your suggestion. But in fact there is no need, as I shall be here looking after the dog as Mr Lundgren asked, and paying for his food out of my own money, and taking him for walks as I promised. Would you do that?"

"Don't be cheeky. I want you to leave. Now."

"And Mr Lundgren doesn't. And it's his house."

"I'll bring the Police."

We looked round at each other. Joe gave a slow grin.

"Would you be wanting a Scenes of Crime Officer?" he asked. "Because if you do I can arrange it. My Dad can come and look round."

For some reason that floored her.

"I could arrange a solicitor," said Alex suddenly – it sounded as if he was speaking from between gritted teeth. "He could search for the deeds of this cottage and prove that it belonged to Nils. I wonder who the houses belong to, the houses where you live? And I wonder where the ground rent is paid?"

I hadn't a clue what he was talking about, or why it mattered. But the woman deflated suddenly.

"How long do you intend to stay here?"

"Until Mr Lundgren can look after Lars," replied Arif smoothly. "How long does a broken ankle take before it can be used to... to walk a dog?"

She looked daggers at him. "So we have got to put up with five boys on our doorsteps until then, have we?"

Once again I could feel Alex bristling. But Steve spoke first this time. "I don't know what you mean about putting up with us, since you're in the hamlet and we're up here. You were happy enough to let us in before – my Explorer Scouts – so there's really no difference, though actually the six of us will probably be quieter. By the way you're dressed you must be out at work most of the day, so I'm sure we'll be able to avoid each other most of the time."

"You mean you've trespassed here before?" she asked indignantly.

Steve actually laughed. "Our leaders made arrangements for us to use the Estate for a hike. That's not trespassing. And they asked if any of the kids who live here wanted to come along too, but none of them did."

"No children live here," she said flatly.

"Sorry to hear that," Steve rejoined.

For some reason that seemed to shut her up. She turned, almost barged into the woman who'd come with her and who hadn't said a word, and the two marched out.

We looked at each other. "*Well...* of all the bloody cheek..." started Alex.

"I could see you were about to explode," I told him.

"What a cow! What do they think we're here for? Doesn't she realise we just saved Nils' life? That Arif is looking after the dog?" He subsided, muttering words that I'm really glad the woman never heard, professionally unpleasant though she had been.

"So what *are* we going to do?" asked Joe. "There's not really enough room for us all to stay here and I'm not sure about using Nils' bed, somehow. I suppose one of us can stay and look after the place, and make sure Lars is okay. But we should really go back to the camp, shouldn't we? We'll be more out of the way there.

I realised he wasn't talking about the woman or the others in the hamlet. We were still meant to be in hiding.

Something else suddenly occurred to me, and I think the others felt it at the same time. Hunger. Lars had woken us very early, and although we'd never had the chance to check the time then it must have been before 7.00. It was now well past 11 o'clock and we'd not had breakfast. Nor the usual drink and biscuit mid morning. Nor an early lunch.

What had occurred to me was that I was extremely hungry.

"Is there anything to eat here?" I asked, aware that others were looking round the kitchen too.

"We'll talk over a meal. Let's have a look. We can always replace stuff before he comes back." Steve was being honest, as always. I would just have eaten whatever we found; after all, we *had* just saved the owner's life.

A thorough search of the kitchen found bacon, eggs and bread, along with butter and lard.

"Lard?" asked Alex, "what the hell's that?" We put it back.

Finding the cooker was the next thing. None of us had seen a range before, so the idea of burning wood in this big black thing at the back of the kitchen was a new one. It had really not struck us that living with no electricity or gas meant that there was no light you could switch on, and that cooking required serious pre-planning to get the range hot enough.

The thing was by then just slightly warm, having been out since the previous night, or so we supposed. After a lot of poking around and unspoken questions to ourselves we finally realised what had to happen, and to our amazement managed to light it. There was at least a supply of wood handy. Rather cautiously, we applied bacon to a nearby frying pan, cremated some bread and nearly-dry-fried an egg each; woofed it down and gave the last two uncooked rashers to Lars who looked happy at the prospect and asked for more. Arif searched again and found some dog food so as to complete the job of breakfast for the dog. We filled up on bread and marmalade, not wanting any further accidents with damaging yet more of the loaf with the range.

"I *think* lard is a sort of cooking fat," said Steve when we'd finished. "Perhaps we could have cooked the bread in that like you do oil."

"Do you?" I asked, my cooking skills being somewhere just above zero; I could by then more or less boil water without burning it. The rest of us weren't certain about using the lard either. I was ignored.

It seemed that we were just hanging around in the cottage. There was nothing to do. We were at a loose end. Our unadmitted leader was at a hospital somewhere, giving moral support – or so we imagined – and we were rather rudderless. At last Joe brought it to a head.

"What are we meant to be doing? We can't just stay here and twiddle our thumbs. We should be camping, and out of the way."

"Okay, then," Steve started, "let's go back to the camp, then we can do… I don't know… have a swim, or something."

"How will Tom know where to go when he gets back?" asked Arif.

"He'll guess," Alex decided. "He's not stupid."

"No, but he doesn't know the way." The quiet Arif was quite positive about that. "In fact, I wouldn't know the way. Lars would, if he knew where we were trying to get to."

The dog's head came up as he heard his name.

"Well, what do we do, then?" Alex asked.

"I think we should go back and leave Tom to get Lars to bring him up when he comes," Joe said.

"He's not that clever!" said Arif.

"Who? Tom or Lars?" Alex asked innocently.

Arif grinned. "Neither of them. I'll stay here with the dog and you four go up to the camp."

"Don't you want some company?" I asked.

"Well…" Arif thought. "…if you want to stay as well, that's fine. But it'll be boring, just waiting."

"I don't mind," I answered, though I wasn't sure why I was offering.

And so it was decided. Steve was about to lead them off, with the map which he had at first forgotten, when Arif suddenly stopped Joe.

"Don't forget to phone later. If we're not back with Tom by then you'd better come and see what's happening before reporting in."

Joe, currently the holder of the phone, nodded. They set off and we watched them out of sight. I was aware that Arif's strangely dark eyes were looking at me. I raised my eyebrows, having seen this expression before.

"Come on then," I said.

"What?"

"You're planning something."

"No…well, yes. Should we take the dog for a walk?"

Lars's ears pricked up and he looked at him.

Was that it, I wondered? Or was there something else?

"And…?"

"Well… if we saw some of those fungus things – truffles – we could pick them, couldn't we?"

"Why didn't you just say 'Let's go truffle hunting'?"

He looked sheepish. "I didn't know if you'd want to."

"Try asking."

"Shall we go truffle hunting?"

"Yes."

"What about Tom?"

True… "Leave a note on the door."

"What, saying we're on a truffle hunt?"

"Okay, okay… I'll just say "Wait here, walking the dog."

Lars was now up and on his feet… paws. We found some paper and a pencil, wrote the note, wondered how to secure it and eventually just trapped it under the knocker.

"Lead?" I asked.

"Don't be silly! I shouldn't think the old man even owns one. There's nobody else around and anyway Lars knows his way around better than we do. Come on!"

At first I thought we might actually have needed a lead. Lars bounded off and was quickly out of sight. I looked reproachfully at Arif, but he just smiled and soon enough the undergrowth shook and the dog ran back to us. If ever a dog could be described as smiling, he was doing so. He led off again, then looked round at us. We followed.

It soon became clear that we weren't taking Lars for a walk, he was taking us. We agreed that he'd managed to defeat our sense of direction, and were starting to worry when we reached a clearing where the dog was sniffing around excitedly. There was one patch, near a huge, ancient oak tree whose roots seemed to be struggling to reach the surface, where he was most interested. He started scrabbling at the earth as if digging for a bone, then looked round at us.

Arif crossed to him and saw, with only a few claw scratches on it, the knobbly top of what could only be our target. Carefully he excavated the earth around it, hands being better at delicate digging than paws and claws. At last, he held up a rather unpleasant looking lump of…well, stuff …and grinned at me.

"Success!" he crowed.

"Really? Is that a truffle?"

"Lars thinks so. Good boy!" He ruffled the dog behind the ears, and once more he seemed to grin.

But it wasn't over yet. Lars was sniffing around again and soon started pawing at another piece of ground. Soon we were looking at another of the rather odd looking, slightly knobbly lumps.

After about hour we decided we needed to return to the cottage and wondered how we were going to find our way back.

"Just head downhill, I suppose," said Arif hopefully.

I thought I knew better. "Lars? Home!"

The dog just looked briefly at me, then fixed his eyes on Arif.

"He's right, Lars. Home, please."

And incredibly the dog left the clearing, looked to check we were following, and trotted purposefully along what we could just distinguish as, if not a path, then as a lightly used route a little like a rabbit path. Unconsciously we walked in single file and tried to disturb the foliage as little as possible.

Sure enough eventually we started catching sight of the roofs of the old house – where they still existed – and knew we were near. We rounded the corner and came to an abrupt halt. At the cottage door stood a man.

10   Tom

We ducked back under cover, thoughts of the gang we were trying to avoid coming immediately to mind. But Lars seemed to have no such reservations and ran forward, tail wagging. The man saw him, put down the laptop case he was carrying and bent to greet the dog as an old friend. That reassured me rather. We looked at each other, raised eyebrows, nodded simultaneously and walked out to join Lars and the stranger. He noticed us, and his welcoming smile turned to a frown.

"And who are you? And why…" he looked at our armfuls of truffles. "Do you know you're trespassing, and stealing if you've got those?"

Arif said nothing, just smiled and opened the cottage door. The dog headed in, so did Arif, and the man's expression turned to one of astonishment. I followed Arif inside, and the man followed cautiously.

He looked around. "Where's Nils?" he asked.

"We found him earlier this morning. Lars came to find us and took us to where he had fallen. He'd broken his ankle. We called an ambulance and he's in hospital with another of us to keep him company."

The man blinked. By this time we had both put our truffles in a basket to join those already there. His eyes followed our movements, a fact not lost on either of us.

"Er…" he started.

We looked at him.

"Er… what are you going to do with those?"

"They belong to Mr Lundgren," Arif told him. Given what he had said when we first were talking about truffles, when he mentioned a new iPhone, I was again quietly relieved.

"I…er…yes. Sorry. It sounds as if you did Nils a good turn. And as to these… well."

He paused, looking at us. "Do you know what they are?" he asked.

"Yes," said Arif slowly, "but do you?"

The man looked him in the eyes. "Begins with a 'T'," he said.

Arif grinned. "Truffles."

"Indeed… but how do you know?"

"I'd seen photos of them. We know that Nils sells them and want to find out who buys them. And the money will go to him, not to us. Except that if we're going to stay here and look after Lars and collect them, we might use some of the money for food – for the dog, if not for us."

Silence. The man continued to look at Arif, who held his gaze. Then he gave a deep sigh.

"What hospital is he in?" he asked.

"We don't know yet. When Tom gets back he'll be able to tell us," I said. It was my turn for the searching look.

"Excuse me," said Arif. "You know about us be we don't know you. Can you tell us…?"

The man interrupted him with a laugh. "I don't know much about you, just that you're in Nils's home, have done him a good turn and have collected some truffles which you want to sell… for him. But me? I'm the manager of the Royal Hotel in Upperden – Marcus Yardley. And I'm the person you're looking for. I buy truffles from Nils Lundgren. At our agreed price. Now you know me, can you tell me about you?"

"Arif Choudhury and Matt Ingham," said Arif. "We live in Upperden too. Er…" he thought for a moment. "Look – do you know the Plough pub?"

"You don't live *there*, do you?" He was obviously suddenly on his guard.

"No," Arif reassured him hastily, "I wanted to make sure you were nothing to do with it."

"I avoid it like the plague, and advise you and your families to do the same."

"Why?"

"It's home to some very unpleasant gangs. Allegedly, I suppose I'd better add."

"Yes… we know, sort of," said Arif. "Look… just a minute."

He drew me over to the other side of the room. "Should we tell him? Is it safe?"

"I think so," I whispered back. "We've got to trust ordinary people some time."

We rejoined him and Arif explained our difficulties and why we were in the estate. At the end he was silent for a moment, then nodded.

"It was only a matter of time before that place got busted," he said. Sounds as if you've got yourselves mixed up in it well and truly…"

I began to protest that it wasn't our fault but he interrupted me.

"I can see that. In the hotel trade we have to weigh people up quickly and it's obvious you're trying to do the right thing. Are you sure you're safe here?"

"As far as we know," I said. "And where we're camping is well out of the way."

"Unless you're Lars," said the man. "With his nose he could find you anywhere. Which is just as well if ever you get lost."

"One of us is a Scout," I said. "He's a good navigator."

"How many of you are there?"

I was ready to tell him, but Arif butted in. "Enough to be able to defend ourselves," he said bluntly. "So how much are you…do you pay Nils for truffles?"

The man laughed. "I can see that trust only goes so far. Fair enough. I suppose you have a phone? Here's my number. When you have enough to make a journey worthwhile, call me and I'll come and collect what you've found. And if there's a problem with anything, call me then as well. I'm known in the hamlet so I can get here at any time."

"How many do you want at a time?" I asked before Arif could. I was thinking about the stock in Nils' kitchen which might well have been there some time.

"It depends. Usually Nils calls me when he's got what he thinks is enough."

"We might have enough already," said Arif.

"Those in the basket aren't really enough."

"There are more over here," he said, crossing to the cupboard where he'd found those Nils had collected – Nils and Lars.

"Ah… that's better. That makes about enough, I should think. Okay, I'll take them."

He held out his hand for the two baskets in front of him, but Arif held on to them.

"If we're acting for Nils we need to be sure he's getting the right price," he said.

Mr Yardley looked surprised. "We – Nils and I – have an agreed price. I'll give that to him when I visit him."

Arif thought, then said slowly: "At the moment, we have

dug up half of this load and have found the other half. That actually makes half of them ours. When my parents sell anything in their shop they take the money before handing goods over, even to people they know well. They say it's business. We should do the same."

"You just want the money for yourself!" protested Mr Yardley.

"We want the money to buy food for the dog, and for expenses looking after Nils' home. The bulk of it I will ensure is kept safe and is given to Nils when he returns."

"But Nils and I work on trust. I'll pay him the money."

"And we and Nils work on trust, and we will pay him the money."

"But if I walk away you'll get nothing."

"If you don't buy from us, other hotels will. My parents have contacts in London, with wholesalers, and they would be glad to buy some local, fresh truffles. Maybe for more than you pay."

I was gobsmacked. This wasn't the Arif I knew, the quiet one who hardly ever even answered teachers back. I could tell Mr Yardley was taken aback too.

"But… well, don't forget they don't last forever, or didn't you know that? You need to move them on soon."

"My parents…"

"But they're not in the luxury food market, I'm guessing. Look; I pay Nils £9 an ounce. You've probably got about half a pound there. That's £72. I'll give you £36 and the same to Nils when I visit him. How's that?"

It sounded fair to me, but Arif chimed in again. "But we've got the supply and we're selling on behalf of Nils. I need to see him – when I can – about Lars, to tell him how he's doing. So I'll take all the money with me when I go and see what Nils wants me to do with it. How's *that*?"

And this time Mr Yardley laughed. "You drive a hard bargain, Arif Choudhury. All right, I'll pay you the money. But just as you're needing to learn to trust me, I have to learn to trust you. I'll be visiting Nils, and soon, and if he's not had the money it'll be the Police coming here."

"That's fine," said Arif without a murmur. "Probably they'll come here anyway to make sure we're all right. Not that they'll find us, of course, since we'll be spending most of our time at our camp."

He smiled again. "It looks as if, when I next need an assistant, I'll have to come to you. You have a good technique and can bargain without being phased."

Arif's turn to smile. "I just want to be sure of my ground. For Nils' sake."

The trade was done. We had a fistful of banknotes. When Mr Yardley left both he and Arif were smiling. Once he was out of sight Arif and I had a long discussion about how he managed to do what he'd done. It appeared that his parents did the same with their suppliers, so he'd heard the attitude before; assertive, positive, but friendly.

Having put a note on the door in case Tom returned, we took Lars for a walk again, though he did look a little puzzled at the concept. *He* took *us* to the same clearing where he'd found the truffles before, and at last we recognised the point where we'd come into it from a different direction and found the injured Nils.

"Could we find our way back from here?" I wondered out loud.

"Don't really want to try until we really need to, in case we can't find the way. And then where would we be?"

"If we knew where we'd be, we'd not be lost," I told him. Lars was foraging onwards, deeper into the ancient woodland and soon found another clearing where he whimpered and started digging.

"We should have brought a basket or something with us," I was told.

"Shall I go back?"

"I'm hungry. Let's grab something to eat and then come back."

"When do you think Tom will come back?"

"Haven't a clue. In fact, how's he going to get back without being seen? That's what worries me more."

That was a thought. When he got free from the hospital, how would he try to get back to the estate? What would I do? Phone the parents. No - both at work. And I had no phone on me. Ask the hospital to phone... but whom? Police? And did Tom's mother work? Again, no idea. I shook my head.

"I know what you mean," I told him.

We gave up the idea of getting a basket, and again the dog

was puzzled. But we led away from the clearing and wandered aimlessly for a while, Lars seeming to be happy just to snuffle around. At length we found we were getting hot and decided enough was enough. Arif said "Home!" to Lars who just looked at him and set off as if we two knew where he was going as well. Since he kept checking to ensure we were following we were happy we were on the right track, and soon the rooftops hove into view again.

There was a note under the old knocker, written on ours. "Have gone up to camp. See you later."

"Damn!" I said, "and after we'd told him to wait here for us so we could all go."

"Now what?" Arif asked.

"Food. Then we'll track him. Or rather Lars will – I hope."

We rather hurried over food and water. After all, jam sandwiches for lunch isn't particularly 'right' even if we did feel better afterwards. We turned the note over and wrote: "Gone looking for you. Stay HERE if you come back" on it.

We headed off on the path we'd returned on earlier. Arif paused, looking thoughtful.

"How will Lars know we're looking for Tom, and not more truffles?"

I blinked. Okay, Lars was clever, but not that clever. "What have we got of Tom's that smells of him?" I asked. I hadn't a clue.

Nor had Arif.

"If... " he started. "If we take him to where Tom would have come up to the door, would he smell that? Would he follow that back to where Tom's gone?"

Again, I hadn't a clue, but it seemed the only possibility. Carefully, without crossing over the area, we let him sniff around and when he led us off down towards the cottages we thought that at least it could be Tom's scent he'd found, even if he was following it the wrong way. We called him, then set him going in the opposite direction. Again he cast around, found a track again, and headed off on roughly the path we thought Tom might have taken.

We trusted that dog. Indeed we had no option. He led us on paths I couldn't recognise; neither could Arif when I asked him. I was sure we'd been nowhere near the path he was following. It wasn't so bad when there was a track, but when Lars turned off into what looked like the sort of scrubby bushes we had struggled through when we were first trying to find the campsite we had difficulty in keeping up. Our legs got cut by brambles and sometimes stung by nettles. To make it worse the heat seemed to be oppressive again and we were uncomfortably hot despite still having no shirts on. We hadn't liked to wear them after their duty as a stretcher.

We were about to give up when we arrived at a point where there seemed to be a load of crushed grass, and the dog looked up at us expectantly.

"Good boy," said Arif quietly. "Is he nearby?"

Lars just threw his head back and barked, startling us.

Nothing happened. Then, from the thickest, most thorny line of bushes we had seen, there was a sniff and a rustle, and a blonde, tousled head appeared, looking most dejected – if relieved. It was followed by a torso and legs that were so scratched that I winced in sympathy.

It was then that I noticed the red eyes, and I knew that even Tom was near the end of his endurance. The shout and teasing died on my lips.

"Hallo," I said uncertainly. Arif just nodded at him.

In a shaky voice our leader said: "I thought you were *them*. I thought they could see where I was going."

"No. It's just us," Arif said, just as quietly. "Led by Lars. We couldn't have found you otherwise."

Lars just went to him and looked at him, then nuzzled against him.

It's an odd feeling, witnessing someone your own age, someone whose leadership you take for granted, shed tears. He sat, hunched up, elbows on raised knees, and palmed his eyes. The dog still sat there, pressing against him.

We waited, rather shocked, knowing instinctively not to say anything.

At last he looked nervously up at us, trying to clear his eyes without it being obvious what he was doing. The dog looked up at him. We looked down.

"Sorry," he said, still shakily. "I got completely lost and was getting worried when I heard someone after me. I didn't realise it was you two."

"Three," said Arif, determined the dog should get the credit.

"Three," repeated Tom with a pale smile, and put his arm

round the dog, who looked at him again and leant into him.

"Do you think you can start back?" I asked.

"I think so," he said, "But my legs hurt like hell and itch too."

"Wonder if Nils has a first aid kit?" said Arif.

"Water would be okay," replied Tom. "Inside and out."

Even a feeble joke like that seemed to show he was recovering.

Lars, fortunately, knew the word "Home". Fortunately, that is, because even in the ten minutes or so since we had pushed our way through to Tom's resting place most of the foliage seemed to have returned to normal, obliterating all signs of our earlier passage through it.

Tom seemed oblivious to the further damage to his skin. Perhaps he was in so much discomfort that more had no effect. Arif and I muttered constantly to each other with the occasional curse thrown in for good measure. Tom said nothing, just followed the dog closely.

Returning seemed to take far less time than the search had. We were surprised when we started to recognise signs of a trodden path, then features we recognised – not from earlier, but from the journey with Nils all that time ago.

"How didn't I find the way?" muttered Tom, more to himself than us.

"Well," I said as cheerfully as I could, "I most certainly couldn't. And I'd have been in a far worse state than you were."

Tom was silent again.

At last roofs started to appear, and we knew the ordeal was all but over. Lars barked and ran off, and soon a chorus of barks rather alarmed us. But Arif said they weren't angry barks and it was probably the others, though how he knew wasn't obvious.

Tom stopped suddenly, looking round at us. His face was defiant. At least his eyes were back to normal.

"Please…" he said, and hesitated. "Please.. don't mention what happened back there." He turned back, as if to follow the dog.

"Tom!" Arif called, quietly as always but in a tone that suddenly had authority. Tom stopped, his back still to us. Arif went to him and did something none of us ever did: he put his arm round Tom's shoulder.

"Tom, we may tease each other and insult each other, but

when one of us has been in trouble we're always there. Always have been, always will."

I was with them now, and hesitatingly put my arm round his shoulder too.

"And as far as I'm concerned, nothing happened. You missed your way, Lars and me and Matt found you. That's it. End of. Okay Matt?"

"Okay," I confirmed with certainty. I didn't want to be some kind of snitch. It wasn't in my character. And the more I thought about it, the more right it felt.

So it was that when we came across Steve and Joe, armed still with both map and phone, all that appeared to be the matter were some thousand or so scratches to our legs and arms, particularly to Tom's. Steve had somehow managed to think of the first aid kit as well as finding his way – Joe told us he hadn't fallen over once – and we had a painful 45 minutes with water, sterilising wipes and a few sticky dressings until The Scout was happy that we weren't going to die on him.

Armed with dog, map, compass and increasing familiarity on the part of Joe who had made the journey a distressing number of times that day, we arrived back at the camp site with a massive feeling of relief. To our delight there was a stew nearly ready – Steve had given instructions – and all we had to do was to wait for the potatoes. He hadn't instructed about those.

11 Storm

It was Lars who would have been unfortunate. No one had thought to bring any of his food. But we all contributed a bit, especially Tom who had particular reason to be grateful to him. He ended up with a good plateful of his own, which was gone in a tenth of the time it took us to eat. Like all dogs, he then visited each of us in turn to watch us eat, and must have heard "you've had enough of mine already" many times. He did get to do the washing up, though, following which we did it again, with clean water and some little effort.

We badgered Tom to tell us about his experiences with Nils and the ambulance. "They had to keep giving him gas in the ambulance," he started. "He'd keep gasping and was in agony until they gave him more." He looked almost scared. "I've never been in that sort of pain in my life. Hope I never am."

We nodded sympathetically. I couldn't help but wonder what a wounded soldier felt like.

"They had to cut his shoe off – it was in the way and they said it'd have to come off later anyway. Then they put this plastic thing on his leg to keep it still.

"We got to the hospital – the General – and they got him into a cubicle. The woman in the office said it was good it wasn't a Friday as they get all the drunks then, followed by the footballers on Saturday." He grinned.

"The next thing I heard he was being taken up to a ward, so I followed and when some guy in a white coat tried to stop me Nils just said 'No. Let him come', and they did. They gave him an injection and that stopped the pain so we had a chat. Seems he was really surprised that we helped him. Don't think he has much time for other people usually.

"Anyway, he told me a bit more about himself. He actually spent some time in Holland, got married, but she died, so he came back here. His stepfather, the old owner of the big house, gave him the run of the place and made all sorts of promises, then he died too and it turned out he had been the last of the old family. There was no money left, and the house and the estate were just left to fall apart."

"Except his cottage," Alex put in.

"Yes. But some of the promises were that he'd get

electricity and running water and heating, but he says they never happened 'cos the money ran out. So he's still there, years later, just living on the basics.

"Anyway, we waited for a bit and he kept asking me what was going to happen, but I didn't know. At last a doctor came and said they were going to operate and put it right, but it would take a bit of time to heal. That worried him, mainly because of Lars and having to gather things called truffles. He didn't tell me what that was all about. But I told him we'd look after Lars, and he seemed to think Arif knew something about truffles."

He looked at Arif, who smiled innocently back. "Might do," he said.

"What are they then?"

"Ahh…" He paused, grinning, and then just as Tom was getting up to launch himself at him, he explained what he'd found, how we'd collected some – and then almost immediately sold them. When he produced the money, Tom's jaw nearly hit the ground.

"*How* much? You're kidding me!"

But he had to agree that £72 was rather more than Arif's weekly allowance.

"Bloody hell – I can see why he's anxious. Can we get them for him?"

"There's plenty there at the moment," Arif told him. "It took Lars no time to find the supply we sold to Yardley."

"You should have heard Arif bargaining with him," I told him. "Yardley was gobsmacked!"

I'm not sure if the look I got was The Look, but if it was it was tinged with something like pleasure.

Tom grinned. "There's more to Arif than meets the eye, it seems!"

"What happened next?" asked Joe.

"They came and put him on a trolley, and this time told me I'd better go because he would be under the anaesthetic for some time. He didn't want me to…" He paused.

"He… he got rather emotional and I had to promise to come back when he had had the operation. He… well, shook my hand."

"So?" asked the irrepressible Alex.

"Well, he more grabbed my hand and wouldn't let go, but

they were wheeling him away and all I could say to him was that he'd be all right." He paused again. "I just hope I'm right."

A longer gap in the conversation this time as we all tried to think ourselves into Tom's situation.

"How did you get home?" Joe asked suddenly.

Tom pulled a face. "I was so caught up with Nils that it wasn't until he'd gone that I started thinking about that. I knew I had to avoid the town. That meant I couldn't walk or get a bus. So I phoned your home, Joe. Your Mum made an emergency call to your Dad who spoke to someone in the Police. Plod...". We grinned. "... and the next thing I knew there was a Police van with blacked out windows arriving at the hospital's staff entrance.

Several eyebrows shot up.

"So they took me away with lights flashing and siren going, until we got to the Police station. Then they asked me what had happened, so I told them about Nils." Another pause, then he added in a rather embarrassed tone: "They seem to think I'd done rather well, but I explained it was all of us."

That was all right, then.

"They asked where I needed to get to, so I told them about the hamlet. I had to wait a bit, and drank so many cups of tea... it just seemed rude to say no. At least I know where the toilets are there now!"

We laughed.

"Some time later Tim – your Dad, Joe – brought me a couple of bags of food from your Mum. It seems she thought we might be starving. So we've got that too. And then, a bit later, they brought me to the hamlet in a Police car. It caused one or two to come out of the houses to see what was happening, and the Police told them that I was entitled to be on the Estate, so were the rest of you, but that if any other strangers appeared they were to call the Police immediately. He even gave them a code word to use.

"It seems we're important. But he also told them not to talk about us to anyone else. Then he took them on one side and said a lot quietly. The look on their faces when he'd finished was... well, different."

"Any idea of what's happened to the men who got us into this mess?" asked Steve.

"A bit. They did their raid, but they only got one or two girls and the men with them. The main people had just sent them to the pub to meet the girls."

"Anyone we know?" asked Arif with some urgency in his voice.

"I didn't ask," Tom told him, "It didn't seem right, somehow, and I was sure I wouldn't have got an answer."

"So you don't know if…" Arif trailed off.

Suddenly I guessed. "She's too sensible, Arif," I told him. "And she's got higher standards than that."

He glanced at me gratefully. Tom grinned. "I'll second that," he said. "Even if she's decided she likes you it doesn't mean she's going to make any other mistakes."

Arif stuck his tongue out.

We chatted about his experiences and, uselessly, the details of the raid and its outcome as we knew it. Nothing came of it, but I suppose we all felt better afterwards. We knew as much or as little as did Tom, the last of us to have encountered civilisation.

It did strike me then that here we were, deep in the countryside and surrounded by nature, with good friends, eating well and looking after ourselves; and regarding ourselves as 'outside civilisation'. In contrast there were men and girls in our own home town, trying to get... what? Money? Street cred? A quick pleasure fix? What?

I think we all knew which we would prefer. I did.

It was by then late afternoon. We'd been woken early by Lars, kept awake by Nils, ambulance people, villagers, a truffle buyer, Tom and each other. Small wonder, then, that conversation became scarce and we gradually lay back where we were and... well, relaxed.

I woke, eventually, and was aware that the light was different. It was no longer sunny. In fact the sky was definitely grey to the extent that it said "rain" as clearly as if someone had shouted the word at me. If I'd had my normal phone I'd have looked at the weather app. But I didn't, and it was out of bounds for very good reasons. All I had to look at was the cloud cover, and that looked decidedly greyer, lower; a dark grey where before there had been sunlight.

Having just emerged from sleep I was only half aware. For some reason my skin said "splodged spiders" to my brain. With no common sense intervention between sensation and brain, I gave a shout as the first large drops started landing on me.

At least I'd woken the other five, and when we'd finally secured the tents against the weather, with all of us in one of them, there were congratulations on having given a timely warning, even if one or two thought that what had emerged from my mouth had been a scream. I was dry – ish – so didn't care and made no comment. The moment passed.

As the summer thunderstorm started properly we looked at each other, I think rather nervously. If I'd been on my own in a tent I would definitely have been nervous, but with the others there it felt better. As they say, we were all in it together. No change there, I thought.

The rain hardened, became a downpour, then something approaching a torrent. It was quite an event, with frequent lighting flashes illuminating nervous expressions even inside the double wall of the tent.

We never touched the walls of the tent. Steve had warned us early on not to do that, but in the downpour there was a steady, fine spray penetrating both flysheet and inner. The inside of the tent got more and more humid and we had a few anxious looks round to see if anything was getting actually soaking wet. It didn't seem to be. I wondered what the contents of the other tent would be like.

After about twenty minutes of this the gaps between lighting and thunderclaps increased, and the intensity of the rain decreased. Finally it grew lighter outside, the rain stopped and Tom raised his eyebrows. We nodded, he opened the tent and we looked out on to a sodden world. The waterfall was already making a different sound, angrier than the gentle, soft background music we were used to. This was Wagner rather than Delius (Yes, I know. Blame my parents.)

Getting out of the steamy tent was a wet experience, impossible to do without drips landing on you and the wet ground seeping up through your shoes.

"Should have worn boots," The Scout was heard to mutter. We more or less knew he was talking to himself. We looked toward the point where the waterfall had been falling on to our mini-lake all the time we had been there. Water was now hammering its way over the little cliff, ignoring the rock ledges that had broken its fall before, and landing in the lake with a force that none of us would have believed.

We had all been periodically gobsmacked by something or other over our time at camp. For me it had been Nils' out-of-true ankle and the pain attached to it. For others... well, I knew that surprise had figured high in their list of emotions. But to see the difference between the previous gentle fall and the torrent that had replaced it made us all stop and stare, and try to make sense of the difference.

"Is the water level rising?" shouted Alex. Quiet chat was ineffective at that point.

Tom and Steve looked at the edge of the lake.

"Don't think so," Tom shouted back, "but I wouldn't want to be swimming by the exit point."

We looked. Before, the water from the lake had left with a courteous trickle over many metres of ledge before running through rocky outcrops and reaching the continuation of the stream. At that moment there were what would be described in adventure stories as foaming rapids, whose force would dash you to your doom at the bottom if you were caught in them.

"Wouldn't want to be swept over that," Alex said.

"Wouldn't want to swim in it either," I said, having dipped my hand into a lake that suddenly felt as if it was emerging from a freezer. Everybody had to come and do the same, of course, and make some exclamation. I suppose I'd have done the same if another of them had discovered it.

Over the next thirty minutes the clouds drifted away, thinning as they did so, and at last the sun reappeared. As it grew in strength mists rose from the undergrowth around us, from the lake and, so far as we could tell from occasional glimpses of the estate, from everywhere else too.

It was unusual enough a sight for us to stand and watch, not least since there was little else we could do. As I discovered when I needed to visit my bush, all the leaves – and everything else – was still soaking wet. So was I when I rejoined the others, attracting many suggestions about learning to aim properly. Steve interrupted the comments, making his own suggestion that we collect firewood so he could dry it out in time for use later.

"How are you going to start a fire to dry it, then?" asked Joe.

"I might use the dry wood I stored in the store tent in case it rained," he crowed. "Good idea. Yes?"

Various people gave him The Look, but he was right. We set to, knowing that no fuel meant no food. Much of what we collected was very wet indeed, and so were each of us by the time we arrived back with it. Steve was regarded as a tyrant, though we did realise he was sitting by a pile of dry wood, trying to get it to light. "The ground's so wet it just soaks into everything I lay on it," he complained.

"Try some dry ground," suggested Alex.

"Show me some."

"Dry it?"

"Hang on," said Tom, "if you've got some big sticks, dry ones, how about putting them down first and lighting the small stuff on top of them?"

"I should have thought of that," he muttered, and did so. Soon the first whisps of smoke rose, and we were in business again. It took a long time to dry the collected wood, although the heat of the sun helped quite a bit.

Another, rather unexceptional meal was cooked, eaten, and washed up, then as always we gathered by the fire and there was nearly silence between us. Lars had taken up station beside Arif, who was often seen to drop a hand to the dog's shaggy coat. Desultory conversation happened, certainly, but we were all once again tired by the early start and the day's events. Even The Scout could find nothing to bully us about,

12   Hospital

I was dreaming, and it wasn't a pleasant dream. A dark, wrinkled mass had leapt from the earth and fastened itself to someone's ankle, disfiguring it. I was carrying a stretcher with the patient on it, and at every bump of the stretcher the ankle seemed to grow, and come towards us, but each time it happened a dog whimpered and scared the ankle back to just a normal disfigurement.

I woke. My right arm felt odd. The hand stretched its fingers and found fur. The brain gradually caught up and recognised dog. Lars. Lars was sleeping between me and Arif. My stomach was aching a bit – there were other symptoms too. I struggled from the warm sleeping bag and went to visit our toilet arrangements. The dog accompanying me was half a comfort and half an embarrassment, but we each did what we had to and soon we were back in the tent. The others hadn't stirred.

At least it was a reasonable time when I next awoke. By that I mean that it was about 9.00 am. At weekends I usually get up later than that unless I'm being forced to get up by Parents. And I knew better than to visit any of the other Suspects before about 11.30 over the weekend or during the holidays – it was an unspoken code between us.

I lay back, feeling warm, thinking about the events of the last... what? Three days? Was that all? But yes, my watch said this was Saturday, so it must be.

During the parental phone check the previous night we had said we were cooking and would phone back next day as we had some news – not bad news – and needed to arrange for still more food. After breakfast our washing up was interrupted by the phone and as it was his parents who had provided the thing, Joe answered.

It was starting to be a long, involved conversation and Joe was getting rather agitated. Tom mouthed "Battery!" at him and he swiftly used it as an excuse to end the required explanations. He did get a promise that they'd phone at about 3.00 that afternoon to arrange a parcel drop of shopping, but would want a face-to-face explanation of the happenings.

"Damn," said Alex, "that means we'll have to remember to switch it on again in time."

"Where are we going to meet them?" asked Tom.

"They didn't say," Joe told him.

"Hardly surprising as they don't know where we are exactly. They can hardly wander up here and drop it off, followed by several polite gang members."

There was silence at this.

"It's going to have to be either at the wall where they dropped us off, or at the cottages," he continued. "Either way we can meet them there."

"Cottages for me," said Arif. "We can go on a truffle hunt again. And get some money to Nils. That Yardley will be visiting him soon, and we need to make sure he knows what's happening."

"Easier there," Tom admitted. "But easier for anyone following them to find us. And if they see us going into Nils' house…"

I saw what he meant as soon as he'd mentioned it. "It has to be the wall, then,"

"Can you get us back to the spot, Steve?"

"Yes. Can Joe get his parents to it, and hide them while they have a conversation? And apart from yesterday, what else do we tell them about?"

Tom looked puzzled.

Arif took up the conversation. "Someone's got to get to Nils to give him the money. It can't be one of us. And Parents will realise as soon as they talk to him who Lars is. And they'll know we've… er… not told them the exact truth."

"We haven't lied!" I said indignantly.

"No," said Tom, "but we've let them think what they wanted to. So it'll look as if we have."

We digested that.

"Well," Alex started, "if you ask me we didn't have an option."

"We didn't."

"What?"

"Didn't ask you."

"Shut up. If we'd not done what we have we'd have been kept indoors or something, or sent away to relatives, and that's even worse than camping with you lot."

There was the inevitable scuffle and Alex seemed to end up on his back.

"See what I mean?" he asked once back sitting on his log.

"He's right, of course," said Tom. "And we need to get them to realise it. But I think the wall is the only place, so long as we get them to drop off the stuff quickly. If they hang about someone might see them."

"But they're going to want to know what happened yesterday," Joe reminded him.

Tom thought. "We can't get them over the wall," he said.

Joe snorted. "Fat chance. Not either of them."

"So what do we do?"

A pause, interrupted by Arif. "I need to go and see Nils in the hospital. He needs to know from us that we're collecting money for him and looking after Lars and the house."

"But…"

"Yes, I know. But we almost promised. And we certainly promised Yardley that we would give him the money. I think I should go with Joe's Mum or Dad and get them to take me to see Nils. Then they can bring me back to the wall and I'll climb over with your help and bring the bags of food."

"Or we can take the food when they arrive, so when you come back we'll have a meal ready."

That won him over.

"But isn't that risky?" I asked.

"It doesn't show where we are. And anyone getting over that wall won't be able to find the camp easily. And we could hear them coming, and Lars would warn us."

Another silence. I was waiting for someone, anyone, to say something like: "But that's not what we've all agreed." But no one did. I wondered how the others were thinking we could take on the gang - or even one of them – if they did invade the Estate.

Arif carried on as no one else spoke: "So if no one has any better ideas that's what we'll do. When your parents phone, Joe, can you tell them? Then we need to get up to the wall as soon as possible afterwards, and you can get the food. Once I'm done at the hospital and we're on our way back I'll phone again – we'll decide a time, and you can guide me back down, please. I'm not as good with the map as The Scout is."

To my surprise there were no arguments, though I was mentally screaming out "It's too risky!" But I don't think any of us could fault Arif's logic.

The day was warm and dry again, thank goodness. We tested the water temperature and spent a happy late morning messing about in or by the water. We had the football with us so managed a game of water polo – of sorts. Its drawback was that hard contact between a football of plastic, and skin of...well, skin... was painful. It caused red marks and loud shouts of pain.

We changed. By now we seemed to be even more comfortable with each other than we'd become through the long years spent together at school and at each others' homes. It followed that first one, and then all of us, rather threw caution to the winds when changing into dry clothes. I decided I was running out of dry underwear.

We revived the fire, cooked, ate, and washed up. Steve 'suggested' someone could help him make some sort of hurdles to go round the pit. "I'm fed up with wondering if one of you is going to wander round the corner when I'm...er..." We all felt the same, so he got quite a few volunteers.

Just before 3.00 Joe switched the phone on. The call came through on the dot, and Joe explained what we'd decided. There seemed to be some resistance on the grounds of it being dangerous for any of us to be noticed, but he was quite positive. Although the argument wasn't exactly going his way he made some clicking noises and covered the phone from time to time, then explained that the signal wasn't brilliant and he couldn't really hear them but that he'd see them in about a couple of hours if that would give them enough time to get the food. Oddly that part of the conversation went without a hitch. Eventually he rang off and looked round smugly.

"They weren't keen on Arif's plan," he said. "In fact Mum said we weren't to go anywhere outside the Estate. But... well, the signal sort of broke up on me."

We all said versions of "Hmmm..." and grinned, glad we hadn't been in charge of the conversation.

"If it's only two hours we'd better set off," said Tom suddenly. "It'll take us some time to get to where we're going to meet them, and we might as well give The Scout some map reading practice on the way." Steve just looked at him and gave a sign which indicated he was still capable of operating a longbow.[1] At least it made a difference from The Look.

He must have been improving, as not only did he fail to fall over when reading the map, but we didn't get lost at all. After so many days – well, it felt like it – away from civilisation, it was odd to be walking along beside a wall over which could be heard traffic noises from a road we all knew. Indeed we were so early that we sat under the wall, near the rendezvous point, to wait, and to rest. And promptly each fell asleep.

A slightly familiar voice entered my head. It was saying things I didn't understand but that I felt I should because they were important. A hand grasped my shoulder and shook it; a disembodied voice nearby called again: "Hallo! we're here!"

The rendezvous had been made. Joe had to embark on another argument about it not being safe to leave the Estate. We only won it when they realised that the longer the car and they were waiting, with shopping bags as well, the more likely it was that the wrong people would realise our presence.

Our stores came over the wall one way, Arif went over the other. We were down to five for the two hours Arif was allowed to visit the hospital, plus Lars, who whined when Arif vanished above him, and wasn't keen on coming back with us.

For the sake of form we returned to the camp and laid about, nearly going back to sleep once or twice. But all too soon Joe gave the signal to Steve and he set off. The rest of us started cooking as we'd promised. We'd been given explicit instructions what to do, as well as how to do it. By whom? The Scout, of course. We almost followed the formula, though it did look a bit suspect even if the smell was good. It was ready before Steve and Arif reappeared, and Steve looked at it and gave as good a Look at each of us as he could muster.

"I'm getting to know that route now," he said. (We thought he was going to criticise the cooking but it turned out he was too hungry for that.)

"I haven't," Arif admitted. "It confuses the hell out of me."

We ate, at Tom's insistence, before listening to what Arif

---

[1] *It's said that in the Hundred Years' War against the French, any captured English bowmen had their second and third fingers cut off by the enemy to prevent them being able to use their longbow any more. Able-bodied English archers used to wave their second and third fingers at the French to show they were still able to shoot arrows, to the devastating effect so feared by their enemies. So it's not a rude sign at all. So there.*

had to say. And he had a lot to tell us.

Nils was okay. He was still rather groggy from the operation but... and here Arif became characteristically quiet. We pestered him and wheedled out of him that the old man was almost pathetically grateful to Arif for coming, and to all of us for "saving my life" as he put it. One of the nurses had asked who Arif was before he was allowed in and when he admitted that he'd been one of the people who had carried him to the ambulance she was almost embarrassing about it – again, Arif's words. It seemed that Nils was becoming sleepy when a doctor came and told him that what we had done had almost certainly saved his patient's life, and... and here Arif became dismissive about it apart from telling us that we'd all done rather well.

Nils wouldn't accept the money for the truffles. Arif had done his best to persuade the man but he wouldn't. He didn't think it would be right. He'd muttered that we had expenses and that the dog needed food. And at that he became anxious, until Arif told him that Lars was happily with us and was well. That quietened him again and he seemed to fall asleep.

"I realised I'd said nothing about the restaurant man..."

"Yardley. Marcus Yardley," I put in.

"Him. So I wrote a note to tell Nils about what we'd said, and left most of the money there, with an apology. The nurse came and put it in the cupboard where the rest of his things were."

"So we've got none of it?" asked Alex.

"I took £15 out of it to buy dog food," said Arif, "and put that in the note too."

"How are we going to get dog food?" asked Tom.

"Your Mum got some," Arif said, looking at Joe. "She was a bit astonished."

She still didn't know that Lars was a dog, thinking instead that he was the landowner under whose permission we were using the land. She would have been a little put out if she'd known. And as if he had indeed been human we'd fed Lars with some of our food, which he seemed to enjoy, though I've hardly ever known a dog not enjoy any food. Not that I was any kind of expert.

But Arif was carrying on with the news. "Your Dad, Joe, told me again what he knew, that they did the raid last Wednesday. He says that actually they found quite a few girls, some almost kids... " He looked at us with a worried expression. "Some of the men they were with were caught, but they know that others there were involved too. At the moment they can't do anything because we're the only people who've identified the others."

"Can't they just arrest them anyway?" asked Alex.

"Not without evidence, or some adult pointing the finger like we did. They don't want to use our statements and involve us."

We all nodded. That was the last thing we wanted, and the Police had told us our statements were required just for a 'paper trail'.

"So the Police are concerned that we're safe. So are Joe's parents, and I told them we were and not to worry."

"Did anyone see you at the hospital, or follow you here?" I asked.

"Not so far as I could see," he told me, "but the roads are quite busy and so was the hospital. But even if they did, no one could find us deep in the woods here."

We nodded. Knowing the difficulty *we* had finding the way around we were pretty sure no one else could.

"And if they did, Lars would tell us there was someone near," I said.

Arif grinned. "He certainly would. The only stranger he's not warned about was Yardley, and even then he barked. It was a different bark, though."

The dog had lifted his head at the mention of his name and was looking round at us hopefully. Arif rummaged in a bag and found something that he held out. The dog rose and sniffed, and then very, very carefully took the bone from his hand, went over to a bush and started work on it.

"Your Mum got it, along with all the food," he told Joe. "She said that she hadn't a clue what was going on but if we needed dog food, and it wasn't going to be eaten by us, we were welcome to that one fresh from the butcher."

We smiled, mainly at the idea of Joe's mum wondering if the dog food was for us.

The phone rang. Joe answered. As he listened his face grew serious.

"When was this?" he asked. We all watched with growing alarm, although we hadn't a clue what was going on.

"How about everyone else?" he asked the phone.

A few more one-sided exchanges later and Joe ended the call. He looked round at us.

"Arif's house had a brick chucked through the window this afternoon," he announced. "His parents are furious and want to know what the Police are doing to protect them - and Arif - from the culprits."

Arif was plainly shocked. "I need to borrow that phone, please," he said in a tone that was as unlike the usual quiet, laid back friend we all knew as it was possible to get. Joe handed it over without a word. As he punched in his home number he walked over to the bushes so he could talk privately. We stayed sitting round the fire but could hear only snatches of what was being said.

When he returned he looked as if he was back to his usual self again. The phone was returned and he sat down. We looked at him expectantly.

"They're all right," he said. "They wanted to know more about the people who were involved. The Police wouldn't tell them any more than what they've told your Mum, Joe. Dad asked if anyone he knew or dealt with was involved, but I couldn't help him there either. We know their faces – the faces of two or three of them – but we don't know who's been arrested and we don't know any names. He wasn't happy, but I just told him that if I knew, I'd say. But I had to tell him I – we – were all safe and please could he tell everyone else's parents the same."

It was a development that we hadn't foreseen. As Tom said, though, a bit of parental negotiation was preferable to anything the rest of the men chose to do to get their own back or persuade us not to say anything to the Police. He changed the subject.

"Why don't we go truffle hunting tomorrow and get enough to earn a good amount of money for Nils? About time we contacted Yardley again. And do you think, Arif, that if we got a good supply your family might be able to get a good price? A better price than Yardley, perhaps?"

"We could try. Lars is up for it, aren't you? Hondje?"

The dog looked up from his bone, head on one side as if understanding what was being said. We all laughed, but politely. It seemed wrong to offend a dog like that.

"What was that word?" asked Alex.

"I asked Nils in one of his more awake times. It's '*hondje*'. Dutch. It's a sort of term for 'good dog'. A sort of endearment."

We digested that and tried the word, as we'd heard it, in our minds. It had a good sound to it.

"Hondje?" I tried, looking at Lars. He looked me in the eye and cocked his head on one side. I smiled. He got up and barked.

"Wants a walk," I said.

"Come on, then," said Arif, "we'll all go."

So we did, and I have to admit that in the falling light and with no map it was only because of Lars that we found our way back. And the relief at following his strong, hairy hindquarters and to see our tents dimly reappear was really rather great. We grew an even greater respect for his abilities.

13   Hunting again

"Do you know it's Sunday?"

It wasn't the normal way I'd choose to be woken. It wasn't the normal time I'd choose, either.

"Shut up, Arif," I muttered.

"Wassatime then?" he murmured, more quietly this time.

I struggled a bit and found my watch.

"Half past five."

"Shut UP, you two. I need my sleep." Alex felt as I did. I'd normally argue with him, but as I agreed it seemed hardly worth it. We all lay back – well, I did – and the next thing I knew it was a lot lighter and I needed to get up, as usual. What had caused Arif to become an early alarm clock neither he nor I knew.

The day followed the usual pattern – at least in the morning. I suppose swimming was becoming our version of a shower except that none of us stripped off or used shower gel. My own underwear shortage crisis had been solved by reusing my swim shorts and wet pants from before, and I guess some of the others were doing the same. We dried off, changed and decided to look for some truffles.

Lars seemed pleased to be on a long walk and led the way, apparently without difficulty. We were starting to recognise the path and sections of it were showing signs of having been trodden before, hardly surprising seeing the density of the undergrowth we had to go through. Our efforts, particularly when hurrying to and from Nils' cottage were starting to leave a mark.

We looked into the cottage, Lars particularly searching around as if to look for his master. He was satisfied there was no one there and returned to the kitchen where we were enjoying a drink of spring water. He crossed to a corner of the room, looked down and pawed at a flagstone. To our surprise there was an iron ring set in it, something we hadn't noticed before.

"Where do you think that goes to?" Alex asked the question in all our minds.

"One way to find out," Tom replied, crossing to it and giving it a tug. "Bloody hell!"

It hadn't budged. Now despite his thin build Tom wasn't a weakling, so if he couldn't move it, none of us were going to be able to. We tried two at a time; any more than that wouldn't have helped as only two hands could fit on the ring.

"How does Nils raise it then?" I asked.

"Dunno. Either he's superhuman or Lars does it." Tom was nursing his shoulder where he had wrenched at the ring, expecting it to follow the jerk of his arm. But Lars was just standing there, looking at us as if to tell us we were being stupid.

"Hang on," said Alex suddenly, "what's that bright bit for on the inside edge?"

We crowded round. The ring was mainly of the sort of old metal colour you'd expect of something that was... well, old and metal. But opposite its hinge, on the ring's inner surface, there was a centimetre of bright metal.

"Does something go there? Something to help lift it?" Joe's turn to play detective.

We looked around the kitchen, unsure what we were looking for. Everything we saw we had already investigated, all apart from what looked like a small cupboard at the bottom of a sort of upright beam. We cautiously opened it.

The Scout looked at its contents with dawning understanding. "It's a block and tackle!" he almost shouted.

That meant nothing to me. Nor did any of the others look any wiser. All I could see was some ropes and a large metal thing.

Steve straightened and looked up. Still almost shouting he said: "Look – there's the other end. We never looked at the ceiling."

We still failed to understand, so he explained. "If you release this end, the hook against the ceiling comes down. You hook it on the ring. Then you can pull the rope back again and the stone will come up."

"How? We couldn't lift it." Alex was indignant.

"'Cos it's a block and tackle. It triples the force you can have with it."

He could see that we were still none the wiser, so demonstrated by letting the coil of rope in the cupboard go through the metal parts, and sure enough the hook above the stone started coming slowly down.

We humoured him by attaching the hook to the ring on the stone when it was low enough. He pulled at the rope again, the hook started up again *and pulled the ring and the flagstone up with it.* Steve was pulling quite hard, but it was obviously nowhere near as difficult as when we had tried to lift it.

"Stop there," Tom ordered when the stone was upright. "There's steps going down. Who's got the torch?"

We all remembered guiltily that we'd left it at the camp.

"Will this lantern do?" asked Steve innocently, holding up a battered old hurricane lamp he'd fished out of the 'cupboard' where the ropes were. He got The Look from Tom.

When we had found our way down and adjusted to the hurricane's dim light, we found we were in an Aladdin's cave of tins and non-perishable food for both man and dog. There were some gaps, but not many. It was obviously Nils' way of ensuring that he and Lars would never have to starve if they were snowed in.

"Well," Arif started, "that solves a lot of problems."

"Certainly does," Tom confirmed. "If we can use these we won't be having to rely on parents, which means they won't have to come and drop stuff off, and give us away."

A doubt crept into my mind. "Just how long do you think we're going to be staying here?" I asked. Some nervousness must have crept into my voice, for Alex immediately piped up.

"Not more than a year or two, I should think."

I just looked at him.

"Not more than a week, maybe two. It depends on whether Plod manage to get the whole gang locked up."

I wasn't sure I could last two weeks of doing nothing apart from walking round the Estate, collecting truffles, swimming and all the camping stuff. But then I also realised that for safety there wasn't really an option apart from staying somewhere miles away – with god knows what to do there.

We rescued a lot more dog food and some tins to supplement what we'd just been given by parents.

"Now all we've got to do is get this lot back to the camp," said Tom cheerfully.

Five hearts sank. Probably six, actually.

"Can't we leave some of it here, and collect it later?" asked Joe. "That way, it'll look as if Nils is still here if anyone comes in."

"Okay," said Tom. "All we need do now is collect some truffles to sell, then phone Yardley and get him up here. Would he come on a Sunday?"

"One way of finding out," Arif told him. "Phone him."

"Where's the phone?"

"In camp," said Alex.

"Damn. We need another one, really. So that anyone down here who has trouble can contact the rest of us. And if someone is down here and we need some food brought up, we can call them."

"Won't that waste batteries?" asked Alex.

Joe was positive about that. "No, the one we've got has still got 95% battery left. It's so basic it hardly uses any. And if we've got two we *could* send one home to be recharged. I'll phone them when we get back and tell them to get one."

"*Tell* them?"

"Well, you know what I mean. It's to their benefit as well as ours – they don't want their little boys hurt."

And this time we all gave him The Look, until he put up his hands in resignation.

"Is it worth collecting truffles if Yardley can't come?" asked Arif suddenly. "Isn't it better to get them on the day he's due to collect them? That way they're freshest. And if he does come today we can come down again, Lars and I at least, and get them."

There was no argument on that one. We found a bag for the food and returned to camp, taking turns to carry it. A short-ish rest, and Joe was prompted into making the phone call.

Apparently it made sense to his parents and the promise was made that they would give it to him next time we needed food.

Arif grabbed the phone and called Mr Yardley who said that as it was in the middle of his hotel's evening dinner service he couldn't come immediately, but would be there at 11.00 the following morning. He told Arif that collecting some that afternoon would be fine as they'd last overnight if kept cool.

"So when are we going to get the phone?" asked Alex plaintively.

"When we next need to get food from parents," I told him, though it was obvious.

"But we've got all Nils' stores."

That was a problem.

"But I'll need to go and see Nils," Arif remembered. "I need to give him the next lot of money and make sure Yardley knows it. I could pick it up at your place."

"Too dangerous," said Tom at once. "But if your Dad, Joe, could get it to the hospital while you're there, that would work."

"It'd mean a load more explanations," growled Joe after a pause, "but it's a safer way. I wonder if they'd wear it?"

"We need to try," Tom told him. "Otherwise it means visits, either to homes or to here, and we have no idea if or when these people will be watching, or where, or how many are looking."

A long pause this time. Lars got up and scratched.

"Let's wait and see what Yardley says," Arif said at last. "That might give us a lead. In the meantime, I'll go and get some truffles. Anyone coming?"

We'd all just returned to the camp, carrying food, so no one else volunteered apart from Lars, who had scrambled to his paws as soon as the word "truffles" was mentioned. For some reason I volunteered too.

"Hang on," said Steve suddenly, "what about lunch?"

We looked at each other and I realised with something of a shock that I was hungry. We cobbled something together hurriedly, ate it and fed Lars some too. Washing up, like being made to wash your face in the morning, was inevitable, according to Steve.

Lars, Arif and I set off back down towards the clearing where we'd found Nils all that time ago. Well, two days ago.

Although we found a few...

We found a few? Lars was the one who did the finding. We just dug where he told us to.

... found a few in the clearing where we'd discovered Nils, Lars kept looking at the undergrowth at the back of the clearing and whining, looking back at us. We got the hint and tried bashing our way through the thickets of prickly foliage. Even the dog kept backing out and trying another, less damaging part of it.

"Hang on," said Arif, when we had paused for the third time to examine our increasingly numerous red, skin perforations, "there must be another way in to where he wants to go."

To the dog's disgust – shown by some disgusted, deep barks – we left the clearing and tried to find a way round to the back

110

of where he wanted to take us. It was a struggle, and had not Lars reluctantly rejoined us and, who knows, realised what we were trying to do, we wouldn't have found the only, half hidden, thinner part of the thorn bushes.

"He seems to need to get in there, and he's so intelligent we ought to try." Arif was echoing what I was thinking.

It took time and lot more bush beating and skin punctures but we got there eventually. "There" was another clearing, full of fallen branches, where once again rabbits had delved over many years making the going risky. Risky for heavier humans, that is; Lars just walked in, dodging the branches, and immediately started digging. We carefully crossed to him and immediately unearthed our first truffle.

An hour later we had a good two basketfuls and decided enough was enough. Even the dog seemed tired. He was certainly dirty. Struggling out of the clearing was... well, a struggle. We wondered about making it easier to find next time but decided that keeping it hidden was a better bet so as to protect the valuable contents.

We hiked down to Nils' cottage, carefully stowed the baskets in his cupboard, drew some water from the well and drank, then returned to camp. The rather bored four had gravitated to card games but were pleased to hear of our success. Steve told us to patch up the worst of our injuries and clean them. "I don't want to have to get you two to hospital with septic wounds. We might get seen," was his sympathetic response to our protests. We complied. He'd only have bullied us otherwise.

It was still only late afternoon. There was nothing we could usefully do. Not even The Scout could come up with any jobs he wanted doing. Arif and I entered into the card games. But eventually Steve rallied and started bullying us into wood collection and help with cooking. We ate, washed up, stretched, then sat round the fire, idly chatting, but with long periods of silence. I don't know about the others but those were periods when I just enjoyed being there. The gathering dusk, the twilight, the now quiet sound of the waterfall, the knowledge that my friends were with me, the general good feeling, the ambience... what is there not to enjoy?

Incredibly, it was 10.00 before we woke the next morning. As soon as I nudged – well, hit – Arif and told him the time he was up as if a wasp was sharing his bed.

"Yardley!" he exclaimed, "he's coming at ten!"

"Eleven," I said. He looked at me hopefully.

"It was ten, wasn't it?"

"Eleven. Definitely eleven."

"Well... if you're sure..."

"I'm sure."

"Then we can just about get down there and look as if we're organised. Come on!"

"Why me?"

"'Cos you collected them as well."

Tom had been listening from the next tent. "Sort yourselves out, you two, and get going. Or he'll think you're messing with him."

He was right, of course. But then he would be. That's why we did what he said most of the time. We struggled into clothes, called "Hondje!"at which Lars bounded up (which didn't take much time as he shared the tent with us), and hurried off. The route was more familiar now, and it certainly was to Lars, so we arrived at Nils' house with about ten minutes to spare.

"We can get the rest of the supplies up to the camp when we go," Arif said.

"Yes... " I replied reluctantly, "we can, can't we?"

He looked at me with a grin. "Well, some of them."

I grinned back.

There was a greeting from Lars in the garden, answered by a man's voice. We showed him what we'd collected and he was most impressed.

"That's a good load of really excellent looking truffles," he exclaimed. "In fact they're probably worth more than the usual amount I pay."

That was good news. He dug out his wallet, then paused.

"Have you given the first money to Mr Lundgren?" he asked rather sharply.

"When I was there he was still recovering from the operation," said Arif. "He didn't want to accept it – something to do with our food costs and Lars' food. He was very tired and went to sleep. So I left most of it in... near him with a note explaining."

"So you haven't seen him since?"

"Not since then, no. But that was only Saturday."

"I see. And when are you going to see him again?"

"It's difficult, as you know. We explained. I don't want to keep going there or someone will notice. And then Nils will be at risk too."

Silence.

"How do I know the money will get to him?"

My turn. "We've been through this. Nils has the first instalment. He'll get the remainder of what you're going to give us as soon as we can safely get it to him. And all the other amounts he'll get as soon after you pay us as we can. We play fair."

He looked at me.

"He's right, you know," said Arif quietly.

Perhaps it was just that quietness, and his sincerity, that made Yardley's face clear into a slow smile.

"Okay, okay," he said. "You win. You have my trust. No doubt we'll both be visiting Nils as soon as we can anyway."

He counted out another handful of banknotes in front of us and gave them to Arif.

"Hope that's satisfactory. You look as if you struggled a bit to get to the new supply, if that's what it is."

We looked puzzled.

He laughed. "When I last saw you, you weren't covered with sticky plaster and scratches. That says 'thorns' to me. And no doubt Lars could do with a brush too to get the remnants from his wiry coat."

We looked at each other, then at the dog who was grinning up at Mr Yardley.

"Never thought of Lars," admitted Arif shamefacedly. "We'll find a brush and give him a good going over."

"Nils would appreciate that if you told him. And Lars will enjoy it too. Now I must go."

He said his farewells and left. We went into the cottage and had another search around, eventually finding an old towel, a brush and comb which had fairly obviously been used for the dog. Armed with those and some of the provisions we made the journey back to camp.

14   Hospital 2

Our arrival with such a large amount of cash was greeted with warm joy and slightly cooler breakfast. We were puzzled as it was by then getting on for a normal lunch time, but they guiltily explained that they had gone back to sleep and then overslept even more than we had.

We explained what Yardley had said and proceeded to groom Lars thoroughly, even if he did yelp on occasion when a particularly knotted part of his coat was dealt with by a caring Arif. By the amount of thorns, weed and other stuff that came out with a lot of moulted hair, he must have felt better. He certainly looked it. From being an average, slim but unremarkable Labrador he now looked as if in show condition.

He stood, grinned at us and shook himself. We decided it was our turn to get clean, which meant the usual undignified scramble into pre-loved underwear and a run to the water to avoid embarrassment (though we were getting less self-conscious about this as the days passed). Our shower / swim time involved Lars who played alongside us as before. Whether it improved his state of grooming or otherwise I haven't a clue, but we weren't going to stop him enjoying himself. We all did, as always. I quite envied him his dry and change at the end of it: a quick shake and that was that.

I wouldn't mind the shake, if it was effective, but as to the permanent fur coat...

"I really should get to see Nils again," Arif announced out of the blue. "It's this cash – I just can't feel happy with so much money bumping around in my pocket."

"We'll have to wait until later when they're home from work. And that's the earliest," said Tom. "They can't just stop work for us. And how are you going to get there? Hitch a lift and hope no one's watching?"

"I can't really believe that they'd be as...as..."

"Persistent?" I asked.

"... persistent as that," said Arif, with a glance at me.

"Pity no one in the houses seemed to like us," said Alex, still bruised at the way we'd been talked to.

"We don't know them well enough. Not at all, in fact," said Tom. "We can't just give large sums of money to anyone and ask them to keep it. Or bank it…" He tailed off. We waited. Pearls of wisdom might be coming, we each thought.

"Of course," he said casually, "if Yardley could be trusted to do a bank transfer each time…"

We thought. "I think he could," said Arif. "If we can get Nils' bank details the money could go direct there."

"Then we need to get them, said Tom. "And for that we need to contact parents."

"And then what?" Alex asked.

"And then Arif had better go with whoever comes, then visit Nils. And come back with someone else's parents. That way there's no connection. And none of the parents can be his own."

"Why?" asked Arif.

"Because you have the shop van with its name all over it," Steve explained.

Arif just nodded.

I'm ashamed to say that the rest of the afternoon was again spent playing cards. Okay, the weather was clouding over, but The Scout kept saying we should really get out and explore so we knew where we were at a glance. I didn't think that was ever likely to happen, the area was so big. And even Nils, after many years of living there, seemed unaware of our camp site. Although Lars had managed to find it… Hmm. Odd that.

At last it was time to make the daily phone call. Amazingly they'd managed to get the phone – an even cheaper one than the original. Joe, whose father it was we were talking to, rolled his eyes in disgust but said nothing. We all grinned.

When he told them about Arif's need to visit the hospital, there was some stalling. They didn't think it was a good idea at all. But Joe said sweetly: "But Arif just *needs* to go, to make sure the old man knows his dog's okay, and to make sure he's okay himself. I mean, he could go on the bus, but that's a bit… er… *exposed…*"

By the squawks on the line I think Joe had hit the right note, because when he rang off he said that we were to switch it back on at 7.30 and arrangements would have been made.

And so it turned out to be. Arif would be picked up the next morning at 7.30, before Joe's parents went to work. He would be given the new phone. My Mum would call at the hospital in her lunch time, phone Joe, bring him back and push him out of the car in the usual place, as near cover as possible.

115

"Does this phone have an alarm on it?" asked Arif grimly. "It seems I have to get up at 6.30 to fight my way up to the wall. And I'll need Steve, because my map reading isn't that good."

I think Steve was pleased at the compliment but appalled at the prospect of another early morning.

"We'll all get up," announced Tom, though rather doubtfully. "It's only fair."

And even we, all aged between 14 and 15 and experienced delayers of parentally required bed times, persuaded each other that we should get to sleep early.

And even managed to do so.

I was in a submarine. It was in the war... no, I don't know which one... yes I do: the second world war. I know that because a bell rang and that meant an old submarine on an emergency dive. I could feel the buffeting of the depth charges as we dived down, down.....

"Wake up!"

"Not 'til we're out of danger... What? Who? Oh..."

Arif was shaking my shoulder. The bell had stopped. Memory returned with a rush. I just felt the remains of the submarine slipping away and was glad I was no longer on it. Though the reality of half past six was nearly as bad, just safer.

He raised the others – after all, Tom had said so, hadn't he? It was a shame the one who clung on to the sleeping bag the longest was... er... Tom.

Breakfastless, we set off. It must have been early in the mind of the navigator because he made some mistakes and started falling over again. But having Lars with us, a slightly puzzled Lars, was comforting. We reached the wall and Tom made a platform for Arif, who once again proved to be rather more solid than he expected. No car.

"Damn," said Joe. "Where is she?"

We milled about a bit, nearly accusing Steve of coming to the wrong part of the wall, though to be honest we recognised the spot as we'd been there more than a few times before. Finally, Lars looked at it and barked. Tom's back was used again, and this time Arif disappeared over the wall again, to Lars' amazement. He gathered himself and jumped up at it, but fortunately couldn't make it more than two-thirds of the way.

He looked at it, then turned to me.

"I'm not making a back for you, Hondje. He'll be back for lunch, anyway."

We heard a car start and fade off into the distance.

"Come on," said Tom, rubbing his back, "I want some breakfast."

We almost recognised the route on the way back. Steve had little to do, just a reference or two when discussions (aka scuffles) broke out about what we thought we recognised as the right way.

There's something about a strenuous walk before breakfast to give you an appetite. Bullied into more wood collecting than we could shake a…er… Well, we collected a lot of wood. The Scout, helped by anyone he could grab, cooked the remains of the bacon, including Arif's[1], sausages, including Arif's[1], eggs, fried bread and anything else we could lay our hands on that was remotely breakfast-ish. With some hesitation we even tried black pudding. It met with mixed fortunes, so the servings that didn't get eaten we put on one side for Lars.

It was really rather nice. We made up our minds to gloat when Arif reappeared, then remembered we had no bacon or sausages left. Another phone call was made, this time to my Mum who would be bringing Arif back. It was quite nice talking to her, although as she wasn't allowed to take personal calls at work it was rather a hurried conversation. I came off with a grin on my face, anyway.

"What's she say?" asked Joe.

I thought back. "Well, basically just 'Are you all right?' and 'Yes' when I asked her to get some more bacon and sausages."

"What are you grinning about, then?"

I didn't know, really. "She's not meant to take personal calls at work, so it was a bit awkward and one-sided," I said. That would do.

Despite the recent heavy breakfast we went swimming. The air was cooler than it had been and the water seemed not to be as cold as usual. Joe said it was a contrast between air and water

---

[1] *Yes, I know: but Arif had decided to try it, liked it, wanted more and his parents weren't there to remind him he was part of a Muslim family. It's his life: ask him. Okay?*

temperatures – he's a bit of a geek like that.

"Toilet needs replacing," said Steve once we were dressed.

"What with?" I answered innocently.

"Ha ha. We need to fill in the old one and dig another. Otherwise we'll be digging up the…"

A chorus of "Shut up!" and similar stopped him. We took the point, and very carefully filled in the first one. Need made us dig a second, some way away, and all that took the rest of the morning. It was fortunate that we had the mobile switched on, and in Joe's pocket, when it rang.

"They're on their way back," said Joe. "That was the new one."

"Save its number, quick." Alex was quick off the mark.

Joe did, and we made the long journey back to our wall crossing place. I was placed on top of the wall ("You're lighter than Arif," said Tom) as a look out. We waited, and waited, and waited…

After what seemed like an hour but was actually only about fifteen minutes, Mum's car appeared, but from the opposite direction from home. It stopped opposite the trees, Arif jumped out with a bag, Mum sped off and he crossed the road as quickly as he could. I could barely lift him up – he was as solid as Tom had hinted – but managed it eventually.

The bag was of great interest to Lars, so we kept it well out of his way.

"I think we were followed," said Arif grimly. "I got your Mum to carry on to the end of the route and turn round near the bus depot. She was good; there was a bus about to come out and she timed it so we got past and the other car didn't. Then we doubled back to here fast. No one followed us on the way back. If they did, we didn't see them."

That was grim news. Perhaps they *were* as persistent and desperate as we'd feared. Privately, we had assumed that that sort of thing happened only to other people, to adults, and even then in story books.

With little chat we returned to camp.

"Lunch," said Tom, trying to brighten the mood. "Sorry Arif, we ate your breakfast."

"That's okay, I had one in the hospital."

"How's Nils doing?" I asked.

"He's bored already, but he gets tired quickly. The injury

seems to be doing okay even if it can't be seen because of the plaster. He was pleased to hear about Lars, and really pleased we'd found a new area to get truffles though a bit disappointed it wasn't him who found it.

"He says that Marcus Yardley is trustworthy. He still thinks we should keep the money but I told him we couldn't; not all of it. I said we'd keep enough to keep Lars fed and, when he insisted, us too. Though I think we need to charge him very little."

We nodded. So far as we could see, truffle money was the only thing Nils had to live on.

"But he doesn't have a bank account. So what he agreed is that Marcus would give us…"

"Who?"

"Marcus Yardley. They're friends, it seems; that's why he trusts him. He would keep the money in his bank, tell us and Nils how much it was, and then it would be given to Nils when he comes out of hospital. He'd tell Marcus to give us a regular amount first, though."

Not ideal, I thought, but at least it solved a problem.

"Had Yardley – Marcus – been to see him yet?" Joe asked.

"Not yet. But don't forget there's just been a weekend, he said, and it's the busiest time for hotels."

And with that we had to be content.

"We'll have to go and see him with Lars when he's allowed out," I said.

Arif laughed. "He'll be allowed out in about two weeks, but on crutches and with a heavy cast, so he won't be able to live here," he said. "He's fighting that, as there's nowhere else for him to be."

"Where's he going, then?"

"No one knows, yet. Nor does he."

"But what I meant was, when he's allowed out of bed so he can see the outside world."

"Oh, they're getting him into a wheelchair tomorrow, with the ankle supported, so it might be then."

There was plainly nothing much we could do – not at that point, anyway. No doubt the hospital would sort something out.

We had a scratch lunch, washed up and wondered what to do next.

"Explore," announced Tom, but in that way of his which

meant that it was a suggestion, not an order; but nevertheless is was a suggestion you wanted to fall in with. We did. We set a course to 'our' bit of wall, where we got in and out of the Estate, for the third time that day. Once there we explored the land alongside the road that would eventually lead us to the hamlet, figuring that they were reluctantly allowing us to be there now.

"Did Nils say anything about the people in the hamlet?" asked Alex suddenly.

"No. Why?"

"If he knows any of them well, perhaps they could help him when he gets out of hospital."

"He didn't say anything about them. I suppose I shan't get another chance to go and see him now. Not when we know these people are really trying to find us."

It had been Tom's idea to explore that way, and I suppose perhaps to end up at the hamlet. Maybe he wanted to encounter some of the residents and see what their attitude was. He didn't say anything to the rest of us at the time, though.

It was an unremarkable walk. Perhaps because to our left the whole time there was no view, just a brick wall. To our right, mainly, there were trees and bushes growing thickly, so there was little to see. At one place, once we had lost a lot of height and – according to Steve – swung round to the right a bit (he actually gave a bearing, but we ignored him), there was a quite deep-looking stream flowing through a similarly deep gorge.

"This must be where the streams flow out of the Estate," he said. "We saw where one of them came in, and then there's our own. They join just up there –" he pointed into the undergrowth – "and go under the road here."

We looked at it, impressed. A lot of water seemed to be flowing through it.

"Is that the bit of the road that floods after really heavy rain?" asked Joe.

"Could be... yes, there's nowhere else it could be. It's the only place where there's a stream near the wall."

Another pause whilst we digested that.

"Er... " I started cautiously, "er... how do we actually cross it?"

Steve seemed a little hesitant.

"Er..."

"Well, I said that," I muttered indignantly.

"I don't know," he had to admit. "We can't scramble down that, and the water's too fast to try and swim."

"I suppose The Scout is going to build a bridge," said Alex sarcastically. Steve ignored him and chose to look at the map instead.

We let him stew for a bit. And just as Alex was about to say something else he said: "Ahhh…"

"We have an 'er', and now an 'ahh', I said as I moved slowly away. "Any advance on 'ahh'?"

"Got it!" he exclaimed, once again indicating to me the presence of all his fingers. "We follow it along this side and cross somewhere."

"It gets shallower and slower, does it?"

"Haven't a clue," he said cheerfully. "It's a map, not a coastal chart."

I looked puzzled.

"They mark depth soundings, dummy," he said, getting his own back. I indicated that I, too, was equipped still with all eight fingers. We set off along the stream, pushing our way through the bushes, going around what we couldn't push through, and generally getting cut to ribbons. I remembered our truffle hunting efforts, our struggle to find Tom, and his to escape from us thinking we were the gang chasing him when he'd returned from the hospital.

The mini-valley containing the stream soon became a gorge, and the water seemed even faster and deeper. There were mutterings of "this is ridiculous!" and "how much further?" interspersed with frequent "Ow!" sounding expressions whose real words I won't repeat here. But not once did "bother" come into them.

We were all a bloody mess when we first saw the roofs. Now, that's not remotely rude: we were each extremely untidy from head to foot and bleeding gently from every exposed piece of skin. The only one who seemed still to be his normal self was Lars, and he was just panting to the extent that if his tongue was any further out of his mouth he'd have tripped on it.

I didn't know whether to feel relieved or anxious. It was good to know roughly where we were, but I had no idea what reception we would receive from the inhabitants.

15   Raided

We found, after a bit more struggling, that we were the opposite side of the hamlet from the stream, which was still really too uninviting to cross without some risk. We were looking over the fast moving water into back gardens, mainly. Of people there was no sign. I was rather glad. Instinctively this made us not want to attract attention by making a noise, so we moved as quietly as the undergrowth would let us. In practice it meant muttering curses at further skin punctures under our breath.

With relief we found that we were passing by the houses and heading off again.

"We've gone right round in a sort of U-bend," Steve announced. He was the one with the map, as usual.

"We must all be round the bend to be doing this," muttered Alex. I rather agreed with him. But we had to keep going. Camp must be somewhere on this river, though it was considerably bigger than the stream from our lake, even given the gorge we had discovered lower down.

Steve fell over.

Now, although not a new occurrence, this meant that he was concentrating on the map more than where his feet were. That meant we were in danger of getting more lost than we currently were. We stopped. It seemed kind. And we needed his skill.

Having retrieved map and compass, and rubbed bits of himself that were more damaged than before, he spoke.

"Got it. In a moment a stream heads off to the left and goes up to the top of the Estate on the other side. Some way after that the stream we found ages ago and followed for a bit branches off, this time to the right, and goes through the wall – you remember? That leaves ours, and we know we can cross that."

"Yes," said Tom, "by climbing up beside it, over the boggy bit, and down the other side."

We digested that.

"You mean we've got to follow it all the way, past the camp, then down again?" I was not happy with the prospect of all that walking.

"That's about it," he said. "Sorry."

"Anyone got anything to eat?" Tom was feeling the

pressure.

We looked around. At school one of us usually had something in a pocket somewhere, maybe a bit fluffy, but still edible in case of need or boredom. This time none of us had anything.

We'd have mutinied if had been any point. We knew we had a long, exhausting and still prickly walk ahead of us. Resigned to it, we set off.

"Anyone seen Lars?" Arif said after about ten minutes of struggling. We had diverted away from the river by some distance so as to avoid a particularly nasty large clump of high thorn trees (Blackthorns, I discovered later. They live up to the name.)

We looked around. No sign of the dog.

"Damn," said Alex. "Well, he'll find us."

"I'm not leaving him here," said Arif firmly, and called as he'd heard Nils do: "*Hondje! Hondje!*" Close to it sounded – well, just foreign, but I could understand why at a distance it came over as "O – e".

A bark, then some rustling a little way ahead, and the dog stood looking at us, grinning as usual.

"Good boy," said Arif in the tone he used with the dog when he'd done something clever. We walked up to Lars, and found he was wet. Where he'd emerged the end of the blackthorn wood coincided with an easier path which led back down to the river. Better, its water here seemed wider, and we could see the stones of its bed.

"Does that mean he's crossed?" asked Joe.

"Maybe," Tom replied. "Can we get across, do you think?"

"Hang on!" Steve was looking at the map again, this time without moving so that he stood a reasonable chance of remaining perpendicular. He looked from the map to the stream and back again.

"Can you see? Just over there a stream leaves the main river. That's the one we haven't explored yet. We need to get between the main river and it, follow the main river for a bit, then strike off to the right and we'll get to Nils' cottage."

Tom looked at the map. Steve's grubby finger traced the route and Tom looked up and nodded.

"He's right. We just need to go paddling a bit. Lars has been over, haven't you? So it can't be too deep."

"Perhaps..." Arif started. We waited. "Perhaps it'd be better if Lars went first and showed us his way. After all, he's shorter than us."

Why did he have to be so sensible?

We stood at the water's edge and Arif looked at the dog. "Go on, Lars. Home!"

We all watched carefully as the dog waded through one part of the water, swam the next, and then leapt from boulder to boulder on the last part. And yes, he was making for the other side of the main stream, ignoring the smaller stream leading off to the right.

Carefully we followed him, having taken off our shoes and socks. I was glad to get the cool water on at least the lower part of my legs where the stings and scratches seemed worst. As I went on it seemed that the upper part of my legs were in danger of being cooled off too, whether they liked it or not.

"Lars swam here," Tom noted. It was something I was a little worried about too. Cautiously we felt our way into the deeper part and gasped as the water came over the hem of our shorts, freezing our thighs. But it was nothing to the intakes of breath and yelps as the rest of our shorts were submerged too, bring cold water into contact with items guaranteed to feel the cold the most.

But we were soon climbing back into shallower water, then up the bank itself, shivering and muttering about life, the universe and everything. Particularly we were discussing the male body and the effect cold water has on it. We ignored our socks but pulled on shoes so as to protect our feet from the stony ground.

Soggily we tramped after Lars, who at least had the good grace to wait for us to emerge from the water. I was sure his grin now wasn't just good nature: he was actually laughing at our discomfort. We found that we were on a path we recognised, that between Nils' cottage and the hamlet. We dripped our way up and let ourselves in. Without any hesitation Tom and Arif went searching for towels. They returned from the first floor with a few.

"That's all he's got," said Tom. "I think there are six but some of them are a bit small – and a bit old."

He wasn't wrong. There were actually eight, but two were small hand towels which were of little help. The problem was that we had to remove clothing down to the skin for it to be any use, so those who found themselves with two small towels had... er ... too small towels. However, no comments were made.

Our wet stuff was wrung out at the sink but of course there was no way of drying them any more. So when Lars began to look at his water bowl and then at us Arif groaned. Tom had no sympathy.

"You're the dog whisperer," he said. "Down to you, I'm afraid."

So Arif pulled on his shorts and then paused. "Anyone care to give me a hand?"

"When are we shifting back to the camp?" I asked.

"When we've had something to eat, I hope," Joe growled.

I sighed. "Okay, Arif. I'll come and wind." I pulled on my own shorts which still felt cold and clammy, though not as horrible as they had when soaking and with underwear underneath.

"Bring the bucket?"

I did. He opened the door wide and there was an immediate chorus of phrases such as "Do you *mind*?" from the remaining four in their various stages of nudity.

We filled the bucket and returned; fortunately no embarrassing areas of body remained on display.

Rather than spend time lighting the range again we opened some corned beef and found a tin of savoury biscuits. Most of us queried the corned beef, but Arif with his grocery shop experience told us it was all right and people did eat it. There was also some Spam, which he knew about but had never tried. We avoided it.

It wasn't much, but we liked the corned beef and it made a good snack until we could get back to camp and cook something bigger.

Lars enjoyed it too.

The route to the camp was becoming almost familiar, especially to Joe whose speedy efforts at running back to get to the phone and calling the ambulance had saved Nils so much time in pain. When we were safely there we flopped down and ignored Steve's half-hearted attempts at bullying us to get wood so he could start a fire. Rather less privately than before when it had been just changing after a swimming session, we changed, dried properly and exulted in the feel of underwear and dryness again.

Then I think they all did the same as me. I just lay on my sleeping bag and half dozed, half listened for someone else to move. When eventually my stomach told me that it was time for a meal I looked at my watch and saw I'd been there for an hour. The light seemed to be rather dimmer than I remembered, too. I managed to kick Alex on the way out of the tent – by accident, obviously – and got some muttered words, and saw that it was nearly sunset. So I fetched some wood and, having seen Steve's efforts at fire lighting a few times, started one myself.

It only took about ten matches.

I went to the other tent and called "Fire's alight. Anyone else hungry?", and waited. Steve's tousled light haired head looked out, said "About time. I asked some time ago." Then he woke properly and exclaimed a bit about the time and the fact that he hadn't started a meal yet.

The resulting noises of activity persuaded the rest of them to stir, help, eat and clear, and then we were as usual sitting around the fire, idly chatting, looking into the flames and, eventually, yawning. Another of those times when you know it will stay with you as a time of quiet happiness and comfort. Eventually we crawled off to bed.

I knew it was early morning. It was one of those nights when a late night pub leaver starts a motorbike some streets away, and all you know is that it's woken you and you wish they'd just ride off on the thing. But this time the sound was wrong, there were gaps in it, and that shouldn't be possible with a running engine.

My puzzlement grew and at last I woke. In what little light there was from a fitful moon I could see Lars on his feet, growling, looking at the tent entrance. There were distant sounds of someone crashing through bushes, a sound we'd all experienced on a personal level and at much closer quarters. The cause of the noise was making no attempt to move quietly, so after one particularly loud and prolonged such sound effect I shook Arif and Alex into wakefulness – or something approaching it.

That's easy to write, but they took a lot of stirring, far more stirring than I had. At last I had their attention, sort of, and as quietly as I could told them what I'd heard. Lars was still standing, looking at the tent entrance, quivering, but of noise outside there was now no trace.

"Stay there," said Arif quietly, "and I'll go and wake the others."

"I'm coming out with you," said Alex quietly, "so there's two of us out there if it's... anything untoward." He hadn't mentioned the gang, and I didn't believe it could be them, but then who else could it be?

"So am I," I said. "We're in this together, you know."

The others were only a little easier to wake than my two had been. To underline the need for their attention the bush noises had started again, then stopped, then restarted... At last all six of us were up and ready, but for what we didn't know.

"Where's it coming from?" Alex whispered.

"Shh... don't know. Listen out for it..."

When you're woken from deep sleep by something unknown that you realise could probably affect you, and only you can deal with it, your heart thumps in your chest. Mine was so loud I was sure the others could hear it.

To make matters worse there was then silence for a long time. Nerves grew tighter and tighter. The slightest, normal, night noise made us jump.

And then, away to our left, somewhere near the waterfall, there was a groan and the bushes thrashed about again. We looked at each other, then five of us switched on our torches and led by Lars, rushed off in that direction. The sixth, Steve, grabbed the phone and some rope, then followed after us.

It took some finding. At first, all we could see was a tangled mass of bushes, the same as we had been struggling through the day before. But a groan and a weak cry gave us a direction and we got a little closer. Torches eventually discovered some clothing held securely by the dense blackthorn growth. In it, someone was a prisoner. The dog had reached it first, and stood near it – nearer than we could get – growling menacingly.

All movement stopped.

"Who's that?" Tom's voice was as confident as he could make it.

"Get me out of here!"

"We need to know who it is first."

"Can't you see I'm injured? Get me out, you..." The rest of it consisted of words we knew and used, but they have no place at home, in a classroom with a teacher in it, or usually even amongst ourselves.

"No. You can stay there." I wouldn't have dared say it, but Tom was on form. And, as we learnt later, angry.

"What?!!"

"You're rude, have interrupted... the dog's sleep and you're trespassing."

Silence.

"Please would you get me out of here?"

That was better. "Who are you?" asked Tom.

"It doesn't matter who I am. I've fallen into this... this..."

"Blackthorn."

"What?"

"Blackthorn, It's called Blackthorn. It grows sloes."

"What?!"

"Sloes grow on it. They're dangerous."

Silence.

"Please can you get me out of here? Someone else is nearby and I think he's dead or something. He hasn't moved."

All torches were on the bushes, but still we found ourselves looking at each other.

"Who are you?" asked Tom again. "No name, no help."

Silence. Then, weakly: "Tom Cruise."

"In that case you're a film hero and get yourself and your friend out. You're still trespassing, though."

"Please help me." It was weaker now.

"Give me your name."

He called out a name. Immediately Tom looked at Joe and whispered something. Joe nodded, slipped off a few yards, and I could eventually hear muttering. He returned in about five minutes, phone still in hand, and nodded. I heard the whispered answer.

"Yes, that's one of them."

"Are you coming to help?"

"We've been looking at how to. Who's the other one?"

"Why do you want to know?"

"Do you want help?"

Another name was given. Joe repeated it to the phone in a whisper, then looked up and nodded.

128

"How many more are there with you? We need to know for the rescue."

Weakly: "It's just us two."

"Okay. We'll get help."

"What do you mean? You can do it."

"We live in the village," Tom lied. "We need to get stuff to be able to reach you."

"But you can see us."

"And to get to you we'll need cutters and ropes, or we'll end up like you."

There was some more thrashing around, and movement which we could see clearly in the light of our torches. "He'll get out soon. He's nearer the outside than he thinks," Steve whispered. "I've got some rope. We could tie his arm to the next trunk along, and a leg to that one. That should do it."

"You sure?" Tom hissed back.

"Watch me! But stay around in case he gets free, eh?"

"Of course. I'll be behind you."

"Okay," Steve called, "I'm coming."

The different voice roused the man. "How many of you are there? You sound young."

"Just us two. It's our dog who heard you."

Cautiously, because of the bushes, not the man, he prodded his way towards him. Lars was still on station, but quiet now. It would give the man a shock to be reminded there was still a dog there, I thought.

"Going to tie a rope to a couple of big branches," called Tom, his torch still on the man's face most of the time. All ours were, thanks to a whispered instruction from Tom. "That way we can make sure they stay where they are."

And you with it, I thought with a glow of hope.

There was a grunt above him.

Carefully he secured a rope round a trunk, low down, then the other around the one nearest the man's right arm. He was in the process of gathering his nerve to bind the arm when his torch fell from his mouth. Instinctively two torches were shone downwards and lit his face.

"You're one of them!" yelled the man, and tried to thrash his way out of the bush again. Steve recoiled, but then just went for the arm and all the smaller branches that still held it captive, put a loop around the lot and pulled. There was a shout, and some more interesting language. Hurriedly he got another loop around, and a third, then secured it round the trunk again.

Ignoring the stream of abuse from above he ducked down to the first rope and with some difficulty managed the same basic idea there too. Then his torch – which he'd recovered – flashed around, and he ducked out of the cavernous root system and faced us, dishevelled and bloody, but grinning.

"Trussed chicken for lunch tomorrow?"

Really, the language that was coming from the bush was most interesting.

"I could see the other one," he told us, now in a normal volume, "but I can't see how we can get to him. He's right in the middle of the plantation – looks like they've fallen there."

We looked up. And for the first time since arriving on the scene we saw the cliff, the continuation of 'our' waterfall cliff. It looked a really impressive height by torchlight. We'd seen it often enough in daylight, so knew it wasn't a good height to fall from.

In a gap in the stream of curses, Tom shouted to the man: "Did you fall off the cliff?"

Silence.

"Oh well, we'll take that as a 'yes' then. Never mind, the Police will get you out, somehow."

All this time, Joe had been busy on the phone. "Which way should they come in?" he asked Tom urgently.

Tom thought. "We're about half way between the road and the hamlet. Difficult call. I suppose we know the way from the hamlet better. Need someone to direct them in. Joe? Steve? Can you both? Maybe take Lars, if he'll go. Just in case."

"I'd better go, then," said Arif. "I know the way too."

Tom dropped his voice. "The oldest should stay here, really. Just in case."

"I'll go with Arif and Lars," I said fed up with the torrent of abuse that was still coming weakly from the bushes. "I can remember most of it."

"Pick up the other phone from the tents down there," ordered Tom, "and tell us what's happening down there when you can."

16   Police

The estate at night was a very different place from its friendly, daytime self. Direction finding was difficult. Had it not been for teamwork between Arif and me, our memories, the fitful moon, and aided as always by Lars who seemed to realise which of his two homes we needed to reach, I'm not sure if we would have made the trip so quickly. As it was, two Police cars, Tim Hammond's official van and this time a fire engine had caused pandemonium with the residents of the hamlet by the time we arrived, and almost immediately various of them were complaining about us and how we'd brought chaos to their quiet lives. The senior Sergeant listened for a very short time, then drew out a whistle and blew at it. I didn't know that the Police still carried whistles.

There was an instant silence, apart from Lars who barked.

"I'm sorry you've been interrupted, but you should know that these boys are known about and are helping us. At the moment you are interfering with the Police in the course of their duties, and I'm sure you've heard that expression before in Court. Please return to your homes and keep out of our way."

He turned to us. "They've got themselves caught in blackthorn bushes, the others have told us..."

"And they've called the Police just for that?" asked a querulous voice from the crowd.

"Your name, please?"

"Well, it's a waste of Police time. And why you give such credibility to these hooligans is beyond me."

"Name please?" asked the Sergeant again. "Jim, go and talk to that gentleman and read him his rights, please. I'll talk to him in the morning."

The crowd started melting away.

We started leading, tiredly, back to the camp. It was good to have Joe's dad with us and to assure him that everything was all right. Relatively speaking.

"Arif," I said suddenly, "we need to phone them, tell them we're on our way."

He whipped the phone from his pocket and found the number, concentrating on the phone so much that he did a Steve.

"Falling Man," I joked as Lars nudged him and he struggled back to his feet. It may have been silly o'clock but I still got The Look.

"Pardon?"asked Mr Hammond.

"In-joke," I muttered.

That walk, in the dark, leading the Police, was surreal. I felt like pinching myself to make sure I was awake and actually taking four Policemen for a walk... as I said, surreal. We were finding our way with difficulty in the dark and it was only a combination of Lars, a few recognised features, and luck that got us back.

I know I keep mentioning the dog, but he just seemed to know that if we weren't going to one 'home' we would be going to the other: Nils' house or the camp site. Amazing dog.

We passed through our camp and, suddenly unsure of where they all were, I gave a shout. An answer came – to my relief - and before long we were standing where the others had decided to lie on the ground and rest. Mr Hammond crossed to Joe and hugged him.

"So... said the Sergeant, "where are these people, then?"

As one we shone our lights on to the nearest of them, and we could just see a drained face, its eyes closed.

"How the hell did they get there?" exclaimed one of the Police. We made no answer but swung our lights up to the cliff. There were exclamations from behind us.

"And there's another one? Where?"

"He's through there," Tom answered, weariness in his voice. "I think he's been unconscious since we discovered them. We can't get to him. He's not said anything."

"This needs more than just us," said the Sergeant. "I'm not sure if a helicopter isn't the best way of getting them out – if we could get them released from the thorns."

"I think the one nearest could be helped out from here," said Tom quietly. "We had to tie him to the bush to stop him moving."

The man looked at him in surprise, then back to the bushes, then back to Tom.

"This is Boys' Own adventure stuff, isn't it?"

Tom looked puzzled and the man had to admit to knowing about the old magazine. Tom didn't. Neither did the rest of us.

"Get on to the Ambulance and Fire, please Smith. Give

them a full description of what we've got and stress to Trumpton that they'll need chainsaws and skins like rhinos. Then you'll have to go down and direct them."

So tired were we that reference to Trumpton took several seconds to sink in. Even then we could only manage a smile.

"I don't know if I can find the way, Sarge. It's like a maze."

He looked at his officer with an annoyed expression. "For goodness sake, Smith!"

"He'd get lost," said Arif quietly. "We only found our way here because of the dog. I'll have to go down with you."

"No, no... there's too much equipment needed to walk it in. It'll have to be done from the air. Is there a space where we can land a helicopter?"

"We've been exploring most days," said Tom, "and there just isn't. The only flat area with no trees is our camp and that's just not big enough."

"Damn. It'll have to come by road. But then… look…. there must be a place by the main road they can offload, then the aircraft can ferry men and machinery here."

A weak curse came from the bushes.

"He's awake again," said Joe,

The Sergeant detailed off three officers to try and free the first man. "Handcuffs at the ready, please, although I shouldn't think he'll be in any condition for running. And when he comes out, you boys make yourselves scarce. I don't want him recognising you."

"Too late for that," said Steve. "He's seen my face."

He muttered something under his breath. "Whatever. I still want you out of the way – and no, I don't mean far, I mean I don't want him seeing you and getting angry."

We were getting so tired now that the danger was all but past, that my brain was in danger of shutting down. Dimly I could see that Joe and Alex were swaying, and I could tell how tired Steve was as he was sitting against a bush, fortunately with a thick jacket on, adding nothing to the conversation at all. Tom's voice had given away how tired he was, and I guessed Arif was relieved not to have to make another journey to the hamlet to direct the rest of the emergency services to us.

I made a decision. "Sorry," I said slowly but firmly, "I'm going to bed."

"Me too," came simultaneously from four of the others.

"Someone wake up Joe?" I suggested. "Tell him we're going."

"Wouldn't you prefer to come home?" Mr Hammond asked his son.

"Just wanna sleep," was the slurred response.

"We'll all come," said Tom. "Come on, Arif."

Given the chance I think Arif would have stayed. It was probably just loyalty to us that made him walk with us.

We were just about to leave when the Sergeant stopped Tom and handed him a card.

"Sorry – but have this and give me a call late tomorrow afternoon, would you? We want to get as much information from you then and make sure you're all right. Okay?"

Tom just nodded, joined us, and we went to our tents where we must have been asleep just about instantly. My dreams were troubled dimly by a prolonged aircraft noise which I couldn't understand, but apart from that the only thing that woke me was Lars whining. The tent was like an oven and he was panting as hard as I was sweating. But I really didn't want to get up. The next whimper from Lars woke Arif, though. He looked blearily at the dog and then at me.

"You could have let him out... god it's hot in here."

"Only just woken up. Yes, it is."

"Wassertime?"asked Alex. We ignored him.

None of us moved. Then Lars barked and looked reproachfully at Arif. He groaned and manoeuvred to the tent's zipped entrance. The dog bounded out, air rushed in and immediately we felt cooler. Arif laid back.

"Don't want to get up," he said.

"Nor me."

The next thing I knew was Lars' tail tickling my ear as he was licking Arif's, who was awake almost instantly. There was a face at the tent door. Tom. Grinning.

"Come on you two. It's nearly afternoon. The Police and everyone have gone and I'm hungry."

"Tell Steve," said Arif lazily. "He's The Scout."

Next thing he knew Tom had pulled his sleeping bag out of the tent, Arif still in it. Lars barked and jumped around like a puppy, and Arif's chosen words, interspersed with some we didn't know but which sounded like Hindi (his parents' original language, as we knew from school), would probably have landed him in deep trouble elsewhere.

It seems all six of us were getting up. Bleary eyed we might have been, but perpendicular we were, though it did take Arif some time to struggle free of his sleeping bag, return to the tent and dress.

While we were getting our brains in gear we went to look at the scene of the previous night's "excitement". A lot of damage had been done to the large area of intensely tangled blackthorn. It gave the impression of having had some vandals venting their emotions on it – or whatever's in the mind of people who do that sort of thing. Complete cut bushes lay round the outside of two areas where the dense thicket had been hacked down. Sawn branches and pieces hardly bigger than twigs littered the floor waiting to penetrate the feet of anyone silly enough to walk through with no shoes. The more remote semi-cleared area even had blue and white crime scene tape around it, looking completely out of place in the middle of a forest. We wondered who was going to return to it, and how, without our help.

We also wondered how we managed to sleep through the noise of a helicopter and chainsaws and normal saws, all of which must have continued for some hours.

"How on earth did they find their way back?" Alex wondered. "I suppose they're not still wandering around the estate!"

"All last night. Maybe even this morning" I joked.

At one o'clock we had breakfast.

At two o'clock we were interrupted by the phone five times in succession. There were variations, but the main theme of them went like this:

"Hallo Joe. Can I speak to X please?" (Where X = the name of one of us.)

"Are you all right?" "Yes thanks, fine. Just got up."

"Joe's Dad told us what happened last night. Are you sure you're all right?" "Yes, we're fine. We've just got up and had breakfast."

"Do you want to come home?" "No, we're fine."

"Do you need anything?" "Dunno yet. Maybe more food."

"How about some clean clothes?" "Well, okay then."

"Can I come and see you some time?" "Dunno. We need to talk to the Police later to see what's happened." (This was usually after a quick consultation amongst the six of us.)

"How can you not want to come home when something awful like this has happened?" "Well, we're okay here, it's good, and we're enjoying it."

The sixth call was from Mr Hammond to Joe. Many of the questions were the same, but apparently he said he was proud of what we'd done and how we'd done it. Oh, and inevitably: "let us know when you've had enough and want to come home."

"We need to phone that Sergeant," said Tom when the flurry of calls had died down. "Are we all right for battery?"

Joe looked at it. "Seems okay. It's so basic it doesn't use much, like I said."

"Well, let's phone him, then."

"Do you want to?" Joe wasn't keen.

"Okay then, pass it over, and let's have his number as well."

Once again, hearing just the one side of a call is frustrating. Many of the questions asked of us were similar to our parents' questions, but one floored Tom. Had we seen the other man?

"Well no, not really. We could see where he was but we couldn't get to him 'cos he was right in the middle of the bushes. Why?"

The answer came. Tom's answer was just "Oh. Oh bloody hell. Sorry to hear that."

Another pause whilst he listened.

"Oh. Oh, I see. Hmm."

It went on a bit, then Tom just said "Okay then. So that's all of them accounted for. We can be seen in public again."

Another pause at our end. Then: "The cow! How could she have done that? To us?"

A short answer, then "You're welcome. Bye then."

He rang off and looked at us. We looked back expectantly.

"They've got everybody, he said. Getting the names was important, so well done, Joe on that..."

"You got them. All I did was repeat them. Quietly." He grinned at the memory.

"Well, the one we were talking to was so fed up that he told the Police rather a lot, including that the other man was the one who started it all off. He'd already done the same sort of thing in parts of London – you know, housing estates and things – and the Police were getting close to getting the evidence they needed. So he headed north to try his luck with the girls here.

And with the boys, say the London Police."

"Boys!" I said incredulously. "Bloody hell."

"So have they arrested him, then?" Alex asked.

Tom hesitated. "Well.... er ... no. It seemed that he broke his neck when he fell."

"So... so all that time, he was dead?" I asked.

"Yes."

"Oh. Oh bloody hell."

"That's what I said."

"So that's why the area is taped off," said Steve. "Perhaps someone *will* want to come back.

"So what happens now?" Alex asked.

"Okay. So if we want we could go home – it's safe now. Or we can stay here. Or spend some time at home and come back. And by the way, the reason they knew where we were was because bloody Emily Long told them. Though how she knew they didn't say."

"What a cow!" said Alex.

"That's what I said."

"What are we going to do about Nils?" Steve asked.

"What can we do?"

"Help him," said Arif unexpectedly. "He's not going to be able to get around for a bit, so he'll need food, water hauled up, truffles collected, and the dog exercised."

"The dog's down to you," said Tom.

"After all he's done for all of us?" I accused him. "We'd still be lost between the hamlet and here from last night if it hadn't been for him. And what about getting back from Steve's grand tour yesterday? That was down to Lars."

The dog looked at me expectantly. The others muttered a bit. Arif looked embarrassed.

"Okay," said Tom, unperturbed, "We'll all help. But how are we going to make it work? We can all walk Lars but we're not nurses."

"We don't need to be," said Arif quietly. "He's coming out of hospital because he can walk, I suppose on crutches, but he'll be able to do things. I don't know how he gets food in, but we can help there. We need to get fuel for his range, carry on truffle hunting, draw water and make sure he can feed himself. We don't need to stay in the house or anything."

We digested that.

"But doesn't that mean we can't do other things?" asked Alex.

"He won't want all of us round all the time, or every day. He might not need us at all if he has friends in the hamlet. Though their attitude to us didn't seem to show they were interested in helping him."

"So what does that mean?"

"I don't know yet," said Tom. "I think we need to see him in hospital and tell him that one of us will come down and help do things whilst he can't. If he says that the villagers will help, we can do what we want and can decide to stay here, camp near his cottage, go home and come in when we're needed, or... I don't know what else."

Another long pause whilst we all thought.

"Should I go and see him again?" asked Arif. "I could tell him everything that's happened, why we're here and so on. Then I could tell him what we've decided and see what he says."

"May I come as well?" Tom asked. Now this was a surprise, as Tom was the one usually who was decisive on behalf of all of us. But this involvement with the gang, and with another adult who might or might not want our help, as well as all the other issues we'd encountered, was outside his – our – experience. We were feeling our way through it.

"You went with him in the ambulance," said Arif, "It's only right. We should all go, really, but the hospital wouldn't appreciate that. Nor would Nils, probably."

"I'll tell you one thing that someone could do," said Tom. "Bring Lars, and have him outside the right window so Nils can see him."

Nobody else said anything, so as I was the one who had had more to do with the dog apart from Arif, I volunteered.

"When?" asked Joe.

"Don't know about anyone else, but I'm still knackered after last night," said Steve. "And it's a bit late to start thinking about heading into town now."

"Have a doss-about day, then?"Tom suggested.

"Sounds good to me," I said.

It turned out to be the laziest day – half-day – we'd had there so far. We started off with several games of cards. Had we been playing for money I'd have won quite a lot – a change for me. Then we had a swim, flopped around to dry off in the sun, and collected wood for the fire. That made us hot and sticky so we pulled our wet underwear back on again ("Must get Mum to chuck in my swimming things next time," said Alex.) and had another swim. Fire lit, Steve and I cooked (I just did what I was told.), we ate, played cards, sat round the fire, then crawled back to bed.

In the night there was some shouting.

Looking back, I think many of us were more affected by the previous night's events than we admitted to ourselves. I woke to find Arif calling something, and Lars was nuzzling up to him. That woke him; he looked scared at me, then the dog, then his face cleared a little.

"Sorry. Bad dream," he mumbled, put his head back on his pillow and seemed to be immediately asleep again.

For me it wasn't shouting, it was a lot of twitching about and fighting what, in my dream, were blackthorn bushes. I kept on trying to say "but it wasn't my fault! I shouldn't be here!", but no sound would come out. For some reason my left ear was warm and wet, and I woke, feeling as scared and disorientated as Arif had been, to find it was my turn to be comforted by the dog.

Alex just slept on... and on... and on...

There was some noise from next door, too, which woke me at one point. I didn't know who it was, but heard Joe talking in a low voice as if he was comforting his little sister. Surely it can't have been the ever-strong Tom? Then I remembered that time when he was lost in the bushes... Perhaps he's just as human as me, I thought.

The next thing I knew it was light.

17   Hospital 3

Nearly simultaneously we crawled out of bed, stretched, found bushes and returned to get dressed, getting into each others' way as we did so.

"How are we getting to the hospital?" Joe asked over the eventual breakfast.

"We could go by bus," Tom said through a mouthful of bacon and egg.

"I'm not making a fuss," Joe retorted. Tom just looked at him. "Does that mean going back to our exit point or can we go through the village, do you think?"

"Easier through the village," I said hurriedly. Going the other way would mean skirting round the bushes where the men got trapped – and where one had been killed. Though we'd gone to explore it the previous day I wanted to avoid the area and I think the others thought the same.

"It probably is," Tom agreed, his mouth now empty. "And we can check everything's okay with the cottage too. And how about some more truffles, Arif?"

"See what time we get back," said Arif. "And what time Marcus Yardley can get here."

"Would he come the same day?" Joe asked.

"Don't know. But at least we can tell him when we've got some."

The excitement of being able to leave the estate and join in with the public anonymously still didn't stop Steve bullying us into washing up, clearing up and getting still more wood to be kept dry in the store tent.

"Look at the sky! It's not going to rain for a month!" I complained.

"Ever heard of dew?"

I shut up.

It must have been close on ten o'clock when Arif, Tom, Lars and I made our way down again to the hamlet. There was no one there, or perhaps they were so used to us they didn't bother coming to tell us off. Without challenge, we found our way to the bus stop.

Sitting together, chatting quietly because we still felt that our experiences should be kept to ourselves, we became aware of some odd looks, though no one said anything to us. I looked at my reflection in the window when I could, just to make sure I'd not grown another head, or forgotten to get dressed, or something. But there was nothing obvious. Surreptitiously I checked my zip. Nope: no problem there. I shrugged.

Finally we arrived at the hospital. One or two more looks from people as we went in. It's a big hospital, big enough to have a small shop. It sold paperbacks, snacks, newspapers, sweets and so on. Idly I glanced over at it and was shocked into a sudden halt.

The other two looked back at me.

"L...l...look!" I stuttered, pointing at a stand that was dedicated to the local newspaper. On it, the new edition bore in pride of place on its cover a photograph of the six of us. We looked very scruffy, and were obviously in a woodland setting. Over it was the headline: "LOCAL CHILDREN FOIL PEDOPHILE GANG".

"Oh no..." Tom groaned.

"What the... where the hell did they get that from?" Arif asked.

I was horrified. Not only was being identified exactly what we'd been trying to avoid, the last thing I wanted was any sort of fuss made of the whole sorry saga.

"Walk on!" commanded Tom suddenly. "If we want one we'll buy one later. But the more I think about what we said yesterday the more sure I am that Arif is right. We need to help Nils and we need to sort it out with him before he sees all that crap."

We had completely forgotten that Lars was with us and that I was meant to be waiting outside a window with him so Nils could get up and see him. It wasn't until a large figure with 'Security' written on his cap hurried over to us that we realised.

"You may be bleedin' famous, but that dog ain't allowed in 'ere," was the cheerful greeting. We understood this sort of approach, grinned, apologised, and turned back to the exit.

"And good on you for what you did to those bleeders!" came after us. As one of 'those bleeders' had suffered rather more than a loss of blood, it wasn't something we particularly wanted to be recognised for.

Outside again, Arif looked around, trying to find where the windows of Nils' ward might be.

"I don't really remember," said Tom. "That was before the operation. He'll have gone somewhere else after it."

"Try and remember the view from the window," I told Arif. "See if you can find what you were looking at."

It seemed we walked almost all round the main building before he said: "There! That band of trees. That's what I saw."

"Okay. You stay here, Matt, and we'll try and wave from the window when we can."

It's boring, just hanging around with a dog. Even Lars. Eventually he just lay down on the grass and went to sleep, and I almost wished I could do the same, but I had to watch for movement at a window.

It seemed like ages, but eventually one on about the third floor was flung open even wider than any others seemed to be, and Arif's face looked out, an arm waving by the side of it.

An older face appeared lower down, and another arm waved.

"Lars," I said, and the dog looked round. I pointed up at the window and the dog dutifully looked where I was pointing. He didn't seem particularly interested, and I wondered if he realised it was his master up there.

The window partly closed. I sat on the grass next to the dog and tried to remember all the things we'd done over the previous – what? Week? Ten days? It seemed like ages ago that we first became... I tried to think of a word. Outlaws? Sounded good, even if we were on the right side of the law. But we couldn't call ourselves In-laws, that was certain.

'Suspects' would have to do.

My daydreaming was interrupted by a voice. It called "Hondje!"

Like a spring, the dog was on his feet and running before I had a chance to grab the piece of string that was all we had found to use as a lead. It was probably as well, because either I'd have been dragged along the ground by my arm, or have become another dislocation patient. Or both. Rising from the grass I looked in the direction of the voice.

A wheelchair was at the edge of the car park nearest me. The occupant seemed to have a leg supported by a plank, a leg that was thicker than normal and wore a very odd looking sock on its end. With the wheelchair were two figures I recognised and a dog that was bouncing around like a large hairy football on steroids.

I crossed over to the group and found a hand was being offered to me to shake, and a face with an open grin on it. I shook the hand and returned the grin. Lars nuzzled at me, then went back to his master whose hand immediately resumed massaging the dog behind the ears.

We learnt that our supposed fame had preceded us.

"Once we had asked at the entrance to the ward whether we could talk to Nils," said Tom, "we were treated like royalty. We got cups of tea, biscuits, and of course a private audience with their patient. Then we remembered Lars and you, came to the window and caused a bit of a stir in the ward by opening it too wide. That's when they decided Nils could use the wheelchair he's just been lent, go down in the lift and see Lars properly. And you."

"Thanks!" I said in mock indignation of being thought of second to a dog.

Nils looked at me and smiled again. "He has been my only companion for longer. There is no harm meant."

"I know," I said. "I was just joking."

"I have talked to only few people for years and this week people in the hospital are talking all the time. And they are so serious. They complain. And I tell them that they are being made better, they have food coming and drink, and they pay nothing. Pah! It is good to see again people who know what is right in life and show a life of their own."

There seemed nothing we could say to that, so we said nothing, though I was trying to find something that I *could* say.

Tom found his tongue first. "You see now why we had to come back to our camp in the estate. The gang would have done something to us if they'd found us – we went to the Police after they'd approached us to get some girls for them."

"They are *stront*[1]," he said, then looked up and said "Sorry. But they are. And I am not sorry one of them broke his neck trying to get to you to attack you."

"I think I am," I said timidly, after a pause. "I don't want to be the cause of a death."

"You are NOT!" said Nils vehemently. "That *stront* caused his own death by wishing harm to you. You are without blame

---

[1] *Er...well... Human excrement.*

and must never think any different. He would be still alive now if he had accepted it was over. He might also still be free. He is a *stront* who has damaged so many lives that he needed punishment."

I'd not looked at it like that. I supposed he was right.

"And yes, you had to escape from home to the estate, where it is wild. And it is as well that you did, otherwise I would be dead."

I looked embarrassed and muttered something. The other two smiled politely.

"And thank you for saying nothing about truffles when you spoke to the newspapers. People would have come and invaded and taken them for themselves."

"But…" I started.

"We've spoken to no one," Tom butted in, indignantly. "We don't know where all that stuff in the paper came from. Even that picture of us was taken without us knowing."

"But it is in the estate."

"I know. And it was taken on… when did it all happen?"

"Don't know," I admitted. "Don't even know what day it is today."

"Thursday," said Nils.

"Tuesday night, then. Well, Wednesday morning. And you can see it was in the dark."

"They had those big lights," I reminded Tom.

"You look tired in it," said Nils, "as if you were asleep."

"We were," I told him, "It was about two in the morning and Lars had woken us up."

"Then who took the picture?" asked Nils.

"Police? We don't know. We don't know how the paper got hold of it."

"You need to ask." We nodded.

Tom took the initiative. "We need to decide something. We're going to help you get along until you can do everything yourself again. You know – walk Lars and collect truffles, haul up water, collect wood, maybe even do some cooking…"

He stopped at the look on the man's face: sheer astonishment. So he continued, hurriedly saying: "Unless one of the people in the village would do it for you, of course."

A pause. The face slowly changed to one of scorn. "They hardly talk to me. They want me to go and live somewhere else.

144

I heard how they talked to you when you brought me down to the ambulance."

"They've ignored us too," I said. "We've seen none of them."

"But they haven't told you to go, or called the Police?"

Tom laughed. "If they'd called the Police they'd have been told to mind their own business! Joe's Dad is a Scenes of Crime officer. And the night of the – incident – one of them had his name taken by one of the Police for... what was it? Obstructing a Police Officer?"

He smiled. "That is good. If they try and turn you off tell them to see me. I shall return in a few days."

"So what can we do for you?"

"I cannot believe you want to help me like that."

"Well... "Arif started. "You can't just come out of hospital and carry on as if nothing has happened. You won't be able to stand much, I suppose."

"They say I have to keep my leg supported like this for a long time. I cannot, of course."

"But if they say that..."

"Pah! They don't know me."

"Well, once you know when you're leaving, you need to tell us so we can decide how to do it."

"But you cannot camp on the estate just for me. It wouldn't be right."

We looked at each other.

"We don't know how we're going to do it," admitted Arif. "But Lars needs looking after, and I can't just leave him there. And if I'm coming to look after him I can do things for you."

"We all can," I said. This was all of us – wasn't it?

But a nurse was walking towards us.

"I know you wanted to see your dog," she said, "but you mustn't let these children tire you out, even if they are heroes."

"Don't be silly," Nils said with sudden spirit. "These fine *jongens* have saved my life and are now saying they will help me when I am home again."

"That's nice. I'm sure your wife would appreciate their help."

"My wife... Ah yes, my wife would appreciate that I am having help."

"Well, it's time to come in again now. You haven't been

outside for a few days, and we don't want to get cold, do we?"

He just looked at her, straight in the eyes, and she looked uncomfortable.

"You are new, I believe?"

"I'm new to this ward. I used to look after older people."

"I am not older. I am just not young. And I can look after myself. I will come back in when I am ready."

"But…"

"But no. I will come in when I am ready."

"The ward manager told me to come and get you. A doctor wants to see you."

"He could come out here."

"He is a busy man."

He considered that. Then:

"Very well then. I will return." And to us: "Will you come back? Tomorrow? I need to find out from this doctor when I am going home."

And that was that. With a final scratch at Lars' ears he was wheeled away. The dog's tail drooped as Arif stopped him following. We felt rather let down, too. We still didn't know what we were going to do.

"Shall we go and talk to the Police?" asked Arif.

"I want one of those papers," said Tom. "I want to see just what they've said about us. Just a minute… nobody asked us any questions – apart from the Police – so where did they get it all from?"

"No idea," I said. "None of us spoke to anyone else and anyway, we were all too tired."

We went into the hospital again – Arif stayed outside with Lars this time – and bought a local paper. Tom read bits of the report to us as we walked away towards the rest of the town. Comments about being called "children" and "young boys" and a lot of other phrases caused much disgust and between us we were angry and upset by the time we found we were heading towards the centre of the town and having to pass the Police station.

We looked at each other, nodded, and went inside. Getting to talk to the Sergeant was not simple, particularly as we wanted to say as little as possible to any other of the Police there. But we managed it eventually, and poured out our disgust.

146

At the end, he looked at us and nodded. "I can't control what the Press say, let's get that's clear. They can use whatever words they like so long as they're not badly inaccurate or defamatory. But it *does* worry me that the information and that photograph got to them. I – we – thought you had spoken to them and sold the story."

As one we protested that we would never do so and we didn't want anything reported.

He held up his hand. "And the other three?"

"They're the same," said Tom indignantly. "And anyway we've been with them, we have no phones… well, we have two but Joe has them both usually and we've been together all the time. And anyway, how did they get the photo?"

"If you want me to follow this up, I'll need to talk to each of you, formally, so that I have it on record that the information came from none of you. Then I can ask our officers, the fire and rescue service, the pilot and anyone else I can discover who was there. It'll be a lot of work."

"But we have been hiding, and trying to hide who we are, for over a week," said Tom deliberately, "and then suddenly when all – it is all, isn't it? – the men are in prison our identities and our pictures are there for anyone to see."

A pause.

"I take your point. Can you get the others to come and see me?"

"Is it possible you can come and see them, please?" asked Arif. "You see, we are going to help Nils when he comes out of hospital. We need to be around the camp or at his cottage."

"Who is Nils? Is he the dog?"

"No. Nils Lundgren is Lars' owner. He lives in the cottage by the hamlet. We rescued him a week ago and he's coming out of hospital soon."

The man looked puzzled.

"He broke his ankle when he was looking … when he was looking for his dog," I corrected myself.

"So you arranged for him to be taken to hospital. And they called you "the usual suspects" at your school…"

It was our turn to look surprised.

"Ah yes – it was me who came to see your headmistress then. I've grown a beard since, so you perhaps didn't recognise me. But I was pretty sure I recognised you."

We all smiled, faintly.

"Anything else I don't know about you?"

No one mention truffles, I said to myself. But it seemed that no answer was expected, and soon we found ourselves walking away from the building, wondering what to do next.

"Anyone want a shower?" I asked suddenly. "Parents are out and my place is nearest."

It seemed only right that I should go last. Fortunately the other two didn't take all the hot water. Lars didn't get a look in.

18   The Royal

Clean and refreshed, I left a note for parents explaining about the bathroom floor and the number of towels, and we joined a bus back to the hamlet. It was by then early afternoon, we found we had missed lunch ("Should have grabbed something at your place," said Tom) and were hungry. So we made do with sandwiches and cake once we were back – they joined us, of course – and gave a rather incoherent account of the morning's work. It's difficult for people to understand you when you have a mouth full of food and for some reason Joe objected to being showered with crumbs when we got to the part where we had got angry, and why. They read the piece in the paper about us and the shower of crumbs became so great that Lars started looking hopeful.

Afterwards Arif and I, with Lars, made the journey back to the truffle hunting grounds and collected a really good supply, then phoned Marcus Yardley. Again he promised to visit the following day at eleven o'clock.

"We visited Nils, today," Arif told him. "Have you been to see him?"

"No, I've been too busy. I was going tomorrow but it'll have to be Monday now."

"He might be out by then."

"Out… you mean, home?"

"They think so. He hopes so."

"Can you call me if he is, please?"

"Okay."

"Thanks. And well done on getting those perverts locked up. Single handed, according to the paper."

"Huh! That paper…"

"Not known for its accuracy. But whatever you actually did, congratulations."

"Thanks. See you tomorrow, okay?"

"Will do. Bye."

"I think I'm getting to like him," I said.

We wondered whether we should take anything else from Nil's stores but then remembered he was coming home soon and decided not to. The truffles were left in baskets in the cupboard where we had found the first lot awaiting collection.

We made our way back to the camp where Steve was in bullying mode about getting wood collected. To give him his due, when he saw how tired we were he muttered something and set us to prepare vegetables instead.

"We haven't had a swim today!" Joe remembered whilst we were eating.

Tom, Arif and I looked at each other. "We had a shower at my place," I admitted smugly.

When three people give you The Look it really is quite withering, but we grinned anyway.

"Should we give the others a 'home day'?" Tom asked. "After all, we enjoyed a shower."

"It'd be nice to get away from fires and cooking," admitted Steve, even if he seemed to be flourishing at bossing us around and being a housewife (Well, camp-husband, then. No; that sounds worse).

"We could all go down to the cottage, meet Marcus, then go into town and have lunch," Tom declared. "Then perhaps spend a night at our homes and come back here tomorrow – if everyone wants to come back?"

We all thought..

"Don't forget Lars," said Arif.

That was a point.

"He'll be okay," said Tom.

"I'm not leaving him here on his own," said Arif indignantly.

"I didn't mean that. I mean we can take him with us."

"Do cafés accept dogs?"

"Hmmm. Good point. I know – we'll ask Marcus tomorrow."

We washed up, cleared up, collected more wood for the morning, then Joe, Steve and Alex decided they were going to swim. We joined them. After all, they had had a second lunch with us, so it seemed polite.

We seemed to wake at more or less the same time the following day. "Far too early," as Arif said. A rather slow effort at breakfast meant that we were only ready to leave at about ten o'clock, but at least we had remembered to phone the various homes and tell them our plans. Joe was told to take the phones home for charging. We all remembered, somehow, to ask for more food and were told they could provide some but the rest we could jolly well buy for ourselves.

Arif had to plead with his parents to be allowed to take Lars home. After a discussion that seemed at times to reach near-argument levels, they unbent eventually. It sounded like that was when he said: "He's a working dog, though, and they're allowed." He was told that *they* didn't mind, but that when his grandfather visited the dog would have to go outside. We looked at him when he'd rung off.

"It's an Islam thing," he said uncomfortably. "Some Muslims think that a dog's saliva is poisonous, more or less, and that dogs have no place in a Muslim household. Me, I think it's crap. My parents are a bit easier about it, but Grandad is a first generation immigrant."

We looked at him in wonder. Arif was just Arif. One of us. Being Muslim didn't come into it. And besides, he needed nothing special or even asked for it.

"Does… does it stop you doing much?" Alex asked.

He laughed. "Not me! But Grandad thinks I should be made to toe the line, go to the Mosque and be 'special'."

"What do you mean, special?"

He paused. "Not be a normal person. Not muck in, eat bacon, love dogs, spend my time with… well, people, the English friends that he would call 'infidels'. And dog's saliva? Maybe thousands of years ago, but now? Hardly! Or a lot of Europeans would be dead by now." Another pause. "Look, it's just a stupid, family thing, that's all. I'm one of you. One of us. That's all that matters. Just don't tell them about the bacon thing, okay?"

"He wouldn't… wouldn't try and get you to be a *terrorist*, would he?" asked Alex, the ever blunt.

"He'd have a bloody job! I'd run a mile. Probably back here, with you lot."

A cue for a general laugh, a rather relieved one as a discussion outside the experience of any of us was defused. Tom just nodded, grinned at him, and we took his lead. As always. After all, we were The Suspects, and all of us were mates, and in it together, as Arif had said.

We met Marcus, after a walk through the grounds that we were starting to know without help from Lars' nose or Steve's map. He was amazed at the quantity and quality of what we'd collected.

"I'll give you what we agreed," he said, "but these are really good and there's enough of them to be able to offer them to London hotels. If I can get an interest there it'll be top dollar and I'll give you the extra. Are there any more like this?"

Arif admitted that there might be, but we were only just exploring parts of the estate that hadn't been visited for years.

"Well, I won't ask you to take me to where you get them from," he said, smiling. "After all, if Nils and you need this chap here to find them, I'd have no chance."

We smiled, rather more warmly this time. The promise of the extra money, made without a prompt, notched him up in our estimation. Arif remembered something.

"We're going into town now it's safe," he admitted. "Do you know if cafés allow dogs in, please?"

"Why do you need to know? Anyway, it depends what café. Usually, no. But some pubs do."

"Oh," said Arif. "That's a nuisance. We were going to give Steve a break and have a meal out."

"Steve does the cooking, does he?"

"I do." Steve confirmed. "I've done a bit before, at camps and things, but this lot think I'm Gordon Ramsay."

Marcus grinned, looked at him and thought.

"Well... if you're happy to make do with what my hotel staff have for their lunch, I'll find a small room at the hotel and you can eat there, and Lars is welcome. No charge. Just a sort of 'well done' for your exploits the other night, and what you're doing for Nils."

Twelve eyes bored into him. The Royal... good grief!

Steve got his voice back first. "At the Royal? Really? That would be... well, thank you."

Marcus looked almost embarrassed. "It's eleven now – quarter past – so if you can get there about twelve thirty that'd be good. That's just before we get really busy. Ask for me on Reception and if you get any looks, ignore them. I'll sort that out."

A chorus of further thanks and he left. We hung about until he'd gone, and then walked to the bus stop.

Six people waiting for one shower takes ages, even when told by Tom to take as little time as possible. It was my house again, of course, as it seemed to be the only one with no parents, small sisters, small brothers or grandparents. Clean, and I must admit, smelling fresher, we reached the Royal just about in time.

Six still quite scruffy fourteen to fifteen year old boys descending on the Reception of what we learnt was a five-star hotel did cause a few heads to turn. We stuck to our guns and were expecting the smart guy behind the desk to order us out. But he took a look at us and instead of raising his voice and pointing to the door, smiled.

"You'll be wanting Mr Yardley. Wait a moment, and I'll get him."

Marcus answered the phone summons and swept us off to a small room with a large round table already laid for six. And we were plied with soup, thin but juicy steaks and sausages and potatoes and vegetables, with ice cream afterwards. Lars too was catered for, despite it not really being his normal meal time.

At last we were done: I felt really full.

When the last bowls were being cleared away, Marcus returned, asking if had been to our satisfaction, just as if we were paying, adult customers. We were enthusiastic and he received another gale of thanks. He just held up his hands and said that he was glad that we had stood up to 'some really evil men'.

Outside, we decided that we would compare notes by phone later and arrange a place to meet and return to the camp.

It was odd, going home alone, sitting in my own room. I lay on the bed and relaxed on its softness for the first time for ages, and thought. Home, or camp?

Here there was no bush I had to hide behind to pee, or a thicket I had to – er – use for other requirements. Instead there was a bathroom with what are called 'the usual facilities'. There was no wood to collect so we could start a fire to cook the next meal, and no Steve bullying us into doing so. But there was no lake to swim in – to get clean, yes, but also to have fun in. There was no wildlife to be spotted now and again. There were none of those times where sights and sounds and smells combined to give a memory that was so special they would penetrate the soul and last a lifetime. There was no dog… and I suddenly realised how much I missed the dog's constant, unquestioned and unquestioning company. And I missed discovering new qualities about these people who I was so used to that they had become almost Family.

Arif with his quiet unassuming ways, yet who was well able to stand up for himself and for us when it was needed. Alex with his ready grin and frequent impetuosity, not to mention his familiarity with his father's legal jargon and ability in arguments. Steve whose practical skills and abilities we had discovered and had grown to rely on so completely. Joe with his general good nature, the master of the phones and of the ability to arrange food stocks at the drop of a hat. Tom with his happy demeanour and unspoken leadership abilities, but also his surprising vulnerability.

And me? What on earth did I bring to the group? Perhaps I was just what the more dismissive history books call a foot soldier. Though the others didn't seem to regard me with any such condescension.

With that, I fell asleep.

The closing of the front door and Mum's voice woke me. Before I knew it she was in my room treating me as if I was still eight. Apparently she'd missed me. Oh well, I thought when she'd gone, muttering about food, I suppose it was better than the opposite. *Food!* I suddenly realised what she'd said, and struggled to my feet to rush down to tell her not to bother, and why. She was most impressed.

The rest of the afternoon passed in doing not a lot in front of the TV, and it wasn't until later that my resurrected, proper phone started ringing. The other five had enjoyed a similarly chill-out type day, had also switched their phones on again, and were wondering if another day off was on the cards. I added my agreement.

Arif's call had been in a highly amused voice. "My parents *love* Lars. They've really taken to him. And when Grandad came round I could see he was impressed, but he never said anything. But when he thought we were all out of the way he went out into the yard and sat with him – Lars had his head on his knees, looking up at him like he does; you know? We were all watching from the window laughing, but he never realised. When he came back in and saw us he tried to be all high and mighty but we all just teased him. So Lars is indoors again now. And Grandad loves him too."

That was good news. I just hoped the dog didn't try licking anyone. Not that he's a very licky dog, unless you're a food bowl.

The parents were rather put out that I'd only be around for another day before we headed back. "Haven't you had enough yet?" Mum asked.

"It's good," I told her. "We've got plenty to do, and even when we walk round the estate and get lost, it's fun."

"I've seen the scratches on your legs…" I was wearing shorts again as it was hot. "…and really you should look after yourselves better. What happens if they get infected?"

"We go to the hospital, get checked out, and visit Nils," I said cheekily. She looked at me – in fact it may have been The Look – but Dad just grinned and said "And good riddance!"

I have to admit that my own bed, a real bed, was a lovely change later, but I really missed that last hour around the fire before clambering into the tent.

So the next day was another dossy day, and towards the end of it I started getting bored. It was my turn to phone around and it seemed from the welcome the call received from the others that I'd been right to take the initiative. We agreed to meet up to buy some food first, then get the bus back to camp. Then came the business of cajoling money from parents to buy the food. Some parents, we discovered, felt that as the danger had now passed we should give up on the camp, bring everything home and stay there like good children.

We weren't good children. We were The Suspects. But that apart, parents should know that by the end of the school holidays we get bored, then they get fed up with us under their feet or using play-stations all day… you know.

We each reminded them of this.

We got the money, and the next morning met in a supermarket and stocked up, big time. Then we begged more rucksacks as we knew from experience that carrying shopping bags to the camp site – from either direction – was a long and painful process.

The wait for the bus seemed to be longer than usual, and it was only after some time that we realised it was Sunday. Finally it came, we were the only people on it, and the driver was surprised to be dropping us off near the entrance to the Forbidden Estate. So he called it, and expressed surprise that we had a permanent invitation to go there.

"That's the old man's dog, isn't it?" he asked. "Not

155

kidnapped it, have you?"

Arif told him, rather coldly, that 'the old man' was in hospital and we were looking after the dog and his house. He said no more; we got off and the bus sped away.

We called at the cottage but found nothing untoward, then walked slowly up to the camp. It was like coming home, especially as the first thing Steve said when he'd dumped his rucksack full of food in the stores tent was "We need more wood!"

"Can't get more," I protested, "'cos we haven't got any to get more of."

He returned to the store tent and rummaged, emerging with the bunch of dry wood he'd stashed away. I looked at it, he looked at me.

We went to get more wood.

Cooking a meal – a rather quick stew because we were hungry – told me even more that we were back home. The meat was tough, and it took ages to eat, but it tasted all right.

"Must find out why that was," Steve was heard to mutter.

"What?" I asked innocently.

"Why it was so tough. It never is at home."

"We've got our mobiles now," I reminded him, "You could always phone a friend."

Ignoring the catchphrase he muttered something about probably doing just that, and went to supervise the washing up - some things don't change. He was seen on the phone later, said "thanks", put the phone in his pocket and said a rude word.

"Solved it?"

He looked annoyed at me, rather annoyed. "You heard?"

I nodded. "Got your answer?"

"Yes. Should have been two hours, not twenty minutes."

"Ahhh..."

He had the grace to grin. "Sorry. All the other stews have been out of tins."

I shrugged, grinned back, and carried on picking my teeth.

It was almost good to go back to being bullied by him – the stew episode didn't stop him from making sure the washing up was all done to his high specification. We repaired a few of our creature comforts – his phrase, which meant the tables and things to sit on – and built a few more little gadgets under his slightly impatient direction. So... plate racks, mug hanging things and so on got built. Then he muttered something about building an oven.

"Can't we just go for a walk?" demanded Alex.

19   Grandad

It wasn't so much of a marathon as before, though we got to places we'd not seen. The general layout of the estate was becoming clearer. Its long road border at the southern side we were reasonably used to by now since we had used a part of it as our entry point. There were still expanses of the wall to either side of that point that we hadn't walked yet.

Opposite, the field border to the north was where many of the little streams entered under the wall and flowed confusingly through the estate. Approximately opposite anyway, we thought, as that's what the map said.

One end, the west, was plugged by the hamlet. Another stream ran at the back of the hamlet and joined all the streams there (as we had damply experienced). The only area we hadn't visited at all was the opposite end from that, the east. By now, using the map and a lot of trial and error and cursing, we had a good idea of where it went. What we didn't know was what it looked like or what was outside it.

There was a wall, just like all the other boundaries except the hamlet end. Beyond it we discovered a pattern of fields which continued upwards to the distant skyline. At the wall's remotest points, parts of it had fallen, wholly or partly, with many bricks not just fallen but by now completely missing. It was worst where one of the little streams we'd come to expect entered the estate.

"Not so well protected here," Alex remarked.

"Glad those men didn't choose this way."

"Too remote," said Tom cheerfully. "Think of the distance they'd have had to walk from the road. They're townies, don't forget. Countryside is foreign to them. Especially at night. And don't forget they don't know it as well as we do."

"Who *does* know it better than us?" It may have been a silly question, but it struck me that not even Nils and Lars could have been everywhere around the walls. The undergrowth that threatened to swamp the parts that were high enough to be called walls showed no signs of human penetration. We were discovering this by acquiring a fresh harvest of skin punctures.

Tom looked at me. "He's right, you know. No one's been here for years. No one knows the condition the walls are in nowadays. There's no money to repair them, even if someone did."

"We need to draw a definitive map." Alex sounded like his own father when talking to a client – we'd all been at his house when Mr Stephenson had been in official mode, and his tone on the phone at times made even our ferocious headmistress sound tame. At all other times he was just a normal Dad, as easily talked to as anyone you'd want to meet.

"Why can't we just make notes on Steve's?" asked Joe

"'Cos it's my Dad's," Steve answered him shortly.

"So what do we do?"

Silence.

"Don't you know, Steve?"

"Why me? I read the things, I don't draw them. You want an expert for that."

"We've got one. You."

They eventually stopped their tussle when Tom pointed out that the nearby slope down to the wall was really quite steep, and that if Steve was rolled down it and got injured, we might not find our way back.

"We've got Lars," Joe pointed out. Steve brushed the leaves and twigs from himself and glared at him.

We made some mental notes, and Steve jotted down one or two lines on an old till receipt he found. With that, we continued until the wall gained in height again and became better maintained, blocking our view of the surrounding terrain. But soon we started to hear traffic sounds, and knew we were at the road boundary again. Sure enough, about a half mile further on there was our original way over it and the start of the 'path' down to the camp.

"Is this where the men got over?" asked Alex.

"Who knows?" Tom responded. "Not something I want to remember."

"No, but perhaps we should be aware," Arif put in. "If there *should* be anyone else at any time, that might be a way in for them."

The thought was greeted with silence, as well as a reluctance to consider the possibility.

"Should we... should we try and block off our unofficial way in, do you think" I asked.

"We don't need it again," Tom admitted. "but how do we

block it off?"

"But *do* we need it again?" Arif asked. "It's a useful way out in an emergency, too."

"But what do we do, then?" I asked.

"Barbed wire over the wall and along the ground? Make an exit further on, or further back?" Joe was thinking. "If it's just for us as an emergency *exit* we could build it up this side and make sure there's a big drop the other."

"Sounds like a lot of digging... Anyway, have we got any barbed wire?"

"We need to have a look at both sides first, find how we're going to do it."

"Job for tomorrow," Steve said firmly. "I'm knackered and we should be cooking soon. And trying to get a map on paper if you think you can."

"I notice you said 'you'..." Joe responded.

We followed our usual path downwards, carefully avoiding the edge of the small cliff and the thicket beneath it where our would-be attackers had come to grief. Back at the camp there was a short respite before Steve urged us to collect wood. We groaned and did so. He smiled evilly.

Amazingly, he managed to concoct something else new, something we'd not tried before. Although it looked like boiled tapeworms with corned beef, green bits and cheese on top, he said firmly it was tagliatelle and pesto, with other bits he didn't mention. It was still cheese on top, though. He got a 'highly commended' from all of us.

"Thank Mum for that," he said smugly.

Once again it had been a long day and conversation around the fire, despite being such a welcome part of the day, didn't last long. We were soon in tents; me with Arif one side, Alex the other and Lars lying across all our feet. We slept.

At an ungodly hour called eight in the morning, one of our phones rang. Lars growled at it. I felt like doing the same.

But it was a rather odd sounding Nils speaking: speaking as if he was unused to the phone. Indeed, it was one of the first things he admitted.

He told us that the hospital had accepted that his stepson would be able to look after him if they could get him delivered to the cottage.

"I didn't know you had a stepson," said Arif cautiously.

"Does that mean you actually don't need our help, then?"

He listened. "Sorry? I didn't hear that."

A few seconds later his jaw had dropped. "*Me?!!*"

He listened some more.

"Oh... oh, I see. Oh well, we'll come and meet you and get you sorted out... Yes... okay... about three this afternoon... Bye."

He took a deep breath. "He's told them that I'm his stepson and they think I'm going to look after him until he can get around on his own."

"Bloody hell," Tom said. "I know we all said we'd help, but really... how long is he going to need help?"

"Weeks," Arif replied dismally.

"We're all in it together, Arif. It's not just you." I was certain of that. There was a mumble of agreement.

"I don't mind, especially as we volunteered, but if it was just down to me...well..."

"Okay." Tom sounded positive. "Let's get breakfast done, then go down to the cottage and sort it out – make sure it's clean and tidy. Then we can get some more truffles and have them ready for collection so he can see we've been busy."

"We need more wood!" was Steve's response.

The cottage, when we finally reached it, was as we'd left it. We had a joint think, then set to. Water containers were filled, a truffle expedition was mounted, and Tom and I, with some trepidation, went up to the bedroom to renew bedclothes. It was actually not too bad. We made a pile of cast-offs to take home to get washed. The bathroom was very tidy; we just did a bit of cleaning and that was that.

"The range!" exclaimed Tom suddenly. "It needs to heat up."

"We need more wood!" Steve responded, happily.

This time, he found himself collecting it. With help from Joe and Alex.

We proved the range was working by making a cup of tea and 'cooking' lunch – that is, making sandwiches with what we found there.

"What's he going to do about shopping?" Alex asked.

"Send me, I suppose," said Arif.

"Send one of us, you mean," Tom responded. "It's not all down to you, as we keep on saying." Arif looked at him gratefully.

"Who's going to get his washing home?" I asked, somehow dreading the idea of inflicting someone else's dirty bedclothes on my working parents.

Nobody answered. Arif just shrugged. "Stepson's privilege," he muttered.

"No," Tom commanded, "we take it in turns."

The phone rang. Joe answered it – it was his, after all. The emergency number had been given to all our parents, and even now the danger was over some of them regarded it as the way of contacting us all. He looked puzzled, then relieved.

"Hang on, I'll pass you over." He extended his arm and looked at Arif, who took it as if it was a hot potato.

"Your Grandad," said Joe.

He looked astonished. "He doesn't do mobile phones.... Hallo?"

Pause.

"Er... today, about three. Why?"

Pause.

"Er...well... I don't know."

Pause.

"Well, I suppose so. But it's very basic. No electricity. Water from a well."

Pause.

"Well yes, of course... Yes, he will... I don't know, you'd need to ask him."

Pause.

"No Grandad, I'm not trying to put you off. If you'd like to come and talk to him that'd be fine, I'm sure. But he'll tell you if he wants you to go..."

Pause.

"I'm not saying that, Grandad; but he has just come out of hospital, and he doesn't know you."

Pause.

"Okay, then: we'll see you later."

He hit the button and rolled his eyes.

"He wants to come and meet Nils and jolly him along a bit. I think he really just wants to meet Lars again and believes that his owner might be a nice person. Oh, what have I done? What has *he* done? What will Nils think, having someone else come and invade his house?"

"Will he bring your gran along too?" I asked. There was a pause.

"She died last year. Grandad's never recovered properly. He gets lonely."

There was no answer to that, so we all made sympathetic noises.

Nils arrived sharp at three. He looked tired, but said he was relieved to be back. Lars went quietly wild when he was allowed to get close and welcome him properly, but was far too well behaved to do anything as puppyish as jump up.

The ambulance men looked around for Nils' stepson but could see no adults, so asked. Primed, Arif stood forward.

There ensued an argument. In the middle of it a throat was cleared and an old man, of coffee complexion similar to Arif's, appeared. Lars made a fuss of him, Nils didn't have a clue what was going on, and the rest of us guessed. There were various exchanges and at last the ambulance men were beaten into submission.

After they'd gone Arif introduced his grandfather to the tired and now dazed Nils, who nodded politely and was taken indoors to sit down. To our surprise his Grandad knew when to say nothing, and said the minimum. Five of us left and congregated in the garden; Arif stayed for a while then came and joined us.

"I've known him all my life and he's never, ever, been as good with someone as that. He usually bullies us."

"What's he saying?" asked Tom.

"Nothing! Lars takes it turns to nuzzle up to first one, then the other. Grandad keeps saying he's a good dog, a great dog, and Nils just grins and agrees. Grandad's just put the kettle on and Nils realised that the range was alight. Grandad said that was down to us, and they then started saying that we're good, we're great, just like Lars. They've obviously hit it off, so I left them to it."

It seemed extraordinary to us that two so totally different people could just meet and get on. To make sure that's what was happening we thought we'd go and make ourselves another cup of tea. We felt that we should knock, and did so, even after having just walked whenever we needed to over the previous week. It would have felt wrong, going to the door and opening it, knowing that for a change there was someone at home.

"Good, said Arif's Grandad without reference to Nils. "Nils wants to get some sleep, and I think we should bring his bed downstairs for the time being, so it's easier for him and safer than getting up and downstairs. Please will you get it for him?"

"Ne...ne... I will not put any more on these people. They have done so much already..."

"They can manage a bed, though!"

I'd seen the bed, and I wasn't too certain.

"Ne... no... besides, I prefer to sleep upstairs."

That floored Grandad, but pleased me.

"Well, then. If it must be, it must be."

Nils leant back in his chair, exhausted.

"Grandad..." Arif said quietly to try and stop him. Then to Nils: "We'll leave you, Nils, and come back in an hour."

"Yes," Grandad butted in again. "What he needs now is just to be left to relax quietly. He's fine there for a while. Leave your phone with him, Arif, and if he needs anything he can call us."

"No use, mijnheer Arif, I cannot use these phones."

"They are very simple, Nils. Look..."

"No," Arif interrupted, "Not now. We will come back later. Is there anything else you need?"

He shook his head and smiled. "Ne...ne danke. Please return in an hour or so and I shall be all right."

With that he closed his eyes. We all trooped out, including Grandad, and looked rather foolishly at each other.

Grandad gave a smile, according to Arif later a rare event in itself.

"I am unkind to my Grandson sometimes," he admitted, "but this time he has done well. And Nils is a good man and a lucky man to have him – and you – as his friends. It is a pity he is an infidel, like all of you except Arif. And I am unsure nowadays about him..."

"Grandad!"

"I am joking, my son. I have lived in this country for most of my life and I am no longer blind to the goodness of those who do not embrace Islam. I have not the strength, the youth and certainly not the will to be a fundamentalist. And I know the young do not follow slavishly the ways of their parents... or grandparents..."

He smiled again, and we did politely even if we weren't sure what he'd *really* meant.

"What are we going to do for an hour?" Tom asked in a matter of fact tone.

"What *were* we going to do?" I wondered out loud.

"Welcome Nils home and look after him," Arif told us.

"And then?"

"God knows!" said Alex, the blunt.

"Well, *I* want to look around the village and some of the woodland," said Grandad, townee that he was.

"We're not welcome in the hamlet, Gran... I mean sir" said Tom. "They tried to turn us out. It's not happened since, but we walk through it as quickly as possible when we come that way."

"But you saved Nils' life!"

"I know. But they are that sort of people."

The man sighed. "It is strange. It is their loss not to know you. And to you, all of you, I am Daneesh, not Grandad! That is for Arif."

We digested that.

He was taking us down to the hamlet anyway, and stopped to look at some of the cottages. Though he said nothing I knew he was thinking. But he turned without a word and came back, sensing our reluctance to stay there.

We took him over the old house and its garden, and showed him the damage that the years had caused. Again, he said little. When we came to the start of the long path to our camp he stopped.

"Where are these truffles that Marcus Yardley tells me about?"

We gaped at him, even Arif.

He laughed, obviously pleased at the reaction. "Marcus and I know each other from the grocery trade. I knew he was able to get truffles, but I never knew where. When Arif became interested in a wooded estate, and was camping there, I put two and two together. He is no fool, this boy. I hope they are making you money."

"Grandad," Arif started, almost aroused to annoyance, "they are Nils' income. When he was injured we started collecting them, yes, but for him. The money we have collected from Marcus has been put into Nils' hospital storage. The only thing we have kept is for Lars' food, some of ours, and anything we've had to pay for Nils."

It was the old man's turn to look astonished.

"Well... I'd still like to know where they are."

"Why, Grandad?"

"Well... I mean..."

"I thought you were Nils' friend, not someone hoping to steal from him!"

"You forget yourself, boy..."

"No, Grandad; I don't. But I *know* you."

The two looked at each other. And despite the age difference and the family hierarchy Daneesh broke eye contact first.

"This is the honour you have, is it? Honour for your friends, not your family? How things have changed." Despite his words I thought I could see the light of amusement in his eye.

"I honour my family, Grandad, but I also honour my friends. And if it means doing right by both, I do. If I were to steal from my friends, how would my honour within the family be seen?"

The rest of us listened to this with embarrassed interest. We had heard of the Muslim honour, but always in relation to other things... unpleasant things.

"Who teaches you to think this way?" asked Daneesh.

"I do."

"You do not take teaching from your elders."

"Would they teach me to steal?"

Silence. A silence that held until we crossed a path that would have led us to one of the truffle collecting areas. We passed it.

It was by then late afternoon. Our general direction was toward the camp, but I hoped we weren't going that way. It was ours; too private to be shared with anyone unless they had to see it, as the rescue parties had had to on *that* night. But Tom, now in the lead, was heading off to the meeting of the two streams where we had been forced to wade or swim. We reached the water's edge.

"What are we doing here?" asked Daneesh.

"We were walking the other day and had to swim through that," said Tom airily. "It was a bit cold."

"You think I am going to swim? At my age?"

"It's the only way across," said Tom.

You will have noticed, of course, that Tom had told no lies whatsoever. We *had* had no option but to swim through it. It

166

was the only way across.

If we wanted to get across.

Daneesh did some muttering, just as most of us had done over the previous two weeks, and announced that he wasn't going to cross it for anyone, even if they asked him. So we didn't, but turned and headed back to the cottage. Only about thirty minutes had elapsed, so it didn't seem right to wake Nils.

"I'll come back tomorrow to see if he's all right," Daneesh announced.

"We *can* cope, Grandad."

"I want to. He is a friend."

"It's not just that you want some truffles then?" Arif was unrelenting.

The old man looked at him and was about to say something. But his eyes held Arif's for some time, and he at last smiled openly.

"Do I have to take religious instruction from my own grandson? Does he need to instruct me what is honour in this country that I must surely be able to call my own after all these years?"

"I don't know, Grandad. Do you? Do I?"

"All right, boy, you have made your mark, and it gives you credit that you live by it. Now come with me to the bus stop and see me on my way home, or I will of course sneak back and steal some of my new friend's income..."

At this he laughed, and there are certain tones that tell you whether a laugh is genuine or fake. We believed him.

20   Police again

We wasted a bit of time on the way back, then Arif exclaimed "Truffles! Who's coming?"

I said I would, and indeed so did all the others.

"Only one or two," he said. "If there are any more we'll be treading on more than we collect."

I suppose he had a point. Alex was chosen, his first time at collecting them, and then we remembered that we had no baskets to put them in so as quietly as we could we congregated outside the cottage. Arif undid the door and tiptoed in. The next thing we knew was that we heard the two of them talking.

Arif came out after a while.

"He says he's still tired, but is concerned he doesn't know what to do about food. I told him not to worry, that we were going to collect some more truffles and would think about it when we got back."

"*We* should think about food too," said Tom.

"I could cook for seven, rather than six," Steve volunteered.

"Those other bags full of food that we got the other day are still in the cottage. Any chance you could cobble up something with what's in them?"

"I'll have a look. Is it all right to go in?"

Arif pushed the door open again, and Steve vanished inside. Some muttering happened, then he poked his face out again.

"I need more wood," he announced happily.

We all laughed resignedly. "Come on," said Tom, "Alex, Matt and Arif to the truffle fields, the rest of us on a wood search. Back here in half an hour."

And so it was. Now we had developed a way through to the new truffle area getting there was a lot less painful. Alex was keen to see what happened, and although a bit of a spare part was able to help gather a good supply. Arif stopped us after a while.

"We've only got a few more minutes, and if we get too many of these Marcus won't be able to sell them for what they're worth."

Lars was reluctant to leave, but leave we did, and this time we led him – for a change – and managed not to be too late. Nils looked at our collection of truffles and exclaimed that they were better than he had seen anywhere on the estate. We tried to explain where we had found them, and how, but he couldn't remember having been in the area. They obviously impressed him, especially when we told him what Marcus had said.

"Is there a good supply?" he asked.

"Ask Lars," Arif suggested. "He didn't want to come away tonight."

"That means there are more to be found. Good. You must take your share when Marcus pays."

"We'll see about that when the time comes," said Arif.

Steve had cooked up another massive stew, though this time with tinned meat. Our teeth were safe. Nils had only a little of it.

"I have been sitting for so long, I need less," he said. "But it is good, very good."

The trouble was, he had only one plate, and not even we felt it was acceptable to use spoons dipped in the large stew pot Steve had used. We apologised and wondered what to do.

"You must take it to your camp and eat there," we were told. I shall not need the pot yet. Perhaps you might, if it is here…" He said it wistfully, looking at Steve.

Tom got the hint and laughed. "Some of us will come and cook for you – don't worry. And if it's simple, any of us can do it."

"You could bring down your plates too… I have eaten alone too long."

It was a simple thing to say, but it meant a lot to us.

We had remembered to feed Lars too, to Nils' pleasure, and I wondered whether the dog would return to the camp or stay with Nils.

"But you should return now," said Nils. "You have things to do, and a meal to eat. And I must learn to get myself around."

Nobody argued with him. We checked that he could get himself up and down the stairs, and once again Joe tried to show him how to use one of the phones so he could call in an emergency. He would have none of it, though, and said that if it was that urgent Lars would come to us.

We couldn't argue with that logic, so, stew pot in hand, we made our way through the estate and to our camp.

"I need more wood!"

We groaned and set to, and soon –ish– were settling down to

the reheated stew.

"What a day!" Tom exclaimed.

We had actually done very little, but it seemed as if we had. I just hoped Nils was all right.

"We never told Marcus about the truffles!" Alex remembered.

"Is it too late now?"

"We could try," said Arif. Joe handed over the phone.

Marcus was pleased to hear that Nils was home and said he would be there at the usual time to see him and collect our findings.

"Another early start!" groaned Arif.

But it didn't stop us sitting round the fire as always, talking over the events of the day and insulting each other as we always had.

It was late when we woke the next morning; there had been no Lars to whimper at us and remind us that he needed a bush of his own.

As soon as we could, Tom and Arif went down to see Nils. The rest of us really just wasted the rest of the morning playing cards, reading, and not feeling guilty about it. The sun wasn't shining, for a change, and we felt lazy. When finally the two reappeared they reported back.

"Nils is okay. My Grandad appeared and is really being rather good. He and Nils have hit it off again and seem to talk to each other happily for ages. They could be good for each other. And they both dote on Lars, so that's good. I took Lars out to add a few more truffles to the pile – and give him some exercise – and Marcus appeared to collect them and give Nils the money. He said that he knew that we had given the other two lots to Nils, so he wasn't going to bother asking, but Nils told him we had, of course."

Tom took over. "I asked what Nils wanted us to do, and Arif's Grandad just said 'Nothing, I can do it all.' I asked how long he was staying and he said he'd go after he'd made an evening meal tonight. When he'd gone out for a pee Arif asked Nils if he was happy for that and he told me he really liked him, and they both knew when to stop talking if the other one was tired! So I think we're more or less off the hook."

"Except for Fridays. Friday Prayers. He has to go."

"But surely he can't come in every other day? And the

170

weekends?" asked Alex.

"He thinks he can," Tom said. "But I'm not so sure Nils won't want a day's freedom now and again."

"Nils can look after himself, I think," said Arif. "He's quite capable of telling Grandad to leave him alone so he can have a rest."

We digested this. Steve said "I need more wood," so we threw a towel at him. But Alex, Joe and I went foraging, the others being excused because they'd been working.

Sharp on 6.00 that evening, when we were wondering when we were going to be attacked by Steve for the next supply of wood, one of the temporary mobiles rang. 'Our' Police Sergeant. He rather apologetically, according to Joe who answered it, asked if we could show a group of Police and Scenes of Crime up to the area that was cordoned off. "You mean my Dad," said Joe. "Yes, we can do that. When?"

Pause.

"Nine tomorrow! Blimey, that's a bit early."

Pause.

"Oh. Oh okay then. Hang on."

"They want us to take them up here tomorrow so they can do some work on that lot." He pointed to the distant scrub and woodland.

"It means another early start," groaned Tom.

"That's what *I* said."

"I suppose we've got to. How about giving Lars a run at the same time?"

"I'll go," Arif volunteered.

"So will I," I added. I wanted to see how Nils was getting on, and being with the dog was always fun.

Joe relayed the message and shut off the call. "Just you two to get up early," he crowed.

"We'll want breakfast," I said innocently.

And that was when I discovered that Steve is quite strong, and heavier than me, but he let me go when I volunteered to get wood for the meal.

Once again we lazed a bit, then enjoyed that magic hour or so of peace and fellowship before the yawns started and we crawled into our pits.

Apparently people are meant to wake up and get up once an alarm goes. We didn't. It was only the need for a bush that

171

made me realise the time and dig Arif out fast, get dressed and start our journey to the hamlet at the run.

Passing Nils' cottage we set Lars barking, and Arif muttered something I didn't hear. He faded into the distance as we ran down toward the houses, and eventually stopped.

"You're late," stated one of the waiting Police, one we hadn't seen before.

"Sorry," I mumbled, "We overslept."

"I knew it was wrong to expect kids to be reliable enough to help us," he continued to another of the officers.

"Well, we are here now," said Arif calmly.

"And we've been wasting our time here for fifteen minutes," he said, working himself up. "Perhaps you know it's a crime to waste Police time."

"Yes," said Arif. "Should we just let you find the crime scene on your own, then?"

The man took a step towards him, but Arif stood his ground. He was as tall as the Policeman, and held his eyes calmly.

The man turned aside.

It was a few moments after that that the Sergeant appeared in a car. "Sorry to keep you," he said. "Hope you haven't been waiting long. We got held up at the station."

"That's okay," I said, trying to keep as cool as Arif. "We were late ourselves, as one of your officers has just reminded us."

It may have been chance, but the Sergeant looked straight at the right man, who had the grace to blush.

"Okay then. It's good of you to help us like this. We'd waste a lot of time trying to find it if it wasn't for you."

With that, we started off. Our route meant passing Nils' cottage again. Arif looked at me. "I can't just leave him barking, and Nils wondering what's happening."

He turned to the Sergeant. "I've got to collect the dog and tell Nils what's happening. Can I catch you up?"

"Understandable," he said, knowing the situation. "We'll wait here."

Arif was quite a short time in the cottage but appeared with the dog and a still astonished Nils on crutches. He turned and told the old man he wouldn't be long, and that the Police would be off the Estate as soon as they had finished. He nodded, and watched us until we were out of sight, the dog almost reluctantly with us, and probably only going along because of Arif.

Walking in single file doesn't do much for conversation. Arif and Lars were in front, me behind him, and the Police following as they would. We were on one of the steepish climbs when the Sergeant called, his voice some way behind.

"Hold up, lads! I'm older than you!"

"We'll stop at the top," I called back.

The Sergeant had a red face by the time he joined us, but was grinning. "I'm not as healthy as you. Or as light on my feet!"

We smiled back. All the others were in a similar state, including, I'm glad to say, the man who had been unpleasant. But he wasn't smiling.

When they'd recovered we continued, and managed to make the camp without another stop. Fortunately the others were awake by then and were cooking breakfast. Tim Hammond greeted Joe, who looked glad to see him. The two chatted on their own for a while.

"Ahh…" started one of Policemen, "any chance of a cuppa? It's hard work, getting up here."

"Bacon sarnie'd go down well too," said Tim Hammond.

Steve looked at us all. "I'll put more water in the kettle."

"Take no notice of Tim. You don't need to cook for us – he's just being greedy."

Tim laughed. "He's just being polite. You should see him in the canteen."

The Sergeant cleared his throat. You could tell he was giving his version of The Look.

"I can probably manage to do that. There's only five of you."

"Four," snapped the rude one.

Tim chipped in. "Without anyone knowing it, I bought enough bacon for everyone. And a loaf of bread. I thought if this lot… I mean, my esteemed colleagues… don't want it, all you people could use it."

Steve looked at him, surprised. "Four, then. Do you want tea?"

The answer seemed to take a long time coming: "Yes… please."

"I need more wood!"

Alex and Tom gave a look of resignation and went off into the woods. Joe, Arif and I took the Police up to where the men had been caught.

"Okay, lads, you've done your bit, thanks. This is up to us. We can find our way back to the camp when we're done. If it's ready before we appear, give us a yell, or blow a whistle – that's what we're still used to reacting to – and we'll come running. Well, walking, anyway."

"Okay," said Joe, talking mainly to his Dad. "Good luck."

We returned, and helped with getting a really good supply of wood together to try and shut Steve up. The kettle boiled at last, the bacon cooked in almost no time after that and rather than yell Joe ran up to fetch them.

Bar one person, it was a pleasant, sociable snack. Actually it was breakfast for us and Lars, and a snack for them as they'd started work at six. They all (bar the one, who sat aside from the others and just sipped at his tea) treated us as equals. It helped that Tim was Joe's dad, and knew us well, and that despite not being actually uniformed Police he treated them as equals too.

Once finished, Steve poured the remaining hot water into the washing up bowl and looked meaningfully at Tom. Tom grinned and just said "Washing up time! Volunteers, please."

I knew how hot the water was so grabbed a tea towel. The Sergeant looked at the silent one.

"Give them a hand, would you? They've been good enough to feed us. It only seems right we should pull our weight."

Wordlessly the man crossed to the bowl with his mug and dipped it, and his hand, in the water, only to swear and jerk it out again. I retrieved the mug.

"It's just come out of the kettle," I said innocently. "You're meant to put some cold in with it."

If looks could kill... It put my mates' meaningful glares into the shade.

But the washing up got done and they all seemed as impressed as Joe's dad that we had a draining board and then a place for everything. "Blame The Scout," said Tom when the Sergeant remarked on it.

"Who's that?"

"Steve."

"Ahh... in that case..." He crossed to where Steve was

supervising the final bits of tidying.

"Congratulations. I hear you're the one they have to thank for keeping them healthy."

"Er…" Steve was a bit gobsmacked.

"You're in the Scouts."

"Yes."

"Local?"

"Yes."

"So was I, forty years ago. Shake."

And to my surprise they both did. With their left hands.

It took them another hour to finish their measuring and searching, return and say good bye, and then remember they needed guidance down to the hamlet.

Joe and Tom, with Lars and Arif, took them back this time.

"What's that business with the left hand?" I asked Steve.

He looked a bit embarrassed. "Everyone in the Scouts does. It's tradition."

I nodded. Oh well. Scouts are different. Useful, but different.

"When are you leaving?"

We spun round. It was the unfriendly Policeman.

"Excuse me?" asked Steve.

"You realise you don't have the owner's permission to camp here, so what you're doing is illegal. You need to pack up and go."

Alex appeared from his tent. He'd been 'resting'.

"Er… well, we had to be somewhere to get out of the gang's way, and it's such a good place that we want to stay. And actually we do have permission," Steve continued.

"Who from?"

"Well, our parents, the Police and Nils."

"But none of them are the landowners."

"Can you tell us who is, please? I'm sure they'd give permission. After all, we have saved one life, got the Police evidence to jail some criminals, and started to map the estate after all these years."

"It's not my job to trace land ownership. That's your problem."

Alex chipped in. "Well now, technically it could be. You see, the Police can't prove whether the owner has given permission or not, as they don't know his or her identity. So until proof is available to offer to a court that we are here without permission, we are innocent of any crime. Basic principle of English law. So if you're able to trace the owner and obtain a written affidavit to show us that we *have* no permission, then it might be possible for you to persuade the Director of Public Prosecutions that it's worthwhile persecuting… I mean prosecuting … six minors for a minor, civil crime. If it does come to court, my father, who would take the case for the defence, would ask your Sergeant to act as a character witness, and a witness that we are camping to a high standard. And from our conversations with him, and especially Steve's, I'm sure he would be delighted to do so."

Steve and I by this time had our mouths open, looking shocked. We were not the only ones. The Policeman had gone red. We were unsure what he was going to do, but to our surprise and relief he turned on his heel and followed the rest of the party.

"Bloody hell, Alex," I exclaimed, "where did all that come from? I thought he was going to explode!"

"It's no use having a solicitor as a father if you don't learn how to talk to people," he said smugly. "I had to swallow hard before I started, I was so angry at his attitude. But it seemed to work."

"Is what you said right?" asked Steve.

"Maybe. Don't know. It sounds like sense to me. But most importantly *he* didn't know either, and he's not senior enough to know. Have we got a phone here?"

I went to Joe's tent and rummaged around, avoiding the underwear, and returned triumphantly with it.

Alex found the Sergeant's number – fortunately it was the main phone, the one we'd had through our 'exile'. He made the call and explained what had happened.

"No," he said eventually, "He's not still here. Isn't he with you?"

It appeared our unfriendly man had been left behind, had missed his path, and was presumably now lost.

Alex hung on. In the distance was a loud, prolonged squawk, and a near-simultaneous curse.

"We heard it," he reported.

Pause.

"Yes, okay. Hope he's nicer with us this time."

Another pause, then he laughed and rang off.

"We have a rescue mission, men. Find a Policeman time!"

As we set off down the path the others had taken, we could hear periodically the same long squawk from the man's radio. Eventually Steve posted me on the path whilst he and Alex followed the sounds. Ten minutes later I head crashing and curses, so I called out.

"Keep shouting every half a minute!" came Steve's instruction.

What the hell do you shout when you have to act as a sound beacon? I finally decided on the time. It sounds very odd when called at high volume, but hey, it's better than just 'Hallo'.

They got back to me and I just pointed to the path... or what counted as a path to us, who had walked it so many times.

We delivered a silent, obviously embarrassed and hopefully tamed Policeman to his colleagues, who grinned at us when he wasn't looking. To make his embarrassment worse, Nils, Daneesh and Lars were watching, and laughing silently.

"Come in, come in!" Nils ordered. "The Police, they were here when you called and we heard every word. You did well."

"It's a pity we found him so quickly," said Alex. "I'd have liked to see him get really lost for a few hours. He's what my Dad would call a jobsworth Policeman. Not like that Sergeant who's taken a shine to Steve."

"He was a Scout too," Steve muttered.

"That's what I mean," Alex said without a blink.

"How are you getting on?" Tom asked Nils, as if it had been weeks since we had seen him, and not just a matter of hours.

"Very well, very well. Daneesh is good for me. Too long I have spent in my own company – and with Lars, of course." The dog's tail swept the floor. "It was only having to talk to silly people in the hospital that I realised that when I found someone worth talking to, it was good."

"And it keeps me out of your mother's way, Arif," added his grandfather, trying not to smile. "And now I have found how good it is to have the friendship of a proper, working dog, and of another person my age who has come to this country from his own – well, it is good and I will enjoy it until Nils gets fed up with me and throws me out."

"So long as you realise, Grandad, that he needs to rest so his ankle mends. You know how you can talk when you get on to one of your pet subjects."

"My own grandson tells me off, Nils. You see how it is. But he doesn't realise that the best company is almost always someone of your own age. Even from a different country. But perhaps he does. For he has been with his friends, the friends of his own age, for the last two weeks."

Arif grinned. "And we argue and spar with each other... but yes. I know. We get on. But we can walk away when we get really fed up, or want some time alone."

Daneesh looked at him fondly. "Nils and I – we are not so different. Anyway, the kettle has boiled. I will make tea."

We spent some time with them planning. Friday was the first time that Daneesh wouldn't be there. "Friday Prayers," he said as if that was an obvious reason.

"So we could have a couple of days at home, really, said Arif.

"You could. You should. Amy wants to see you."

It was Arif's turn to be astonished, and it showed.

"How... how do you know about her?" he managed eventually.

"Ahh...simple. She came into the shop and asked if you were all right. I may be old, but I can see when someone is more than just a school friend. She is not of our race, nor even a Muslim, but I suppose I must put that aside. Especially as she is so pretty."

"Grandad... You old..." Before Daneesh had a chance to say more he was in a great embrace. We watched, astonished.

They separated, but Arif still looked at the old man. "I was so scared you might object..."

"I know how Britain works, after all these years. And how the rest of Europe works. I am not one of those who believe in Shariah law being brought to Britain. But most, I want my grandson to be happy, and to like me still. I know how *he* works, too."

I can't remember Arif looking dazed before, even when he'd been tackled hard at football.

We decided to have the rest of the week off, spend the weekend with our families, and phone on Sunday to talk about the following week. Tom and Steve would visit on Friday morning to make sure Nils was all right, and Arif and me in the evening.

178

"We'd better have a tidy up in the camp," Tom suggested. "I think some of my stuff might need washing."

"You mean, before it walks down and catches the bus on its own?" Alex said innocently.

So we returned, cleared up, took stock of the food situation and packed a lot of clothing and near-date stuff into rucksacks. The journey back down to the cottage was uncomfortable as a result. We rested there, said our goodbyes to Nils, Daneesh and Lars, then walked through the hamlet and caught the bus home.

"We never thought about truffle collection, did we?" asked Joe.

"That's true. Perhaps we should call Marcus and ask him when he wants another lot."

"Matt and I could do a collection on Friday," Arif offered. "I'll call him, shall I, and ask?"

"If Amy lets you," said Alex.

Tom said we'd all get chucked off the bus if the two of them didn't behave.

Getting home to an empty house was a bit weird, even if I had spent a night there only recently. I seemed to have been away for so long that realising I was actually going to stay there seemed peculiar. At least I could shower and change. I wondered what to do with the dirty stuff, so just left it in a pile in my room. Mum would know.

Oddly, when she'd come back, found me in front of the TV and greeted me, and heard about the washing, I received her version of The Look.

I now know how the washing machine works, where the pegs are, and how to work the washing line. On the plus side, it was good to see the parents again, have a meal I didn't have to collect wood for first, or help to cook. Despite the previous night there, TV was almost a novelty and once again a bed that was kinder to my bones was a pleasure.

I still missed that gathering around the fire as the night drew in, though.

21   Mapping and curry

I met Arif at the bus stop and was a bit gobsmacked to find Amy with him. I knew they were friends – possibly a bit more – but the estate seemed to be somehow at arm's length from families and others – from people who weren't The Suspects. But then, thinking on (as a teacher who had come from Yorkshire would have put it), Joe's dad had been there as a Scenes of Crime Officer; and Arif's Grandad had been there, attracted by Lars and then befriended by Nils. So really, why shouldn't Amy come? My mind thought further on: would she want to come to camp with us? Would she and Arif…

No. That was too far for me to think. But intriguing.

Nils took one look at her and smiled. "Like my daughter might have been, you are, and as pretty." The smile faded. "But she died with my wife."

We all looked at him. This was news.

"I'm so sorry," she said quietly. Arif and I murmured agreement.

"Killed in a car crash, both of them. And the man whose driving killed them, died too." He cleared his throat. "That is why I came back to England."

There comes a point where words aren't enough. We just nodded, and stayed silent.

"Never told anyone that," he said rather chokily. "Thirty years ago it must be, and still hurts."

Another pause, and he started again. "Lars needs a walk, if you want. And Marcus probably needs some truffles."

We interrupted and told him we'd thought about that. Arif had called him and he had arranged to collect them the following day. Nils smiled.

"You are very good to me. Thank you. And Daneesh is coming tomorrow too. Good."

We took the dog and introduced Amy to the estate's tough woodlands, particularly to the new area for truffles. She took it in her stride and watched in amazement, first at what Lars was doing, then at the odd, ugly lumps that we so carefully collected. Carefully she lifted one.

"Arif says that this is worth… what?"

"About £30."

"Why?"

"Dunno," I admitted. "Chefs use them. I've never tasted one."

"Better cooked," said Arif. "Used mainly for sauces, I think. I'm not going to waste Nils' money by biting into one, though."

"I took a pinch out of one once," I admitted. "It just tasted like mushroom to me."

"I won't bother, then," she laughed. I noticed Arif smiled at her in a way I'd never seen him use before, if you see what I mean.

Anyway, we gathered what we thought was enough, and returned to Nils' cottage.

"They are the rare ones again," he said. "Thank you. And Marcus will fetch them tomorrow?"

We confirmed that.

"What are you doing for food?" Arif asked. I had forgotten we had to prepare something for him.

"I have gathered some beans this afternoon," said Nils proudly, "and if you get some potatoes and start them, I will be able to do the rest."

"We will. Do you like Indian food? I could bring something now and again if you do."

He laughed. "In some parts of Holland are people who came from Suriname originally. They can cook very hot food, and we loved it. I have not had proper Indian food for many years."

"My Grandad still cooks. He is not from there but from northern India. As a Muslim he was persecuted when Pakistan was formed... but that's for him to tell you. I'll ask him to bring something for you, and I will too."

"And I will pay, of course."

Arif looked uncomfortable. "Well, that's between you and Grandad. But now let's get some water and start cooking."

So we fetched water, enough to tide him over, and put some of it on to boil potatoes. He seemed to have some meat from a can, and some fruit, so it seemed he wouldn't starve. We made sure he was happy and could cope, then made the journey back into town. I left them at the bus stop, though when I was nearly out of sight I turned back.

They were holding hands.

The weekend went quickly. On Saturday I was at the shopping precinct, just for something to do, and nearly bumped into Emily Long. She looked shocked to see me, but recovered quickly enough to give me the finger. I found it impossible to understand how she, at just a year older than me, would willingly do what she'd presumably done, just to get some money. It wasn't something I wanted to think about. I ignored her after the initial shock of recognition and rather left her, standing finger still extended.

We met up again on the Sunday afternoon, this time at Steve's. With a slightly embarrassed look he produced a large piece of paper and spread it on the table. We looked, and as one started looking closer as we saw what it was.

He'd started on a large scale plan of the estate. "The outline is accurate, and the places where streams cross the walls are as well. The hamlet's in the right place, and so is the big house. I think I've got Nils' place right but it's a bit difficult to tell which of the buildings on the Ordnance Survey map it is."

The definite places, including our lake and campsite, had been done in ink, but the paths and where we had explored were in pencil "so we can change them without leaving a mess," as he said.

We were impressed.

"Dad's done some copies so we can mark them as we want, and only put things on this one when we know they're right," he said. We were even more impressed.

"I thought you said you only worked with maps, you didn't draw them?" Alex accused him. "This is really good."

For Alex, the insult merchant, praise of any sort was rare. Steve looked pleased.

"How do you feel about going back?" he asked.

I nodded immediately. It was a lot nicer than just wandering around the town. The others thought, and then agreed. Arif looked worried.

"I... well, I'd like to come back sometimes," he said rather shyly. "It'd be good if Amy could come with us, but that's not going to happen. And...well..."

There were some ribald remarks which he bore with good grace. I silently agreed that adding someone else to the mix was not really on, and having her in one of our tents was probably not going to be allowed. And not least, not allowed by her.

"She's got a holiday job anyway," he said, "so what we could do is spend the week there and the weekends at home.

That way we could sort Nils out when Grandad's not there on a Friday, and if parents have anything on, that'll be at weekends. And Amy doesn't work weekends…"

It seemed like a good compromise. Tom saw a problem.

"We need more…"

"Wood!" Steve and I chorused.

"…food," he finished, but smiling anyway. "And some of the shops we want are shut. It's Sunday. We need to shop tomorrow, get our stuff together and catch a bus in the afternoon. Then we can start mapping on Tuesday."

For a change we made lists of the food we needed. Parents had been rather fed up – or should that be exasperated? – by the amount of nearly out-of-date food we'd brought back. So we tried to be a bit more scientific. It gave Steve the chance to bully us into choosing things he could cook. Arif had already asked for a curry from home so he said he'd add to that and divide it between us and Nils – and Daneesh.

"Better not give any to Lars either," he said. "It'll be a hot one. We don't want a rocket fuelled truffle digger."

It doesn't look particularly funny, written down like that. But at the time we were nearly rolling on the floor. At least we now knew that we all enjoyed the Choudhury family hot curry.

We met, as planned, at the usual bus stop after lunch on the Monday, loaded down with full rucksacks. We weren't looking forward to the trek up the hill to the campsite, so stopped to call on Nils as an excuse to rest. Daneesh was there, and silently handed us a stew pot which smelt as if it had curry in it.

"Thanks, Grandad, but we'll have to come back for it. We're laden down with everything else at the moment."

"Come later and eat it with us," asked Nils, "but bring your own plates and things. Then Daneesh can return on the bus with you."

"But we're camping again," said Tom. "We shan't be going home until Friday evening." He explained what we'd decided. "But we'll certainly come and eat with you – we'd enjoy that."

So long as we can sit round our own fire afterwards, I thought.

The slow walk up to the camp was as tiring as dodging the foliage in the early days when we had come down from climbing over the wall. When we got there not even Steve had the heart to yell for firewood, so we just opened the tents to air them and lay around at rest. Finally, though, there was the inevitable cry for wood; we all groaned and went to do Steve's bidding. He brewed a cup of tea and we sat round with it, unwilling to get on with anything.

"Come on, guys!" Tom was being decisive. "We need to get down to Nils' cottage and eat. There'll be time to get busy at being lazy when we get back."

He was called a bully by most of us and cheerfully ignored us all. Steve started building the fire up higher than usual, then putting earth around it and on top of it.

"To see if I can keep it hot," he explained. "Save lighting it later."

Still groaning, but armed with plates and cutlery, we made the journey back down and were immediately accused of being late. The cottage smelt like an Indian restaurant, which I suppose it more or less was.

The concoction Daneesh had come up with was challenging, even to those of us who liked their curry hot. Some were seen drinking copious amounts of water despite Daneesh's warning not too as it made the spices seem even hotter. Both the old men were laughing at those of us who were suffering. Annoyingly, neither of them was. Finally, eyes streaming, we tucked into some very welcome ice cream from Daneesh's cooler bag.

Nils was the most cheerful and forthcoming we'd seen him, and was telling us stories about Dutch customs, but carefully avoiding the war years. It was a remarkable change from the unsmiling, nearly taciturn man who had thrown us out of the estate originally. In a gap in the conversation I mentioned it.

"In hospital I learnt that talking to some of them was enjoyable. And then you people. And then Daneesh, who is being a good friend. It is good, talking. I have been alone too long."

At last, very late, Daneesh said that he must go if he was to catch a bus. "I don't want to have to sleep at your camp, and Nils needs to be free of me sometimes." We too made our way back, and settled down by the fire which Steve resurrected from the heap of steaming earth. Dusk glowed around us, then gave way to darkness and the night noises of the woodland. And once again we enjoyed that time where little is said, except by the fire, conversation becomes sporadic but friendly, and the cocoa cools in the mugs.

At last we dragged ourselves off to the tents and slept.

Tom was annoying in the morning. Steve had been annoying first by disturbing us all with a shout about needing wood, and then, as breakfast was being cooked, Tom started planning. And this was happening before any of us, presumably except those two, were properly awake.

It seemed that if we were going to be serious about surveying the place we needed to be organised and accurate.

"Come on," said Joe, "this is the holidays. You sound like a teacher."

"Well, you can do it badly if you want to. It's not something I've done before. Nor has Steve, not properly, so if we're going to do it I think we should try and do it as well as possible."

There was sense in this, but I knew what Joe had meant.

We left the camp cleared to a standard that met with Steve's approval and set off to the top of the waterfall, ignoring the area whose unpleasant memories still hadn't fully left us. We took a bearing from there to where our original wall crossing place was shown on the map.

And once there, it became obvious that Steve and Tom had been planning. They showed us distances, bearings, and how to plot them on the map and find other distances, and a lot more that went over my head. I'd done maths at school – obviously – but this went beyond what we'd been taught. I suppose if we hadn't been the sort of people we are, we'd have scoffed and wandered off. But the way they showed us what to do made us sit up and take notice. We would have to use the teaching we'd had at school and discover holes in it. And that made us more interested in making it all work.

When you're trying to count paces, follow a straight line and simultaneously keep someone else in view, two things happen. You fall down a lot, curse a lot, and ignore stings, scratches and even small bushes. By the time we'd done a morning's work and one part of the photocopied map was starting to look like a spider's web, we were hot, thirsty, hungry and bleeding.

"Can't we just go back and play cards?" asked Alex plaintively as he bathed his shredded leg with our precious drinking water.

"Yeah, okay," said Tom. "But we'll need to come back here

tomorrow rather than just carry on, and we might not get it finished."

Alex was about to say something but thought better of it. We carried on.

Another few hours of doing the same thing and even Tom was starting to get fractious, and finally, to our relief, called a halt.

"We know where we are now," he told us. And for once, we all actually did. When you watch your progress on a map you *really* know where you are, and we could all see, not just that we'd actually covered a good amount of ground, but there was a reasonable looking way back to our lake.

"Just as well the gang didn't find this," said Joe as we followed a quite level straightish line through woodland – woodland rather than scrub – which the map said should lead to just below our camp. Much to our surprise, pleasure and relief, it did. We crossed the stream, followed it for a few hundred metres and found the tents.

"Swim!" announced Tom.

"Fire!" said Steve. And for once there was enough wood, he uncovered the earth banking, blew on the exposed bits and smoke appeared, then flame, which he fed, then came and joined us wallowing and washing in the water.

We'd all remembered to bring our swim things, but were so keen to get the refreshing water to our lacerated skin that we just stripped off to underwear and dived in, just as most of us had done from the start. We were used to doing it that way by now.

Feeling better, we were drying off in the hot sun, still dressed in very little and holding mugs of tea, when there was a bark. Lars rushed up to Arif and nearly got scalded, then came to greet the rest of us.

"What the...?" said Arif when he'd recovered.

"This doesn't mean that Nils is in trouble again, does it?" asked Steve. "Or your Grandad, Arif?"

"No, it does not, but if I'd known it was so far and so steep I would not have come," said a voice, which turned out to be a very out-of-breath and hot looking Daneesh. "That dog is a wonder, but he's younger than me and stronger. How I can make the return journey, I don't know. And why are you all naked?"

"We're not, Grandad," said Arif reproachfully. I suddenly realised that I was, nearly, and felt uncomfortable, even if the old man wasn't serious.

"Would you like a tea?" asked Steve hospitably.

"Ah, one of you is a gentleman: yes please, I think it might just save an old man's life."

Despite his partial lack of clothes, Steve went to the fire, brought the kettle to the boil and brewed a mug of tea. He had to wash his own mug up first, though, as we had only one each. Daneesh sipped it, muttered about its temperature, and held it.

"Nils is going to start cooking," he told us. "Knowing you were late last night I said that I would come and fetch you so that you weren't late tonight."

"Grandad, we have food, and we know how to cook..." started Arif.

"One of us does, anyway," Steve muttered.

Daneesh heard him and smiled. "Nils wanted to do something for you, something he is able to do, to thank you for being kind to him. I said that you would probably prefer to be independent but he insisted."

"Is he doing a curry?" I said incautiously.

"Too hot for you, was it? You will get used to it. But no, he is doing something, a Dutch recipe, that he used to do a lot. But he'd like it if you could come down soon. With me when I've recovered. And with something on."

We all had to laugh at him. After the initial shock I'd ceased to be worried. After all, it was only as if we'd been in swimming shorts. More or less.

We were more or less dry, so just hauled on shorts and shirts of various sorts. By the time we were shod the tea was finished and Steve had allowed us to leave the mugs dirty, but hung up. We started down toward the cottage. It was useful having to go at Daneesh's speed; we were all still tired from the day's efforts.

As we neared the cottage we heard voices. And one was female. Arif, nearest to the door, leapt forward and opened it, and there, chatting happily to Nils, was Amy. Hardly to our surprise, though it might have been to hers, he crossed the kitchen in very few strides and hugged her, then looked embarrassed. They separated. We just smiled, as did Nils and Daneesh.

Amy looked at him, somehow glowing. He just looked back at her.

"I… I'm not coming every night," she said. "But your Grandad persuaded me tonight."

Arif seemed tongue tied, but he was still looking at her.

"Arif!" said Daneesh, sharply. "She's not a film for you to watch, she's human and you are embarrassing her."

Arif shook himself. "I'm just so surprised to see her… to see you."

"Blame your Grandad, as I say."

"Come on, you two," pleaded Alex, "we're all hungry."

Nils was in good form, his recipe was wonderful and Steve was glad not to have to cook. Once done, Tom volunteered to wash up – in fact he volunteered Alex and me to dry as well, and it gave Arif and Amy some time to chat.

Once they had left to catch their bus and we'd said our good nights to Nils and Lars, we walked slowly back up through the estate. I noticed that Arif was very quiet. Once back at the camp he vanished with his mobile, then returned, looking unhappy.

"Problem?" I asked him.

"Battery gave out," he said tersely. "Forgot to charge it last weekend."

"Borrow mine if you like."

"Thanks. But I managed to say good night. And she's coming after work tomorrow."

I digested that.

"Up here?"

"No, to Nils'. Seems she likes him a lot."

"Nothing to do with you, then."

He had to cheer up at that. When we were flame watching as usual he seemed to be his normal self.

22   New owner

The next two days followed the same pattern. Breakfast, packed lunch construction, a walk to the next area of the estate boundary to survey. Packed lunch. More surveying. A weary return to camp. A swim with soap options. Tea. Walk down to Nils, talk, eat, talk, go.

It got to Friday. We'd decided to have a half day at our surveying, partly because our scratches were getting uncomfortable and partly because we'd nearly had enough. Steve and Tom said they wanted to start adding what we'd discovered to a master map, something to be done at home, in peace. Arif had Amy on his mind and the rest of us wanted some creature comforts.

We returned to the camp at about lunch time and decided on a quick swim and wash. It was during this that a splash interrupted us and we discovered Lars was cooling off in the water as well. Not only that, but a female voice called out: "So this is what you get up to!"

Shocked, we did an about turn; not easy in water without going under. It was Amy, as we'd guessed. Arif was already swimming towards her and I wondered if he'd remember he was, let's say, only technically decent. He must have been fond of her, because he just marched out of the water and was about to give her the sort of hug we'd seen at the cottage the previous Monday, but she backed away, smiling.

"You might get dry first," she laughed.

Arif suddenly realised his state of undress, I suppose, because he made a rush for the tent. Amy looked at the rest of us, still grinning widely. "Are you wearing anything? Should I go?"

"We are," Tom called back, "but I think we'd like a bit of privacy whilst we dry and get dressed."

She laughed again and vanished back down the path. We emerged cautiously and called to Arif: "Ok, she's out of sight." He came out of the tent, towel round his waist, and looked round.

"I forgot I was just in underwear... Damn."

We all followed the usual routine of getting dry, but this time changed into dry stuff as it didn't seem right to lie in the sun and dry off as usual. Once he was officially decent, Arif ran off to find Amy, reappearing with her far too soon, before the rest of us were properly dressed.

Her being there certainly hurried us up, though.

"She was only just down the path," said Arif, almost accusingly. "I'm sure you weren't watching behind the bushes, were you?"

"Me? Good heavens no!" But she gave a sort of grin that made me wonder.

Steve started a fire and was so flustered that he forgot to bully us into fuel collection. He put the kettle on, and Amy immediately asked him if he had enough wood.

"Don't encourage him," pleaded Arif, "he's been nagging us ever since we got here: 'I need more wood!' It's like living with a parrot."

"I need more wood!" obliged Steve.

"I'll get some," she volunteered. We all groaned. "Come on, Arif."

Once they had gone, Alex made the obvious sign of someone being under the thumb. "Already!" he said. "Poor Arif."

But they were efficient, and quick, and Steve was pleased. "Enough for next Monday too," he said.

We sat round with the tea.

"I suppose Lars showed you the way?" asked Arif.

"Yes. He's a clever dog, isn't he?"

"You don't know the half of it," he answered her.

"There's a reason I came up," she started. "Something's happened. Marcus Yardley has brought a man up to see Nils. He's from Australia and he has a pile of papers from Nils' father. He says their family has been given the estate in a will."

Mutterings of surprise all round. "Nils' father? That's going back a bit. Is he legit.?" asked Alex.

"Seems so. It's not Nils' father who's come…"

"Well obviously!"

She raised her eyebrows at Alex. "He's talked to Stephensons, he says. That's your father's solicitors, isn't it?"

He nodded. "If Dad says it's legit., then it is."

"He and Marcus are explaining it to Nils now, and the first thing Nils asked was that I come and get all you down so you can hear too. He says it's only fair."

I didn't know why. It was his business, after all, but it was nice of him to include us. Made me feel important.

"What else has he said?" Tom asked.

"Nothing when I was there. I came up here – Lars did and I followed – straight away."

"We'd better get down there," said Tom. "Someone else to be on Nils' side."

We gathered up our dirty kit, a lot less perishable food than the previous Friday, and set off. I was walking in front of Amy, who had Arif behind her.

"You look good in just your undies," she said quietly, thinking, I suppose, that I wouldn't hear. I grinned to myself.

We arrived at the cottage and went in with the usual perfunctory knock. The room seemed already busy. A dazed looking Nils was sitting, his foot supported on a box. Marcus Yardley was there with a strange man; bronzed, wrinkled, and with long swept back fair hair. He seemed about the same age as Nils. Conversation halted as we appeared.

"Er… sorry…" Tom faltered. "Er…"

"Come in, come in. You are no strangers here. And you need to hear what has been said to see what you think too… I have no more chairs, but…well…" Nils tailed off.

Marcus smiled at us, looking rather perplexed. "Nils was anxious you should be here. So probably best if I go over what we've learnt again. Nils has had a lot to take in. Repeating it will help us all understand things."

He paused and looked around, making sure we were listening. But before he could start again the stranger spoke.

"Excuse me…" The accent was definitely Australian. "…but are you the guys who were in the newspaper? Who got that child molester ring put inside?"

We looked at each other, rather uncomfortable again. But Tom just said: "Yes, we are."

The man grinned. "Then it's you I have to thank for getting Upperden in the press so it rang a bell with me and got me off my butt to do something about it. I'll start the ball rolling this time, Marcus.

"You see, years ago my Dad got a packet of papers from Britain, but he was very ill at the time and did nothing about them. When he died, a couple of years later, I got all his stuff but there was so much all I did was have a quick look and stow it all in the attic to look at later.

"Later never happened. You know how it is. I forgot about it all most of the time. That was about twenty years back.

"Then a couple of weeks ago there was this report in the national press about a group of young Brits who had stuck to their guns and got a load of perverts stuck in jail where they belonged. I read it, and the name of Upperden meant something to me, but I didn't know what. It bugged me, so at last I figured it might be something to do with those old papers I'd stuck in the attic. I dug them out, looked, and there it was. And the more I looked, the more gobsmacked I got.

"It was a bunch of stuff from a guy called Gillespie in a place called Upperden Manor. Here. And Gillespie is my name too. Seems he was about to peg it, didn't have any money, his stepson didn't have any money as he was in Europe where there had been some sort of personal tragedy. He hoped his relative – my Dad – would take over the estate. He even sent a copy of the will and the deeds to the place, telling my Dad where to ask for the originals."

It sounded to me like a fairy story. But Marcus took up the tale.

"Mr Gillespie came to stay at the hotel and mentioned it to me, and I was as surprised as you all look. Now, you'll know I have an interest in the estate – that is, Nils and his supply of truffles. So I took some time off and we visited the firm of solicitors that the papers mentioned."

He laughed. "I'd never been in there before, and it was like going into something out of a Dickens novel. Very courteously they asked us to wait, spent ages in another room, then came back and told me it was in their archives and they could get them out next week.

"That was the wrong thing to say to Mr Gillespie here..." Marcus grinned wryly. "He's something of a businessman and doesn't take to delaying tactics like that too well. I've not seen a partner in a law firm squirm so much, ever, with what he said. Before long he had vanished into their store. He came back, covered in dust, with a box of papers and told us there was a shelf full still to bring up.

"We told him to look after them safely as we'd be back, took the file he'd given us, and went to see a rather better firm of solicitors called Stephenson's – I think that's your family firm, Alex."

Alex nodded.

"Now I'll start at the other end of the story. It all came out when Stephensons had gone through it – and it must be said that they were as quick as the other lot were slow.

"Over a century ago there was a family called Gillespie who lived in the big house here, Upperden Manor. The two sons had a big falling out over a girl, though it sounded as if they hadn't liked each other much to start with. The younger son was engaged to the girl, but the elder son…well, let's just say he took advantage of her. In a major way."

We were all used to adult-speak for rape, so understood perfectly.

"The father insisted that it be hushed up to guard the family honour, but the younger son understandably wouldn't accept that. So after having a full-on fight with his brother that apparently left the brother badly injured, he and his fiancée eloped to Australia where they got married. Oh, thank you so much."

This last comment had nothing to do with the story. Amy had handed him a mug of tea.

"They settled down in Australia and had a son and a daughter. The son got married eventually and they had a son of their own, and he's this Mr Bill Gillespie who you see in front of you."

We all muttered something. Or it could have been a collective sharp intake of breath.

"The family had worked hard and owned several farms…"

"Sheep stations."

"Sheep stations, and on one of them they found oil. So old Mr Gillespie became very wealthy, almost overnight. News of the find got out to Britain where the son of the elder brother, the brother who had started the split, heard about it. He had been an army officer in World War II and had married a Dutch girl at the end of the war. He had brought her and her young son back to Britain to live with him. She had died, but the son still lived there."

He bowed to Nils, who nodded. I was making connections and was starting to see where all this might be leading, as were the others.

"Eventually, because of the vast expense of repairs of the

house in Britain, some unlucky investments that went bad there in the 1930's crash, the money was starting to run out, but despite his wife's death he still carried on with the estate, somehow.

"By this time Nils had met a Dutch girl who was on holiday in Britain. He visited her in Holland, stayed there and married her. They had a daughter and all was well until…"

"Until a mad, bad driver crashed into the car when Anja was collecting my lovely daughter from school and killed them both." After all these years Nils' emotions were still raw.

Marcus continued. "Nils' stepfather had become ill by this time, and just after this tragedy he died. So in the course of a year Nils had lost his whole family.

"He'd heard about it too late to be there, but returned as soon as he could, not just because of his father's death but because he wanted to escape the bad memories in Holland."

"I found here a little cottage that would be enough for me," said Nils, "and here I stay."

"Seems he's been living here alone ever since," Bill resumed the story. "Amazingly he's still got none of the basics you take for granted, like running water and electricity. But his step-father had promised him that he would have a home if he ever returned to Britain. That was before the money ran out."

Silence. There was a lot to take in. Lars scratched himself.

"And now I have to decide what to do." Bill Gillespie had taken over the story again. "Seems that the old solicitor has accepted that the papers I have are genuine and I am who I say I am. And Stephensons have too. So it looks as if I've had a bit of old England dumped on me."

He grinned round at us as he said it.

"So the family lands have come back into the family – not that the family really left, anyway. Not with Nils living here. And in my book that's no bad thing. Comes as a bit of a shock, that's all."

"It is a shock to me as well," said Nils.

"Yeah, well… whatever happens you'll have your home here. No sweat. Blimey, you're the one who's looked after the estate and know it and… well, it's your home. And you'll have electricity and running water and warmth and – well, all the things you'd expect in this century."

"May I interrupt?" asked Alex. I could tell by the tone that he was in trainee solicitor mode. "How is it that Nils' father didn't just give it all to Nils?"

"I didn't want it," said Nils bluntly. "Dad – my stepfather – wrote when he knew he would die, but I was in no mood to agree to anything. My own family, my beautiful wife and my only daughter, had been killed the month before and I was numb. It wasn't until afterwards, when I realised that grieving, with no job, was making me weak and ill, and I had to return to the only other place I knew. Here. When I was a boy I had discovered there were truffles here. At the time nobody wanted them, they had no value, but now I knew that things were different. I was right, and they have given me a living and a reason to get out of bed."

Bill Gillespie continued: "And then he goes and busts his ankle, and starts talking to people, especially the ones who saved his life. You people. And, I guess, the papers. So the news gets to me.

"Now, I can't just leave the big house here to carry on with its rotting. It needs a roof and some guts, and people looking after it, and a way of paying for itself. I've got kids and grandkids in Oz, and I have no idea what they'll all think about it. But at least they can come over and have a look. Who knows – we might all uproot and move to England. I'm getting old, and probably could do with an easier climate. In the British summer, anyway.

"And my grandkids – well, they'd love being in the estate. It's a sort of English version of the outback, but safer. When school's out they run wild in the outback at home anyway, though we don't let them go too far. Sounds like you people might be on the same wavelength."

I wondered what the reaction would be to having to share the estate with a load of other kids, no matter how wild they might be.

There was a natural break at this point. We remembered that we needed to cook for Nils. Steve asked him what he'd like but Marcus interrupted.

"All you need do is to put a pot in the oven – it's still in the car. Whilst it heats, the vegetables can boil. There's enough there for everyone."

The pot was big, and smart, and when the top was removed the contents smelt wonderful and made us all hungry. We'd only had a snack at some time in the morning, so were famished. As usual.

Whilst it was cooking we chatted idly and made sure we understood everything as fully as we could. Alex was scornful of the solicitors who had seemingly ignored the estate for so long, and Bill was scathing about them.

"The only thing they did do was sell the houses down there to cover the death duties. They managed that, and no doubt ran all the way to the bank with the commission off that lot."

Death duties? Did it cost you money to die? Bloody hell.

When we'd eaten our fill Joe and I washed up and listened over our shoulders to the conversation.

"What are you going to do now?" was the burning question from Nils.

"Early days," Bill Gillespie said. "But firstly, you need something a bit more comfortable. I can't get water and electricity here like yesterday..."

"The water is good. I need no piped water that has been infected with chemicals."

"Yeah... but you *do* need a pump so you don't have to wind it up. Our boys on the station are used to living rough, but they'd tell me where to go if they didn't have water in a tap. Trust me."

"But a pump you have to switch on. And pipes..."

"No. A clean plastic pipe that doesn't taint the water. A pump that only starts when you turn the tap on. Easy. We do it all the time."

"Well..."

"Good. We can get on with that. But until you've recovered fully we need to do something that will give you fuel to cook with. And that's not so easy."

Bill thought for a bit. The rest of us were just listening, apart from Arif who butted in.

"I can get wood for him when I come and take Lars out. So can my Grandad."

"You and your Grandad are being ace," said Bill. "You all are. But whether he realises it or not Nils deserves even better, like gas powered warmth and cooking. And in the winter, when he can't move around as well as usual, he'll need instant warmth in this cottage."

"I can manage," Nils protested.

"Next year, yes. But you won't be so mobile this autumn. And don't forget that Arif and his friends have to return to school soon. This will be a busy year for them if it's anything like Oz. It's the year before they take some pretty full-on exams and they'll have a lot on their plates."

Silence from us. The reminder of the sentence of school, after so much real freedom, was a blow to our spirits. And Bill wasn't the first to mention GCSEs. It had been drummed into us during that boring last week of term.

"Well, I'll still be coming over," said Arif at last. "And I can study as well here as anywhere else. Better, probably. If that's all right with Nils."

"You have a girlfriend now. She will want to see you."

"I can come as well," said Amy simply. "I'd like that."

"And I like the idea of you being here, Nils," said Bill. "And by the way, Nils and I are related, so I'm Bill, not anything else. And it's good to know I'm related to someone as independent as you."

"Danke… thank you. But I have Daneesh who helps me too, and I can manage."

"Sheesh!" said Bill, "who's Daneesh?"

We all explained, and he looked totally confused.

"So how does he come into the equation? One person only, please!"

"He's my Grandad," said Arif quietly. "He grew to love Lars…"

"Lars is the dog, right?"

"Yes. Then he came to meet Lars' owner, and they got to like each other."

"So this Daneesh, he's about the same age as Nils and me?"

"Yes, I think so."

"Then he needs warmth as well! And if he's cooking he needs better than a wood stove that you have to get fuel for before you even start."

Steve grinned faintly.

"Look… how long will it take to get LPG installed here? Deliveries can get up here, yes? And can this stove be converted? And surely there's electricity to the settlement down there? They can run that up here, no problem. And the water? That's a piece of… that's very easy. Nils, I'll come back tomorrow and bring someone with me and we can get this place made easier and warmer for you pronto. Right?"

By that time, Nils was looking shell-shocked, and just nodded.

"But who will pay for all this?" he asked faintly.

"The owner of the estate. He's going to honour a promise made bloody ages ago by a relative he never met."

23   Incident

Bill, Nils and Daneesh must have had a lot to talk about the next day. Arif texted us all that evening and we met up at his house, with Amy of course, and a curry (but not as vicious a curry as Daneesh had made for Nils, I'm glad to say).

While Daneesh was explaining all that had gone on we listened open mouthed to the immediate plans that Bill had made. Nils still wasn't sure that he wanted all the conveniences, but Daneesh – and Bill – had talked him round, so that eventually he agreed and started to sound almost excited. Bill had told him he'd get things started as soon as he could, and for him, that meant immediately.

We had each been told at home that we had the next week to ourselves, and then our families, without exception, wanted us back home to sort out uniforms and other boring things about the start of the new school year. We had all groaned when we'd heard, but knew it was inevitable. Term started in the middle of the week after that, after the teachers' training days.

"Though if they don't know what they're about by now," said Tom, "God help us."

"Some of them don't," Alex offered. "And we know who they are."

"So are we going to try and finish off the surveying, next week, then?" asked Tom.

Secretly I'd rather have spent some time at home, but nodded when all the others did.

"Does Bill know you're doing this?" asked Arif's mother.

"No," Tom admitted. "It just seemed that it'd be an interesting thing to do. We already know the estate better than anyone else, so it's just putting it down on paper."

Steve looked at him.

"Well, when I say 'just'… It's a bit more difficult than that. But that's what we decided to do."

"Bill has talked to his wife and their children and families," said Daneesh, changing the subject. "They're looking forward to visiting, but not until October, probably. It's school holidays then."

"Do they know what he's planning?" asked Joe.

"Apart from Nils' cottage I don't think he's made any

definite plans for anything else. He means to put the big house into order and use it, but apart from that, nothing."

"So this might have been the only year we could have camped there," Arif said. "By next year he might have built houses on it, or something.

That shocked even me. Surely that wouldn't be allowed?

"He would not do that, I believe" said Daneesh. "He is a man of honour. That would not fit well with his beliefs."

I didn't know what he meant by that, but sometimes Daneesh could be difficult to understand.

"Talking about houses," Alex started, "what about the houses in the hamlet? What's going to happen to them?"

"They are not owned by him," said Daneesh. "Why should he do anything about them?"

"According to my Dad the houses were sold, but not the land. So there should have been ground rent collected on them."

I remembered this being talked about before, to one of the owners, and they went very quiet.

"We must talk to Bill," said Tom.

"I'd like to see them taken down a peg or two," Alex commented. He remembered people who had looked down their noses at him, as some adults to an unwelcome child.

We arranged to go shopping yet again the next Monday morning and travel to the estate as soon as we could. "Half a day is better than nothing," said Tom, meaning the surveying. That gave us Sunday to be free at home and oversee – or in my case to do for myself – some washing. I was told that I was needed back the following Sunday night at the latest. It seemed that we were all given the same deadline.

In fact when we finally struggled from the bus stop to Nils' cottage it was to find Bill outside, with Nils on crutches, looking at the adjoining outbuildings. Bill welcomed us with a "G'day" and got us all grinning. It was like watching one of the Australian soaps.

"Nice neighbours Nils has got!" he said with a grin. "They seemed to want me off the premises as soon as possible. I had to tell them I was the landowner and would be looking at the legal situation in the coming weeks. That shut them up."

"Have you asked about payment of the ground rents over the last…er… well, however many years?" Alex asked.

"Er… no. But the houses are with the estate, surely?"

"Don't think so," Alex started.

"They were sold to pay for death duties," said Nils sadly. "I was told they were when I, too, had just moved back and asked what my business was."

"I need to find out," said Bill. "Thank you both."

"My Dad can help on that," said Alex.

"Very efficient, your Dad. I'll be talking to him. You're going back to the camp, are you? I might come and visit, if you don't mind."

"We'd need to come and get you, or Lars could bring you up," said Arif. "You'd never find it otherwise."

Bill laughed. "I can find my way round the outback, more or less. I should be able to find my way round a few hectares of Britain."

Nils broke in. "No, you need the dog. Or a guide. Not even I know where the camp is."

"Isn't there a path?"

"Nope. One of us can stay here and guide you up," Tom said with a laugh. "See if you can find it or not."

"Deal!" said Bill.

"Bill has arranged for someone to come and see if my stove can be changed to gas," said Nils. "The bottles are going into one of these buildings. But they need new roofs first."

"Start of the repairs," said Bill happily. "Then we get some good big electricity mains up here and put a transformer into another of the buildings. That'll feed the big house too, when it's ready."

"I am pleading with him to bury the cables, not put pylons up," Nils said.

A van appeared on the track from the hamlet. From it climbed a man with a clipboard and, to our surprise, Daneesh. Clipboard man was to look at the stove, Daneesh was there to keep Nils company. Arif hung around to wait for Bill and the rest of us went to the camp to start cooking lunch.

"I need more wood!" The cry of the lesser-spotted Scout rang out its usual complaint. But this time we were ready for him.

"You said on Friday that Amy and Arif had collected enough wood for today!" Joe responded. "Look at that lot."

'That lot' was a large woodpile that Steve had stashed under some nearby bushes. He shut up. It didn't stop him from detailing me to help cook, though.

We were in full eating mode when there was a shout of "Where's ours?" from the edge of our clearing.

"There's plenty in the pot – it's boiled tapeworm again."

The first time Steve had done tagliatelle we'd enjoyed it, so this was a repeat performance. He had – as usual – miscalculated his quantities, and this time there was plenty for Arif – and for Bill. Arif had asked if he was hungry on the way up and had obviously not bothered to check that there would be enough. This time he was lucky. Otherwise they'd have gone hungry as Steve wasn't the same sort of flexible cook as Joe's mum who had conjured up extra quantities on demand seemingly without effort.

"And could you have found your way up here alone?" asked Tom when Bill had a mouthful.

He shook his head, swallowed and said "No bloody chance. The outback's mainly flat. It's confusing, 'cos the bush all looks the same. But here it's confusing 'cos it goes up and down like a switchback and all the bushes are different."

"You'll learn," Tom told him. "We had to. And we had to find our way here the first time."

"Good on ya for that."

"Blame The Scout. He knows what he's doing with a map and compass. It's just that he falls over a lot when he's using them."

"Crikey!" Bill said at Steve's expression. "If looks could kill!"

"Ah, said Tom, "that's known as The Look and using it stops people being hit. Usually."

Bill laughed. "So how well do you actually know the estate? Can you find your way round it?"

"Some of it," Steve admitted. "We're trying to map it, but we're running out of time."

"*Mapping* it? Bloody hell. Can I see?"

"We've only got our draft. The good one's at home."

That was news to me too. I'd not seen the main one. Steve went to fetch our working copy. Bill looked at it, studying it.

"This scale – is it accurate?"

"It's taken from the Ordnance Survey and scaled up with the map," Steve said (rather smugly, I thought).

Bill looked at it some more, then put it down.

"And this is just the draft?"

"Yep."

"Strewth. If you can sell me a copy it'll save me a hell of a lot of time – and money."

Sell? It never occurred to me it would be actually worth money. I mean – we were still at school. It was hardly going to be the height of accuracy, despite our best efforts.

"Well… We're carrying on this week," Tom told him. "There's more we want to try and do. If that's all right with you."

"All right? I'll say it's bloody all right! Stay here as long as you want."

"We can't," I told him. "School starts the week after next."

"School… Blimey, of course. Despite what was said last week I hadn't connected you lot with having to go to school. Yeah… well…"

He paused again and looked round, not just at us but at the table and the washing up arrangements, the fire, the tents, the woodpile – which was by then so low I expected The Scout to emit its call again – and then back to us.

"We do a lot of camping back home," Bill continued. "But I think you could teach us a thing or two. Can my grandkids come up and join you when they get a holiday? October some time?"

I think we were all about to say something, but Tom, the realist, took the lead.

"Depends on the weather. October's getting close to winter."

"Ah yes… I'm forgetting. It's spring in Australia."

"Best if we meet them first," said Joe.

"Yes." Tom sounded more upbeat. "But we can certainly show them the camp."

"They'd like that. Soon as you like. But the map – can I get a copy of the complete thing?"

'Get' sounded more like it. "Yeah… no problem," said Tom, speaking for us all as usual. "As soon as we've got everything we manage to do this week on to it. But…."

He faltered, and I could almost hear the cogs turning.

"Go on! I did say I'd pay you for it!"

"It's not that. But…well…what are you going to do to this part of it?"

"What, the map?"

"No, the estate. I mean… what's going to happen to our campsite?"

Bill looked at him for some time, then at the rest of us, a grin slowly spreading across his face.

"Well… I thought maybe a big estate of little town houses, with a good, wide road down past the big house…"

We started to grin at him. He laughed.

"It'll be left alone. Most of the estate will be left alone. We'll have to carve out some garden for the big house, but this will be left for you – and my grandkids if you like them – to come to at any time. And the only way in will be through the hamlet, so it'll still be untouched. That way we can encourage wildlife to stay – if there is any."

We assured him there was, and told him about the deer. He seemed impressed.

"I'll tell you something else too; anywhere we find truffles will be left, so Nils, and you, and I, can take a dog and go and find them and have a little side line. We owe that to Marcus, too."

I think we all said versions of "Wow," but quietly.

"If it hadn't been for you lot doing what you did, I'd still be in Oz playing with sheep and oil, if you see what I mean. So I owe you big time. Anyway, I'd better let you carry on with your mapping, and don't forget to sell me a copy when it's done. Thanks for the tucker, and I'll bump into you soon, deffo."

He got up, then looked at the lake again with its waterfall.

"Good for swimming?" he asked. "No nasties in the water?"

"It's great," Joe assured him. "Cold, but great."

"So if I come up here – if I can find the way – and hear you lot splashing about I'd better be careful in case you're skinny dipping."

We looked at each other.

"We don't," said Tom.

"Yeah? Well, my grandkids do, just as my kids did. You should try it. Perfect place for it, here. Anyway, I'll be careful, just in case. Don't want to embarrass you! G'day now. Oh… can someone be a guide for me again, please?"

"I'll go," I said. I was getting used to it by now and found my way back up to the camp quite quickly, having avoided the washing up and tidying – and the wood collection.

"Just in time," said Tom when I returned. "Let's go mapping."

That Monday afternoon, starting late, proved not to be very productive. We had by then gone almost all round the wall; the only part we hadn't done was nearest to the hamlet. Not only was that a long distance to travel before we started, we wanted to be as quiet and unseen about it as possible. Even if we now had the landowner formally on our side another encounter with some of the unpleasant people living there seemed inevitable.

"How about the stream, going upwards?" I asked suddenly. "Do we know that the waterfall is the only supply to the pool?"

It seemed I was the first to ask that question. Steve looked at the official map – not the one we were compiling. It showed nothing else. He said so.

"Okay," I said, "but the water coming out the other end looks more than just what's coming down the cliff."

They looked at me, then all around. I led – yes, me! – up past the fall. We used the same path we'd come in on when we'd entered the camp from the road having climbed the estate wall. The big area of blackthorn bushes was carefully avoided because of its memories.

At the end of the pool the path veered away. Between it and the water was a small beak of flat land ringed by ferns. And in the middle of that was another small stream quietly flowing towards the camp. We tasted it. It was freezing.

"Well done, Matt," said Tom. "That's part of our temperature control. Block that off and swimming might be warmer."

I was pleased, and started following it through the arching ferns. The ground became soft, and I paused, trying to separate the plants so I could see. A few more steps and one foot sank to the ankle. Hastily I pulled, and with a sucking, gurgling noise it came free, causing me to lose my balance and fall on my back in the mud.

My colleagues were most concerned. When the laughter had subsided and they had all ignored my colourful language in their direction, Steve cautiously attacked the area from a little further on. He found solid ground, though there were reeds growing there. Eventually they discovered that the water actually bubbled up in a stony area, overflowed on to the swampy bit, then created the slightly less soft ground before becoming a very short feeder stream.

"Another spring," said Steve triumphantly. "We'll call it Matt's. Matt's spring."

I was pleased. Uncomfortable, but pleased.

"Call it Mattress," suggested Alex. "He was the first to lie on it."

I actually succeeded in causing him to fall in the mud, causing even more mirth.

"Where does it come from?" asked Tom when he had recovered.

"Upwards," Alex muttered, looking dangerously at me.

"Yes, but where from?"

"Well, it can't be from the path," said Arif, moving between Alex and me. "So logically it must seep down from the top of the cliff, but underground."

"So how do we find out?"I asked, keeping out of Alex's way.

"We don't," said Tom. "You need special equipment to do that so we'll leave it to the experts who are paid to get wet. Come on, let's carry on up the path and see what else we've missed. And you two… if you fart about by these bushes you'll get damaged, like the last two guys who fell into them discovered."

That rather shut us both up.

The rest of the afternoon found nothing untoward apart from another path we had missed which led away from our original unofficial route in. It wasn't actually a human-size path, having probably been made by deer, but we followed it – and for mapping purposes did our best with its constant changes of direction. It led us up to the end of the estate opposite the hamlet, and we soon discovered the stream entering through the broken wall that we'd seen before.

"I suppose this isn't the stream that goes through the thorny bits near us, and seeps up into that marshy bit?" Steve asked.

"We've mapped this wall, so we could follow it back down again."

"Doesn't it just run parallel to the path?" asked Alex.

"Didn't see it as we came up. Did you?"

He shook his head.

"Should we investigate?" I asked.

Tom thought. "How about you, Alex and Steve follow it down and try and map that? Arif, Joe and I will go one way or the other... er... probably back to the south wall where it's rough country. We've not done much apart from map the direction of the wall."

It seemed a good plan. Increasingly, as we became more used to the surveying, some of us were starting to feel rather like spare parts, so having a proper job to do was attractive. Agreeing to make contact by phone if necessary, we parted.

We walked by the side of the little stream, doing our best with its changes of direction as we had with the path earlier. It was quite small, and there were patches where it all but vanished into a runnel covered by reeds or ferns. I was trying to note on the map where these were whilst still marking the course of the water.

My feet seemed to be easier to push forward and I realised I was going downhill. Then I seemed to be going downhill fast. Simultaneously there was a shout and I hurriedly looked up. Too late, the ground was approaching, fast, and just as it and I were due to make contact I had a vision of a large, sharp looking rock at a hand's distance from my nose. It and I met, I had a searing pain to the head, there was a roaring in my ears, and everything went black

24   Hospital 4

I read a book once, where the subject returns from unconsciousness and thinks he has a man with a little hammer hitting his forehead – from the inside. That's how I felt, and it hurt. I shut my eyes, an odd sensation when you then discover they're already shut.

"He's awake."

I knew the voice. I know I did. But it was loud, and hurt. And I couldn't put a name to it. I tried to open my eyes this time, and it felt as if I was looking straight into one of the school theatre's spotlights, and hurt. I shut them again.

"Where am I? What's happened?" My voice seemed not to be mine either. It was weak and oddly croaky.

"In hospital. You had a crack to your head."

A name resolved itself. Alex. But why hospital?

"Am I all right?"

"Seems so. Do you remember what happened?"

That was wrong. "I asked you that."

He laughed, and it sounded like the old Alex, not the rather worried-voiced one who had answered my first question.

"You tripped, fell, and your head hit a rock. If it had been a centimetre lower it'd have hit your eye." Now the scared voice was back again.

I did a sort of examination of what felt right and what wrong. Head... well, it hurt. Arms... okay, legs... pain in my right knee and thigh but nothing major. I wriggled a bit, and everything else felt normal, except that it made my head ache worse. I stopped doing it.

"What are you doing?"

"Seeing if anything else was hurt."

"Are you going to open your eyes?"

"Tried that. Hurts."

"Hang on..."

It went quiet. I tried opening them again, but it was still piercingly bright. No good.

I was woken again by voices. One was Alex and one a stranger.

"Hallo Matt," said the stranger. "Alex says you're awake."

"Who are you?" I mumbled, still croakily.

"I'm Linda, and I'm a nurse. Can you open your eyes?"

"Too bright."

"That's what I said," said Alex indignantly.

"Just a minute, I'll turn off the bed light."

Of course. Bed. That was why movement felt strange. I hadn't connected the two. My eyelids let in a bit less light. Cautiously I partly opened my eyes. It was still very bright, and I half closed them again, but gradually I got used to it. Some of the searing brightness that hurt so much grew less.

"You gave us a scare," said Nurse Linda.

"Bloody hell, did he." I heard Alex mutter.

I smiled.

"How did I get here?"

"Helicopter." Alex, joking as usual.

"Ha ha," I said painfully.

"Yes, really. Helicopter. We phoned and told them where we were, someone at the hospital remembered the others who had to be air-lifted out of the estate and decided a helicopter was the best way."

"But I never got to see it…"

"I did," said Alex triumphantly. "Best thing that's ever happened to me."

"They took you too?"

He paused a moment, then sounded embarrassed.

"I wasn't going to let you go on your own, was I? Who knows what might have happened?"

This from the guy who wanted to push me back in the mud earlier that day. That day? Was it?

"How long have I been here?" I asked.

"About six hours."

"What time is it?"

"It's about midnight."

"*Midnight*? But how come you're still here?"

Another pause.

"We're all Suspects, remember?"

There was a slight commotion by the door.

"Your parents are here too. They just went to get some coffee."

Oh God. It was a weekday and here were my parents losing their sleep. I felt them nearby.

"Hallo," I said, rather uncertainly.

Fortunately the kisses were careful. I discovered then that there was a bandage across my forehead.

There were all sorts of things said, but when they started saying things – in a humorous way – about not being able to be trusted, I closed my eyes again. Alex chimed in.

"We were all *being* careful," he said indignantly. "It's not easy, putting stuff on a map as you're trying to walk along. We've all been falling over things. He was just unlucky he was on a slope and there was this rock in the wrong place. Could have happened to any of us."

I left my eyes closed until I'd heard the answer. It seemed to be favourable, so I opened them again. Parents were smiling. Alex was looking serious.

"I think," nurse Linda broke in, "it'd be as well to let him sleep. We've been monitoring him, and he seems to be fine. All we need is to make sure there's no concussion so he needs to be in here for another night, then he can go home and take it easy. The skin graft…"

Skin graft? What the hell?

"What skin graft?" I interrupted.

She laughed. "Nothing to worry about. You took quite a bit of skin off your forehead, you know. So we had to take some skin off your thigh and replace it."

So that's why there was a pain in my thigh. Now I was more aware, I could feel a bandage round it. It felt rather high up…

"Oh," I said.

"The skin graft will need a day or two to heal and that's best done without putting strain on the thigh or the head. So… no exertion for two weeks, and no sport for a month. Then go gently for another month."

My mind raced. "When can I go back to the estate and join the others?"

"About October half term. You can't just come out of hospital and go and join them. You need to heal properly." This was Dad, talking in his no nonsense voice. My spirits fell.

"But I could go back in a couple of weeks," I protested faintly.

"You'll all be back at school by then." Mum this time. Damn. I'd forgotten school.

"So that's it," I said. "We'll never get the map done."

"There's October," said Alex. "And Bill's family will be

here by then, so if they're okay we can all go and camp. And take it in turns to go and survey or play cards in the tents."

I had to smile at that.

"Steve will have so many wood collectors..." I muttered. Alex laughed, then stifled a yawn. I was getting sleepy again too.

"You need your bed, Alex," Mum said. "You'll be good for nothing in the morning."

To my surprise, he nodded. "I'm sleeping at home tonight. I'll go back there in the morning."

"Do they know you're coming?"

"No. I'll wake them, though."

"You can come back with us rather than that. I don't think Matt will be using his bed tonight, and it's got clean sheets. We won't be up early in the morning, either."

They left shortly after, to my relief, having been assured by Linda that they would be told if I got worse.

They woke me at six-thirty the next morning! Six-thirty! Apart from the time we were trying to outwit the gang I had forgotten it existed. I did *not* want to be awake, kept drowsing, but someone would always return and offer me tea, a wash, a bedpan (me! A bedpan! I used it anyway. If they wanted me to use it, I would. It wasn't the same as using my own bush, though), and then breakfast. Oddly for me, I wasn't very hungry. My head still ached, but less than the previous day.

I was moved to a ward later. That wasn't much fun as everyone else seemed either asleep or very old or rambling. Or all three. It was that evening when boredom really set in. I discovered there's a limit to the amount of time you can sleep. I couldn't find my phone and I never remembered to ask for it when there was a nurse nearby. So there I lay. I sat up at one point and was told to lie still. For goodness sake...

Parents came in again after work. "Home tomorrow," said Mum. "Looks like I'll have my work cut out looking after you."

"I don't need looking after. I just need my phone and something to do."

"Your phone's here. We found it in your pocket."

"What pocket?"

"Shorts pocket."

"And my shorts?"

"Over there...oh."

I hadn't been out of bed. How could I have got to some shorts I hadn't been able to see? Grrr.

While they were there the nurse came and told me I could sit in the chair, but wanted to know where my dressing gown was. I was about to give a frustrated answer but Mum delved into a bag and gave me my own that she'd brought from home. With help, because I seemed to be as weak as a kitten, I struggled into it, thankfully since it cut down the number of people who could see I was only in underpants. Okay, that meant Parents and the nurse as the curtains had been hurriedly drawn round the bed. Some of the previous day's headache returned with the effort but eased off as I sat still in the chair. They opened the curtains again.

Also out of the bag she brought a book and one of the old electronic games I'd had when I was a kid. But I was just so glad for anything to do that my eyes must have lit up and the movement of my eyebrows hurt. Note to self: don't do that again for the time being.

They'd just gone again, promising to be in the next evening to take me home, when Tom arrived, with Alex. It was great to talk to them, and Alex seemed so stupidly happy to see me so much improved since he was last there.

"'Course, you realise Amy's using your sleeping bag now?" he said airily. "I've been chucked out into the other tent so I don't cramp Arif's style."

I was aghast. Even I had realised how much that sleeping bag needed a wash.

"You're joking!" I exclaimed.

"Yes."

"You…" And then I remembered I was in hospital.

Tom laughed out loud. "Your face just then. Even with a bandage on – you look like Paddington, by the way."

"Do I get as much money as he does?"

"Only if you appear on TV as you are."

"Yeahh…okay. If you do the same."

"So… are you actually okay?" Alex sounded anxious again.

"Think so. They say the brain will take a little time to settle down again. I had a brain scan whilst they did the operation…"

"Did they find one?" asked Alex.

"What operation?" Asked Tom. I put my tongue out at Alex and described what they'd done.

"It looked pretty unpleasant," Alex admitted. "We didn't know what to do, not even Steve, apart from check you over. But it was good to get a medic to you."

"Good to have a helicopter ride, too!" I said accusingly.

He looked a bit ashamed. "Once I knew you were okay, that there was no skull fracture, I could look out of the window. But it'd be nice to do it without having to worry about… about you."

He was looking decidedly embarrassed by now. I changed the subject. "Talking about hospitals, how's Nils?"

"Oh, okay, I think. Daneesh is still looking after him, and they get on really well still."

"I wondered if him being there so much might bore Nils."

"Doesn't seem to. And Bill's been visiting a lot too. He's getting electricity laid on soon… but you know that."

"They've not started, surely?"

"Not on that, but he's got a load of gas there now, and all they're waiting for is an engineer to alter his stove. Or get him a new one."

"Is he going to do away with the paraffin lamps when he gets electricity?" Somehow, the old pressure lamps that Nils was using seemed a part of the old man.

"Probably. Wouldn't you if you were told you could get light at the flick of a switch again after all these years?"

I nodded. Not a good idea because it started my head aching again. I could feel my eyes drooping, much to my annoyance.

"You okay, Matt?" Alex again.

I was about to nod, but remembered in time and said "Yes…" But it was no good. I was falling asleep on them. Oddly, though, I could still hear. Tom said something rude in an alarmed tone and I heard his chair scrape back and retreating footsteps. Alex grabbed my hand and pressed it so I gave his a squeeze back.

Then there was a gap before two sets of footsteps approached. A nurse said "Matt? Can you hear me?"

I slurred "Yes" to her.

"Are you tired?"

"Yes… sorry…"

"Okay. Get some sleep. They can come back tomorrow."

Then, talking to Tom and Alex: "He's just tired. The brain needs rest and his is telling him he's had enough for one day.

He'll feel better tomorrow but it'll take time…"

They had to help me to get back into bed. I must have been properly asleep in seconds.

When I woke it was because it was bloody 6.30 in the morning and *they* were waking me again. Grrr.

I did feel better, though. Despite all the checks, washes, breakfast, and using the game and reading the book, I was bored by midday. I phoned Mum.

"Am I going home today?"

"Yes, I've got the afternoon off. We'll be in at about 2.00. That's when they asked us to get there."

"Thank God. I'm bored out of my skull."

"You could have cracked your skull open."

"But I didn't."

"Hmm… I'm at work until 1.00 so I'll get there after that. Okay?"

"Okay. And… thanks."

"Love you."

She was as good as her word. They made her take me downstairs in a wheelchair! I ignored offers of help getting in the car and found it oddly difficult. My legs seemed to be disconnected, somehow. At home, getting up the stairs to my room had to be done stupidly slowly, and I just collapsed on to the bed and shut my eyes. At least the headache had gone.

The remainder of the week, and the weekend, found me feeling better each day and I was increasingly surprised how much a bump on the head and its treatment had taken out of me. All the Suspects visited on Saturday morning. I had come downstairs and was sitting reading, a thing unheard of for any of us on a Saturday in summer.

Tom came straight to the point. "We've done quite a bit more surveying, even without you, and we've come to the conclusion that there's no one better than you to do a neat job of transferring the notes on to the good map. What we've been doing is to transfer it to this one…" He unrolled a piece of A3 paper. "Then once we're happy with that it goes on the real one."

Even I was impressed with the work on that. I mean, the first one was good, but the start they'd made on the version for Bill was really smart. I looked carefully at both of them. Yes, I could do that okay.

I said so. "That's good," said Tom. "You see, yesterday was our last day there. Parents seem to have been talking to each other and want to get us kitted out for next week."

He stopped, slightly embarrassed. "I tried my school trousers on yesterday and there's a five centimetre gap at the bottom. I knew they were short, but not that bad."

"He's talking about the bottom of the leg," said Alex.

It took us all a few moments to latch on. Tom glared at us.

"We're all in for a shopping spree," said Joe, with the others muttering their agreement with suitable groans.

Once they'd left, I took a good look at the maps and the drafts done in the field. Here was something I could get my teeth into. By that time I was feeling almost back to normal, but got tired very early and was often in bed by 7.00 pm, from choice. Well, if not from choice then because my eyes refused to stay open.

On the dining room table I did some experimental lettering and drafting in, and found it oddly rewarding. I could almost see the sort of terrain they'd been in when transferring the information as they did the measurements. It may not have been as good as being there but maybe the best I could manage at the moment.

Until October.

I pushed the unpleasant thought from my mind and thought about mapping. Nobody had thought of a key to the drawing, so I started concocting one.

I actually got to walk outside that afternoon.

By the following Thursday the parents thought I was well enough to go shopping. Oddly my heart didn't sink; it was ages since I'd been out and about in the town. By then I felt nearly back to full strength, though I still needed to get to bed early. And I had an appointment with the doctor the following day.

Remembering what Tom had said about school trousers I tried mine on.

Blimey. Talk about skinny fit. Embarrassing fit, more like. We needed to go shopping. And school was due to start the following Wednesday.

The doctor had looked at my head and removed the bandage, replacing it with a large sticky dressing. Great!

He'd also looked at my thigh and re-dressed that with something similar. More embarrassment. My mother and a nurse were there watching. I was glad I was wearing privacy-maintaining trunks-type underwear.

He'd also written to the school confirming that if I felt tired I was to be allowed to go and rest, and that any sport or PE was out of the question until he said so. Damn. But I didn't want to risk any more damage.

The weekend found us all at Joe's again, much to my joy. The other five seemed really pleased to see me.

"I think you should put the bandage back on," said Tom. "You make a very effective Paddington."

"Apart from the lack of yellow fur, you mean?" Joe quipped. Well, it was his house and we were demolishing one of his mother's cakes, so I couldn't complain.

I made them all go and wash their hands, much to their surprise, then unrolled the second draft map – the one before the final version. They looked at it and were impressed with what I'd done to clarify things and enhance colourings.

"Bill will like that," said Arif, who had bumped into him the previous Friday. The final of the map so far was hidden in the cardboard tube that I ensured it was kept in when not in use or being worked on. When the five had pored over the second draft I removed the final version and carefully flattened it on the table.

I felt really pleased at their reaction. I'd gone to town on it with really fine mapping pens (thanks, parents), and the result looked presentable even to me. They were gobsmacked.

"Paddington couldn't have done that," said Tom.

"He might if he had hands instead of paws." Alex, inevitably.

"Nah... he can only see out of one eye."

I had a vision of that rock rushing towards my own eye, and thought what might have been.

25   School, maps & cottage

Wednesday and school rushed unstoppably towards us. Despite the ban on camping we managed to persuade them that we ought to go and see Nils the evening before. Parents insisted I had to be taken by car as they thought the bus might be too bumpy and do some damage. No amount of pleading would change their minds. With Arif and Alex, my tent mates, we arrived first.

Nils and the parents were introduced and we all hurried off when Nils and Daneesh started saying how good we were and so on. When they'd finished we were invited in to inspect the new cooker which Nils said was so much better than the range, though Bill had had to unblock the chimney and get it lined, then put a wood burning stove in for heat. We looked at each other, wondering how that was going to stop Nils having to collect wood. He pointed proudly to a pile of split logs nearby, and told us to look at the side of the cottage.

Enough prepared logs had been delivered to last him all winter.

"I am used to a live flame," he said simply.

Bill had been busy, it seemed.

Together, we took my parents up to the camp, more to visit it than to show it off to them. They expressed surprise at how tidy it was, though my sleeping bag was called into criticism for being rank. Actually, it was no worse than any of the others, but they never mentioned them.

"We need to get all this back home," said Dad.

"Not yet!" we all chorused. He looked surprised at such a unified reaction.

"We can get it back one weekend," said Tom. "Possibly we'll be using it some Friday and Saturday nights."

"That could be useful," said Arif. "Daneesh can't come on Fridays, so we could come in the evening, make sure he's okay, walk the dog and collect some…"

"No!" Tom shouted to drown him out.

"…wood," he continued, his eyes raised.

"But Nils doesn't need wood now," said Mum.

"He'll need kindling," Arif explained, still digging himself out of trouble.

"I suppose we could leave everything here until September's out," Dad said thoughtfully. "But we need to get things back then. And please, do you think it would be sociable to take the sleeping bags home for washing? They've had a month's solid use and – well, *really*."

Secretly, coming back to it now with the benefit of many (careful) showers behind me, I could see what he meant. Smell what he meant.

So we each gathered up our bags to take home.

"Need to do another pit this weekend," said Steve.

"I'd been meaning to mention that," I said.

"You should have done that rather than hit your head. It's a hell of a way to tell us the toilet pit's full," retorted Steve. My parents joined in the laughter.

And so we made our journeys home. I will admit to going straight to bed: I still wasn't completely 'there'.

And so, next morning, to school. A shirt with the top button done up! A tie! Smart shoes! It all felt totally foreign. I made my way, gathering other people, many I knew, some I didn't, on the way to the bus stop. (Suddenly buses were okay for me to travel on, apparently.)

I was bombarded with questions about how we'd beaten the gang single-handedly and found I was telling the same story over and over. Gradually the rest of the Suspects boarded the bus and got the same treatment. What was it going to be like at school?

The presence of teachers welcoming us stopped too many more questions, and it wasn't until assembly that the matter came up again.

The Headmistress gave the news as if no one in the school had heard of it, and said that we had been able to help the Police in their investigations. That was it. So that was meant to save us from persistent questioning. Rather disgusted, we went to our first year assembly. On the way a thought struck me: where was Emily Long? Alex was nearby and I asked him if he'd seen her.

"Nope, thank goodness. Hope she's been chucked out."

Our new Head of Year (September: we were now in Year 10) was Mr Windebank, one of the good teachers. A human being. You knew he would treat you fairly. On the other side of it he was known to expect a lot and not take prisoners. But you knew where you were with him.

To our surprise he started by telling everyone what we had been through and how, in his book, we were nearly saints. That wasn't his phrasing, but he was talking us up a lot. Then he surprised us. Teachers don't usually talk about individual pupils.

"Emily Long has left the school. She has left home and travelled to London. Frankly it saves us having to expel her. Her part in the disgusting events of earlier in the vacation would have made her presence here impossible. We know of one or two others now in the Year 11 and the Sixth who are being carefully watched, so if any of you notice any unpleasant or problematic behaviour, you need to let me know. This isn't a school request so much as a legal one. You've now reached the age when your understanding of right and wrong is tested regularly and you have decisions to make which may affect the rest of your lives. Don't mess with those decisions. Any doubts, talk to me in confidence.

"Lastly, a word of caution. Matt Ingham…" I pricked up my ears. "…had a nasty accident a week or so ago and has to take things easy. No doubt he will be supported by the usual suspects…" there were laughs at that "…but everyone needs to be aware he's not allowed to do sports or PE until he's fully recovered. Anyone else with any medical problems we don't know about, please tell the office. Or me."

He went on to talk about GCSEs and their importance – you know, the usual stuff, and that was that. We started school proper again, with only the prospect of half term and our campsite, then Christmas, to console us. I went home after school, rather fed up and more tired than I chose to admit. I didn't even remind parents that I was getting on for fifteen when they caught me nodding off over the TV, I just went meekly upstairs and went to bed.

The next thing that happened was that I wasn't allowed to go with them to the campsite the following weekend. I was really angry, especially as I'd visited Nils with them the previous Friday and even gone up there then. But no… nothing would persuade them. "Maybe next weekend" was all I could get. I went to my room and sulked.

The next weekend, autumn started early. It was pouring down. No way were any of us going to the estate in that. To make it worse, after a full week of school I felt so exhausted on the Friday that I couldn't even face going to see Nils.

For the next two weeks, after that, nothing happened.

I don't mean *nothing* happened. I mean nothing *happened*. Nothing worth talking about happened.

And then…

Our new head of year teaches geography. "Geography," he told us, "involves maps."

Get away.

"Now you're no longer proper children you need to get an understanding about mapping, and where better to start than with one of the best mapping systems in the world, our own Ordnance Survey."

My ears pricked up, and stayed pricked when he started showing details of mapping conventions and symbols. I wanted to shout "But we've just spent a month doing all that!" but he kept bringing in stuff that I'd never realised existed. Others near me – not any of the other Suspects – had the usual lesson expression on their faces but I was just trying to drink in the information and retain it.

And then he started talking about surveying techniques. He started talking about the specialised equipment you need to be able to get the measurements to make maps. He talked about the years of experience you needed…

I made an odd sound, but I can't remember what it was. But he focussed on me as if I'd just yelled an obscenity.

"Matt? Anything to say?"

I couldn't stop. "Yes, sir. We've been mapping the… er… an area for the last month of the holidays. I just…er…" I trailed off.

"Just 'er', Matt? Do you think you can do better than that?"

I had to think fast. I knew Tom was sitting behind me, and the others were scattered around the room.

"Sorry sir. I'm not being…er…"

"Rude?"

"No sir. Just interested. Er… involved. As I said, we've done a lot of this over the last weeks and…well…"

"You can do it better than me."

"Yes… er… no. I mean, we've been doing it differently."

I drew a breath.

"There are six of us who are really interested in this and

want to know if we've been doing it right."

I'm the youngest Suspect. It wasn't really my place to be saying any such thing. But I had been given the job of making the final map and they'd all said how good it was.

"The Usual Suspects, I suppose?"

There was a general laugh.

"Yes, sir. Us."

"Okay. Let me carry on for now – I've done the lesson plan, after all. But when we next have time as a class, bring in your map and you can tell everyone how you tackled it. Deal?"

I wasn't used to being talked to like that. I was used to a sort of "Do-this-because-I-say-so" teaching. I listened hard for the rest of the lesson and made lots of notes. Afterwards we all met up.

"Do you know what you're doing?" asked Tom.

"Not really. But it's about what we've been doing and I was just … dunno. Caught up in it?"

I knew what I meant. When someone is talking about the details of a topic you'd been trying to tackle for weeks on your own, and you've been coming to it from a different angle, an angle developed out of necessity, then…well, yes. I felt involved in a formal lesson about mapping. I tried to explain it to them.

"I know what you mean," said Arif slowly, and after some thought. "I knew that what he was saying was important for what we've been trying to do. But Matt's been combining our notes and descriptions to try and make a proper map out of it. So yes, we're all very involved in what The Farter[1] had to say."

Footsteps approached. The man himself.

"What's all this then? Have you really been making a map?"

"Surveying, then mapping," said Tom. "Matt's been doing the final copy. It's good."

"Basic surveying? Instruments?"

"Compass, bearings from one point to another. That sort of thing."

"How about heights?"

I pulled a face. "Only from the O.S. map. It's one of the things that's been bothering me."

He nodded. "Sounds as if you've done your best, starting

---

[1] *Mr Windebank. Our new Head of year and Geography teacher.*

from scratch. Bring it in, would you, and let me see?"

We nodded. He'd sounded enthusiastic.

A week later I took in a photocopy that I'd got done at the Library. I could tell he was impressed, but when we told him he couldn't display it since it gave information about a very private tract of land he was less impressed. Oh well. You can't please all the people all the time.

"Is it finished?" he asked, looking at a particularly blank piece of it.

"No. When they get a chance they'll be doing some more. I'll add it after that."

"Would you bring it in each time?"

I thought. Would it get damaged? I couldn't get a photocopy done each time, not at the cost they were.

"Well…"

"I promise I'll keep it safe in my office, and you can take it home the same night. I'd really like to see how it's developing. Do you think you'd enjoy a career in this sort of thing?"

That came out of the blue. I didn't really know, and told him so.

We settled into the school routine. Was it me, or was there a nicer atmosphere around the place now that Emily Long had gone? The influence she had on the others in her year had vanished with her, and their rather 'off' attitude to the rest of us seemed to be diluted.

The weeks to October's half term were only punctuated by several bouts of rain, by the Friday visits to Nils, and by Steve's report of the reaction to the map by his mates in the Scouts. They could hardly believe that he'd been a part of the mapping process. His leader said that whoever had done the artwork showed a real flair. That made me rather proud. I wondered about joining. But each weekend, under parental orders, I had to return home while the rest of them continued to camp – on the weekends it was dry.

Oh, and every Monday after a weekend of surveying I was given the notes and added what I could to the map.

The Saturday of the week before half term Joe summoned us to a meal at his house. He'd been prompted by Arif, he said, and his house had the most space. Bill would be there. So would Nils and Daneesh. Eleven people! I hoped they had a big table.

As soon as we got there Mrs Hammond told us not to stand on ceremony but to take what we wanted from the table, find a seat and balance the plate on our knees. It was nearly like being back in camp, but the cooking was better. I didn't say that to Steve.

It was a relaxed way of holding a meeting; so much better than a formal sit-down affair. To start with conversation was limited to matters of importance, such as "Can you pass that to Matt, please," and "Anyone seen the salad dressing?" By the time we had mainly finished, which meant that we were just grazing on things that needed finishing (in our eyes), Bill started.

"That cooking range for Nils was put in just about in time. The old one was – well, old. It was also dangerously thin. So once his ankle's healed we can all go round there for a meal." Nils looked alarmed at the prospect.

"The electricity people have found an old sub-station in a cellar attached to the old house. They've condemned it, but agreed to replace it at their expense when I told them we would be refurbishing the manor house. It also means replacing the cable – also at their expense – so all we have to do is provide a feed off it for Nils' cottage, and for the outbuildings when we get that far. The work starts the week after next.

"Then we have the minor matter of running lighting and power for Nils around the cottage, and pipes for central heating…"

"A lot of fuss for nothing. I have light. I have my Tilley."

"And although Nils is putting up some objections I think I might be able to persuade him." He looked at the old man and smiled. He got a grimace back, but there was a sparkle in the old man's eye.

"So there's a lot going on. And best of all – for me – my family is arriving soon. They'll be staying at the Royal Hotel, and while all the work is going on at the cottage I want Nils to stay there too."

This was news to Nils, who looked as if he'd been struck by lightning, though without the burns. And to stay at the Royal! Bill must be extremely wealthy, I thought.

"So would you all, with your parents, be able to visit us there one day? Marcus Yardley caters for large groups. I'm told his kitchen does wonderful things with truffles."

We all laughed at that, except the Hammond parents who weren't party to all the facts.

"And would you people take any of my grandkids who are interested up to your camp? And anywhere else you think would interest them? They'd really like that."

I could see Tom thinking. "How many are there?" he asked.

"Blimey... well, Andrew and Jess have got Toby and Jane, they're 12 and twins, then Mike who must be 15. Drew and Nicole's family are Ava who's 12, Grace who's 14 and Cooper who's also the grand age of 15 and makes me feel old."

"Sorry," said Tom faintly, "how many is that?"

Bill laughed. "Six, with the twins. Do you think you can cope?"

Tom looked round, eyes raised. I nodded when he looked at me.

"We'll give it a go," he said.

"Great," said Bill. "Now, how's the map coming on?"

I'd remembered to bring it with me. Some of the others hadn't seen it for a few weeks and it had changed a lot since I'd first been given it.

"Bloody hell, Matt, this is good!" exclaimed Bill. "You have a flair for this. Drew needs to see this. He's a surveyor."

I wasn't sure if I wanted our obviously amateur, schoolboy attempts at something as advanced as mapping to be seen by a professional. There wasn't any choice, though. Bill had been promised a copy of it, so his son would see it.

"You son will probably laugh at it," I said disparagingly.

"Blimey no – he won't. Lots of the plans of the stations are drawn by guys on horses. Mostly they look as if they've been done at the gallop. Yours is based on the official map, so that's a good start, so you know you've got the right shape and the house and village are in the right place. So's your swimming pool and its river. So don't put yourself down."

"No, Matt, don't put our efforts down!" Alex was at my left and I knew Bill's words had given him more enthusiasm for the job.

"Well..."

"He's right, Matt. It isn't Ordnance Survey standard, no, and even if one of you was an O.S. surveyor, he couldn't do much more with just a compass and a bit of paper. But it's bloody good, and it gives me a real overview of what the place is, and that's what I'll need. And thank you for it."

Well, that seemed better. Perhaps the Farter was right and it *was* good.

We continued talking for some time, then found our ways home. This time it was Alex who came with me to my door, even if it was out of his way.

"You don't need to see me home, Alex," I chided.

"I know, I know. But if you'd been there and seen someone crack their head on that rock, and hear the sound it made, and then see the person lie still... well, you'd want to make sure they stayed okay after they managed to recover from it."

All those wisecracks, and teasing, and scuffles – including being put on his back in the marsh that afternoon – and he came up with that. I smiled.

"It's kind of you, really. But I am back to normal, you know."

He nodded. "I know. More or less. But... oh, I don't know. Good night."

"Seeya.

26   Australian Invasion

Half term arrived in mid-October. So did the rain, and it was on the Tuesday of its first week that Bill said his family were arriving. I wondered what their first reactions would be, coming from a scorching South Australia (as I thought). I was back to normal, apart from the scar on my head which occasionally people noticed and remarked about, and another on the inside of my left thigh which they didn't.

The next day, Wednesday, was miserable, but dry, so we conferred and went to the estate. It seemed a good time to strike camp and bring all the stuff back home. The weather was going downhill fast towards Christmas. We knew we could return in the spring. The idea was that we should get everything down, and then parents could bring it all back home once we had lugged it down to Nils' cottage.

In a rather sombre mood, made more so by the amount of homework we had been given to be handed in by the first Wednesday we were back, we boarded the bus. As it made its way into the countryside we thought the sky seemed lighter. As we neared the stop, blue sky could be seen in the distance. Our mood lifted immediately.

"Could stay over," said Tom hopefully.

"Hmm." Arif wasn't so sure. I think he must have been planning to see Amy later.

"We'd need to get some food," said Steve thoughtfully.

"And some wood!" Alex, Joe and I added almost simultaneously.

Steve grinned. "Thanks for volunteering." We groaned.

The chatting was rather livelier now, and homework forgotten. We made our way through the hamlet, seeing nobody, and up the path towards Nils'. Over the sudden birdsong, we thought we could hear voices, young voices, and the nearer we got the more certain we were.

"They're here!" Tom exclaimed unnecessarily.

The overgrown drive branched to the left, giving access to the path that led to the cottage. It seemed wider now, with tyre tracks on it. We wondered why.

"Gas and electricity people," said Joe.

As we rounded the last bend the cottage came into view.

There were six people talking to each other as they looked down the well. The sound echoing back to them must have drowned the sound of our footsteps, and we were walking deliberately quietly. We stopped at a sort of conversational distance. At last the tallest of the three boys looked up, gave a start, looking alarmed. I suppose six boys standing nearby having seemingly appeared out of nowhere might be a bit off-putting. Before he had a chance to exclaim, Tom spoke.

"Problem? You must be Bill's grandchildren."

The boy nodded, looking relieved.

"You must be the Suspects."

I grinned to myself. We were famous even the other side of the world.

Alex laughed. "We are. The Usual Suspects. We get the blame for everything until they discover who really did it."

"Oh *that's* where it comes from," said one of a pair of them. I say 'one of' because there were two of the same age who looked so alike in face, height and even hair that it was difficult to tell them apart. One had slightly longer hair than the other, but it was not by much.

They must have been used to having the focus of attention on them when meeting new people because immediately they launched into what sounded like a well-rehearsed routine.

"Yes, we're twins."

"Yes, we're identical."

"Yes, we think the same way."

"Yes, we go around together all the time."

"No, I'm the boy: I'm Toby."

"And I'm the girl: I'm Jane."

"Sorry," said another of the older ones, a pleasant looking boy with a deep tan and short, dark hair. "They've developed that speel between them. So many people they meet say the same things to them and ask the same questions, they get fed up with it. I'm their elder brother, sadly. Mike."

We nodded.

"I'm Tom," said Tom, "And here are Arif, Steve, Joe, Alex and Matt."

I was aware that one of the girls suddenly looked at me when she heard my name. I suppose it was unsurprising as each of them were looking at us just as we were looking at them. But it felt as if she'd been waiting to hear my name.

She was about my height, perhaps a little shorter. I don't know how to describe her face, but I found it... instantly pleasing. Framing it was tightly curled, light brown hair.

For the first time in my life I felt a sudden lift to my spirits that was the result of seeing one person.

But another of the boys was talking. "Hiya... I'm Cooper, the one with the frizzy hair is Grace, and the other one is Ava. They're my sisters. Sadly." He shot a look at Mike and grinned.

"He's rude," said Ava. "We love him like an elder brother and he's just rude back to us."

"You should hear them sometimes... When the twins and Ava gang up on me... strewth."

We were grinning at this exchange. "Sounds like me and my sister," said Joe. "Seems that when she's not carrying on about unicorns she's attacking me. That's why I escape and spend time with this lot when I can."

"And I thought it was because you loved us," said Alex. Joe just looked at him.

Cooper continued. "You're the blokes who had the aggro with those nonces and got your names in the rag? Grandad told us. Sounds like a bit of a do."

"Bit more than that," Arif said quietly. "Going around knowing that people could be watching you, and knowing where you live, is horrible. And having to hide out here in case they find you and do something to you was the same."

"But we've had fun," said Alex the irrepressible. "Bill said you might like to see the camp."

Mike and Cooper looked at each other.

"We'd love to. Grandad says you might let us camp up there too. If you don't mind. You found the site, he says, so it's yours really. But we do a lot of camping at home, so it'd be good if we could."

"Well, we'll go up later and you can have a look," said Tom without promising anything.

"Ace. But we're not going to be flavour of the month if we don't get the bucket up the well again."

"What's happened?" I asked, thinking I should really say something, and hoping that the girl might talk to me.

"*Someone* didn't tie the bucket on properly," said Mike, looking at the twins.

"Yes, we did," protested Jane. "It just came undone in the

228

water."

Cooper rolled his eyes to the skies.

"We can't get it out, anyway," said Mike. "And we don't think there's a ladder long enough."

"What does Nils say?" asked Tom.

Mike and Cooper looked at each other, rather guiltily.

"We haven't told him yet."

"Let's have a look," said Steve. They made space for him.

"Hmm. Looks deep. Well's too wide to climb down, chimney style… Have to be an abseil or… I know. A caving ladder."

"Got one?" asked Cooper.

"No, but my Unit has."

"Can you get it?"

"Next Thursday…no. We're not meeting for another two weeks. Damn."

Alex and I looked at each other. The Scout had failed us.

"How about asking if he's got a grapple," asked Grace. She had a low, smooth voice that seemed somehow different from how you'd think she'd talk, looking at her face. I was fascinated.

"What's a grapple?" asked Toby.

"Bit like an anchor, but it's got three hooks on the shaft instead of two," said Tom.

"Or perhaps we could make one." Steve was back in the game.

But Nils was so tidy that there was nothing outside the cottage that we could use to cobble one together.

"Nothing else for it," said Mike. "You'll have to go in and admit it."

The twins looked at each other and it looked as if they were having a silent, private conversation. And without another word they went to the door and knocked, then went inside.

"It piddles me off when they do that," said Mike.

"What?"

"Talk to each other without saying a dickie. It's so annoying."

"A dickie?" I asked.

"Dickie bird. A word. They don't say it in words, but they still know what they decide."

Bill came out, with Nils hobbling after him.

"You have lost the bucket. Well, how am I going to make tea now? And I have all that new gas to heat it, too!"

"We're very sorry. But it was an accident."

"Ah well, it was an accident when I first did it, too. And the next time. And the time after... Come with me."

He hobbled back into the cottage. A few minutes later the twins returned, carrying, of all things, a grapple.

"Do you know what you're doing with it?" he asked.

"Yes," said Cooper, "we're not letting Toby or Jane tie it on."

The two culprits smiled faintly at him.

"Let's have a look, then," said Steve. He looked at the end of the rope, then at the grapple. It had a loop at the end. Swiftly he tied a knot round it, and tested it. "That'll go nowhere."

They looked at him with something like respect in their eyes.

"You sure?" asked Mike. "I thought it'd need more rope round it than that."

"Bowline," said Steve tersely. "Old sailors' knot, taught to us all."

"All of you?"

"Yeah... not the Suspects, the Explorers."

"Explorers? You belong to some exploration club?"

"Explorer Scouts."

"You're in the Scouts?"

"Yeah... okay, let's get the jokes out of the way now, shall we? I used to get enough at school. I enjoy it, and it's come in useful this summer."

"I'm not going to joke," said Cooper. "Not if it makes you as useful as that."

Steve looked pleased.

It took quite a bit of fishing around and cursing. We quickly got used to some words of Australian we'd not heard before. Finally there was a weight on the end of the rope and up came the bucket. As a bonus it was full of water. Mike unhooked it carefully and sent Toby and Jane in to see Nils again.

Bill came out with them, grinning. "You know, I think those two will be good for Nils. He's fallen under their spell already."

"They're a pain," said Mike, with resignation. "You have to live with them to realise how much."

"They're my friends!" exclaimed Ava. "They're only

horrible to you 'cos you're horrible to them."

"You see, Grandad, even my cousins gang up on me."

"Do you want to come and look at the camp?" I thought it might be time to avoid a family argument.

There was a chorus of "Yes, please."

"Tea first? Or just go? And are you taking some tucker with you?"

"Our stuff's still up there, so we could cook." Tom was in Leader mode, leading eleven rather than his usual five.

"Sounds good to me," said Cooper. "What've you got we can cook?"

"I brought a load of burgers and stuff so you could have a barbie," Bill admitted. "You do have a barbie up there, don't you? Though I didn't see one."

"No. We've just got a fire," said Steve. "But if Nils has something we can put on it to turn it into a barbecue I'm sure we can cope."

Nils provided a grid, clean, but what it had started life as I didn't ask. Carrying it, and sharing round the provisions that Bill had magicked up as if he was expecting his family to be doubled, we set off. He promised to join us, with Daneesh, and Nils if he thought he could make it. Nils's ankle was apparently sound, but now it was down to the muscles and their attachments to repair themselves. And as it was about 2½ kilometres to the camp, we wondered if he could make it.

Tom, Arif and Lars led off. The dog had decided he'd get some exercise. The rest of us spread out after them. I found myself at the back and it seemed that Grace had also decided to make sure that none of the youngsters got left behind.

I didn't know what to say to her.

We had been going for about five minutes when she broke the silence. "Are you… I mean, is it you who's done the map?"

"Yes, we have. We're still doing it, when we can, at weekends."

"No, I meant is it *you* who's drawing it?"

"Oh… yes. I'm putting it on paper. I had the time, you see."

"After knocking yourself out."

"Yes. Bill told you about that, did he?"

"Yes. He seemed to think that… I mean, he knows that I like maps too. And drawing and painting. I suppose I should call it art now. I just love the way you can make something that people like, doing something you like."

I'd never thought of it that way, but having been complimented on my mapping efforts I at least understood that side of it.

"Yes, I know. They gave me the map to do when I was stuck at home, being bored, because someone needed to do it. But the more I did, the more I got involved – in the map, I mean. And having been there when we measured it – most of it – and got the angles and stuff, it made it easier to put it down on paper."

"Can I see it some time?"

"Yeah, course. I could bring it here, or to the hotel, or…"

"I don't want to be a nuisance."

"Oh, you're not," I said fervently.

"I could come to see it at your house."

I wondered if my heart was all right.

"Okay," was all I could say. "That would be good, if you want."

She smiled.

I thought of the cred I'd get with the parents if I brought a girl home with me. But then she wouldn't want anything to do with me, not really. I was a medium sized, brown haired, pasty faced 14 year old with a strange shaped scar on his forehead. She had the pick of all those tall Australians with their bleached blond hair, muscles and attitude. Although her brother and cousin weren't like that I was sure she'd know some from school or somewhere.

We were silent for a time. Again I wondered what to say.

"Did… did Bill tell you all about us?" I managed.

She laughed. "He's very good at 'getting' characters, so yes. He did a sort of character sketch of each of you, and you all came over rather well, especially Tom, Alex, Arif and you. He seemed to think you were really good with a pen, and with design. 'Better than he thinks he is,' were his words. And he's a nice, quiet bloke too. Just the…"

She stopped mid-sentence. I looked at her and her face was red.

"You okay?" I asked."

"Yes," she said, "just a frog in my throat, that's all."

"What were you going to say?"

"We'd better catch the others up," she said rather hastily.

"We seem to have fallen back a bit."

She set a pace which, a few weeks back, would have had me tired. But I was fully recovered, the doctor had said, although the muscles I'd built up over our exercise-heavy summer seemed to have faded a bit. We caught up the twins and Ava. Toby was looking at his knee.

"He's ripped his jeans," said Ava. "And cut himself."

Toby looked at her and us with a serious expression.

"Is it okay?" Grace asked.

"Bit of a rip," he said. "Hurts a bit."

"There's still quite a way to go," I said. "Can you last another twenty minutes?"

"How many clicks is it?" he asked.

Clicks? Sounded like a sci-fi book.

"He means kilometres," Grace explained.

"About another two," I told him.

"He's a man, not a mouse," said Ava loyally.

"Okay," Grace said. "So we won't stop unless we hear squeaking, is that right?"

He grinned.

"I've…er…got a couple of plasters on me," I offered. "Could help keep the dirt out."

He looked at me gratefully. "That'd be cool."

Treated by his sister, he looked better. We walked on behind them and the initial theatrical limp vanished over the next three minutes. I thought it better not to boast about our lacerations when we'd been trying to explore, measure and map simultaneously.

Despite his protestation we were some way behind the others and found them scouring the area for wood.

"I need more wood!" exclaimed the Scout as we hove into sight. "Hallo, are you all right?"

"Just a cut leg," said Grace.

"Who, you? Oh no, I see. Let me have a look."

His turn to lead. Toby let him examine the knee.

"Did you clean it?" he asked. Toby shook his head.

"Probably be okay but I'd rather take this off and swab it. Do you mind?"

Toby looked doubtful. I've been dealt with by Steve before so I had an idea what was coming.

"Won't take a mo. Might sting a bit but at least we can be

233

sure it won't go poisoned. How big's the wound, Matt?"

I demonstrated on my own knee.

"So that's stuck to good skin?"

"Yeah."

"Okay." And before Toby had a chance to say anything he'd ripped off the plaster in one movement. Toby shouted, surprised and stung, but then looked at Steve.

"Ow," he said.

"Hurt now, does it?" asked Steve.

"No."

"Better than a slow pull, then. Hurts too much, that. Stay there."

He came back with our first aid kit and Toby's eyes opened as he saw its size.

"Can you use all that?" he asked.

"Hope so," said Steve cheerfully. "Not many things in here, just a lot of the same thing. Mainly disinfectant wipes so we clean up the worst of the cuts and things we've picked up on the estate. Usually we go swimming first, and that helps a lot."

"Yeah," I said, remembering one incident. "Stand under the waterfall and the cold takes away all feeling."

"Not today," said Toby.

"Not till next summer, I guess. Swimming'll be too cold until then."

"Looks a great place to swim. Anything dangerous in it?"

"Only Alex," I said.

"What's an Alex? Oh, I see," he grinned. "But he's not that dangerous, right?"

"He's okay," I said thoughtfully. "When I hit my head he helped all the way and stayed with me until I woke up at midnight, in hospital."

"Good guy."

"Yes. They all are. Just don't tell them I said so."

He grinned again.

Steve returned. "Another bit of stinging, then it'll shut up and be fine."

Toby had no time to say anything, just shut his eyes and let Steve get on with it. A new, larger sticky dressing was put on and Toby was sorted.

We wandered over to the others.

27   Raid 2

"Just saying you've done well here, Steve, this camp," said Mike, who thought he'd better stay near his injured younger brother, so wasn't collecting wood. "Looks really good and comfortable. Lots of good ideas. Better than we manage most of the time."

Steve nearly purred.

"Done quite a lot of it before," he said. "We were here a long time so it paid to go for some comforts. I'll get a fire going."

"No wood yet. They won't be long." Cooper could hear crashing around in the distance.

"Just you wait," said Steve.

He went to get his secret stash of dry wood from the stores tent, to the amazement of the Australian contingent (and me. I didn't know he'd carried on keeping some). He arranged it, set light to the firelighter and by the time the first of the wood appeared he had flames.

"Strewth," said Toby. "Quicker than you do, Mike."

"I don't use firelighters," his brother retorted.

"When you're here for ages, hiding from criminals, you want to be sure it'll light even in the rain. Else you go hungry."

"Was it scary?" Jane asked.

"What? Hiding here from them? Not really. We enjoyed it – until they discovered we were here and crashed down from the cliff."

"Where did that happen?"

"Oh, further along. Past the end of the pool where the blackthorns are."

"Are blackthorns dangerous, then?" Toby this time.

"They are when you land on them from a cliff," I said grimly. "They're not nice to fight your way through, either. You get punctured."

"But they're not poisonous?"

"No. Just sharp."

Mike, Grace, and Cooper were talking to Steve, who was describing how the tables and things were made. I'd always assumed that Australians were the experts at being outdoors, but apart from the inevitable barbecues it seemed that camping was a thing done of necessity or when on holiday rather than just for leisure. Unless you're a Scout or some sort of Cadet, perhaps.

Armfuls of wood had appeared, Steve had a good fire going and was arranging more large stones, wet from the slightly swollen pool, to support the grid for a barbecue.

"Do you want us to do this?" asked Cooper. "It's a bit of a ritual in Oz."

Steve grinned hugely and waved him on. It seemed to be an all-male occupation, barbecuing, as Mike and Toby joined in without a second thought. Grace, Jane, Ava and even we Suspects were redundant, though Steve was seen to extend the fire so he could put the kettle on.

"I saw some crosses in the bushes back there," Grace remarked to me. "Did someone die?"

My mind flipped between the man who had fallen and broken his neck, and the real reason for the crosses. "No. Er… they are…er…the old pits we had used for toilets."

She understood. "I saw what you're using, behind those hurdles. A bit basic!"

"Well, it was only for us, so just a screen is okay. If you see someone's head over the top, you don't go in. It worked over the summer."

"Yeah… but… oh well."

"What would you have wanted?"

"Oh, a fancy, blow-up dunny with pink walls and a basin with running water… You know. The works. With fluffy towels."

I raised my eyebrows.

"Sorry, we're fresh out of… what did you say? Dunny?"

"Strine for toilet."

"Fresh out of them, then. But if you want to improve on what we've got, The Scout will show you how to make a hurdle. Or I will."

"He's nice, but I'd rather you did."

In my mind, my jaw dropped. I don't think it *actually* did, but I can't be sure.

Surely she didn't *like* me?

In a slightly husky voice, which made me clear my throat without making much difference, I said "I'd need to go searching for wood first."

236

"Oh, we could both do that. No biggy."

At least I knew that was Australian. We used it between us at school sometimes. She wasn't referring to me. I hoped.

I heard a phone ringing. Mike's. He listened, then laughed.

"That was Grandad," he called. "He wants us to make smoke so he can see where we are. Or better, send Lars down to find them. They're lost."

"Lost!" exclaimed Tom. "We do know this place better than Nils, then! Okay, I'll go down with Lars."

"Best if four go," Steve suggested, "Then you can give Nils a chair if he's limping too much."

The rest of us looked at him.

"You mean a two-handed chair," offered Mike.

Steve looked at him with renewed respect. "Yeah. You know how to do them?"

"We get taught at school. Come on, Cooper. Let's show these Poms we know something. They can't make all the running."

"Hell yeah," Cooper laughed. "Who else is going?"

"I will, said Tom. "Joe? You're my height. Steve's better off here with the kettle."

"We can look after that!" Ava exclaimed. "Jane, Toby and me. We're not useless, you know."

"Okay," said Tom. "You're here looking after the fire and everyone else comes down to help."

"Lars!" called Arif. The dog looked up reluctantly from his place in front of the fire, raised himself and stretched, even more reluctantly, and padded over to Arif. Waving to the others we made our way down the path.

Arif's phone rang. He dropped behind. For a few minutes, then caught up.

"I was meant to phone Amy," he said. "What do you think about her coming over this afternoon?"

With difficulty, as we were in single file on something that was nearly a path, we decided that it'd be unfair on Arif to exclude her, particularly if Grace, Ava and Jane were part of the equation now.

Grace! She hadn't been included in the stay-behinds: where was she? I looked behind me when we were on a rare straight bit, and just saw her head behind Mike's broad shoulders. Oh well. Perhaps she preferred her cousin's company to mine.

We reached a natural clearing.

"Any idea how far they'd come?" asked Tom.

"Not a clue," said Mike. "He never said. I'll try calling."

I expected him to reach for his mobile, but instead he cupped his hands to his mouth, faced the way we were going, and in an amazingly loud, shrill voice yelled what sounded like "Queue-eee!"

"Bloody hell," said Tom. "What was *that*?"

"Shhh," he said, hands now to his ears. And sure enough, in the distance there was a similar sound, though rather cut off, as if the yeller had been interrupted.

"That way!" he directed, pointing straight into the undergrowth.

"Okay…" said Tom doubtfully, "but we've been here weeks and had our fill of scratchy undergrowth. We'd better go down a bit further and find a path or something that leads off that way."

I'd taken the chance to move behind Mike. It was less ear damaging given Mike's yells, and Grace was there. I smiled at her, and got an answering one.

"Quieter here than having Mike shouting in your ear," I offered.

"We all live outside the town," she said, "and sometimes in even the bit of bush we have near you just need to find where you are. A 'cooee' is the best way – travels for miles."

"Not surprised, that loud."

"Oh, we can all do it that loud. Just that the bigger lungs you have, the better. A girl's travels further 'cos it's higher pitched."

"Please don't try! Not with me standing by you."

She laughed. "I won't. Don't want to scare you away."

I looked at her, and she looked back.

"We'd better catch them up," she said. I looked round and just saw Mike disappearing round the next bend. We followed. I felt rather warm.

We were still some way behind when Mike's next call rang out, and we heard a rather less strenuous response than before. We caught them up.

"Can you stay here?" said Mike to Grace – or it may have been to Grace and me. "We need a point to get back to."

"Okay," said Tom, "good thinking."

"If you hear two calls, it'll be me wanting you to call back, Grace. Okay?"

"Right," she said.

"If she does, move well away," said her brother. "She's piercing!"

She put her tongue out.

"It was a compliment!" he protested, and grinned.

Steve muttered something about having left the compass in the tent.

And off they went.

The next twenty minutes were, to me, extraordinary. True, they were interrupted by a more and more distant "Cooee!" every now and again but that made it even more extraordinary.

I'd never been a natural conversationalist – not up to that point, anyway. But the time passed in what felt like thirty seconds. And all we did was to talk, Grace and I. Talk about our lives and what we did, our schools and what we thought, about friends… and she made me think that a group like The Suspects was unusual, but in a good way. She had no band of friends or a group like ours and was rather envious, I think. I'd just never imagined that there was anything special about us.

We would probably have continued had it not been for a double "Cooee!". Almost immediately Grace faced the sound and put her hands to her mouth. And the lovely, quiet, soothing voice that had enveloped me for all that time gave vent to a "Cooeeeeeeee!" that nearly split my eardrums.

"Bloody hell, Grace! You might have given me a chance to duck!"

She grinned at me.

"Cooper did warn you."

"Yes, but blimey…"

There was an answer from the heart of the estate. Hastily I covered my ears so the next call of the lesser spotted Grace bird didn't cause my ears any further damage. The call and response carried on for some time, and at last footsteps were heard and they appeared, looking dishevelled. Nils had been carried for some time, apparently, and he and the others were looking tired. Bill and Grace were slightly hoarse.

"It's nearer to get to the camp, I think," said Tom. "At least Nils could sit down there and have a tea and a bite to eat."

Bill and Nils nodded.

"Have you got enough to help Nils if I go and fetch Amy?" asked Arif. "She just phoned and she's waiting at the cottage."

"Okay by me," said Tom. "Matt can take your place."

Can I? Oh, of course I can. Tom has spoken... No, it was only a fleeting thought.

Arif was off like a shot. "He's got it bad," said Alex in a resigned tone.

"Oh... like Grace and Mike," said Cooper.

Grace hit him. No pretence at The Look, just a good solid hit.

"Ow!" he said, rubbing his arm. "What's that for?"

"Don't stir. You know it's not true. He's my cousin and he's too old and I don't like him... not like that."

Not only was she furious, but she'd gone very red too.

Tom intervened. "Come on... peace all. Let's get to the camp and see how the others are doing with the kettle."

Grace looked at me meaningfully, still red, and grasped her left wrist with her right hand. I looked puzzled.

"You do the same," she said.

After a wrong start during which she ignored her brother's comments about not being strong enough, I got the message and we made the chair. Nils sat on it gratefully, his hands round our shoulders and we started off up the path again.

It was the first time that Grace and I held hands. It was actually the first time that I'd held hands with any girl.

I wish it had been under different circumstances.

It's a tiring occupation, being a four-handed chair for someone. I could tell, after a fairly short time, that Grace was tiring and I knew I was. Walking almost sideways for any more than fifty metres puts a strain on the back. It wasn't Nils's weight, it was the posture. But she seemed to have something to prove and really wouldn't let go. It was me who called a halt first – I had no option because my hand was slipping off hers and I didn't want to drop Nils.

"Well done, you two." Thank goodness it was Cooper who said it. "Tires you out quick, doesn't it? You okay, Nils?"

"I am sorry to be a bother. I should have stayed and cooked for you at home."

"No worries," Cooper assured him. "We'll get you there and back. No biggie"

We got them back to camp. There was no one around.

Cooper gave a loud "Cooee!" but there was no answer. We looked at each other, puzzled.

"They're probably in one of your tents, kidding us," said Mike, laughing. Tom went to each, but no one appeared. We called, saying that food was ready – even though it wasn't. The kettle, though, had nearly boiled dry.

"They've been gone some time, then," Joe observed. Cooper and Mike looked at each other, then at Grace.

"They didn't say anything to me about hiding," she said.

"Just a minute," said Bill, "they've been gone some time and aren't able to hear us… Surely…no… They know better than just wander off into the bush. They're better trained. Grace – your voice travels further, have go?"

I took some steps back. It was too serious suddenly for an amusing covering of the ears.

Grace called, and it was so insistent that she broke off into a cough. Lars looked at her, threw his head in the air and joined her with a howl. Despite ourselves, we had to smile.

"Lars will find them," said Nils suddenly. "Have you something that is theirs? The twins, or Ava's?"

Bill gave a start. "They left their back-sacks behind. Let's see."

"Do not touch anything inside," Nils warned. "Let the dog use his nose."

Bill opened one of the three rucksacks that had been dumped on our table and called Lars. Nils went too, took the bag and held it so Lars could sniff at it. The dog obliged, putting his nose deep into it and snuffling.

"Lars? Lars, *vind se! Brave hond*!" [1]

The dog looked at him and barked, then cast round, sniffing the ground. There was a whimper and he took off down the path we had all come up earlier. Nils called him back.

"*Ne, ne… de andere weg…*" [2] He took the dog past the fire and gave him a gentle push. The dog repeated his snuffling, went round in circles and returned, then did the same again.

"It's where we were getting wood," said Steve.

But then the dog was off on a different direction, going fast along an animal track, one that we had mapped.

---

[1] *Find them! Good dog!*
[2] *No, no… the other way…*

"Nils, Daneesh, can you stay here so that if they come back they know to stay? Do you want Grace with you too? If we need help getting back we can call and she can answer." I was torn, part wanting her kept safe and part wanting her with me. To my surprise she stayed.

The dog checked that we were following and in sight, then kept going. He kept looking, checking back.

"I think this is the path we explored a few weeks back," panted Steve. "Seem to recognise it."

No answer. We were all trying to keep the dog and each other in sight.

Half an hour of part running, part struggling through undergrowth, and the dog let out a torrent of barking. It wasn't the occasional bark we had heard from him before. This was an urgent, angry bark. And it was answered with voices. Men's voices, shouting. We stopped and grouped together.

"Are they moving?" Tom asked in a whisper. We listened. Nothing could be heard apart from the dog, now growling and barking at times, and the occasional shout. No footsteps.

Tom whispered again. "Bill, if this is anything to do with the gang they think there are just six of us. They don't know about you, Mike or Cooper. Can we try and get all round them and hem them in?"

"Don't know how many there are. We should get the Police."

"But they'd take ages to get here. And who knows what they're going to do? They've got the twins and Ava, don't forget. And we can at least find how many there are."

"True," Bill muttered, "but I can't put you youngsters in danger."

"We're not in danger just finding out how many there are. And we can't just wait here."

Bill was obviously reluctant. "I'll go first, then. You follow me at a safe distance and be ready to run if anything happens to me. No point anyone else getting hurt."

"There's a sort of path round this way," I said quietly, having just noticed it. The dog had gone straight on through what looked like a path fit only for rabbits.

Bill thought. "Okay. Cooper, stay here with Matt. The rest of you, come with me."

They carried on, the sound of their footsteps fading. I

wondered if whoever it was could hear them.

"If they come this way, go for their knees," whispered Cooper. "Like a Rugby tackle. D'you play Rugby?"

I admitted that I was a footballer, and not very good.

"Okay. But going for the knees is best."

Silently we waited. It seemed the opposite sort of wait from the time I'd spent waiting with Grace. Not just because Cooper wasn't Grace, but because the urgent need to find the youngsters was uppermost in our minds. Also, we couldn't really talk in anything apart from a whisper. It grew quieter, apart from Lars' warning, angry growls.

At last there was a chorus of whoops that interrupted the dog. There were angry sounds, some shouts, some crashing, and some running feet.

"Get ready," whispered Cooper, "get out of sight and when you can, try and trip them up, then make lots of noise."

Now we didn't have long to wait at all. Footsteps were running towards us, crashing through undergrowth and occasionally a voice gave out a curse. It sounded as if the person – or people – were nearly on us when there was a louder crash than usual, and a groan, then silence.

We looked at each other. Cooper started off. I followed.

We came on across a man, on the ground, trapped by a long trail of brambles that seemed to have wound itself round his left leg. His head was bleeding where he had hit it on a root. I smiled. I knew about hitting your head.

"Pity," said Cooper, settling himself down on the man's back. "I was looking forward to a good Rugby tackle."

The man groaned.

"How many more are there?"

Another groan.

Casually he reached out to the man's arm and pulled it behind his back.

"Now, if I pull this carefully, I could just about dislocate your shoulder. You might find that rather painful. It'd certainly need anaesthetic to get it back in place, and even then the shoulder will be weak for the rest of your life. I want to know how many more are following, and *where the youngsters are!*"

He gave an exploratory pull to the arm and the man shouted.

"They've got them! In the clearing. There are two more."

'The kids' could now be heard, talking, much to my relief.

But more footsteps were now thundering our way. I got out of sight of the path, behind yet more brambles, and was about to muster what courage I have and jump out when Steve's voice rang out.

"You got him! Well done!"

I was so relieved I nearly lost control of my bladder.

"Matt scared him so much that he wrapped his leg in some leaves and gave up," said Cooper. "He liked Matt's scar so much he wanted one of his own too. Look."

He pointed to the man's forehead, which was dripping blood. Steve grinned. "Don't blame him. Matt scares me too, sometimes."

"Last load of wood I get for you, then."

"Cooking for yourself tonight, yeah?"

I just hopped from one foot to the other and ignored him, overtaken by another need. "Can you manage?" I asked. "I need a pee."

"Prob'ly can," Cooper grinned. I moved into the bushes and suited the action to the words.

28   Grace

There was a good deal of telephoning done then. Police, parents, Arif, Daneesh… We had to wait where we were for the Police to arrive. Fortunately the path was one that led to the west end of the estate, so it was simpler for everyone to get to us from the road, along the west wall and over the stream, then over the wall itself. Finally we were able to call Arif, who by that time was at the camp, and tell him we were on our way back.

"We'll start the burgers off," he said.

It was a tired crew that, hours later, sat around the fire, finally able to eat the provisions Bill had provided. By then the sun was setting. In October with the sun so low it had never lit on the undergrowth, the sky, now clear, glowed in pinks and reds so vivid that, if you saw them in a film, would make you say "oh, come *on…*"

Grace was sitting next to me. Our arms were touching…

Food and drink had to come first. No, we didn't forget our *hondje*, Lars, once again hero of the hour; and I just hope he liked burgers. He wasn't complaining. Arif was so pleased to hear how he had found Ava and the twins that he almost ignored Amy for a time in his efforts to congratulate the dog.

Food and drink are great healers for fright. When we were round the fire, drinking in the atmosphere as always, we heard their story. They had been feeding the fire when they heard footsteps, but from the wrong direction.

"We thought you were trying to surprise us," Jane said. "But then we found there were three men surrounding us. We tried to run, but they grabbed us. There's only three of us and when they'd tripped Toby up we thought we'd better not struggle too much until we knew we could all escape. They said something about thinking we were older and asking us where the other three were. Then they put ties round our wrists, and stuff across our mouth so we couldn't shout, and just marched us away."

"And then we heard you calling," said Toby, "and that phased them big time. They had to put their hands over our mouths to make doubly sure we couldn't yell back. They stopped in that clearing and argued about what to do. Took 'em so long that the next thing, Lars was standing in front of them, barking. They didn't know whether to keep hold of us or try and attack him. Strewth, wouldn't like to come across him on a dark night."

"Not if you'd harmed one of those he liked and wanted to protect," came a quiet voice.

We swivelled round to Daneesh. He smiled back.

"That is one very special dog," he said simply.

Toby cautiously called Lars. The dog went and sat on his feet, looking round. Toby laughed. "And to think he scared me!"

"When we had got them on the ground..." Mike started

"Huh!" said Tom. "You make it sound easy!"

"Okay... how about 'after a struggle we got them on the ground'?" Mike grinned. Tom nodded, grinning back.

"...we threatened them with injury unless they told us how they'd not been caught when the rest of the paedos were arrested. That rather caught them, I think. They said they had no idea who the men were, just that they got a call to do a job, and a promise of good money."

"Just about what the Police said to them later," said Bill. "They asked them if they realised they'd answered to a call from some paedophiles to take revenge on some youngsters. It rather shut them up."

I wasn't the only one puzzled, so Bill carried on.

"When you get people like that in prison, they get a bloody hard time of it from the other inmates. Even blokes in for murder take it out of paedos. Unless they're in for killing a child. Then they get an even harder time. They all have to be isolated, usually. Anyway, once they knew they'd been employed from prison by nonces they started talking, and it was all good stuff. The Police know even more about the gang now, and their friends, and those blokes will pass it round to all the other hard nuts they see that the guys in jail are... well, what they are."

"And do you know what they were going to do if they found you?" asked Ava. "Kidnap one of you and try to do an exchange for the main leader of the gang."

"And the guy who's the brains behind this latest attempt at spoiling your fun is about now getting the shock of his life," said Bill happily. "He was one the Police knew nothing about, who got away from the original raid because he wasn't there.

He had a cold." He laughed. "He's certainly catching one now!"

Not too long after that, seeing Jane, Toby and Ava get nearer the fire, Bill said that he really should be taking his family back. We decided that an increasingly chilly October night was really not an encouraging time to be camping. I was secretly glad. I think The Scout was too, because he made only a half-hearted attempt to scoff at us being fair weather campers. Then he remembered that none of the recently washed (and according to Mum, fumigated) sleeping bags was in the tents.

The air was still. We removed fuel from the fire and thoroughly wetted it (though various of us were heard to mutter things like "had to collect that wood, you know", and left the embers to burn out safely. One thing about a barbie – there's no washing up apart from mugs, and a swift dip in the lake was enough for them.

Following Lars' tail and our own bump of direction – Lars being the more accurate – we played follow my leader down to Nils' cottage, taking turns to carry the patient when needed.

"I didn't say, did I?" Bill said. "They're starting work on the electrics on Monday. The cottage is all ready, so a couple of weeks after that Nils will be sorted."

We saw Nils safely home, with Daneesh helping. Bill made two journeys to town, one with most of his family, Arif, Amy and Daneesh ("Don't tell anyone about the eighth passenger," he said) and one with us plus Grace who had volunteered to stay behind. She and I were crammed together. "You're too broad," she said, easing her arm from in front of her so as to put it round my back. Our sides were nearly together. Our thighs were touching. I nearly purred.

Too quick, that car ride. He stopped outside my house, I opened the door. I looked at Grace, she looked at me.

"See you… tomorrow?" I said, wondering what that look on her face meant.

"I hope so."

Arghhh…

"Good night… and thanks, Bill," I remembered to add in a louder voice as I reluctantly closed the car door.

Though it was dark I'm sure I saw her face turn to look as the car sped off.

"You look happy," said Dad as I came into the room.

"Hmmm."

That's all I could say. But it was with a smile on my face I couldn't switch off. Try that I might.

"You scared us rigid us again today," said Mum.

"Yeah?"

"Nearly getting kidnapped by those men."

"They'd got the kids, not us. And we got them back, and the kids arrested. I mean the *men* arrested. And nobody will take any orders from the nonces in jail, not now they know what they've done."

"Matt!" Mum was scandalised. "You don't use words like that!"

"Sorry," I said without thinking, "but the Police do."

"Oh, do they… Well, we're not Police in this house. So please don't."

"Okay, Mum. Not in this house."

Dad made a noise and I looked sharply at him. He was searching for his handkerchief, but I could see he was doing his best not to laugh. Mum looked at him too.

"Really, Harry! You're as bad as he is." But she said it with a grin, and before long we were all laughing, me so light-heartedly I was in danger of losing the plot. But I checked myself in time.

"He is getting on for fifteen, you know, Steph. He's not your innocent little boy any more."

"I know," she said. "Unfortunately he gets more like you every day."

That set us both off again.

"You men!" she exclaimed. "I'm going to put the kettle on."

She'd left the room by about a minute when Dad said: "You've not been drinking, have you?"

Caught on the hop, so to speak, I denied it. But as I did, I knew it was in a tone of voice that was more sincere than one I'd have used if I was trying to dig myself out of trouble.

There was a pause of a couple of moments.

"I hope she's nice, then."

The landline rang early the next morning. Mum answered it and I could hear confusion in her voice. That usually meant it was for me. As I was still in the shower I couldn't just rush down and take over.

"It's Bill," she said from outside the bathroom door. "He's invited us to the Royal Hotel tomorrow night."

Yes, yes, yes... I tried to keep my voice steady. "Friday night? Just us, or all the crowd?"

"Oh, he says all the crowd and their families. That's a lot of people."

I couldn't do the sums, but it was.

"Good," I said.

"You want to go?"

"Well... yes. Of course."

"You don't usually like that sort of thing."

No. Not with all that false 'must have fun, we're paying for it' attitude I don't.

"This is different. We're all mates."

"Even Bill's family?"

"Think what we went through on the first day we ever met."

"Yeeees... Oh okay then. I'll say yes. I'm sure your father won't mind."

"Good."

She went downstairs again, presumably to call back. I continued in the shower, only to be interrupted again by a knock on the door.

"Hallo?"

"This time it's a girl called Grace. Shall I tell her you'll call back?"

"No... no. Just a mo."

I hopped out of the shower and dripped my way over to the door, stood behind it, unlocked and opened it a crack.

"Can I have the phone, please?"

She complied. I bolted the door and crossed as far away from it as possible.

"Hallo."

"Hallo.

"I'm having a shower."

"Now?"

"Yes."

There was a slight pause and a sigh.

"So now's not a good time to ask if I can see the map?"

"It's a very good time."

"What..." There was a sort of giggle. "...You mean *now*? This moment?"

"Well if you like. But I'd be in a dressing gown."

"Awww..."

The penny dropped. "*Grace…!*"

She laughed again. "Took you long enough."

"Huh!"

"Really, do you want me to come round?"

"Yes."

"When?"

"As soon as you like."

"Do you want time to dress?"

"What, five minutes, you mean? Or should I not bother?"

A pause.

"*Matt…!*"

And we both laughed. It felt as though a barrier had just dropped.

In about ten minutes I was dressed – properly – and was almost hopping from one foot to the other. *I* put the coffee on. *I* readied the mugs. *I* even got the sugar ready, just in case, and *I* put some biscuits on a plate, also ready in case.

Then *I* looked at Mum. She was watching me with her mouth open.

"You've never done that in your life."

"I never have guests of my own."

"What about when some of your mates come round? Steve, Tom, that lot?"

"Oh, they're not guests. They're the Suspects. We're… well… sort of family, but not family."

It was actually an hour later that she appeared, with Bill. I wondered why, until Bill asked if he could have another look at the map. We pored over it. Bill was so careful not to let anyone's coffee come anywhere near it that it stressed that he actually meant what he said, that the map was going to be valuable to him.

"Could you add something to it?" he asked. "They're laying on the electricity next week, and I need an accurate fix on where they're burying it. I'll also need to know where the pipework is between the well and Nils' house. We can put that on when we've measured. It needs doing before the earth has settled down, though, as it's not a straight line, you see, because we had to do a detour round Nils' vegetable plots."

Knowing how proud the old man was of his garden I could understand that.

"How about a bigger plan of the cottage and the hamlet?" I

offered, before thinking how much work that would mean.

"That would be ace. And how about adding the old house to it too? There's meant to be an old water supply up to there too, but we'd have to trace it. Don't know where it comes from. Nils says it came into the kitchen, but that's all."

"That's your work cut out over Christmas!" said Mum.

"There's no rush," said Bill. "If we can get it down in rough – his mates are good at that, too – then it doesn't matter when we get to the final. But to start with I'll need to get a big map for him to base the plan on. I think it's the Ordnance Survey do them. This is good coffee."

"Matt made it," said Mum. Was that a hint of pride in her voice?

"Mapping and coffee… any other specialities?"

"Not room tidying, that's certain," said Mum.

"Mum…!"

"Well, you're not. But I suppose you're not too bad, despite that."

"Well, I like him."

Grace hadn't said a word since she entered the house, and now she had a red face and was looking at the wall.

"Thanks," I said. "Good to know *someone's* on my side."

"What pens do you use for mapping?" asked Grace, thankfully changing the subject.

And that was that. From there on in we talked mapping, we two, forgetting Mum and Bill and letting them find their own conversation. She wanted to see where I had been working on it, so, matter-of-factly, I took her up to my room. As I opened the door and went in it struck me what I was doing.

A girl. In my bedroom. Alone with me. The first time.

Some of the time before she had come I had spent clearing clothes and other stuff off the floor and the chairs (I had two chairs for when the other Suspects came round. The bed wasn't big enough for everyone to sit on). And the wardrobe was closed. It had to be: that was where the dirty clothes were. Mum would have been astonished at how tidy it was. How tidy it looked, at least.

I have no idea how long we were at the desk, side by side, looking at the transitions I'd made from the rough field notes, through the first draft to the final map. Grace had some suggestions about symbols and spacings and so on, and I didn't mind because the ideas were good and they were from her.

She told me of the work she'd done mapping parts of the families' stations in Australia and I was surprised and pleased for her that her uncle had asked her to help him by doing them too.

At last there was a knock at the door and Mum put her head in.

"Bill's got to go," she said, "and he wondered if you were coming, Grace. If not, you're welcome to a scratch lunch here, but I have to go to work this afternoon. Or you could have a snack out."

I looked at the clock – midday. "What do you think?" I asked her.

"Shall we go out? We could come back later."

Yesssss!

Mum gave me some money and we went to the mall – inevitably – because it was the natural place for hanging around. And, I suppose just as inevitably, we met up with some of the others. Firstly it was Alex, but he was with his parents on a jolly expedition to buy him some new clothes for school. He looked absolutely cheesed off, and even more cheesed off when he wasn't allowed to stay with us on the grounds that 'we haven't finished yet, dear'.

Joe, also with parents, we saw in the distance, then a few minutes later, turning round a corner we bumped into Arif and Amy.

"You two…!" said Arif.

"Yes? What's up?" I answered.

"Nothing. We were just going for a bite, away from the families."

"Us too," said Grace. "Want to join us?"

They looked at each other, nodded, and Amy said "Why not?"

So we found a large store with a restaurant and amazed the staff there by being young, attached, polite, and able to pay our way. After that they couldn't do enough for us and we ended up laughing with them – and each other.

On reflection it was another first for me. I'd never ordered up a meal for myself and my guest before, and paid for it.

We parted and spent the rest of the afternoon at home. This time we watched a film. Grace was sitting next to me, closely next to me. I was on cloud nine.

Eventually, though, she had a phone call from a parent who said she was expected back for a meal. I walked back to the hotel with her and promised we'd be there the next evening with everyone else.

"You'd better be," she said, looking serious.

"Do you think I wouldn't?"

"No."

"Why?"

"Because all the other Suspects will be here."

"That the only reason?"

She paused and stepped back.

"Maybe not. Depends on you. Seeya."

And, tantalisingly, she vanished inside. And that, I thought, was that.

I was quiet that evening. Parents left me alone, too. I even toyed with some school work, having persuaded myself I had to do it sometime. At last, fed up and frustrated it wasn't tomorrow already, I went to bed and lay looking at the ceiling.

My phone buzzed.

Grace. A message.

Good night and see you tomorrow. Please.

Perhaps she knew there was another reason, after all.

The party was wonderful. Really good fun. So many "yay!" points; where to start? Having your own friends around you in a situation where you were all at leisure. There was no Steve harping about 'more wood', though he did try when one of the barbecue gases gave out. Being able to go round all the different parents accompanied by a girl for the first ever time, and being able to counter the frequent question with "Well, she's a girl, and she's my friend".

And more: The Suspects' being publicly addressed by Bill and thanked, absolutely genuinely, for bringing his attention to the Estate "even due to some pretty grim circumstances". Being thanked again by Nils, who was getting emotional (adults don't *do* that) for saving his life. Each one of us, in turn, taking Lars out for a turn round the hotel's garden. Marcus Yardley quietly putting two dishes of plain pasta in front of we Suspects and telling us that one had truffles in it and the other didn't. We all could tell the difference, but whether we liked it or not…well. At the end, as we were leaving, feeling a hand in mine as we walked down the stairs.

I looked at her. Her eyes held mine. In the foyer we hugged.

I wondered if I should chance a kiss, but the call from outside told me there was no time.

"See you tomorrow?" I said.

She just smiled and slipped away.

Later, it was my turn to send her a message.

29   Departure and rains

Unsurprisingly it was late the next morning when we all woke and the phones started going mad. Parents had seen the weather forecast and insisted that the tents should come back along with all the other personal belongings. And they also insisted it should happen this weekend so that family cars would be available, with drivers. As it was so late, and a Saturday, we begged for the afternoon off and promised to attack it the following day. I was due to hang out with Grace that afternoon anyway.

So mid-morning the following day we descended on the estate once again, this time with parents and heavy hearts. Although we'd not particularly asked them to come the Australian contingent was there – the youngest six, offering help. We accepted. Grace fell in by my side.

For most of the parents it was the first time they'd seen where we'd been hiding out. Those who had done any camping at all fell in love with it immediately, just as we had, and were impressed at how tidy and organised it was. Once again, Steve almost purred.

"I can see why you kept wanting to come back here," said Dad.

Reluctantly we packed all our personal stuff, found missing socks and in my case a pair of swum in, damp, mouldy underwear. The fire, fortunately, had been lit so that disposed of them. It also provided tea, and gave The Scout a last chance to perfect its cry: "I need more wood!"

A pile of rucksacks, cooking equipment, bowls, washing-up cloths and miscellaneous other stuff grew from nothing to what looked like monumental proportions quite quickly.

Steve insisted on help to fill the last…er… pit. With earth. And made a cross to mark it.

We left the stuff we'd built, the tables, racks and storage constructions in the hope we'd be able to use it again. We even left the fireplace, even if Steve said it was unprofessional to leave anything that would show we'd been there. We pointed out the table and other things to him and he shut up, only muttering a bit. We swore we would be back, if not this winter, then at the first opportunity in spring.

And then came the Great Move. With so many parental and other donkeys it was potentially quite light work. We six, plus Grace and Amy, turned at the last bend in the track to look back. To say goodbye. To fix that spot in our memories. A sad moment.

Despite all the help it was a rather tired and dejected single file of Suspects and supporters who made their way, laden, back down to Nils' cottage for the promised cup of tea. To quell his fears, we all told him we would visit from time to time, and Arif protested that he had no intention of quitting his Friday visits. Daneesh promised that his daily presence would continue. Finally, reluctantly, we took our leave.

We had another week of half term ahead of us. The Australian contingent were to leave the following Thursday and every time I thought of it my stomach tied itself in knots.

Those days were constantly wet. We met quite frequently at the Royal Hotel, thanks to Marcus who allowed us to use their sports room when it was free on the promise we'd vacate if paying guests wanted it. Since the guests seemed to use it mainly in the evenings it suited us well. All of us improved our skill at table tennis and proper snooker... okay, we started playing snooker. Not very well.

And the day came for Bill's family to leave.

Part of me wanted to stay in bed and avoid the goodbyes. The part which won wanted to see Grace and promise to write, text, message and, it suddenly occurred to me, Skype. And I didn't even have an account! I sprang out of bed (that's an exaggeration) and fired up the laptop.

Later, armed with 'Mattthesuspect' as a new user name, I hurried to the hotel. Being so keen to talk to Grace, the fact that the family was probably busy packing passed me by. Her room was phoned and she came to meet me, looking rather strained, I thought. She seemed rather surprised to see me looking excited.

"I had an idea," I said.

"What?"

"We can use Skype."

She looked at me. "I'd thought of that. But it's not the same."

"It's better than nothing."

"But it's not the same."

I felt deflated. "No. It's not."

"Can't you come to Australia? For Christmas?"

We were a family who hadn't been able to afford a summer holiday. I shook my head.

"Parents couldn't afford that."

"What holidays do you get?"

I couldn't remember. "I think, when we looked in September, that it was only about two weeks."

"Well that's the same time we've had off now. You could do it."

"I'll ask," I said, feeling a little happier even if I knew, deep inside, that still we couldn't afford it.

"Coming up?"

I didn't need asking again.

She was in the middle of packing.

"I'll want to hear all about what's happening with the estate. And with the Suspects. And school. And I'll tell you all about my boring life."

"Sure it's not."

"It is. Just Ava and Cooper to annoy me and nothing else for miles. Not like here."

"What, boring Upperden?"

"Boring Uppperden with its mall, your friends, the estate, the camp… and you."

"And me?" I could hardly believe my ears.

"You still don't understand, do you?"

"What?"

"Oh…. *Boys!*"

I grinned. "That's me."

"What are you all so… why don't you have any… *emotions*?"

I thought of the last few days and what had happened. I don't mean in the estate, or with the Suspects, or even her family. I thought what had been happening with her, inside my head, my heart.

Yes. That was it. The saying had come to me from books and plays and the TV, but it was the only way of recognising and expressing to myself what I'd been feeling.

All through my thoughts she had been boring my eyes with her own, trying to make me say something, do something. So I took the biggest chance I'd ever taken in my life.

I crossed the two metres between us, put my arms round her,

drew her even closer, and kissed her.

I'd seen it done on TV often enough. It's soppy. Wanting to do it and then doing it are a completely different ball game.

At last I drew back. The look in her eyes was reward enough.

"Those emotions, you mean?" I said quietly.

As if scripted, there was a knock at the door which opened before she could say anything. Her Mum came in, and did a double take as she saw me. I felt my face heat up.

"Matt! Well, I'll be… Been here long?"

"Hallo Nicole; no, about fifteen minutes."

"Okay, but we're due to leave for the airport in another fifteen, and your mates are all downstairs waiting to say goodbye and wondering where you were…"

Oh God. The comments I'll get.

"…and Grace needs to finish packing."

"Can I help?"

"Ask Grace. But hurry up, okay?"

"Shall I go?" I asked, when she'd closed the door.

"No."

True enough, the exclamations when we emerged from the lift, with me carrying Grace's suitcase, were bordering on the ribald. But Bill was there so they had to rein in a bit.

The rest of the family emerged from the bar where they'd congregated over coffee; they were quite a bit more polite but I could see the expression in Cooper and Mike's eyes. Conversation generalised.

"Grace in Oz. One word," hissed Grace in my ear.

It took me several seconds to realise what she was talking about. I nodded.

"I'll set it up tonight. No, day after tomorrow, when we get back. Don't forget the time difference."

Damn. I had. "What is it?"

"My Skype name, stupid!"

"No, the time difference."

"Don't you know?"

"No."

"Nor do I. I'll call you once it's set up, and if it's half past four in the morning, don't blame me."

"I'd like that," I said happily, "it'd give me something nice to go back to sleep with."

"*Matt!*"

I realised what I'd said and felt my face getting hot again.

Despite all our preparations, goodbyes between us were painful. As I watched Bill's car drive away I felt my spirits getting lower and lower. I escaped quickly from the rest of the Suspects and went home. To lunch. And found I couldn't eat anything.

Two nights later my open laptop started making noises. My eyes struggled to open and focus on the clock. Past two in the morning. It could only be one person. I switched on the light, fumbled my way back to it, pressed the answer button and there she was, grinning widely. We exchanged hallos, and I asked her what time it was.

"Four in the afternoon. Told you I would."

"It's half past two here… "

"I know. I checked." A pause. "You look good in underwear. Fit."

I moved closer to the screen so she could only see my face.

"Aww…"

"*Grace!...*"

She laughed. "Do you know, every time we talk one of us says something like that to the other one."

I thought.

"Whose turn is it next?"

"You just did it to me, so it must be mine."

The door opened and the centre light went on. There I was in underwear, in the middle of the night, standing talking to a laptop, with Mum watching.

"*Mum…*"

"If you're going to interrupt your night's sleep, please will you do it quietly and not wake us up? And hallo Grace. And good night. Shush."

She went out.

"I suppose I'd better go," I whispered.

Bill had stayed behind in the town "For a month or two," he said. "There's so much to plan and do, but now the rest of them have seen the place we've decided more or less what we could do with it. For it."

This was at Nils' cottage one Saturday evening in November, with the six Suspects, Nils and Daneesh – and Lars

– there as well. Nils was by then living in the comfort he'd been promised all those years ago. Electric light, propane gas central heating, a good, working cooker, pumped water from his own well, and a log fire to make the main room feel right.

"I've talked to Nils about it," said Bill, "and we've agreed that realistically it can't go back to being a stately home for one family. Those days are gone. We can make it work if we give a part over for families to live in, but use the other, main part as a conference centre and accommodation. That means it can cover maintenance and offer some employment, have a good garden but still ensure the main part of the estate is closed off for wildlife and access by a few friends of mine."

That would put an end to our camp, then.

"Would... who would it be open to?" Tom asked cautiously, just before the rest of us.

"Oh, just close family. Friends, too. I mean, there are six guys locally I can think of..." He trailed off.

I saw Alex's eyes were sparkling.

"He means us, idiots!" he almost shouted. Lars, startled, barked a staccato comment.

Bill grinned. "I think I promised that some time ago. And I meant it.

"What do the people in the houses think about it?" asked Alex. I suspected he knew from his father, though it would have been unprofessional for him to have been told without the client's permission. Bill's permission.

"Odd, that," said Bill. "They don't know what I've just told you. But they're not very happy to have received invoices for many years worth of ground rent. It seems that once the other solicitors decided there was no hope of tracing an owner, someone to pay the money to, they just didn't bother with the business at all. So there's a backlog of thirty-some-odd years of ground rent, and that amounts to a lot of money. Some of them are thinking of selling up and moving somewhere quiet, anyway"

"Quiet?!" Joe, this time. "What could be quieter than here?"

"They got wind of building work – you know, noise and dust and rude workmen. That sort of thing. Fortunately for me as it's only repairs there's no planning permission needed. We'll keep that under our hats for the moment. If they move out they won't object, and if they do I know quite a few local people who'd support our plans for a change of use."

"You know you said 'family'," I started.

"Yes, Nils, of course, and if any of my lot want to come over on holiday there'd be somewhere for them to stay."

"Oh." I wondered for a beautiful moment whether he was expecting any of them to come and live there. Permanently.

"Are you going to stay over here, Bill?" Joe had taken a liking to the Australian and his matter-of-fact way of treating the world. Including us.

"Looks that way, for a bit, anyway. I can leave the oil to be looked after by others – just nip back over there when they're not expecting me and put things right. You know, like a cockeye bob whizzing through. Or in this case a straighteye Bill.

"Pardon, but what is a cockeye bob?" Daneesh asked.

"Another name for a willy-willy. A little dust-devil."

Arif, who paid attention in geography lessons, clarified for his Grandad, not to mention us. "A little whirlwind, Grandad."

I had visions of Bill whirling round his oil well, or maybe its office, creating havoc, and smiled.

"Yeah; lucrative stuff, oil, but boring once you've got it flowing. Other people are better at the day-to-day stuff."

"Don't the rest of the family have anything to do with it?" I asked.

"Nah… Not needed. We just sell to the oil people, really. It's not as if we're Esso or something. Oh, the family are financial partners, but they have sheep stations to run and that's what they prefer to do. And I can't blame them. But it's a younger man's life, that."

I thought of Grace's boredom. But then I was bored with Upperden. Would a swap of places be good? No. Not a *swap* of places. Skype was adequate, but nothing like her being there.

Christmas found Bill about to move into one of the recently vacated houses in the hamlet, though Joe's parents were expecting him and Nils to stay over Christmas itself. Telling us about it afterwards, he described how Mrs Hammond had cautiously mentioned the possibility of the rest of the Suspects coming round on Boxing Day for a meal and silly games, and was surprised at how enthusiastic he was about the possibility.

"She just didn't understand how anyone could possibly want the company of a load of fifteen year old blokes," he said, smiling at the recollection. "She was quite gobsmacked when I told her that usually I wouldn't, but you lot were good friends."

Joe had already told us about their Christmas and the fun that he and his sister had had with Bill and Nils.

"It's like having two grandads with you," he said. "The only thing I really didn't like was sharing a room with Mary, my eight year old sister. Yuch! It's all pink and fluffy and full of unicorns."

I made a mental note to look at Grace's surroundings when we Skyped that evening, to see if I could detect any excessively girly colours. Or unicorns of course.

When we took Nils back after New Year's Day – with Daneesh of course – we decided to take a walk up to the camp for old times' sake. There had been a lot of rain during the week before Christmas, and the holiday itself had been wet too, so it was a soggy experience. Prompted by our tame Scout we wore boots and full waterproofs so were reasonably protected.

As we approached the camp, up the stream, it was obvious that there was something like a flood happening. The stream in its little gorge was hammering down, the gorge being far fuller of fast moving brown water than it had been. Nearer the top we had to take avoiding action as it had over-topped its shallower channel.

All this time we had been aware of a sound in the background, a sound that puzzled us. As we neared our camp it grew in volume until, standing just below the lake and marvelling at what had been rapids but were now a full-blown waterfall emptying from our pool. We thought the noise was coming from there, and it certainly wasn't quiet. But above that was a deeper sound, a roar. So we were still puzzled.

The sight that greeted us as we drew level with our peaceful, quiet, *dry* campsite shocked and impressed us all. We stood, staring.

All that water that had fallen as rain must have collected on the higher levels of the opposite side of the estate. It had gradually spread out, probably forming a new, very shallow, lake near the top of the cliffs. That would explain why we had found that area boggy when we had first tried to find our way down.

The persistent rain had fed the area, and its only means of escape was over the cliffs. Our cliffs. Into our pool.

Imagine a curtain of water, some fifty metres across. Imagine its force as it falls ten metres into an already full pool. Imagine, at its left end, the original waterfall, our waterfall, that now came over the edge with force enough to propel itself a few metres from the edge before falling with an even greater roar into the pool.

Of our gently shelving campsite and beach there was no sight.

"Bloody hell," said Alex, unnecessarily. "I'm glad we weren't in our tents when that started."

"Will it be all right by next summer?" was all I could think of.

Arif is our tame geography expert, in that he's the one who listened in geography lessons from early in our career. I think since Mr Windebank had started teaching us we had all developed an interest. The estate and the mapping of it might have had an influence on at least a part of that.

"Probably happens like this most years," he said airily. "Once the rain's died away the water will drain and the campsite will grow grass again in spring."

"Hope so," I said. "How else are we going to camp here with the Aussies?"

"You're just scared you won't get to share a tent with Grace," Alex chided.

I just looked at him.

30   Return & other things

We met up at Nils's fairly frequently, often bringing a casserole full of something or other to eat with him. It seemed hardly fair to expect him to feed us all the time.

Soon after Christmas he was back to full mobility and full of the joys of spring. Bill had finally persuaded him to accept a phone which, cautiously, over many weeks, he'd learnt to use. I think its main use was to ask us to come over for a meal, or for us to tell him that we would be bringing a meal with us.

Some months later we received the usual invitation to meet up, there. There seemed to be a note of excitement in his voice.

"Bill will be here," he said. Nothing new: Bill was usually there.

We knew now not to bother bringing plates or cutlery as he'd accepted that people would be visiting him – mainly us, but he hoped his new relations from Australia would be dropping in if they came back in the summer. So from having two mugs, two plates and very little cutlery to his name, he was now so well equipped that he'd probably have been able to cater for our entire school year.

As always now, we didn't just barge in, but knocked. We even waited for an answer. His welcoming smile seemed even broader than usual. We wondered what was up. Bill was at the cooker.

It wasn't until we were all at the table, waiting for the hot meal on incandescent plates to cool, that Bill dropped his bombshell.

"You lot all sitting firmly? Okay – here goes. In July, my lot from Oz start on the school's two week winter holidays."

That didn't sound right. Then we realised the significance of "winter" and "Australia". Were they coming over again? My chest seemed unsteady.

"This time, though, they're all going to have a holiday that'll end at the start of September."

Good for them, I thought. And great! Grace will be here for a couple of months.

"At least, I think that's when you lot go back to school, isn't it?"

Silence greeted that as we tried to work out what he very

deliberately was not telling us. Joe, whose powers of quick deduction were starting to show, was the first to latch on.

"Well, either they're not going back to Australia until we go back to school, or they're coming over here permanently and joining us at school."

Bill raised his eyebrows.

I could hardly believe it, but… "They're coming over here? To live? *Really?*"

He grinned. "They are."

Six people – Amy was there too, of course – broke into an excited hubbub of questions and explanations. I just sat, quietly full of happiness. She was coming to join me…

Bill held up a hand. "The kids were all gobsmacked at the welcome they got from you lot, and from other people they met. They live on sheep stations that are next to each other, but it's still a helluva drive between them. School is a drag to get to and from. So there's not a lot for them to do.

"The adults – my sons and daughters-in-law - know there are more rewarding jobs over here than they can reach from where they live in Oz. And they have enough good guys to look after the two sheep stations without them. Anyway, like me they can go back whenever they need to and sort out any disasters. And over here they'll eventually have a rather nice house to live in, with plenty of space. And the kids should be able to live there or have their independence in any houses in the hamlet that come up for sale.

"It was the kids that really got them thinking, just seeing how they reacted together, and with you people, when they were over here, had a few challenges to face and got to grips with the English countryside at its most overgrown."

He stopped for breath.

"Not all of the country is like this, Bill." Tom was being honest.

"Too right," said Steve. "Oh, we get to go to some fantastic, wild places, but you have to travel."

Bill laughed. "We come from a land that's four thousand kilometres wide and nearly the same tall. So we're used to travelling!"

"So when are they arriving, Bill?" asked Tom.

"About mid-July, I imagine. Probably have a few days in the Royal, then they'll be able to move into a couple of houses in the hamlet that'll be empty by then. Once I'd told the people there we were going to be doing extensive building works up at the Hall, they started spitting feathers. Oddly, 'For Sale' signs appeared at two of them. Fat lot of notice they'll get there! But then I put in a couple of offers and they were accepted pronto."

Bill must be *really* wealthy, I thought again.

That evening my regular video call with Grace started with mock indignation in my mind. I accused her of not telling me the plans.

"That would have spoilt it. You'd never have kept it from the others."

"I would. We're not that close that I tell them everything!"

"You should stay close to them. It's one of the things I like about you."

I digested that with a warm feeling inside of me.

"What are the other things, then?"

"Oh, I don't know. You draw good maps."

"That all?"

"There might be a few other things."

And so we went on. For ages.

At the start of the short Easter school holiday The Suspects established camp again and spent two freezing nights overlooking a swollen pool. It was not really a great success, nor was it a pleasure, even if we were each cocooned in blankets and sleeping bags and rather resembled large, multicolour slugs.

Most of the paths we embarked on were soft even if unmarked by human footprints. Getting around was difficult. Trying to stand and use cold hands to make notes on maps was sometimes counter-productive.

Winter winds had produced quite a quantity of fallen branches. The Scout pointed out that these were mostly useless for burning as many were still 'alive'. They bent rather than snapped. He did graciously accept some for more furniture building, though.

"If we're going to have all six of them here, we'll need more table space and stuff," he observed.

"Won't they want to build that themselves?" asked Joe.

"Probably. But we can show them what's possible. And get them some wood."

I was sure that he had a fetish about calling for wood and sending his friends away to collect it. It was still like living with a parrot.

We extended the table. What we didn't do was any more mapping as it didn't seem right to leave sets of footsteps around destroying the wild appearance of the place. Instead there was a good deal of card playing and absolutely no swimming done. We did at last try fishing in the pool, but caught nothing.

It wasn't until May that we started to spend weekends there more regularly, knowing that we'd have a week's half term at the end of the month. At least we wouldn't be taking our GCSEs when we returned. That would be inflicted on us the following year, as we were being constantly reminded.

Arif had been rather reluctant to join us at first as Amy had been forbidden to camp with us on her own. He naturally wanted to see her. She was really put out about it, but thankful that from July three other girls would be there, something which should persuade her parents to let her come. Arif cheered up when he was with us and we had started the surveying again, pushing our way through the undergrowth and gaining information and renewing skin punctures. At least by then night times were warmer. The pool was again swimmable, though we made sure there was a fire alight to warm us when we emerged, dripping, slightly blue, and worrying about certain male attributes.

The map's detailing grew apace. I'd asked Bill at what stage he wanted it as a finished item but he just asked to borrow it, make a copy and leave me to add to it as we got still more information.

"A never-ending job, then," I grinned at him.

"Something like that. You and Grace need something to keep you busy." I blushed. Occasionally he'd say something like that, and each time I rose to it.

He hadn't said anything else about the large-scale plan of The Old Hall, as they'd now formally renamed it. He'd given me the Ordnance Survey plan, with a few photocopies to use for drafts, several months previously with the words "No rush at all. After the summer's fine." That obviously came under the heading of giving Grace and me something to do, as well.

As the summer approached time spent at the camp grew less, not because we wanted it to but because various Parents had decided they should give their families a holiday. Additionally Steve was on a week-long expedition with the Scouts as soon as term ended, about the same time that my parents had booked to go to the sea.

Bill was never forthcoming about the date of his family's arrival in Britain. First it was still 'about mid-July', then it was 'a few weeks after they've broken up', then there was some other excuse. We just couldn't pin him down. At last he gave up all pretence and just told us it was a secret and we'd know as soon as possible. Even when pressed, when we knew about family holiday dates, he wouldn't say. I was half beginning to wonder if they were really coming. But Grace assured me they were, but she didn't know exactly when either.

It was all most unsatisfactory. For all I knew I'd be away with the Parents when they flew in, and I was determined to be at the airport to welcome her. I mean, to welcome them.

But July came, and at the third week of it, freedom returned. School work for the holidays was given out. School ended. Two days of frantic packing activity happened. We drove to the coast, to a small Devon village with a church, pub, three shops, a boatyard, a fishing wharf, a large beach and a Lifeboat. And a view out over the estuary with islands dotted round it.

We registered at the hotel – yes, us in a hotel! Unheard of. Completed the forms, collected the keys, turned round to go to the rooms…

…and saw Arif and Amy laughing at us.

I shook my head as if to clear away the aftermath of a dream, but they were still there.

"What the f… "

I remembered where I was, and who I was with.

"You never said a word! You…you…"

I was so overcome that I went to Amy and kissed her, to my and her amazement. Then I turned to Arif, called him a ratbag and hugged him.

Now, just to get this firmly established, The Suspects don't do things like that. But I did.

"Seems we've got to share, Matt," Arif told me. I felt sorry for him not to be sharing with Amy, but was sure her parents would have vetoed the whole thing had it been any different. Okay, he was coming up to that birthday when an imaginary switch gets pushed and the same human suddenly becomes more of an adult. Overnight. Over a split second, in fact. In practical terms it's so obviously rubbish as to be ridiculous – unless there was a lot of biological stuff that nobody had yet told me about the magic of entering the sixteenth year of life. But I didn't know about Amy, though her parents' opinion would rule what my parents could allow.

As to sharing a room, well, for much of the previous summer Arif and I had been sharing a tent. That qualifies each of us to know lots about the other. Sometimes almost too much.

Luggage was dumped into rooms and we met up with my Parents in the hotel's sea view café, as directed. For some reason they had ordered tea for six. Okay, I was hungry and Arif almost always could eat, but had no clue why they brought a sixth plate.

The rest of them were hanging back, but I was hungry and had my teeth firmly planted into the second piece of sandwich when a gentle, melodious, female voice spoke.

"Hallo, Matt."

I'm told it's not The Done Thing to spray sandwiches from the mouth on to one of your best friends, but it serves him right. The fit of coughing didn't serve to make me any more sophisticated, either.

I'm not sure if the watering eyes were to do with the coughing or to being overcome. As I jumped up and turned to face her everything was blurry. But I didn't need to see her to be able to give her a bear hug.

By the time my sight was nearly back to normal I let her go and looked at her. Then I kissed her properly, breaking off only when I realised that I'd never done that in public before, and my Parents were watching.

And smiling.

"It's a plot!" I almost shouted, still looking into Grace's laughing eyes. "And you're all in it! You rotten, rotten, lovely lot!"

I subsided, panting gently, like Lars when he's been scratched behind the ears.

I have to admit that I spent a long time over that tea with my arm round Grace. It doesn't make eating very easy. At last we gave up.

"Is there anything else you've not told me?" I attacked the world in general. "The other Suspects? Bill? Nils? Daneesh?

269

Have you brought Lars with you?"

"Funny you should ask that," said Arif, mischief in his voice, "because…No."

I punched him. But very gently.

"But when did you fly in?" I asked Grace.

"Couple of days ago. I thought we were staying at the Royal, but they told me you were here and sent me down by train and taxi. I didn't complain."

I hugged her.

"So your parents and Bill aren't here, then?" I asked.

"Bill's not here," said Mum quietly, "but…"

We waited. I could see that this time Grace, Amy and Arif were as unaware as I was what was coming next.

"Go on, Mum!" I pleaded.

"Well, he obviously thinks a lot of you, so he's booked you some extra tuition for the week." Dad was saying this with as straight a face as he could, which isn't saying much. I could see the change of expression (downwards) in the eyes of my compatriots.

We waited.

"You're going back to school tomorrow afternoon."

I was about to say something when I thought of Dad's expression.

He cleared his throat, or it may have been covering a laugh.

"It's a sailing school. Once you can handle a small boat properly you'll be able to use her the rest of the week. And if you get stuck on the mud and have to wait for the tide to turn, it'll be your own fault."

Epilogue

We all fell in at least once. Grace and I nearly got stuck on mud on a falling tide, but just the once. Trying to push off with a leg got me covered in mud to the thigh, though the effort worked. Once we'd learnt just about enough about sailing they let us loose with life jackets and small dinghies and we went everywhere, sailing the estuary. We were just glad it didn't need to be mapped.

The others were camping on the estate, and true to what Arif had said during our winter visit the camp had dried out and recovered. The nine of them did a lot of exploring and some mapping, causing more work for Grace and me the following autumn.

We joined them after our fortnight and had a blast. Steve the Scout organised some silly games for Ava and the twins, then had to reorganise them so everyone could join in. Night time games in the pitch dark were a new experience for all we Suspects, but the sheep station bred Aussies were used to it.

Amy and Arif, Grace and I have had our ups and downs but seem always to come back together.

For a long time Tom followed a tall, blond, rather high-and-mighty girl around like a lovelorn sheep. Eventually she decided to pair up with a recently resigned teacher, causing a lot of raised eyebrows and mutterings. Tom felt worse about it than I had when Grace had flown back home, but was comforted by a quietly spoken, grounded, attractive, girl who just said and did the right things. They seem to be around a lot together.

Alex was often in the company of a guy who joined our school from one in Brighton and finally announced to us that they were a couple.

Steve and Joe are just Steve and Joe. I don't mean they're a couple, just that they haven't changed. Steve told us that he's now a Young Leader, whatever that is, and Joe's thinking about joining Plod.

And Nils and Lars still live in the cottage, but it's really very comfortable now. Neither would want to move.

The big house now gives separate homes to Bill and each branch of the family, along with a really rather special Conference Centre which is starting to do rather well. Various members of all our families work there at times, and it's got other people in the town working there too.

We never saw Emily Long again, nor any of the rest of them.

Yes, we still spend nights under canvas on the estate, even at our advanced ages of eighteen – nineteen. And still we're all The Usual Suspects now, all twelve of us. No one has forgotten.

ABOUT THE AUTHOR

Richard Wright has been, or in some cases still is, a transport enthusiast, church bell ringer, Bluebell Railway guard, Scout Leader, IT enthusiast, narrowboat part-owner, NCI Watchkeeper. He has dabbled in local politics and spends too much time on Facebook. He has earned a living running buses and coaches, being a school security manager and theatre manager, though not simultaneously. In 2013 he saw the light and retired – at least technically.

He is married and has two stepsons and two grandsons. He and his wife live in Sussex.

"The Suspects" is his first published book. He believes in setting his books in real or very plausible places, and most certainly in crediting his younger subjects with intelligence, self-reliance and innate common sense.

Forthcoming books by Richard Wright

There are two other books on the stocks, so to speak. Please don't hold your breath as they will take some time!

Return of the Past (working title)

Set in a version of Salcombe, Devon, in the 1950s. A winter flood causes devastation and kills Stephen's best friend's family. Only the 12 year old sister is saved and she is taken in by Stephen and his father. Anticipating a large insurance payout a relative kidnaps her and sends her to a remote boarding school.

After a 3 year absence she escapes and returns. The two youngsters bond. Life has already changed for each of them and will do so again.

The Youngest Gentleman

Set near Seaford, Sussex in the 1960s. Owen persuades his parents to take on the dilapidated Tide Mills (which actually exists but as a ruin). To start with there is little income and the villagers – including Owen – resort to the old Sussex trade of smuggling. They have to fight weather, Coastguard officers, seasickness and poverty. How will it end?

Make contact

It'd be great to hear your views – positive or negative:

Email: suspects@harbroe.org

Facebook: www.facebook.com/suspects

Web page: rw2.co.uk/suspects